ADVANCE PRAISE FOR *THE*

"A tender and thoughtful exploration of ⸻, ⸻ing-making, and the stories we tell." —Jean Meltzer, author of *The Matzah Ball*

"You can't help rooting for Charlie, for his grandfather, and even for Gellman the dog in this buoyant and generous novel." —Cary Fagan, author of *The Student*

"This coming-of-age story is not only moving, engrossing, and beautifully written, it is also a deeply spiritual account of what it means to be human, searching to be seen and loved. Tell Charlie Minkoff to call me, so we can welcome him as a bar mitzvah!" —Rabbi Lisa Grushcow, Senior Rabbi, Temple Emanu-El-Beth Sholom

PRAISE FOR *ONCE MORE WITH FEELING*

WINNER OF THE CAROL SHIELDS WINNIPEG BOOK AWARD
FINALIST FOR THE MARGARET LAURENCE AWARD FOR FICTION
FINALIST FOR THE MCNALLY ROBINSON BOOK OF THE YEAR AWARD

"[Méira Cook] writes prose so fluid, so effortless, so vivid, you're swept away on its sheer beauty and power... *Once More With Feeling* manages to be both sharp and tender, tragic and fiercely funny, and wholly satisfying." —*Toronto Star*

"Méira Cook has written a fine and funny novel that, like the city in which it is set, pulses with life, love, loss, and so much more. Vital and vivid characters spring from the page, grab your heart, and won't let go." ——Terry Fallis, Two-Time Winner of the Stephen Leacock Medal for Humour

"Brimming with warmth and a wry, often surrealistic sense of humour, Cook's vibrant narrative delves beneath the tenuous surfaces of the everyday, asking us to re-examine the ways in which we see ourselves and understand the world." —Kerry Lee Powell, author of the Scotiabank Giller Prize–nominated *Willem de Kooning's Paintbrush*

ALSO BY THE AUTHOR

Fiction
The House on Sugarbush Road
Nightwatching
Once More With Feeling

Poetry
A Fine Grammar of Bones
Toward a Catalogue of Falling
Slovenly Love
A Walker in the City
Monologue Dogs

THE FULL CATASTROPHE

MÉIRA COOK

ANANSI

Published in Canada in 2022 and the USA in 2022 by House of Anansi Press Inc.
www.houseofanansi.com

26 25 24 23 22   1 2 3 4 5

Library and Archives Canada Cataloguing in Publication

Title: The full catastrophe / Méira Cook.
Names: Cook, Méira, 1964- author.
Identifiers: Canadiana (print) 2022013393X | Canadiana (ebook) 20220133948 |
ISBN 9781487009946 (softcover) | ISBN 9781487009953 (EPUB)
Classification: LCC PS8555.O567 F85 2022 | DDC C813/.54—DC23

Cover design: Alysia Shewchuk
Text design and typesetting: Lucia Kim

*House of Anansi Press respectfully acknowledges that the land on which we operate is the
Traditional Territory of many Nations, including the Anishinabeg, the Wendat, and the
Haudenosaunee. It is also the Treaty Lands of the Mississaugas of the Credit.*

 Canada Council
for the Arts
Conseil des Arts
du Canada

 ONTARIO ARTS COUNCIL
CONSEIL DES ARTS DE L'ONTARIO
an Ontario government agency
un organisme du gouvernement de l'Ontario

With the participation of the Government of Canada
Avec la participation du gouvernement du Canada | Canadä

*We acknowledge for their financial support of our publishing program the Canada Coun-
cil for the Arts, the Ontario Arts Council, and the Government of Canada.*

Printed and bound in Canada

 FSC
www.fsc.org
MIX
Paper from
responsible sources
FSC® C103567

And can a Scarecrow not have, occasionally, a bright idea?
Can a Tin Man not suffer a broken heart?

—*Ethics of the Fathers*
(Look it up.)

BOY WONDER

The trouble with Charlie was he couldn't make up his mind. But as his grandfather, Oscar Wolf Minkoff, pointed out, it wasn't the poor kid's fault. Indecision wasn't necessarily a matter of choice. The fact that the doctors were struggling to assign the newborn a gender, to declare an "M" or an "F," was just one more example of vacillation that was surely not, at this early stage, Charlie's fault.

The way Oscar told it, Charlie Minkoff came into the world shrieking like a banshee, the proud possessor of ten fingers, ten toes, two neat ears, a comically snub nose, a well-developed sense of outrage, and a healthy pair of lungs. A tonsure of pale hair stood out around the infant's head like dandelion fluff, and two large, slightly protuberant eyes completed the picture. "Little frog," his grandfather exclaimed fondly, stroking the baby's cheek.

The child was perfect, Oscar thought, sincerely puzzled by the doctors' insistence that something was wrong, gravely wrong, with the infant's genitals. Neither one thing nor the other, they insisted; too small for a penis, too big for a clitoris. Wincing at the unfamiliar words, Oscar remained phlegmatic.

3

"He just needs time to make up his mind," he said. "Give the little frog time."

"That's not how time works," snapped the surgeon, a ghastly man. Distastefully, he asked if Oscar was the father, and Oscar had to explain that the father was no longer in the picture.

"He's fallen in with a bad crowd," he allowed, which was true insofar as Oscar had always viewed religious orthodoxy askance. But the surgeon was uninterested in Oscar's complaints about the New York Hasidim — the Black Hats, as he called them — reiterating that the family must come to a decision about surgery, the sooner the better. The truth was, with Charlie's father having deserted them, and Oscar's poor daughter in a state of what he persisted in calling post-nasal depression, the decision came down to Oscar — Oscar, with a little help from Weeza, who wasn't a blood relative but, credit due, would always have Charlie's best interests at heart. Weeza, Charlie's godless godmother, as she would call herself, was of one mind with Oscar. In the end, he decided he was disinclined to meddle with perfection.

He had waited too long and too anxiously for this grandchild. His daughter was a change-of-life baby, born when Oscar's dear wife, Chaya Rifke, was in her forties. Now Jules, herself nearing forty, had given birth to this perfect child. The Minkoff women could not be hurried, Oscar thought fondly. They took their own sweet time, time becoming sweet, dripping like honey from a wooden spoon. *But who holds the spoon, Wolfie?* Chaya-Rifke-in-his-head prompted him. She was always reminding him that their lives were in the hands of the Almighty — a gift.

A gift! That was how Oscar had viewed his baby daughter,

even when his beloved Chaya Rifke succumbed shortly after labour to a blood infection sustained during the long and complicated birth, a birth in which two children were born although only one survived. Broken-hearted though he was, Oscar had raised his little daughter as best he could given her perverse nature, her fiercely independent spirit, and her flagrant disregard for convention, all of which Oscar understood was because Jules was an artist, had been since birth. That was how it was, he reflected: you began as you meant to go on.

But when he tried to explain this point of view to Charlie's surgeon, the man convulsed with rage, banging his fist into his palm and speaking so emphatically that he bit each word off at the root. Perhaps this was why it took Oscar a moment to realize the terrible man had called his grandchild a ticking time bomb whose controlled detonation he was willing to oversee but whose "artistic success" he could not guarantee. Sarcasm would never be enough for some folks, Oscar reflected. In addition, they had to use finger quotes to express their disgust.

In response Oscar brought up one of his favourite stories: "Cat in a Box," as he called it. The short of it was that if a cat got stuck in a box you could never be sure what was happening in that box until you lifted the lid. Cat could be asleep, cat could be awake, cat could even be, God forbid, passed away. The trick was to let cat make its own decision, with the understanding that whatever happened, the cat could never go against its nature. It could never, for example, become a dog or—here Oscar turned the finger quotes he'd resented back upon the surgeon—"a bomb."

Fascinated by Oscar's highly original interpretation of

Schrödinger's thought experiment though she was, Dr. Jabbour felt obliged to intervene. A pediatric endocrinologist, she'd been called in for a consultation and, like Oscar, had taken against the surgeon's harrowing sense of emergency. In the flurry of chromosomal testing and analysis of genital tissue that the surgeon had insisted on ordering and the ensuing brouhaha about what to do, what *choices* to make, hers was the voice of reason. "The decision is up to the child," she said. "I look forward to watching him grow into an extraordinary young person."

"Or *her*," she amended hastily.

Now here was Charlie, thirteen years later, still at sixes and sevens. But despite what Jules had written on the Wonder Wall, the boy wasn't angry at God or mad as hell. He didn't hate his mother, he hadn't given up on his deadbeat father, and he hardly ever wished he'd never been born. On the contrary, Charlie was hopeful, prone to hope as others are to asthma or allergies. This dogged optimism verged on foolishness, his grandfather sometimes thought. But foolishness, as Oscar knew, wasn't the absence of light. It was the absence out of which the light could be separated from the darkness and the heavens from the earth.

RIVER

The night before his thirteenth birthday and his first day at Assiniboine High School, Charlie couldn't sleep. He lay awake listening to the ancient building settling around him: the knocking of pipes in walls, gurgle of water through drains, distant ping of the elevator stopping randomly on one floor or another. The few tenants left in the old GNC Building had settled in for the night, but still the elevator roved up and down the creaky backbone of its shaft, emitting electronic signals of effort and distress. *Ping, ping, ping.*

Fall had come early, the wind seeping through badly sealed window frames, radiators giving off a faintly clanking, wholly unconvincing warmth. For once Charlie was glad of Gellman snuffling at his feet, sharing his kibble-breathed, doggy fug, his fur electric with static.

As always when he was exhausted and twanging with nerves, Charlie felt a creeping nausea build in him until his resolve *not* to vomit flared up in response and, with effort, overcame the queasy sensation of saliva flooding his mouth, sweat beading along his hairline, even the way his stomach punched through his diaphragm like a fist. He hadn't thrown up since he was a young kid (five-and-three-quarters, stomach flu, worst three days of his life). The experience of being at the mercy of something nastier and more violent than he could ever hope to be gave him something to aim for: a throw-up-free zone of deep breathing, judicious swallowing, and distraction. A life in which one particular indignity could be controlled.

It had been seven years since the last incident, a winning streak Charlie saw no reason to break. Breathing deeply, he swallowed down the nausea as well as a mouthful of pre-throw-up phlegm and turned his attention to his birthday card. His father's card had arrived, as it did every year, in an envelope postmarked New York City, NY. Charlie had torn it open with barely controlled excitement (was this the year that his mysterious father would reveal himself?) followed by deflation (no, it was not). The card featured a goofy-looking boy gazing into a sky full of stars. It was as if Charlie's father had forgotten how old his son was, thirteen being well after the cut-off for wishes and shooting stars, you would think. "Happy Birthday, Charlie," he'd written, signing it as he always did, "Your Father, Nathan Dervish."

It was an odd thing to send, this childish birthday card, to the son he'd never met, but according to Oscar, Nathan Dervish was an odd man. Even Jules indicated this was so, and Jules was the proverbial kettle when it came to oddness. That's all she'd allow, however, his father being a subject that no longer interested her. Jules's lack of interest was legendary, eclipse-worthy — it could block out the sun — so Charlie was careful to keep the cards to himself, each one returned to its envelope after its solemn birthday message had been delivered and stored in a shoebox beneath his bed. One day, he was certain, his father would seek him out, following the bread-crumb trail of birthday cards through the forest of his indifference. That this hadn't happened yet was no indication that it wouldn't. In fact it was proof that, law-of-averages-wise, it was fated to occur in some undisclosed future of *rapprochement*. As always, Charlie was hopeful.

Storing the card, his attention was diverted by sounds filtering into his room from the street. Car doors slamming mostly, the thump of bass from a stereo, someone telling someone else to get in the fucken car. He was used to the downtown rhythms, the layered sounds that changed over the course of an evening, from the six o'clock lull after office workers and retailers had departed (buses huffing pneumatically on Main, clang of metal shutters over storefronts) to the night city shuddering into gear. First the restaurants opened for business (car horns, car doors, patrons exclaiming in the street; in summer the clink of glasses from patios, salsa, and jazz), then the bars and clubs (more car horns and doors, idling cabs, girls shrieking, police sirens, glass breaking, bass thump from car stereos, hip hop and EDM). The bars closed late (snatches of song, drunken arguments—*get in the car/ no you get in the car/where'd you park the fucken car?*—screech of tires, jeers and catcalls) and then it was just train whistles and imagined country music ballads until the garbage trucks rolled through the alleys at dawn.

Charlie was used to it. It was the way he'd learned to tell time, time being what passed for companionship when you couldn't sleep.

Something blundered through the alley, clattering the bins and yowling. It was only a cat, probably Alexandra on her nightly prowl, looking for rodents or romance, but the drawn-out cry sounded uncannily like an abandoned baby. *Was* it a baby? Charlie wondered. Had someone stuffed a newborn in the Dumpster for Lenny to discover? The custodian could be counted on to rifle through the garbage searching for iniquities on the part of the elderly tenants, whose grasp of blue-box etiquette was shaky. He was always on the lookout for non-recyclable products: Styrofoam containers and plastic bags, Q-tips and pill bottles and batteries, his temper roused when he came across an un-collapsed cereal box or a soup tin that one of the tenants had failed to crush. Old age was no excuse, he maintained; he'd been older for longer than anyone.

The wail sounded again, impossibly high-pitched and plaintive. Charlie didn't like to think of that poor baby being pawed over by Lenny, he really didn't. He wished Jules would come home so he could ask her what to do, and then he wished she were the kind of mother who gave advice, and then he was off on the swoopy trajectory of his wishing, an impulse that only tormented him on wakeful nights. Or cold, blustery nights. Or the night before his thirteenth birthday. Or the night before school began. All of which this night coincidentally happened to be.

The piteous mewling grew louder. He knew he ought to go and rescue the baby, ought becoming could and could becoming would and would hauling him out of bed so that before he knew it he was pulling a fleece over his head and searching for his socks. *That's right, darlink, go rescue the baby,* Oscar would have said in response to the Minkoff propensity for saving abandoned waifs whether such children were real or not. *I'm talking about you-know-who,* he'd allow, winking. But you-know-who wasn't home yet and Charlie was all there was, Gellman, lousy animal that he was, having opened an eye, swivelled an ear, then rooted his way back into dreams of grandeur.

Charlie was still sitting on the side of the bed shaking his big, heavy head and willing himself into heroism when the mewling abruptly stopped and furious hostilities broke out, cats spitting and hissing like oil in a pan. A window banged open below and Mr. Skerrit from 2C, who was definitely not a cat lover, started hurling abuse at the confounded noise merchants (his words).

Mr. Skerrit hurled shoes too, a collection of which he kept at the ready given the swiftness of his ear-to-hand co-ordination. Lenny refused to dispose of the scuffed brogues and stinking sneakers that rained down from above, littering the alley until Charlie, in the course of one of his garbage runs, gathered them up and lobbed them in the Dumpster. What was it all about, the anger, the shoes? Although Charlie was puzzled, it was a familiar puzzlement, so recognizable he wouldn't have known what to do if the secret pulleys and levers of the bewildering adult world were suddenly revealed to him in a blinding flash of light. As abruptly as it had begun, the caterwauling ceased and Mr. Skerrit banged down his window. Once more, Charlie was left in the dark.

Often Jules didn't come home at all, going straight from her closing shift at the bar to the warehouse where she worked on her installations. It was cool, Charlie understood. He had Gellman and his own nervy bravado; he wasn't afraid. He really hoped she'd come home tonight though, and sometime after the 3:15 night train passed through the railway yard, she did. He heard the scrape of her boots on the stairs, the click of a key in the lock, the clatter of coins on the counter as she emptied her pockets. He was so relieved he almost couldn't help himself. Then he remembered how she'd glare at Gellman when the dog flung his loony, needful self at her, and he stayed put until he heard the sofa creak, waiting until he was certain she was sleeping, which she always was the moment she lay down, verticality being the only impediment to her famous ability to fall deeply and immediately asleep.

Sure enough, when he peered through the door she was stretched out on the sofa, arm flung over her eyes, already snoring. Her notebook was on the kitchen counter along with her change and keys and a small stack of twenties. He flipped open the notebook, but it was the usual stuff: a phone number, a bunch of crossed-out sentences, a question mark. She'd passed out before she could yank off her boots, so he eased them off and covered her with the afghan Mrs. Oslavsky had crocheted for his birthday. Looking down at Jules, he felt a familiar kinship. When she was asleep, when she couldn't stare back, her face eased him. It was as if the nerves behind his eyeballs could finally go slack, soften, and lose their painful hyper-vigilance.

A moment later exhaustion hit. He fumbled his way to bed, where the sheets were still warm from his just-vacated self and the dog was turning in his sleep, his fur setting off blue flashes of static in the dark.

—

Voice Mail Message
For: Charles Minkoff
From: Dr. Amala Jabbour,
Department of Pediatric Endocrinology

This is a message for Charles Minkoff. Dr. Jabbour here. It's that time again, young man. Since we haven't heard from you, I assume you are in the pink. Good news! However, we can't forgo your regular checkup. In addition, we're approaching a point where we need to make some tough decisions. I look forward to seeing you again, and not only because I'm so fond of you. Nurse Imelda says call the office to set up an appointment. Telephone operators are standing by!

———

THURSDAY, SEPTEMBER 12, 2019

It was the second week of fall semester and already Charlie's responsibilities weighed heavily, foremost among them the imperatives to escape gym class, choose an elective, and establish a dashing persona. Luckily, Mr. Bezos, the Phys. Ed. teacher, was on board with the first of these chores.

"Yeah, no. Totally," he said, looking Charlie up and down, then grabbing the permission slip and almost tearing it with his signature. Pretending to be his mother, Charlie had written a needlessly comprehensive account of his ailments, informing the gym teacher of his tendency towards flat feet and shin splints. Mr. Bezos must have known all about that, though. He couldn't get rid of the boy fast enough. Charlie got that a lot.

Charlie had once been thin as a rail, his features delicate and feminine, making it difficult for teachers and kids to reconcile the slender girl he resembled with the boy he was. Thankfully no one referred to him as *she* anymore (good), a consequence of not referring to him as anything (bad), ignoring him because some things were too darn complicated (terrible). The cognitive dissonance was too great for unsophisticated minds to negotiate, Dr. Jabbour had explained. *In other words, Charles: not your fault.* But Dr. Jabbour's no-fault clause notwithstanding, Charlie remained downcast. Adolescence was a rake lying in long grass. One minute you were walking barefoot through the garden listening to the birds, the next something smacked you between the eyes so hard you saw double. And if adolescence was complicated by a body that changed in frightening and unpredictable ways (more frightening and unpredictable than most adolescent bodies, Dr. Jabbour confirmed), and if this body was both mortifying and medically problematic, what then? Ten rakes! Twenty! A whole garden of concealed weaponry and rusty prongs.

I wish I could tell you it gets better, Charles, Dr. Jabbour said. *It doesn't get better. You do, though. You get better.*

Charlie would have liked to believe her. Dr. Jabbour had a nifty way of banishing demons with aphorism. Trouble was she persisted in calling him Charles, as if his first name were merely a nickname, a childish hoax she saw through with her X-ray eyes and polygraph instincts. How could he trust a doctor who couldn't remember his name, or worse, refused to believe it?

One of the troubles was that his appetite had outpaced his metabolism. For a while the two had jogged along amiably until slowly, then less slowly, and eventually not at all slowly, appetite pulled ahead, lapping its worthy opponent. The spirit of the thin kid he'd been hung around for a while, accounting for his expression of wide-eyed incredulity but doing nothing to explain his portly thighs, his developing breasts, his high-pitched, reedy voice, the spackle of freckles spreading over his cheeks, or the wild thicket of red hair standing up around his head. You couldn't make this stuff up. A gun loaded with ugly had gone off in his face, Charlie thought every time he looked in the mirror, a habit he avoided whenever possible.

So much for his dashing persona. Putting aside such thoughts, Charlie realized he still hadn't chosen an elective and time was a-ticking.

"You should try Textiles," the guidance counsellor, Ms. Heller, told him. "I mean it looks like you enjoy fashion."

"Well, sure, who doesn't?" he said, taking a gander at Ms. Heller in her post-white cotton turtleneck and baggy-diaper cords.

Charlie was wearing the charcoal-grey sports jacket Oscar had given him, the very first jacket his grandfather had ever made. It was a real beaut, heavy and soft, wide lapels and a loose, boxy fit. The fabric was so finely woven that it felt supple and alive when he ran his fingers over it. It had two front-flap pockets and a vent at the back, but the real kicker was a row of nifty Union Knopf horn buttons down the front. The lining was striped satin that moved with the light. His grandfather had stitched his monogram into the label in neat scarlet letters: OWM. Oscar Wolf Minkoff.

Natty, Oscar called it. It was a little roomy across the shoulders, and more than a little snug over the stomach but Charlie didn't want to seem particular so he told his grandfather he'd grow into it.

"Sure you will, darlink," Oscar said, "but while we're waiting why don't we nab from out here. Maybe extend from out there?" He moved his hands from side to side, measuring. As far as grandfathers went, Oscar was totally boss. For forty-five years he'd been in men's apparel, tailoring bespoke suits for the man-all-around-town, as he put it. It thrilled him to work on the alterations to his grandson's jacket, his spectacles smudgy with exertion, a row of pins bristling from his mouth.

"Well, dear?" asked Ms. Heller. "Shall I just—"

The fact was Charlie didn't want to sign up for Textiles— his grandfather was the fashion maven in the family—and that went double for Creative Arts because his mom was *that* Jules Minkoff. Obviously, Woodwork was an accident waiting for an occasion, ditto Metals, double-ditto Auto Mechanics and Improv and Dance, while something called Life Skills was too hideous to contemplate, which only left—

"Ancestry Studies?" Ms. Heller said. "Sure, why not."

—

Monday, September 16, 2019

To: Parents of Ancestry Studies students
From: Maude Kambaja

By now your child will have explained the "Roots Project" and hopefully you will be as excited as we are. My motto has always been: *To know where you are going you must know where you have been.* In this fast-paced world of "snap chat" and "life hacks" we tend to neglect the past, especially the "olden days," which is what my students call anything that happened before they were born!

We begin with the interview component of our project. As

an educator of many years, I believe in nurturing our students' sense of curiosity. Please take time to answer your child's questions patiently and thoroughly.

Kind Regards,

Maude Kambaja

———

An Exchange of Emails

To: Maude Kambaja

From: Jules Minkoff

What the hell is wrong with you? I don't have time for Charlie's questions. As for his father, good luck with that. The dude didn't leave a forwarding address let alone information on his earliest "memories, hopes, dreams, and accomplishments."

Yours, JM

P.S. Kudos, Kambaja. Congratulations on having a motto. I envy your single-mindedness.

To: Jules Minkoff

From: Maude Kambaja

Good morning Ms. Minkoff,

My apologies for burdening you. I wasn't informed of Charlie's father's absence. How distressing for you both. I shall put a note in Charlie's file explaining that his father is currently "AWOL."

Courage, Ms. Minkoff!

Maude Kambaja

To: Maude Kambaja
From: Jules Minkoff

Don't you dare put a note in Charlie's file. We've had enough trouble from social services and family counsellors. Charlie's father left when the kid was born. Total coincidence, nothing to do with the boy. Repeat: *Do not put a note in Charlie's file.*

What the hell kind of class is this anyway? I told Charlie not to bother me with questions about my childhood and where I went to school and what my parents did for a living. Shouldn't you be teaching these kids useful skills like computer hacking or post-nuclear survival strategies? Look, do me a solid. Give the boy an A for effort and let's move on. He'll know better when it comes to choosing an elective next time. I told him to give Domestic Science a whirl.

Yours, JM
P.S. What is it with you and quotation marks?

To: Jules Minkoff
From: Maude Kambaja

Good morning Ms. Minkoff,
My (correct) use of quotation marks aside, I am torn between sympathy and my duty as an educator. It's not unusual for a student to be unable to complete the "Parental History" module because a parent is deceased or estranged by divorce. In such cases, the student is encouraged to interview the remaining parent. In your case, though, I confess myself to be "brick-walled." I understand why Charlie's father is unable to take part in our project; however, I don't understand your reluctance. Nevertheless, I shall accept it in good faith.

My proposal is to suggest that Charlie ask a grandparent, if such a person exists, to stand *in loco parentis*. May I assume such a solution is acceptable to you?

To: Maude Kambaja
From: Jules Minkoff

Assume away, Ms. K. I wouldn't want to make an ass out of either of us. The boy does indeed possess a living, breathing grandparent of reasonably sound mind. Tell Charlie to knock himself out.

—

Bingo! thought Charlie when he heard the news. Oscar Wolf Minkoff was Charlie's favourite person in the world, his best friend and lifelong confidant.

Jules had just forwarded him her correspondence with Ms. Kambaja. He read it with a sense of awe and misgiving, the usual mixture of emotions he experienced when presented with one of his mother's infrequent forays into his world. Credit due, she didn't usually interfere in his life for all kinds of reasons that mostly had to do with not wanting to be bothered with minutiae, not-bothered being her universal preference. She certainly wasn't the kind of mom to email teachers except in some bizarro world where up was down and left was right, and "I'm proud of you, honey," was kitty-corner to "Keep in touch, kiddo." Something about the Roots Project had irked her, Charlie surmised, irked her mightily, although as always she refused to discuss it.

Not talking about it wasn't her fault, though. Absolutely

the least noteworthy thing about her, she maintained, was her muteness, the fact that she'd lost her voice years ago after a bout of pneumonia. She was an artist, a generator of images and ideas, every last one of which was more interesting than the tetchy biographical details of her life. Though Charlie might have informed her that it wasn't so much the muteness that was noteworthy as the circumstances leading to it: his mother's sallying forth during a freak blizzard, actually going so far as to fall through the ice of the Assiniboine River while the storm raged—a storm that caused power outages and millions of dollars in property damage, claiming seven lives (more if you counted shovelling-related heart attacks) and creating an unseemly bump in population figures nine months later. He'd been five years old the last time he heard his mother's voice, a voice he barely remembered before it too had disappeared into the void of lost things.

Worn out though he was from dealing with stuff beyond his years, Charlie took a moment to marvel at his teacher's persistence. They were all like that—teachers—convinced that kids were wily and parents delinquent, and that the only way to quell revolt was through a system of escalating surveillances: parents over children, teachers over parents. "Why do I have to sign every bloody page?" Jules had complained way back in first grade when Charlie had approached her, a five-year-old with his homework in hand. Jules could speak in those days although she tried not to swear, an enterprise subject to considerable backsliding. She'd start out well—Gee whiz! Gosh darn!—but the effort was the cause of such linguistic fatigue she'd have no recourse but to let loose with the only language that gave vent to the frustration she felt at not being allowed to use it. She tried, though. Give her an A for effort.

That very afternoon Jules had sat him down with a sheet of drawing paper and a pencil. Then she'd scrawled her signature at the top: "There you go, kid. Don't tell me I never teach you anything useful." Sprawling on the dusty floor of the loft beneath the wide, river-facing windows, Charlie had covered the page with wobbly imitations of his mother's signature, his letters resembling an army of ants rambling over uneven terrain. But Jules had merely shaken her head and ripped another page from her sketch pad.

Rip, rip, rip. The sound of paper tearing punctuated the winter afternoon. Charlie's wrist ached and his fingers grew numb. The sun had poked its head, in turn, into each of the windows fronting the GNC Building and was hiding behind the Heck Anderson Warehouse when she paused in the middle of ripping out yet another page and shrugged. Good enough.

That was long ago. Charlie had just turned five and Jules hadn't yet heard the voice luring her out into the worst blizzard in the city's history. *It was a child's voice*, she croaked when they rescued her, the last words she ever spoke. A little girl. Apparently the ghost child had been calling his mother by name: *Jules! Jules! Jules!* For a long time Charlie believed in the child, the cruel sprite who'd stolen his mother's voice by coaxing her onto the frozen river. All that followed — ice cracking, Jules teetering, falling, hanging on, giving up, being rescued (just in time), hypothermia, shock, pneumonia, two days on a ventilator in the ICU, the damage to her laryngeal nerves that the doctor said shouldn't have happened (but had), and shouldn't be permanent (but was) — was oddly beside the point. Even before the accident she'd been a woman of few words.

"She wasn't always like that," Oscar said.

Whenever Charlie asked Oscar what his mother was like as a girl, Oscar said the same thing. "Like a sparrow she would chatter. Enough for two, the little dolly." In fact, there *were* two, once: Jules and her twin sister, who'd been born still, meaning—Oscar tried to explain—still she was born even though not alive.

"Don't cry, zeide," Charlie said. "Please don't cry." He stroked his grandfather's hand, trying to think of something to cheer him up.

"'Only what is made from sugar has the ability to melt.'" Oscar replied, adding: "*Ethics of the Fathers*. Look it up."

Oscar was always making up quotes from the spiritual guide for the perplexed known as the *Ethics of the Fathers* and instructing his grandson to look them up. Charlie appreciated the effort that went into Oscar's humour, but it was strange to think of his mother as a child, even stranger to think of her long-ago sparrow-like chatter.

"True," Oscar said. "One-hundred-and-eighty degrees different from now. No, why be stingy? One-hundred-and-ninety degrees! Two hundred!"

Silence was his mother's superpower, Charlie thought. It transformed *other* people, making them jittery and high-strung. Sooner or later everyone fell silent in her presence, not in solidarity but in shame. Her muteness made them feel ridiculous just as their chatter made her seem profound. The truth was she'd go to any length to keep the world's hee-haw at bay, to live within the silence Oscar claimed there would be time for when he was dead. That was the difference between Jules and Oscar, Weeza joked: they were both artists.

Most nights she came off her bartending shift at the Sans

Souci and walked across town to the warehouse on Railway Road, where she worked on her installations and sculptures, her invisibility machines and memory factories. If anyone cared to contact her, they were welcome to. After all, she always had her notebook, a worn steno pad tucked into the back pocket of her jeans. But technology had advanced in the years since the accident. There were machines that vibrated to vocal cords, smartphones and instant messaging, text-to-speech devices, computer-generated speech synthesizers. If she'd shown an inclination to use her hands in the service of her tongue, Charlie would have learned sign language; if she'd been willing to mouth the words he would have learned to lip-read. She was disinclined, unwilling. Silence was her home, one she carried on her back, spiritual nomad that she was, while all around voices rose and fell, argued and insinuated and raged. In the end *not* choosing to be heard was more powerful than letting machines speak for you (see *Invisibility Machine #9*), although this wasn't something other people, no matter how much they loved you, understood.

"Why don't you have a smartphone like everyone else?" Weeza yelled.

Anyone could text me!!! Jules scribbled on a clean page of her notebook.

"Only the people you give your number to, Mom," Charlie pointed out, and Jules stared at him blankly as if to say, *There's no one I want to talk to. No one at all.* She must have noticed her son's face fall. Shortly afterwards she installed the Wonder Wall, a giant chalkboard that she hung on the back wall of the loft.

Mr. Watson, come here, I want to see you, was the first thing she wrote on the Wonder Wall.

"He's a kid, you terminal idiot!" Weeza scolded when she saw her friend's attempt at motherly chit-chat. "He doesn't know about the invention of the telephone."

The truth was Jules wasn't like other mothers. She never concerned herself with her son's school work or how many vegetables he ate or worried about leaving him alone, which was technically illegal, a technicality she was inclined to view as theoretical. On nights she came off her shift too jazzed to work in her studio, the barely heated warehouse on Railway Road, she loped through the windy downtown streets, listening for the voice she'd heard calling from the frozen river, until eventually she siphoned off her nervous energy and came home to sleep.

Bartending might not have been the ideal job for a fifty-year-old single mom permanently stuck on mute, but Jules made it work for her. Her looks were no impediment: lean women with ropy muscles and high-intensity blue eyes could get away with far less than the curt nods, occasional note-book scribbles, and slow whiskey-burn smiles she bestowed on her customers. She had dark, curly hair, worn short, tucked behind her ears, and large, callused hands, the skin split over her knuckles like a man's cracked and weathered leather gloves. Recently, a dramatic Pepé Le Pew streak had sprung up at her left temple. Jules made no effort to hide the grey, being clear that a damn was just one more thing she wasn't inclined to give.

It was ironic but not unexpected, given the measure of alcoholic self-absorption, that only the Sans Souci regulars knew she couldn't, rather than wouldn't, speak. Some customers swore that they'd heard her speak, others that she was loquacious as hell, a regular chatterbox. But most assumed she was profound, a narrow channel through which still waters ran deep. They tended to use her as a sounding board, which in her opinion was what folks required when it came to a late-night conversation in a hotel bar, or any kind of bar, or indeed any conversation, ever. Almost a decade of muteness had convinced her that what patrons wanted when they asked for advice was the opportunity to talk themselves into a state of sublime justification, to which justification Jules Minkoff happened to be deeply and unshakably indifferent.

On mornings when Charlie woke to discover his mother asleep on the sofa, fully dressed and snoring, too weary to haul her ass to bed, he'd flip open the notebook she left on the counter along with her tips, the stacks of loonies and grubby bills. There was never anything in his mother's jottings to indicate profound thoughts or late-night intimacies. *Jets lost in overtime* might be scribbled on one page, and on the next: *Why the long face, dude?* Each line was crossed through after it had served its purpose, giving nothing away. Charlie knew not to wake her, and even Gellman, hopeless mutt that he was, had mastered the art of silent imprecation. Instead of barking he'd roll his eyes, grimace comically, and finally, as Charlie was leaving for school, hide his huge misshapen head in his paws. *Bye, kid. I'll miss you. Don't forget me when you hit the big time.*

Like Gellman, Charlie was aware of the inadequacies of time, largely that it always seemed to be running out. He could actually *feel* time trickling like sand through his body, rendering him heavy and immobile, fixed in place. *Your mom needs time to herself,* Weeza would explain, adding that all artists needed time. She'd laugh as if to say, *Some dope, huh?* Jules, she meant, not Charlie. But Charlie, smart kid that he was, had received the message. (*Loud and clear, Mr. Watson!*) He was sorry that Jules had gotten stuck with him and made a point of not wasting her time, taking up her attention, or burdening her with the dull, rub-along duties of motherhood.

—

Thursday, September 19, 2019

To: Ancestry Studies students
From: Ms. Kambaja

Learning Template
1) Interview a parent asking **prepared** questions about background, family life, schooling, favourite foods, and music. Does your mother/father feel as if they are part of history? You might be surprised at the answer!
2) Write a biographical report about your parent.
3) You must hand in **both** your transcribed interview and your completed biography.

Due date: **October 3, 2019**
"Your history began before you were born and will continue long after you are gone."

Ralph Waldo Emerson

—

FRIDAY, SEPTEMBER 20, 2019

Charlie loved visiting Oscar on Friday afternoons, when the smell of fresh cinnamon buns wafted through the hallways of the Seth Rowe. Jules would swing by sometimes to play chess, Weeza visiting too when she was in town to sneak in forbidden delicacies from Mr. Ken's. But Friday was Charlie's day; you could set your watch by it. The Seth Rowe was a pretty decent place to live, but Oscar insisted on calling it the Death Row because it was the last stop before the final one. "What's the chance of the governor commuting the sentence to life?" he always said.

"Long odds, zeide."

"What long odds? Long odds is a snowball's chance in hell. Long odds is the Goldeyes making the playoffs. No chance is the correct answer. No chance at all."

Charlie's earliest memory — earlier than signing his mother's name, earlier than the blizzard — was sitting on his grandfather's lap, the old man teaching him his Hebrew letters. The itch of Oscar's woollen jacket and the nose-twitching odour of naphthalene not only kept him from sleepiness but roused him. This was the quality of woke-upedness that he associated with the pages of Hebrew print; each letter resembled a twisted flame, each word a small black fire burning on the page. The flames were outshoots of one fire, a raging conflagration of effort and belief. But Oscar was patient, his gentle finger tap-tapping beneath the lines of back-to-front print, helping Charlie sound out the harsh, throat-clearing syllables, tucking a handful of Hershey's Kisses into his grandson's pocket for every page he mastered. Learning should always be sweet, he said.

Charlie had to duck out of school early to catch the 39 bus that would get him to the Seth Rowe by three, the latest you could arrive if you wanted to snag a cinnamon bun straight from the oven. Oritsia, who worked in the kitchen, sprinkled brown sugar on the buns before they went in and, once they were baked, ladled on more brown sugar before angling the whole puffy, gritty, oozing delicious mess under the grill. When the golden spirals finally emerged, they were rigid with caramelized sugar. You could hear the granules crackling between your teeth.

Once ensconced in a corner of the residents' lounge, a couple of the fabled cinnamon buns before them (still warm!), Charlie told his grandfather about the Roots Project. Oscar was tickled at the idea of being interviewed, less so by the prospect of having to speak into the boy's iPhone, but Charlie reassured him that the "foolish gadget" would pick up his voice, no problem, and that he should just forget about it and speak naturally.

"You got it," Oscar said, immediately lowering his voice from the rousing bellow in which he'd been confiding his deepest secrets on the assumption that the iPhone was as hard of hearing as many of the Seth Rowe residents. It went swimmingly after that, Oscar losing himself in the past as Charlie listened, open-mouthed.

Roots Project
Interviewee: Mr. Oscar Wolf Minkoff
Place: Residents' Lounge, Seth Rowe Care Home

C: Can you tell me where you were born, Mr. Minkoff?
O: First answer is nowhere. Some people, Charlie, they come
   out of nowhere and nowhere is where they end up. That's
   the God's honest truth.
C: No, but really.
O: Already with the objections. Like a lawyer you are. Second

answer is Some Place. Some Place you've never heard of. Some Place that doesn't exist anymore. Ever heard of a town called Some Place, darlink? A secret, I'll tell you. That handful of dust and ashes didn't even have a name until the river flooded. One day the river flooded and washed bales of hay from the fields. All the people hollered, *Vu iz der hey? Vu iz der hey?*

C: What does that mean?

O: Like it sounds, Charlie. They were searching for the hay.

C: Huh. Okay, next question. What do you remember of your childhood?

O: Fires is what I remember. First fire, second fire, and so on, et cetera. Everything was made of wood. The stores, the houses, the school. Every summer there was a fire. One year the tavern burned down, next year the Hebrew school. What can you do? You build up again. And when that burns down, again you build up. Only by the end came the fire nobody could put out. All of us, we all burned to ashes in that fire.

C: Zeide, don't cry.

O: Okay, okay. Hoo-boy. So darlink, give me a good question. What else you got? You want to know a secret? Question: Can a person be dead but also alive? Answer: Yes! Can happen.

C: You mean like zombies?

O: Next question. Can a person be a boy but also not a boy? Answer: Also yes!

C: So not zombies?

O: Answer is disguise, Charlie. *Disguise.* What a person wears on his back and on his head. If a kerchief a girl, if a hat a boy.

C: Ha ha, were you a cross-dresser, zeide?

O: Matter of fact, yes. Hah! A cross-dressing zombie, Charlie. What do you think of that? Now I have another question for you. Question: Can a Jew have a wish? Answer: Certainly, why not? Next question: For what does he wish?

C: Um. Depends, right?

O: He wishes he doesn't.

C: What kind of wish is that?

O: He wishes he doesn't see the German soldiers march into town. He wishes he doesn't hear them shout *all the men stand here, all the women and children go over there*. He wishes he doesn't see the men line up at the door of the Beit Midrash. He wishes his mother doesn't grab him as he tries to stand beside his father. He wishes she doesn't whisper to his sister *give him the kerchief, give him the shawl*. He wishes she doesn't tie an apron on him and say *from now on you are my daughter*.

C: Hoo-boy, that's—

O: Exactly. Hoo-boy. In a nutshell: to save her son's life my mother broke the law and sentenced herself to a hundred years in Gehenna, she must have thought. As it says in the Torah, a man shouldn't wear women's clothing and vice versa. Same goes for boys and girls. No offence, darlink. Times were different but the Torah remains the same.

C: What happened to the men, zeide?

O: Murdered. Shot in the forest. No one remaining.

C: And the women?

O: What do you think? Murdered also. Shot also, later. No one got out alive.

C: So how did you—

O: I was the Wonder Boy. That's what they called me, the resistance fighters in the forest and the doctors at the DP camp.

I should have been dead nine, ten times already. Dead like my mother and father and sisters. Dead like one of the six million, may their blessed souls rest in peace. I'll tell you a secret, darlink. Secret is, I don't know. Secret is maybe I died. Like they say, those who stand on the threshold of death are themselves dead so maybe the Wonder Boy is already dead. A creature of mud and ashes, a golem. Do you know what a golem is?

C: Here, zeide, let me wipe your eyes. Do you want to—

O: No, Charlie. Don't you want to hear more secrets?

C: Of course I do, zeide.

O: What secret am I on? Have you been counting? I was a boy for thirteen years, almost bar mitzvah, then I was a girl for a month. This was after the men were murdered. One day my mother heard they were rounding up the women and children so she told me I must go, flee, hide. She took me in the kitchen and cut off my hair. One minute changed into a girl, next minute back into a boy. She gave me a Chumash and the last piece of bread. I wanted to stay with her but she wouldn't let me. She pinched me on the arm and said hateful things to me so I'd run away. To my shame I believed her. I ran.

C: Please don't cry, zeide. I'm sorry—

O: The last secret I'll give you for free. Ready, Charlie? Secret is you can't catch someone who doesn't exist.

O: Wonder Boy is signing off now. It's almost dinner and I don't want Himmelfarb to grab my place. Did I tell you there's a new widow in town? The Widow Dershowitz, a peach, if you don't mind me saying. Next time you come I'll introduce you.

C: It's been a pleasure, zeide.

O: Mutual, Charlie.

———

Thursday, October 3, 2019

Roots Project
Biography of Oscar Wolf Minkoff a.k.a. Wonder Boy
by Charlie Minkoff

My grandfather says I can say what I like about him, he's got nothing to hide, but be sure to mention the titanium in his hip, the pin in his knee, the arterial stent, and the pacemaker that keeps his heart ticking along. He wouldn't want to fool anyone that he's this good-looking without assistance. What with all the hardware in his system he feels like the Tin Man, he says, except he knows he's got a heart. If there's one thing he knows it's that.

Oscar Wolf Minkoff was born in Lithuania, the youngest of five. He is the only surviving member of his family as far as he knows. But he says you never know, he lives in hope. His mother, father, and sisters were murdered by the Nazis. The town where he was born got its name from the river flooding. I asked him what it's like to come from a town named after an accident with a river. He said he could ask me the same thing. (He means because the Cree called Winnipeg Muddy Waters.) Maybe all cities are named after the rivers they collide with, he says.

Anyway, the town my grandfather came from doesn't exist anymore. All the Jews were killed and everyone else is dead. The worms have already eaten them, Oscar says.

After the war he spent two years in a DP camp then came by boat to Canada and by train to the prairies. By the time he got here he was a scarecrow like Mr. Ray Bolger, his favourite actor. It was a miracle he survived the war, Oscar says. He was thin and his teeth were loose in his head, but the moment he laid eyes on Chaya Rifke Russ (my grandmother) he was struck by the Thunderbolt (love). She was walking down Selkirk Avenue with a friend. Oscar pretended to know this other girl so she'd introduce him to his intended. At first Chaya Rifke didn't exactly take to him but he wore her down. They were married August 15, 1949.

Oscar began as an office boy at Dervish Tailors, but old man Dervish took a shine to him and taught him the trade. He worked there forty-five years and was never late for work, not once. When Oscar wanted to marry Chaya Rifke he went to Mr. Dervish to borrow money for a ring. But Mr. Dervish said if he couldn't afford a ring he couldn't afford to get married. That's the only thing Oscar holds against him, he wants me to say. My grandfather was a master tailor, best in the city. His specialty was custom-fitted suits. He designed the famous Dervish three-button, low-cut waistcoat with knife-pleat pockets. No trick belts, no jazzy patterns, absolutely no fussy detailing. That waistcoat should have been called the famous Minkoff waistcoat, but Oscar bears Dervish no ill will. It was such a wonder it should have been patented, but Oscar was too busy to take out a patent and Dervish was too frugal. There's a vent in the back with just enough give.

Oscar's life has had its ups and downs. The downs you already know (war, Nazis, DP camp, everyone dead) and also the ups (marrying Chaya Rifke Russ, his *bashert*). When she died the light went out of his life. He was like a man possessed. He couldn't eat or sleep or laugh or even cry. His heart was a stone in his chest. All he did was sit and stare into space.

The only thing that would stay down was every now and then a glass of ginger ale. Maybe a couple saltines. It was a miracle he survived, but he had to keep going to look after his daughter. His favourite food is celebration noodles from Mr. Ken's Shanghai Palace. He loves kosher pickles and would give his right arm for another bite of Chaya Rifke's brisket with horseradish sauce. Oritsia's cinnamon buns are especially ace, although he hasn't met a dessert he doesn't get along with just fine.

Oscar's greatest joy was standing under the marriage canopy with Chaya Rifke Russ. His biggest regret was not hugging his mother goodbye. He had to hurry because he could feel History at full tilt, about to collide with him. Perhaps he should have turned back when she pushed him out the door but that was the call he made. Nothing he can do about it now. He also regrets not having a bar mitzvah. The Nazis invaded Europe and boys became men just like that, suddenly, a snap of the fingers. You didn't have to go to synagogue and read from the Torah to become a man. Still, it would have been nice.

—

When Charlie was young and his grandfather lived with them, Oscar would tell him stories. Every night a different story but also the same story: how he, Oscar Wolf Minkoff, a.k.a. Wonder Boy, had defeated, humiliated, and killed the evil Nazis with his bare hands and the force of his intellect. Unlike other superheroes, he didn't have to choose between brains and brawn. Courage he had in abundance, of course, he was the whole package: Scarecrow, Tin Man, and so-called Cowardly Lion after they arrived in Oz, made the acquaintance of the Wiz, and realized they already were what they had always longed to be.

Smart, kind, and brave: that was Oscar. He'd known Charlie all his life; a scrawny kid, he said, but the materials were there. ("Start with a good wool blend and you can't go wrong, darlink.") But Charlie wasn't a kid anymore and Oscar wasn't a superhero. Since he'd always known his grandfather wasn't a superhero, Charlie couldn't think why this confirmation made him feel bereft, as if someone he'd never known had turned out to be someone else he'd never known. But he comforted himself with the thought that smart-kind-and-brave was a combination worthy of superhero status. That was how it began: Charlie's idea to give Oscar the one thing he didn't have, the only thing he lacked.

FROG

Charlie, I'm phoning for Dr. J. Get your ass down here, mister.
I'm not kidding. She's worried about you, and so am I. Would
you or whoever's supposed to be in charge of you be so kind
as to return this call pronto? Pronto means now. Don't make
me come over there.

———

MONDAY, OCTOBER 7, 2019

For a change, Ms. Kambaja was correcting some kid's mispronunciation of her name. Kamb*a*ja, short vowel, name of
a teacher, not Komb*u*cha, long vowel, name of a tea, she was
saying. She went through this rigmarole often, explaining
that her name, like her parents, came from the Democratic
Republic of the Congo, a distant country. "Right, Abdulrahman?" she always said because Abdulrahman too had come
from away, although more recently.

"Right, Ms. Kombucha," he said.

41

Evidently deciding to cut her losses, Ms. Kambaja drew a line down the centre of the whiteboard, making two columns. At the top of the first she wrote "Truth," at the top of the other, "Story." The unbreached line between columns was meant to indicate the difference between accuracy and fantasy, between historical research and what she was forced to call creative lack of searching.

"Some of you," she said, "have been indulging in speculation."

Speculation was Ms. Kambaja's bugbear. Speculation was the road down which, once begun, one had no recourse but to continue through the ever more bumpy terrain of made-up-edness. There could be no turning back, no changing course. As all the students knew, she despised speculation and was now ready to administer yet another worksheet on archival research methods despite having promised to spend this period telling her own story, the story of her roots. Here she halted to receive the groans and protests, the expressions of disbelief and despair that were gratifyingly prompt in coming.

"That's enough palaver, people," she said.

She waited for complete silence before allowing that she would have been sorry to miss an opportunity to share her "well-researched" and "historically accurate" story with the Ancestry Studies class, who, after all, had been generous in sharing their "research" with her. As she talked, she scooped words out of the air with her fingers. She was a neat, modest woman, a decade short of retirement, every inch held in place by clips and grips (hair), rows of buttons (high-necked blouse, winter coat), and sturdy zippers (skirt, purse, book bag). Every inch but those fluttering, skeptical fingers whose characteristic flailing, more than her voice, expressed the incredulity she felt when confronted with stories that were neither accurate nor well researched. Charlie quailed.

Ms. Kambaja's family story—dramatic and wildly incongruous though it was—was no secret. Successive classes had been treated to a recitation of her origins: life and death, politics and romance, drama and moral reckoning, punctuated by occasional slapstick. The full catastrophe, as she often said. It was a well-known part of high school lore that the quiet Social Studies teacher was the daughter of a communist revolutionary and a Belgian nun. They'd met during the Simba Rebellion.

"Who can tell me what Simba means? What's that, Mr. Minkoff?"

Charlie, gazing at her open-mouthed, shook his head. He had no idea what Simba meant.

"Lion, Mr. Minkoff. The rebels chose the lion as their symbol because?"

"Courage?"

"Are you asking me or telling me?"

"...Um, telling?"

"Pay attention, Mr. Minkoff. You might surprise yourself by learning something."

Ms. Kambaja wrote "Simba Rebellion" on the board, and Charlie returned to his daydreaming. Even he, outcast that he was, had heard the story of how Ms. Kambaja's mother, along with hundreds of nuns, was taken hostage by the rebels in the old Victoria Hotel in Stanleyville. Ms. Kambaja explained that the nuns, who'd been abused by the rebel soldiers, were liberated in October 1964. Although the rebel army would disband six months later, her father, already disillusioned by the cause, had followed the Sisters of Saint Vincent de Paul by road from Uvira in the north to the city of Bukavu. Sister

Ursula, however, didn't want to return to Belgium. She and Antoine Joseph Kambaja had fallen in love and decided to flee to Canada, where Ms. Kambaja's father became a railroad employee and her mother cleaned houses. They worked hard and lived thriftily, saving enough money for their daughter to attend teachers' training college.

"Which was supremely lucky for you people," Ms. Kambaja finished, pausing to allow the chuckle of recognition that inevitably followed this observation. It was a chuckle that she relished every year since it acknowledged the moment when a minor character (improbably, magically) revealed herself to be the most important character of all: the storyteller, the narrator.

Smiling, Ms. Kambaja now asked if there were any questions and, as always, a legion of hands shot up. She surveyed her students and said she wouldn't be answering questions of a "personal" nature. She was unwilling to speculate on other people's "love affairs," she clarified, however extraordinary. And that, she observed smartly, was the difference between "Truth" (knuckle rap on the board) and "Story" (double rap).

"Any *other* questions? Simba Rebellion? Belgian Congo? War of Independence?"

The class fell silent as they did every year when deprived of the intimate landscape of romance for the broad sweep of history. Ms. Kambaja, having made her allegiance clear, regaled them with accounts of life in the humid rainforests of the Congo. Experience had taught her that adolescents loved tales of courage, rebellion, and rank squalor. Consequently, she told them of the people's valiant struggle for liberation, of bloody clashes between rebels and white mercenaries, and ended with an eyewitness account, related to her by her father, of a rebel's effort to rid himself of his tapeworm. This involved squatting, grabbing the worm's head as it protruded from his anus, then winding it around a stake in the ground so that it could be pulled, inch by inch, out of the poor man's digestive tract. The procedure took days, the sufferer squatting in the dirt, agonized.

Eww, eww, eww! the class responded as they did every year.

"Such is life," Ms. Kambaja observed as she did every year. "Comedy and tragedy, romance and loss, politics and farce. The full catastrophe."

"The full catastrophe," Oscar repeated, savouring the phrase. He was enchanted by Ms. Kambaja's showmanship, especially when Charlie revealed that she'd shown the class her family crest.

"You don't say. Fancy-schmancy!"

It wasn't a real crest, Charlie said. It was a diagram, a creative (double rap) illustration demonstrating what students must design for their final project.

"So Teacher made up her own family crest?" Oscar was even more impressed.

Charlie described the brightly coloured laminated shield Ms. Kambaja had passed around. In one quarter a lion reared up, in another the continent of Africa was depicted with a ragged-edged country outlined in red, and in the third a maple leaf fluttered.

"And the last quarter?" Oscar asked.

Charlie said he wasn't exactly sure and he didn't like to ask. It looked like some kind of flying nun, he thought, her wimple spread out like wings.

—

Ms. Kambaja wasn't the only one wanting him to research his family history. The last time he'd seen Dr. Jabbour she'd asked how the journal was going. Charlie tilted his hand from side to side.

"I'm not surprised," she said. She seldom was.

For years she'd been telling him — *advising* him — to get his life down on paper. For his own good as well as those who came after, as she was reliably certain many would follow his excellent example. The excellence was all hers, though. Emphatically opposed to medical intervention at such an early age, she'd snatched the baby out of the probing hands of the surgeon (a vile man, a ruffian) and thrust the squalling infant at Weeza.

"Certainly not," Dr. Jabbour said. "Does that sound like something I would do?" (That's exactly what she did, Weeza told him. Lucky for you, *mon chum!*)

Dr. Jabbour shone more brightly every time he saw her. In her starched white coat and dark skirt she seemed to glow, the image of the nun from Ms. Kambaja's story becoming entangled with that of the doctor who'd saved him. She *had* saved him, both Weeza and Oscar agreed, no question.

About the means of his salvation, however, Oscar was vague. "Save, spend, what's the difference?" he murmured, gazing lovingly at his grandson. "You're here, that's what's important."

Weeza was more explicit. "He wanted to castrate you, the bastard," she said when he eventually asked her.

Dr. Jabbour, his saviour!

As soon as Charlie was old enough, Dr. Jabbour took it

upon herself to educate him, sitting him down at his annual physical and telling him that like many babies, more than you'd think, actually, he'd been born with intersex traits. He was a healthy baby, she reassured him, a beautiful healthy baby with a unique anatomy. *Slightly* unique, nothing serious. But she wanted him to know that like all intersex children, like all *children*, he was greater than the sum of his parts: the bits of flesh he had or failed to have, the openings and closings, the imbalance of hormones he produced, even what was scribbled on his chromosomes.

Charlie nodded, confused, slightly tearful.

"Attaboy," Dr. Jabbour said, patting his hand.

The following year she drew sequences of Xs and Ys on her prescription pad. Taking up the story from where she'd left off, she explained that after chromosomal testing the doctors had discovered that his karyotype (XX) didn't match up with the appearance of his genitals, XX being, of course, a female karyotype. Charlie tried to look interested rather than anxious, but Dr. Jabbour had evidently decided that her patient had enough information for the time being. She waited until his next visit to approach the vexed question of anatomy, this time sketching a series of diagrams on the paper sheet Nurse Imelda pulled over the examination table after each patient. The diagrams were puzzling, but Charlie sensed they gave her something to do with her hands. For the first time since he'd known her, she was hesitant.

"Size is relative, Charles. When we say small we just mean smaller than average."

She was referring to his penis; Charlie blushed as she put her cool hand over his sweaty, trembling one.

"The more significant problem is hypospadias." It was a

big word for a simple concept, Dr. Jabbour explained. It meant that his urethral opening wasn't situated at the tip of his penis. His urethra was on the underside of his penis, low down, making it impossible for him to urinate while standing up, as he'd no doubt noticed.

"Pee-hole," she elucidated. But Charlie knew what a urethra was. Hadn't he been sitting down to pee all his life?

"Why's nothing where it's supposed to be?" he asked forlornly.

"Nature is full of variety," Dr. Jabbour replied. "One can only marvel."

That was her position, one she maintained resolutely. To all detractors, to all officious meddlers and unofficial butt-inskies bent on "modification," she replied in the same way: First, do no harm. Second, mind your own damn business. She'd maintained this moral stance from the first day, when, like a sinister parody of the three wise men come to bless the Christ child, the medical team of urologist, pediatric consultant, and vile plastic surgeon had descended on the newborn infant. Taking blood, ordering ultrasounds, drawing inscrutable symbols on the tiny pelvis, they had outlined a series of surgical procedures that were at best invasive, and at worst obscene.

Yes, *obscene*, Dr. Jabbour raged. She told Weeza how, as a medical student, she'd witnessed a terrified child waking up in a hospital bed, bloody gauze packed between trembling thighs. Thirteen years later, when Weeza was once again trying to rescue him, she told Charlie how Dr. Jabbour had described the surgeon going in, knife drawn. They'd opened the child's abdominal cavity and found healthy testes, which they'd removed, discarded. It was no use quoting Hippocrates,

Dr. Jabbour had said. The harm that was the first thing they'd pledged to avoid had already been done.

The last time Charlie saw Dr. Jabbour they'd talked about hoofbeats.

"Say you hear hoofbeats," she began. "Say they're coming towards you. Say you have to identify them to make your diagnosis. Say as a matter of urgency. Say a precious life hangs in the balance—"

When he remained silent she drummed her fingers on the table in imitation of the phantom hoofbeats. *Da-dum, da-dum, da-dum.*

Finally Charlie said, "Um, horses?" the nervous uptick in his voice turning every statement into a question.

She beamed. "Quite right, Charles. Horses."

"Right?"

"Certainly."

Charlie fidgeted. He didn't like to be rude.

"Horses is the correct answer. Nine times out of ten the answer is horses, horses, horses."

"Or, like, buffalo? Cows, maybe?" He didn't understand, but he was in there pitching.

"That's the spirit. What about zebras?"

"Well, maybe. I mean if you were in Africa…"

Once more Dr. Jabbour beamed. "Couldn't have said it better myself. Zebras in Africa, horses everywhere else. That is the credo we medics live by."

In time he understood what she was trying to tell him: when you hear hoofbeats, assume horses rather than zebras, assume it's a natural variation rather than a mutant stripe. This was her way of letting him know he was A-okay in her book, and Charlie appreciated the sentiment. Since that last visit he'd been dreaming of galloping hooves. There was no image, only a soundtrack: the rhythmic drum of hooves pursuing him. *Da-dum, da-dum, da-dum.* In the way of dreams, he understood that his disembodied dream self was sometimes fleeing over the Canadian prairies, at other times over a shadowless African savannah. But whichever grasslands he was scrambling over, the percussive throb was the same. And, inevitably, the hoofbeats overtook him, became indistinguishable from his heartbeat. His pursuer was coming from *inside* the house.

Dr. Jabbour felt about assumption the same way that Ms. Kambaja felt about speculation, Charlie realized. His teacher had urged him to research his story and write it up; his doctor, too, had advised precision. Keep a record, Charles, she told him from the beginning. After all, his circumstances were unusual, unique. For how many children had been allowed to grow—unobstructed and unhurried—into the person they would become, developing in or out of time, by choice rather than chance, into the full catastrophe of their joyful flowering?

"We wanted you to decide," Dr. Jabbour told him. "No right answers," she added.

As he grew into the boy he undoubtedly was, she expanded on her pedagogical model, telling him that the answer was always right but you got extra credit for showing how you had worked it out. Once again she urged him to keep a journal. To pull the story out of himself, inch by inch, winding it around whatever stake was at hand: truth or imagination, jubilance or despair. That way he'd save himself from what in years to come might gnaw at him from inside. Even so, agitation was normal, she assured him. Not because of his genitals or his chromosomes or his hormones, but because he was — here she stopped for a moment, searching for a word, hitting herself lightly on the chest when she found it — because he was human.

—

An Exchange of Emails
To: Maude Kambaja
From: Jules Minkoff

8.5 out of 13! Are you telling me my son's only worth 66 percent?

I read Charlie's interview. The kid smashed it out of the park. Drama, suspense, intrigue, cross-dressing. That piece had everything. Why the reticence, Kambaja? Why the lack of enthusiasm?

Yours in astonishment, JM

P.S. What kind of grade scale is *anything* out of 13?

To: Jules Minkoff
From: Maude Kambaja

Charlie received a mark of 8.5 out of 13 on his project which rounds down to 65 percent (*not* 66 percent). Sixty-five is a respectable grade although, like you, I believe him to be capable of better.

I assure you that as an experienced educator I don't assign personal "worth" to grades. I'm sure you realize how detrimental that would be. Charlie is a bright, curious student with the potential to score well into the high seventies/low eighties in future assignments. With his mother's encouragement perhaps this can be achieved.

Best wishes, MK

P.S. Thirteen is the product of four (research) plus four (grammar and organization) plus five (following instructions). It was chiefly in this last category that your son fell short.

To: Maude Kambaja
From: Jules Minkoff

Whoa, Kambaja! How ironic that Charlie "fell short" in following instructions. What about creativity? What about inspiration? Seems the only thing important in your classroom is that the trains run on time.

That's one. Two is expectations: not, in Charlie's case, great. I'll tell him to aim for the high seventies/low eighties. Don't stop until you achieve mediocrity, kid!

Three (and this is the doozy): I'm shocked at your failure to be moved by Oscar Wolf Minkoff's extraordinary journey from orphaned refugee in war-torn Europe to master tailor in postwar Winnipeg. Where's your heart, Kambaja? Where's your sense of history?

To: Jules Minkoff
From: Maude Kambaja

I take exception to your implication that my classroom is analogous to Fascist Italy. Your tone is—and has consistently been—hectoring. While understanding your concern, I'm not the one standing in the way of your son's academic success. To be clear: name-calling is neither a dignified nor effective means of expressing dissatisfaction, Ms. Minkoff. On the contrary, it is the refuge of wounded adolescents and corrupt politicians.

This misunderstanding must be resolved in person. Please make an appointment **at your earliest convenience**. Our guidance counsellor, Ms. Heller, will act as mediator.

From: Automatic Message

Jules Minkoff is out of town until further notice. She will not be reading her email or answering her phone as she is in a treatment facility specializing in anger management and tolerance awareness. Please be patient at this difficult time.

—

FRIDAY, OCTOBER 11, 2019

Charlie found Oscar sitting in the residents' lounge with his least-favourite friend, Mr. Himmelfarb. They were playing blackjack and Oscar was winning, it hardly needed to be said. One reason was that Oscar was a canny and intuitive player, the other was that Mr. Himmelfarb's legendary bad luck was second only to his poor judgement. He insisted on being dealer, for example, on the understanding that the house always won, a watertight plan that gave him short odds to win in the long run — if he had had an ounce of sense, of course, even if Oscar weren't such a lucky devil. As things stood, Oscar's superior intellect and fluky good fortune only goaded his adversary to ever-greater peaks of desperation.

When Charlie sidled up he saw that Mr. Himmelfarb had just turned over a queen (hearts) and an eight (diamonds). It was an unexpected honey fall from which he could derive no pleasure. Pulling at his lower lip, he mumbled to himself: *Stick or not stick? Stick?*

"Stick," Oscar advised kindly, knowing that he wouldn't. He gave Charlie the thumbs-up. "Hello darlink," he said. "They're still in the oven." The cinnamon buns, he meant.

Oscar was dressed to the nines in a favourite suit, a very nice Harris Tweed in a small brown check. His fedora was tilted just so, the crown lightly pinched, a discreet feather tucked into the band. As usual, his Florsheims were rubbed to a high gloss. The shoes were ancient, older than his *doctor*, he often told Charlie, but he shined them up nice, kept them spiffy. Charlie twirled to show off the vintage Nehru jacket he'd found at a thrift store, and Oscar rounded his lips in a whistle of appreciation. *My, my! Such a fancy-pants!* Bending, Charlie kissed his thin, wrinkled cheek, Oscar gently pinching the boy's cheek in return. "Oy, a boychik," he murmured, knocking him a wink and introducing him to Mr. Himmelfarb for at least the twentieth time. "Himmelfarb, my grandson. Charlie, Mr. Himmelfarb."

"Hello, Fatty," Mr. Himmelfarb said. "I remember you."

"Lookit, he remembers!" Oscar crowed. "Himmelfarb remembers!"

Oscar liked to pretend that Mr. Himmelfarb had shot his last remaining marble. Gott-in-Himmelfarb! he'd chide, his trademark brand of malicious tenderness always in evidence. Oscar's favourite trick was to pretend a face-palming admiration every time Mr. Himmelfarb accomplished something perfectly ordinary, like recognizing someone he'd been introduced to every time they met. Naturally this cranked Mr. Himmelfarb's engine to full throttle and tickled Oscar no end.

"My!" he marvelled. "Such a memory he has. Such a mind!

Like a mousetrap." He was about to go into the dimensions of the mousetrap (small, *tiny*) and the perversity of a mouse falling, again and again, for the same old cheese (stale, *ancient*) when Mr. Himmelfarb came to the outlandish decision not to stick on eighteen. Turning over a card, Oscar let out a hoot of delight. "You're *out*, Himmelfarb. Beaten like a dog. Bank loses again!"

Mr. Himmelfarb's ears turned crimson. They were stuck-out ears to begin with and were starting to look like the handles on the sides of a very angry jug when Oritsia plunked down three plates on the table in front of them.

"Gentlemen," she said, "I don't suppose anyone's hungry?"

"You kidding me, cutie-pie? Only four, five hours after lunch and already you want we should snack?" Oscar expertly nabbed the two biggest buns, pushing one plate towards Charlie and balancing the other on his knee.

"Hey!" Mr. Himmelfarb yelled. "Why does the fatty need such a big bun?"

"Oops, sorry Mr. H!" Oritsia grabbed his plate. "Forgot about the tricky ticker. No bun for you."

Mr. Himmelfarb blinked. "What? I don't have a tricky ticker."

"Certainly you do," Oscar said, catching on. "Absolutely. Says right here on this medical form. 'No calories for Himmelfarb.' Ha!"

Mr. Himmelfarb looked stricken. Perhaps he did have a tricky ticker. Perhaps the napkin that Oscar was waving about and pretending to study so carefully was the readout of his faltering cardiac rhythms. He'd long ago rejected the notion that suffering should be endured without complaint, but for once Mr. Himmelfarb was silenced. Yet still he held out his hand, hoping for a cinnamon bun to appear on an elusive plate. Oscar took out his wallet, solemnly extracting one of his famous IOU markers. *Bun for Himmelfarb*, he wrote. *Redeemable with doctor's note.*

The only thing inelegant about Oscar was his wallet, a bulky brick of a creature, shiny from use, straining at the seams with the coupons and trial subscriptions and free offers stuffed inside. That you never knew when you'd require a bulk-goods discount or a gym membership was his philosophy, you never knew when you'd need to consult a newspaper article or one of Mr. Ken's fortune-cookie slips. Now he tucked the marker into Mr. Himmelfarb's shirt pocket, grandly waving him onwards. "Go. Do. Be," he advised. "Seems like you don't have much time."

Looking worried in spite of himself, clutching at his chest and muttering, Mr. Himmelfarb creaked to his feet and stumbled away.

Oritsia winked at Charlie. "That'll teach him to call people names."

"Fat, *psh*," Oscar said, biting into his bun. "Anyway, fat is good. Good for chickens, good for boys. Hoo-boy, you should have seen me at Charlie's age. A walking skeleton, a scaredy-crow."

Oritsia smiled sympathetically and hurried away to distribute cinnamon buns to those who deserved them. Oscar cleared his throat. "Enough chit-chat. How is the Mother?"

"Jules is good," Charlie said.

Oscar shook his head disapprovingly. Charlie called his mother Jules, claiming she preferred it. But it troubled Oscar that his daughter, who'd never had occasion to call anyone mother, was herself deprived of this dear name by choice. The fact was Jules hadn't planned on becoming a mother, declaring herself as surprised as anyone when she found herself with child — which was certainly not the way she'd expressed it to Oscar at the time. The Minkoff family tree was decidedly sparse and prickly, no question. Every forty years it put out a tentative new shoot, a small but perfect bud. If only the buds could be persuaded to regard themselves as part of a larger organism, Oscar would have been content. He'd sought advice on this matter from his beloved Chaya Rifke. But she, usually so helpful, fell silent on the subject of the daughter she'd held in her arms only once.

Some heartbreak went too deep for words, Oscar knew. Even for a ghost.

On the other hand, he comforted himself, perhaps all this hooey about what to call the woman who was the daughter of one and the mother of the other, the genetic code that spliced grandfather with grandson, the blood hyphen that linked them, was a distraction.

Discerning his grandfather's sadness, Charlie began telling him about the rumpus that had occurred between his mother and Ms. Kambaja. (*Sorry! Sorry! Sorry!* Jules had scrawled on the Wonder Wall.) She'd realized her screw-up the moment she sent the first email, she explained via her favourite chalkboard confidant. Sadly, this hadn't prevented her from sending subsequent emails, after which she'd screwed up again, perhaps royally. She'd solved matters by disappearing, a gambit Charlie was familiar with from long experience. Yet who could blame her frustration at Ms. K's bizarre grading practices?

"Too much speculation, not enough research," Ms. K had written in the margin of Oscar's biography, Charlie reported. "Too much digression, too few details about Mr. Minkoff's family life." Beside the paragraph describing his grandfather's widowhood, she'd prompted: "Did Mr. Minkoff enjoy being a father?"

"Did Mr. Minkoff enjoy being a father?" Charlie now mimicked for Oscar's benefit.

"Don't make fun of teacher," Oscar admonished, adding, however, that he could see Charlie's point. Both points, actually: Ms. K's and Charlie's. That was the trouble with Oscar. He saw everyone's point of view, took in all perspectives, understood where every last blessed fool was coming from. The full catastrophe, as someone wise had once said.

It was a Minkoff family trait, Oscar claimed. A sense of fair play handed down from grandfather to grandson. He didn't have to say "too bad it skipped a generation" because stating the obvious wasn't a Minkoff family trait. Stating the obvious was a waste of breath, pure and simple, that Oscar would rather save for blowing on his porridge or hollering at God. Besides, Jules was his daughter. Don't spread it around, but he loved her despite her headstrong ways. Whether he'd enjoyed being her father or not.

Oscar sighed, sighing being exempt from breath-wasting, apparently. It was time to change the subject, so he asked, as he always did, after the neighbours. Skerrit (2C) and Oslavsky (3B), he clarified, although he didn't have to.

Oscar had once lived at the GNC, during which time he'd grown very fond of Mrs. Oslavsky and less so of Mr. Skerrit. They'd had a grand adventure ending in an all-night vigil, Mrs. Oslavsky and Oscar huddled in the cab of a big rig during the ferocious blizzard. Such tribulations brought folks together, and Oscar never failed to ask how the neighbours found themselves.

"Same, I guess," Charlie said. "Getting on. I worry about them."

"Sure you do. What's not to worry? 'Who has no worries should check for a pulse.' *Ethics of the Fathers.* Look it up." It was only a matter of time before the GNC was condemned, sold for scrap or worse, Oscar predicted.

Most likely, almost certainly, worse.

Worse were the overpriced condos springing up everywhere. Designed to resemble ocean liners, they were inevitably named Seaview or Saltspray, developers pretending that a perfectly good river view was the portal to an ocean vista. It was a perversity Oscar abhorred as much as Jules did, another thing they had in common.

"Eat up, darlink," Oscar said, but Charlie had already devoured his bun and was running a wet forefinger around the plate, collecting crumbs.

"Nice crunch, Oritsia," Charlie called.

"Nice crunch, Charlie? *Nice* crunch? What nice crunch? Why so modest? Why such understatement? Would you say the Taj Mahal is a nice building? Would you say the pyramids are nice little triangles in the sand? Say rather *superb* crunch, say rather *magnificent* cinnamon buns!"

Oritsia laughed, flicking him gently with her tea towel. "Enjoy your coffee klatch, fellas."

"That reminds me—" Charlie took the hint, scampering off to draw two cups from the giant coffee urn that was always replaced at three-thirty sharp by the dreaded decaf urn. Yet one more example of how getting old could kill you, Oscar claimed. When Charlie returned with the coffee—black with a sugar cube for his grandfather; cream, three heaped sugars for himself—Oscar was ready for him.

"Tell me about this bar mitzvah idea of yours," he said. "I'm all ears."

—

To: Rabbi Spiegelman
From: Charlie Minkoff

Dear Rabbi Spiegelman,

Oritsia at the Seth Rowe says you run a fine Saturday morning service for the seniors and that you'll help me with my grandfather, Oscar Wolf Minkoff. He doesn't know when his birthday is so we chose March 21st out of a hat. My grandfather's fedora, in fact. I hope that's okay with you. I know you have to be thirteen to celebrate a bar mitzvah and my grandfather is definitely over thirteen years old. Now that Oscar has a birthday, he'd like to have a bar mitzvah. I don't know how to get him one but I thought, being a rabbi, you'd know. I have $285.23 in my savings account, which is all yours, and there's more in the pig.

Sincerely,

Charlie Minkoff

P.S. The pig is this 2-litre milk jug. When you turn it on its side it looks like a pig, is all.

—

Afterwards, when everybody was asking what he'd been *doing*, who did he think he *was*, and what was his *problem*, etc., Charlie remembered how events had escalated gradually, imperceptibly, until he was in over his head, a frog croaking its heart out in a pot of boiling water.

If you wanted to boil a frog without that frog realizing what you were up to, you had to proceed with caution, Jules had said, as if explaining a recipe. A couple of degrees an hour, the water heating slowly, the frog acclimating to its environment, feeling no pain although it was being boiled alive. She'd told him this story in the interval between his developing the capacity to understand stories and her losing the ability to tell them. For that reason, it was precious, a touchstone to something he couldn't quite grasp because, when you got right down to it, it made no sense: Why was the frog in the pot and who was gunning for it? What was the ratio of heat over time? And, given the circumstances, why not just whack the little green fella over the head with the damn lid and be done with it?

"You can get used to anything," was his mother's take, an inadequate reply to the question Charlie had asked, which was why you'd want to boil a frog in the first place. The truth was, you had to be the frog to appreciate how life could get so intense that before you knew it you were in over your head, the lid clanging shut above you.

Charlie was the frog, of course, and the gradually heating water was life.

"So who's turning the dial on the stove?" Oscar asked.

Charlie was stumped. "Mom?" he ventured.

"Mom is the narrator. Narrator can't do babkes."

"Me? You? The fickle hand of fate?" Charlie guessed, firing wildly.

"Nope. Nope. Warmer."

"Come on, zeide. Give me a clue."

Oscar slapped his hand to his forehead, suddenly angry. "You want a clue, Charlie? Fine, here's a clue. Capital G, capital O, capital D. Got it?"

Charlie was chagrined. Here was his gentle zeide, thumping his fist on the table and hollering out letters like a celestial bingo caller.

"*God*, Charlie! *Hashem*," Oscar hollered. He looked at his grandson, at Charlie's girth, his pale moon-glow face and galaxy of Milky Way freckles. The dry, red thatch of his hair seemed to be growing vertically, straight up from his forehead. His voice was pitched too high for a fellow, no question. The boy had his head down, was staring at the table, gnawing distractedly at a thumbnail. With a pang Oscar noticed the patch of acne flaring on his chin, inflamed and painful looking.

Let the light of your precious self shine out into the world, he thought, gutted with tenderness.

Amen, Chaya Rifke whispered. He touched his grandson on the cheek, tilting his face gently until Charlie's downcast gaze met his own.

"Think of it this way," he whispered. "Frog is the Jewish people, water is five thousand years of persecution, hand on the stove is God."

DOG

WONDER WALL

Earth to Charlie: Gellman shit on the fire escape again. You know the drill. Clean up after the mutt or it's off to the pound with him.

Also, pick up some vegetables at Food Town, would you.

We don't eat vegetables.

We eat olives, don't we? And pickled onions. Those miniature dills I like.

Those are garnishes, Mom. Want me to score a pineapple and maraschino cherries too?

Don't be a smart mouth, Charlie. You're not cute enough. There's cash in the pig.

Some Pig!

Dude, you're thirteen. Why are you still reading kid's books?

I don't read them, Mom. I quote them.

Whatever. Listen—I'm working. Clean up after your dog and stay out of trouble.

Hey Mom, you back yet?

Guess I'll catch you tonight then...

I'm going to school now. See you later?

—

FRIDAY, OCTOBER 18, 2019

After Charlie had reviewed his Hebrew letters with Oscar, the theological sessions began. Friday afternoons, after they wolfed their cinnamon buns, washed down by as much coffee as they could drink before the decaf urn arrived, Oscar would turn to his grandson. "What are we discussing today, darlink? Sodom and Gomorrah? Turning into salt? Cutting the baby in half?"

"You choose, zeide."

"Hoo-boy. Let's see..."

"Tell the fatty about the father who tried to kill his son," Mr. Himmelfarb, an uninvited guest, piped up. He mugged at Charlie, glaring meaningfully.

"That's a doozey," Oscar agreed, opening his Chumash, the same battered book his mother had given him all those years ago. Oscar never opened it without pressing his lips to the worn cover, eyes closed.

"Why don't you read for us, darlink," he suggested as he moved his crabbed forefinger below the letters. He rocked back and forth in pleasure as his grandson obliged, Charlie stumbling over the unfamiliar words and sounding out the syllables.

"Beautiful," Oscar murmured when Charlie had laboured over the first verse. "Such poise! Take five, darlink. Have a Hershey!" He no longer carried candy kisses in his pocket, so he solemnly wrote out an IOU, which the boy just as solemnly pocketed while Mr. Himmelfarb squirmed and made faces as if he had gas.

"Better out than in, Himmelfarb," Oscar advised. "Don't worry, we're all friends here."

When order was restored, Oscar's voice deepened. "There was this fellow, Abraham. That you already know. Nice guy, natty dresser, a good husband. I'm spitballing here, so don't quote me. He's been married a long time, it says here; quote, 'Abraham hearkened to the voice of Sarah.' Hearkened, you understand? That's a married man, all right. Wife tells him what to do, he listens. Other hand, he's something of a listener by nature. Because next thing, he hears a voice saying, 'Abraham, get thyself and thy boychik to a mountain. I'll tell you what I want you should do when you get there.'

"Look, it was olden days, okay? Biblical. People heard voices coming out from all kinds of places — 'issuing forth,' it says here. Quote unquote. Burning bushes, whirlwinds and so on. Abraham saddles up, grabs the kid, and off they go. Three days it takes to get to Moriah. Three days is about a week in the Bible when a donkey is all you got. Only form of transportation. *Nu*, so finally they get to the mountain and the Lord says, 'I want you should sacrifice' — *sacrifice*, Himmelfarb, not kill — 'the boy.'

"Naturally, Abraham pretends not to hear. So the Lord calls again, louder for the folks in the back. '*Okay, Abe, I'm wa-a-a-aiting!*' What you got to understand is Abraham loves his son. It seems Isaac was a change-of-life baby, which means no do-overs. But here's the Lord putting the screws to him: 'Go ahead, sacrifice your son. I dare you.'"

Oscar shook his head, dumbfounded. "And for what? Why kill the kid? Want to know what I think? He wants Abraham to show which side he's pitching for. That's all."

Charlie and Mr. Himmelfarb regarded him, wide-eyed, but Oscar stared serenely into the distance, watching it all unfold. Century after century. Parchment unrolling, books fluttering, calendar pages flipping over. Hashem and His rest-less, relentless questions boiled down to the essence of one burning question: *Whose side are you on? Whose side are you on? Whose side, whose side, whose side?*

"*Azoi.* The Lord's saying it's a bottom-of-the-ninth, bases-loaded situation, Abe. Do me a favour, don't strike out. Naturally Abraham wants to do right by the Lord because, let's face it, the old man's done a lot for him, as it says, smiting and slaying and so forth. He grabs the kid—maybe hugs him, maybe straightens his collar—but just as he's about to draw the knife across his throat, what does he hear?"

Oscar put a hand to his ear, listening for the faint echo of a sound reverberating through the years. Then, as if hearing it, he cried out with full vibrato: "*Baa-baa! Baa-baa!*" After a moment, he continued: "A ram comes out of the bushes and what do you know, the Lord hollers subs and tells Abraham to go ahead and call in a pinch-hitter."

When Oscar drew breath, Mr. Himmelfarb, who'd been sitting on the edge of his chair and shaking his head vigor-ously, seized his opening. "Didn't happen like that, Minkoff. Not a chance!"

Oscar pretended to rear back in amazement, his eyebrows almost at his hairline. "Is that so, Himmelfarb? Excuse me, and why is that?"

"First off, three days is three days. Second, sacrifice is same as kill. *Exact* same. And third, you're telling me ram comes out from the bush making *Baa-baa*? Impossible! Out of the question! Not a sound ram makes. Lamb maybe, ram never!"

"First off, second off, third off!" Oscar shook his head as if he could scarcely believe his ears. Charlie saw that he was enjoying himself hugely. There was a flush on his cheekbones, and he turned to the boy, raising one bushy eyebrow in a "get him" gesture. His voice grew expansive, cajoling. "Okay, my fine friend, answer me something. Who is the dealer? I'll tell you in one word: word is God. Who is the house? Also God. And who is the bank? Three guesses, Mister."

But Mr. Himmelfarb, perennially fazed, was for once stalwart. He'd been dealt a lousy hand, but win or lose he was sticking. "What kind of kid is this Isaac?" he roared. "Daddy says come, he comes. Daddy says go, he goes. Daddy says put your head on the rock, he puts the head. Isaac, hah! Rather say it was Simon. *Simple* Simon!"

It was a devastating rebuttal, but Oscar, true to form, was not rebuked. He spoke with great intensity, emphasizing every word. "I'll tell you what kind of kid. Kid like Charlie here. Good-looking, smart cookie, fine dresser. Oy, such a face!" Reaching over, he gently pinched the boy's cheek.

Both men stared at Charlie, the one triumphant, the other aggrieved.

"First-class kid!" Oscar exclaimed. At the same moment Mr. Himmelfarb yelled, "Fatty Boom-Boom!"

Charlie hung his head and blushed, the heat radiating off his face seeming to quiver in the air between them. He couldn't say what embarrassed him more, his grandfather's praise or Mr. Himmelfarb's taunts. In truth he was abashed by both and, like the frog in the pot, he felt paralyzed as if he were boiling to death in his own juices. But it was too late to escape. Perhaps it had always been.

—

It might have been the exceptionally lame birthday card he received that year or it might have been the story of Abraham and Isaac, but Charlie began to wonder about his old man. What kind of fellow would marry his mom? was his first thought—no offence and he loved her, but she seemed like a lot of trouble romance-wise. He didn't like to ask, though, because he was certain his dad had left because of his son. Who could blame him? Charlie was a difficult kid to love, had been from the moment he was born.

It was an impression formed in elementary school. The first day of second grade he joined some kids on the monkey bars at recess. One minute he was swinging by his legs, the world yanking back and forth in happy alignment with his mood, the next he was pushed, pushed hard. He hit the hard gravel of reality with a meaty thunk, ears ringing, head jouncing on his thin neck, stars blooming in his eyes. All the kids scattered, except for one girl. As he lay on the ground listening to the reverberations of that thunk, she leaned over him. She blurred, doubled, blurred again, then both blurry girls asked him if he knew how ugly he was.

Do you know? Do you?

He had not known. He had not even known such things existed—acceptability and rejection, ugliness and its opposite—that without warning, he'd find himself flat on his back, winded, slightly concussed, and deeply ashamed of the ugliness he'd been unaware he suffered from. With that fall Charlie had entered his long apprenticeship. He would never again inhabit a world where other people's eyes were not the mirrors in which he saw himself. He simply had not known.

Something was wrong with him, he realized, something obvious to other kids, adults, even teachers. "Tick a box,

Charlie, choose a side," a teacher had urged him. It wasn't exactly fair, but it wasn't exactly unfair either, he explained to Oscar, the famous Minkoff trait for fair-mindedness winning out. He dressed like a boy, tough and sturdy, but by the time he grew into his boyhood, adolescence had overtaken conviction. He was still in the boy box, but only sort of—a fat kid of indeterminate gender, high-pitched and sweaty, the most noticeable thing about him being his deeply unappealing self. Those who accused Charlie of not making up his mind couldn't have been more wrong. He knew who he was, had always known. It was just that he'd rather have been good-looking, which wasn't a choice he got to make.

The other kids refused to sit beside him in class or play with him at recess. The bullying was relentless; not a day went by that he didn't go home with gum in his hair or dog shit on his shoes or notes stuck to his jacket identifying him as a freak, a loser. Spray paint on his locker, garbage in his backpack. No self-respecting kid passed him in the hallways without shoving him, the girls giggled behind their hands, the boys sucked spitballs and vied to yank his underpants over his waistband. By the end of third grade he'd developed the cringing demeanour of the perennially picked-on child, a stance that no longer merely announced the expectation of hurt but guaranteed it.

He longed to leave elementary school far behind him, and Assiniboine High proved so large he had difficulty keeping track of his classmates. There were kids from other neighbourhoods, other countries, girls who wore hijabs, boys who flashed gang colours. There were fat kids and dangerously skinny ones, a group of butch girls who dominated the JV volleyball team, and a contingent of slacker boys so dedicated to non-academic coursework that they'd taken over the sewing room. Then there were the theatre kids, who filled in their eyebrows and wore pyjama bottoms to class, and who were rehearsing a daring gender-reversal performance of *The Taming of the Shrew* in which "Petruchia" was played by a grade-ten girl, "Kent" by a talented young method actor rumoured to be transitioning. With so much to choose from, Charlie was hopeful he'd find his people.

So far, though, his plan just wasn't working out. He was still living in a world of mirrors, it seemed, none of them flattering. Whenever he braved the cafeteria, forcing himself to sit with girls from his homeroom, they'd mysteriously melt away and he'd be left alone at the table, sore-thumbish, throat too dry to swallow. Everyone had lab partners of long standing or belonged to study groups formed way back in kindergarten, apparently. So no, sorry, he couldn't join in. The kid whose locker adjoined his had applied for a transfer, and whenever his English teacher announced a group project she added, "Charlie, see me after class." The previous week he'd made cupcakes for the bake sale, frosting each one with flair, his feeling of hopefulness as rich and shiny as the chocolate ganache he'd tempered, then set. They were objects of beauty and remained that way, more or less, until the end of the day — not one cupcake sold, though every last marshmallow square and desultory brownie had long since been devoured. Straight-backed and proud, dry-eyed, Charlie collected the rejected cupcakes and waited until he was out of sight before hurling the whole tragic mess into a Dumpster on the way home, despite his grumbling stomach. For how could he eat what others had so emphatically rejected?

The truth was he'd never had a friend, a friend his age,

someone to walk to school with or sit next to in class. Not having a friend was what made him feel freakish, awkward, and ashamed. It was both similar and different to the shame he felt when Dr. Jabbour began drawing her Xs and Ys. He knew he couldn't help how he'd been born, but the self-consciousness of always being alone — in the hallways, at his locker, in class — felt indescribably worse. As if everything else (monkey bars, crash landing, do you *know*?, dog shit, universal shunning) had been a rehearsal for the pain of being ignored, ignored and yet observed; ignored, observed, and despised. No wonder his father had taken one look at that early version of his son and hoofed it. No wonder at all.

—

WEDNESDAY, OCTOBER 23, 2019

Less than two months into term and the level of suckage was through the roof. Every day Charlie was relieved to escape, to let himself into the GNC, climb the stairs to the fourth floor, feel his shoulders unkink and his stomach unclench. Gellman would be waiting for him when he came through the door, playing it cool although that was a reach. Temperamentally, Gellman wasn't a cool fellow, butt-shaking eagerness being his first defence, slavish devotion his fallback position. Today he simply ran full tilt at Charlie, trying to swallow him whole, and when that failed, aiming to gnaw him down to the bone-sized boy he was evidently planning to bury somewhere safe. Somewhere nobody else would look. Charlie got down on one knee and tried to embrace the dog, but Gellman, once again proving incapable of taking yes for an answer, took fright, skittering away on stiff legs.

Charlie sighed.

The trouble was that what Weeza called Gellman's abandonment issues were not alleviated by the regularity with which he was abandoned, for hours at a time, the humans in his life disappearing from sight with no guarantee they'd ever return. Charlie imagined Gellman's day, hours stretching out like strands of cheese pizza, empty as the Domino's takeout boxes that Jules absent-mindedly replaced in the fridge. No wonder the dog was such a whip-crack of nerves, spit, yip, and pee. Today he'd done just that, peeing all over the loft in panic-stricken spurts. A fetid odour wafted from the fire escape.

Gellman had once belonged to Mrs. Shapiro (2A), but since nobody claimed him when she died, Weeza had persuaded Jules to let them keep him. Weeza could get anyone to do anything, even Jules, which was saying something. He's a stupid dog with a stupid name, Jules maintained. Sure, Weeza conceded, but look at it this way: someone took one look at that clumsy galoot and named him Gellman. *Gellman*, think of that. As if the soul of a neurotic Jewish accountant were stuffed into the sausage-skin casing of the ugliest dog in the world. A dog so ugly even his fleas had to shut their eyes. Jules laughed so hard she tumbled off the bar stool pulled up to her drawing table, one of two she'd "reclaimed" from the Sans Souci. But, as Weeza pointed out, reclaimed was only another word for no one would miss it, and Gellman was much the same thing.

That's how he came to live with them.

Yet despite her advocacy, Weeza wasn't exactly a fan.

Gellman was what would happen, she said, if a wolf and a rat and a shag rug got together with a couple of lawyers and a bottle of Heinz 57.

A mess is what.

Gellman was Charlie's mess, though. He cleaned the loft, swabbed down the fire escape, fixed himself a double-decker peanut butter and chocolate syrup sandwich to go, and prepared to sally forth, a boy and his dog. The pain in his stomach had been griping all day and was becoming difficult to ignore. Not impossible, however. *Nothing is impossible if you refuse to believe,* Dr. Jabbour had said.

As soon as the pair rounded the corner onto Water Street, Charlie saw that they were shooting a movie again. The whole block was closed off by giant wardrobe trailers and catering trucks. A bunch of expensive-looking camera equipment teetered on the sidewalk, and a couple of roadies were laying down lengths of electric cable. Gellman began shaking as soon as he saw the duct tape, although he should have been used to it. They were always shooting a movie on Water Street.

Movie companies had started filming in Winnipeg because the city's urban architecture, particularly its downtown buildings, was well-preserved and labour was cheap. Consequently, the neighbourhood was in the process, once again, of being overrun by the huffing trailers that rolled through in spring and remained until November, parking on both sides of narrow, one-way streets and idling through the night while klieg lights streamed through the broken windows of picturesquely abandoned warehouses. Charlie appreciated the excitement, but Gellman was dubious. Hackles rising at the sight of the dreaded trailers, his fierceness swiftly turned to fear, whimpers giving way to yelps and, finally, a torrent of all-out howls, the transformation so rapid it was as if he'd perfected a new form of canine unease, a sort of whimper-yelp-howl of existential pain.

"You there! Yes, *you*!" An angry-looking man wearing a lanyard and carrying a bullhorn grabbed hold of Charlie's jacket. "That your dog?"

"Meet Gellman," Charlie said. Sometimes you had to own up to trouble, especially if you were holding tightly to the other end of it. Gellman yanked at his leash and Charlie, perennially off-balance despite his bulk, careened into the gutter. Gellman promptly went into full canine meltdown — zero to sixty, whining and cringing and trying to disappear from the world by snouting his way into a discarded takeout bag. Hind legs trembling, he took deep panicky breaths as if he were hyperventilating. It was a plastic bag, though, so the effect was shockingly incompatible with staying alive.

"Yeah, okay, um Gellman," Lanyard said. "Could you kindly get your dog the hell out of here?"

Charlie said sure can. He was down on his knees trying to extricate Gellman from the plastic bag.

"I mean *now*," Lanyard hollered, totally losing his shit.

Charlie started to explain that the thing you had to know about Gellman was that he had a delicate constitution that affected his bowels.

"Look, um, *Gellman*, I don't care about your explosive diarrhea or your shitty no-name dog," Lanyard yelled. "Just get it the fuck out of my movie!"

But the more Charlie pulled at the plastic bag, the harder the dog thrust his great jowly head inside it. It was as if he wanted to vanish from the world, calculating that the quickest way out was in. The resulting spectacle was both tragic and hilarious, basically the terms on which that crazy dog lived his life. Usually Charlie let Gellman get on with the great, unrewarding project of being Gellman, but now he was becoming anxious. The crackly plastic-bag breaths were growing weaker by the second until all he could hear was a faint *crinkle-crinkle-crk-k-k*.

And then nothing.

"Gellman!" he yelled, throwing himself onto his dog.

Gellman was utterly limp, floppy, and warm as a new corpse. Beneath the fug of kibble-breath and dog-fart and filthy shag carpeting, Charlie thought he felt a heartbeat. But the next moment, the dog was in his death throes, hind legs beginning to jibber-jabber, scrabbling as if he were running towards the flickering dream-bone that hovered on the horizon of his longing. Charlie was sobbing so hard he couldn't see through the tears and snot. He thrashed as he tried to loosen the plastic bag. At least let the animal die with the warmth of a human hand on his muzzle.

"Let go!" someone was yelling. "Dammit, just let go!"

"No, Gellman! Don't let go!" Charlie sobbed.

But even as he wrestled and thrashed and panted and wept, he knew that it was too late. Gellman was dead. Gellman and his question-begging ways. Gellman and his eternal *Why Me?* Gellman the magnificent, Gellman the failure, Gellman the tragic mistake. Charlie lay beside the lifeless body, an arm thrown over the rough fur of the dog's hindquarters, his face pressed into its stomach. All the sadness he'd ever felt, a thick grey fog of Charlie-shaped sadness, whooshed into his body and immediately turned to concrete the way depression sets hard when it comes into contact with flesh. He was too tired to move, too sad to cry.

"Easy now," someone said. It was the Let-Go voice. Someone was grasping his arm, trying to tug him to his feet. Charlie resisted, resistance being one way to postpone the hundred years of hopelessness that yawned before him. But he couldn't lie there forever. Who would care for Oscar? Who would look after Jules? Who would take out Mrs. Oslavsky's garbage and keep an eye on Mr. Skerrit?

"He's okay now," the voice was saying.

"No, I'm not. My dog just died," Charlie said.

"Really? Strange way of showing it." The Let-Go voice was coming from an older girl. She held a clipboard in one hand and was pointing to Gellman with the other. Charlie saw that true to form, Gellman had come back from the dead, apparently in order to give his balls the thorough licking they deserved.

"Spectacular itch," she observed.

Whoa. Charlie sensed the hair on his neck standing up, felt the phantom flashes of lightning that preceded — by seconds — the thunderbolt crashing down from the sky. Don't look, he thought, and then — *Kablooey!* — he did. Stars whizzed before his eyes, planets whirred like wind-up toys, and his shirt must have turned transparent because there was his heart, visibly beating out of his front pocket.

He felt as if he knew the girl, a feeling he immediately discounted. For wasn't that always the way with love (or so he'd heard)? She was younger than he'd first thought, and he noticed she was wearing glittery red trainers, black leggings, and an oversize maroon hoodie, the sleeves too long, coming down over her hands and making her seem fragile. A pen stuck out behind her ear; another poked through the elastic band of her ponytail. She studied him for a long, assessing, what-the-heck moment and then, having come to the kind of conclusion that took into account the ratio of pennies to a pound you were in for, said, "Hey, don't I know you?"

Dumbfounded, he shook his head.

She held out her hand. "Mickie Piper. Pleased to meet you. We saved the dog but the plastic bag's a goner. Sorry about that. Had to make a split-second decision."

Charlie glanced down. Gellman was spinning around in the dirt, flapping balls exposed, the torn plastic still wrapped around his muzzle. No question, the Great Houdini was hamming it up, taking enormous, heartfelt, only-slightly-crackling breaths, rolling his eyes in ecstasy. Evidently he was congratulating himself on having survived his ordeal, on having cheated death, on having loped towards the light on shaky legs, claws clattering against the parquet floor of heaven.

Mickie whipped out a pen. "Here you go. Handy for performing plastic bag tracheotomies."

He held out his hand, and she passed him the cheap ball-point as if conferring a magical gift. Then she untangled the bag from Gellman and smoothed it out. "'Mr. Ken's Shanghai Palace,'" she read aloud. "If the food doesn't kill you the plastic bag will. Ba-*doom*!"

Charlie stared, transfixed. The girl made a hi-hat *ts-ts-ts-tststs* sound as if performing, on an imaginary drum set, a riff on the world's corniest joke. "And an hour later you're hungry, right? *Ba-doom, pish!*" She flung her imaginary drumsticks in the air, catching them flawlessly before pocketing them.

"Gotta go, kid," she said. "You cool?"

His stomach was doing flip-flops like the time he hung from the monkey bars. *Whoa! Swing City.* And like that first time, he fell, fell hard. It was shocking to discover that you really did fall when the Thunderbolt hit, just as you really did see cartoon stars when you bashed your head against the hard asphalt of love. Anyway, that's how he was going to tell the story when he told it. To Oscar. To Weeza. To Mrs. Oslavsky. To Jules, if she'd listen. The story of how Charlie Minkoff fell in love. Like the monkey bars but farther from the ground.

"What's the drama queen doing now?" It was Lanyard, little eyes red with fury.

Without giving him time to reply he grabbed Charlie's arm, yanked him upright, and shoved him in the direction of the river. "Get yourself and the incredible shrink-wrapped dog the hell out of here. Capish? I've got a movie to shoot."

Instead of stumbling off with a filthy Gellman wriggling in his arms, a scenario he'd grown accustomed to, Charlie stood and watched the girl walk away in her glittery red trainers, the ruby slippers of his homesick, lovesick heart. Her dark hair was pulled high in a ponytail that arrowed down her back, pointing at the upside-down heart shape of her butt. But before she disappeared into the tangle of film people milling about on the sidewalk, she lifted a hand and, without looking back, waved it over her shoulder. Fingers to palm, a quick open-and-shut motion. *Mickie Piper, signing off now. Goodbye and good luck.*

As if she knew he'd be standing there, as if she knew he'd be watching her.

When he finally turned away Charlie realized he was still clutching the pen she'd given him, clutching it so hard his knuckles were white. The ache in his stomach was worse than ever, the pain bringing water to his eyes and sweat to his forehead, almost driving him to his knees.

—

WONDER WALL

Hey, Mom, what did it feel like the first time you fell in love?

Any lightning, thunder? Other weather-related phenomena? You've been in love, right?

Shit, Charlie! We're out of olives again. Those dark oily ones with pits. Always buy olives with pits, kid. You heard it here first.

We're out of a lot of stuff. There's cash in the pig, knock yourself out.

They didn't have the ones you like so I got the big green ones stuffed with pimentos. I'm visiting Oscar tomorrow. Wanna come?

Tell him I'll see him soon. Tell him not to let the sunshine spoil the rain. Tell him whatever you like but spare me the ersatz olives.

K, sorry. It's just that he misses you.

Look, there's absolutely no reason to stuff anything, least of all an olive, with a pimento. And pitted olives? Charlie, they're only good for martinis. What suburban gals order with their excuse-my-French "appletinis." An olive pit is the grain of sand in the oyster.

We still talking olives here?

When a structure is sound it's in perfect balance. That oily, musky, slightly deranged taste of an olive growing around its pit is what perfect balance tastes like.

Okay, okay. I got the kind you like from the Greek Market. They're in the fridge.

Agh!

You're welcome?

Olives are packed in brine. Brine. A natural preservative.

Not to change the subject or anything, I mean olives are totally fascinating and definitely worth obsessing over, but you know they're making a movie on Water Street?

They're always making a movie on Water Street. Hey, I've been commissioned for a new piece. Just heard the news.

Fantastic!!! I'll buy steak to celebrate. Can I invite Weeza for supper?

Going away. We'll celebrate when I get back.

What's wrong with Gellman? He looks downright mournful. It's pathetic.

Honestly? I think he's in love.

Ha ha. Listen, why haven't you called Dr. J?

You bumped into Dr. J? Wait, don't tell me she swung by the Sans Souci?

I mean it—why haven't you called her?

A rabbi, a priest, and a pediatrician walk into a bar. Wait, says the pediatrician, I'm in the wrong joke.

DUDE! What's wrong with you? I mean what else is wrong with you?

Phone. Dr. Jabbour. Now.

???

Okay, I get it. You're angry at God. You're mad as hell. You hate your mother. You wish you'd never been born.

Charlie?

HAND

ONE HAND

Rabbi Spiegelman had been mightily tickled by Charlie's idea, although he did have one reservation.

"Can't do it, young man. Can't give your zeide a surprise bar mitzvah. Not possible."

"Why not?" Charlie asked.

Oy. The rabbi sighed. With this one he would have to begin at the very beginning. With ABC. With Do Re Mi. With Genesis and the division of light from darkness.

"On the one hand, who doesn't like a surprise?" Rabbi Spiegelman mused aloud. "On the other hand, Torah isn't a room filled with balloons and people hiding behind the furniture."

"So, no?"

"Who said no, young man? Not no! Never no! If zeide wants to be bar mitzvah I will myself teach him his Torah portion. I will myself drape a prayer shawl around his shoulders and lead him up to the bimah. And if zeide can't walk, on these very shoulders will I carry him!" Rabbi Spiegelman had allowed enthusiasm to surge so far ahead of caution that before he knew it he'd committed himself to a scenario that was as undignified to contemplate as it would have been impractical to carry out.

"I presume zeide can walk?" he now asked cautiously.

Charlie explained that Oscar was in fine fettle, as he himself would have said.

"Excellent, excellent," the rabbi exclaimed, rubbing his dry palms together so vigorously that they squeaked. "I look forward to meeting him."

—

FRIDAY, OCTOBER 25, 2019

Oscar and Mr. Himmelfarb were playing blackjack again when Charlie arrived at the Seth Rowe, Mr. Himmelfarb trying to remember not to say "Hit me" when he required another card because Oscar had taken to doing just that. It was obvious that Mr. Himmelfarb was concealing an ace up his sleeve; it had just slid down his skinny arm and was now lying face up on the table in front of them.

Oscar roared with laughter as he nudged his grandson in the ribs. "Well, Charlie, should we run the bandit out of town with a posse or just straight-up shoot him?"

"Lookit, here comes Fatty Boom-Boom," Mr. Himmelfarb said in a transparent ploy to divert attention. Oscar was too happy to pay the fellow any mind and so contented himself with hitting him on the forehead with the expertly lobbed ace and yelling, "Out! Out like a light!"

When peace was restored, Charlie waited for his grand-father to remark upon the proposed bar mitzvah. He had to wait for some time, though. Despite his good humour, Oscar was acting blasé, a state of affairs Charlie might have predicted. He always knew how excited his grandfather was by the effort Oscar put into concealing his excitement. But eventually, as he stole a glance at his grandson's face, Oscar introduced the subject in his ironic way, exclaiming, "Such a fine rabbi you got me. Nice beard, good forehead, excellent voice. But tell me, why only two hands?"

Charlie grinned as Mr. Himmelfarb reared back in disbelief.

"That's right, Himmelfarb. You heard me. Fellow only has two hands. What do you say to that?"

"Bingo, is what I say. Nice counting, Mister Genius." Having not yet delivered himself from the overflow of his personal bucket of sarcasm, Mr. Himmelfarb began listing off the rabbinical attributes: two hands, two feet, two legs, two arms, a pair of lungs, don't forget, and a couple of eyes, my God.

Oscar gave him a long, pitying, tongue-clicking moment. "*Tcha, tcha*, Himmelfarb. I'm not talking left hand, right hand here. I'm talking hands of decision. On the one hand this, on the other hand that."

It was true. Rabbi Spiegelman was so even-handed that it was impossible for him to come down on one side of an argument without immediately leaping the fence to take in the view from the other side, a trait he shared with the Minkoffs. On the *one* hand — to use his favourite catchphrase — he was delighted to teach Oscar his Torah portion so that he could have the bar mitzvah so long denied him. It was an honour to be of service, the rabbi declared. And on the *other* hand, it was a mitzvah, an act of charity, to facilitate the journey Oscar had begun all those years ago. On the subject of Oscar's proposed bar mitzvah, it seemed that for once both hands were in perfect agreement.

Charlie could tell that in his gently ironic way Oscar was pleased too.

"A fine thing, Charlie. A miracle! In three months I will become a man."

But Rabbi Spiegelman, who had just joined the trio, was immune to irony in matters of rabbinic law, and hastily explained that of course Oscar was a man. No question. A Jewish boy became a man when he turned thirteen just as a Jewish girl became a woman when she turned twelve. It was automatic. A bar mitzvah was the boy's acceptance of the responsibilities of manhood, his public avowal that he was a son of the commandments.

Mr. Himmelfarb, who resented Charlie's presence at the study sessions, guffawed nastily. "Nice to be a man, Minkoff. Hope you enjoy it." He glowered at the rabbi and asked him to correct him if he was wrong, but weren't there worse things to be than a man? You might, for example, be a woman. That would be plain terrible. A tragedy.

Rabbi Spiegelman paged through his Chumash, pouncing when he found his place somewhere in the wilds of Genesis. "Let's see now. Here we are on the sixth day and already Adam is lonely. Listen to this: 'So God created mankind in His image, in the image of God He created them; male and female He created them.'"

"Nice," said Oscar, succinctly. "Ve-ry nice."

"Nice, Minkoff? You think you look like God? You think Hashem walks around in a Dervish double-breasted?" Mr. Himmelfarb was fluorescent with happy rage. The blood rose in his cheeks, the hand pointing at Oscar was shaking with indignation.

Oscar considered Mr. Himmelfarb's theological point,

drumming his fingers against his forehead as if to encourage thought. Ostentatiously, he brushed a fleck of imaginary dust from his shoulder. "Good question, Himmelfarb. Congratulations on the question. Answer is maybe yes. Another answer is definitely no."

Sensing trouble, the rabbi intervened. "Gentlemen, please. Let's not squabble about, um, menswear. We know that Hashem is invisible. We are forbidden to imagine His form. So perhaps 'image' refers to something other than physical attributes?" He peered into one face, then another.

Oscar gallantly responded. "Quite right, Rabbi. Beautiful point. Only a fool thinks about clothes at a time like this." He glared at Mr. Himmelfarb as if to indicate exactly what such a fool might look like. "Don't forget, when it comes to clothes Hashem is strictly on the side of nudity. Quote 'And they were both naked, the man and his wife, and were not ashamed.' End of quote."

Mr. Himmelfarb tried to speak but Oscar silenced him with a stern hand. When he was certain that the import of what he'd said had sunk in, he hit the table so loudly that Charlie jumped. "Not ashamed?" he roared. "You're kidding me! Why not ashamed? Why not squirming from embarrassment? Why not dead from humiliation? What does it mean this *not ashamed*?" He rubbed his whiskers the wrong way, making a scratchy sound that somehow focused attention: "Means no mirrors, Himmelfarb. No mirrors in the Garden of Eden."

Mr. Himmelfarb slapped his cheek in mock astonishment. "Right you are, Minkoff. No mirrors in the Garden of Eden. Also no washing machines, no Frigidaires, no handy electric kettles. Such a mind you have, my God. Such insight!"

He whistled in feigned admiration, unaware of the trap he'd strolled into.

Oscar winked at his grandson. "Charlie, what kind of mirror are we looking at?"

But Charlie was silent, thinking about the paradise conjured by his zeide's words. How much happier he'd be if he never had to look in another mirror, never had to reckon with that freckle-blasted face, never had to recalculate, like some perverse GPS, the distance between who he was and how he looked.

"Charlie?" Oscar said.

It was the rabbi who replied. "Gentlemen, the question is what *is* a mirror? On the one hand a mirror is where we recognize ourselves. On the other hand, since Torah urges us to move beyond the physical, the mirror is also where we mistake ourselves. So what am I saying?"

He paused, but there were no takers. "Am I saying that the mirror is a dissembler, a propagator of falsehoods, a snake in the tree of knowledge? As Mr. Minkoff observes, there were no mirrors in the garden, very important point. What happened next?"

"Eve," said Mr. Himmelfarb.

"Snake," said Charlie.

"Bad judgement," said Oscar. "Disobedience, fall from grace."

"All of the above," the rabbi said. "Eve, snake, bad judgement, disobedience, fall from grace. The result? Mirrors everywhere. Like a funhouse, you can imagine."

In silence the three men and the boy contemplated the distorting funhouse mirrors of the Garden of Eden. Oscar shook his head in dismay, *terrible, terrible.* How many had been exiled from the garden over the centuries? That red-eyed angel standing with sword drawn, waiting to cut souls into ribbons. Charlie winced in sympathy for the poor creatures confronted by their cringing, hand-wringing selves. Even Mr. Himmelfarb, putting a hand to his cheek as if to waylay a spiritual toothache, was struck with the horror of self-consciousness. Oy.

Rabbi Spiegelman drummed his fingers on the table. "And what do the sages tell us about this mirror?"

Oscar mimicked the rabbi's even-handed tenor. "On the one hand, no mirror," he intoned. "On the other hand, the world is a mirror, the world and all the people in it."

"And all the people in it," the rabbi echoed. His tone was sad, a melody played in the minor key, as if he were mourning the endless replication of truth in a world of reflections. "The sages teach us that there is divine truth in the Torah, but our understanding is imperfect. We gaze always at a reflection of a reflection. So must we give up our search for divine truth?"

"No!" Mr. Himmelfarb yelled, carried away. "Never!"

"Exactly," the rabbi said, thumping his fist. "On the one hand, no. On the other hand, never."

—

OTHER HAND

MONDAY, NOVEMBER 4, 2019

"Good afternoon, Charles," Dr. Jabbour said. "And this must be Grandfather."

"Zeide, this is Dr. Jabbour," Charlie said.

Oscar waved away introductions. They'd met before, long ago; it was always a pleasure. He stood up to shake her hand, but Charlie was still talking. "And this is Nurse Imelda, and you already met Tanysha at the front desk, and—"

Charlie fizzed like shook-up soda when he was anxious. Jules had promised to accompany him, but she'd had to pick up an extra shift at work. It wasn't her fault, he reasoned. Her hypothetical tendencies always acted up when she was required to be motherly, when she had to sit in a crowded waiting room flipping through germy copies of out-of-date gossip magazines, a television blaring overhead. Too bad they wouldn't let him come on his own. He'd asked, but Nurse Imelda said absolutely not. She said a lot of other things too, but that was the gist.

Now she stood in front of them, hands on her hips. "Mom didn't make it today?"

Her disapproval was evident, but Oscar was equal to it. "Don't worry about the mother, young lady. Oscar Wolf Minkoff is at your service."

"*In loco parentis*," Charlie explained.

"Quite right. I'm the local parent," Oscar agreed, stroking his grandson's cheek. "The mother is prone to discouragement."

Dr. Jabbour laughed. "No need for discouragement, Charles, Mr. Minkoff. Quite the opposite."

"What's the opposite of discouragement?" Charlie asked.

"Couragement," Oscar said.

"Hope," Dr. Jabbour said.

"Ready for the examination?" Nurse Imelda tapped the boy's thick file and then her wristwatch.

"What do you say, Charles?" Dr. Jabbour lifted her

eyebrows. "Would you like Grandfather to accompany us?"

Charlie looked at Oscar. "Stick," Oscar said. "Knock me a kiss, darlink. I'll be waiting on the other side."

Charlie lay shivering under the sheet. Every now and then Dr. Jabbour told him to take a deep breath or roll over on his side. To lift his legs or lower them. *That's right, attaboy.* He always forgot how cold her hands were. She smelled of medicinal soap and spearmint. Did she brush her teeth between patients? he wondered. That would be weird.

Dr. Jabbour removed the blood-pressure cuff she'd secured around his arm. "One-twenty over eighty-five," she said to Nurse Imelda, who wrote the numbers in his file.

"Good numbers?" he asked.

"Great numbers."

"You can take those numbers to the bank," Nurse Imelda agreed. "Are you a betting man?"

Charlie wasn't and he said so; Nurse Imelda allowed that it was probably for the best. Dr. Jabbour kept putting cold hands on him and asking if it hurt. Head (no), stomach (yes, ouch), breasts (um). She asked if he was ready and when Charlie, who'd been dreading this moment, shrugged, she lifted the paper sheet. Nurse Imelda always used to hold his hand at this stage in the proceedings but he was too old now. Instead she went to the waiting room to talk to Oscar. She came back exasperated.

"Grandfather won't sign the form. Says if it can't smile don't photograph. Says to let him know the minute his grandson's privates crack a smile."

Dr. Jabbour giggled. "Not to worry, Charles. We won't go

that route. How about I do a sketch? Didn't know I was an artist, did you? That okay?"

Miserably, he nodded, shook his head, nodded again.

She adjusted the examination light, unearthed a pad of graph paper from her desk, and began to hum. Despite being the focal point of Dr. Jabbour's bizarre still life, Charlie relaxed slightly. The humming was tuneless yet energetic, reminding him of the sound Jules made when she sat at the window half-dreaming, popping Altoids and sketching. Dr. Jabbour leaned closer. She engaged her calipers and angled the light.

"One more diagram, Charles," she said. "You're going to have to help me out."

She took his hand gently, moved it to the shaft of his penis. "Just hold it against your stomach, dear. That's right."

Charlie was dying. Lying under the hot lights, his hand on his dick, he knew how it looked. It wasn't as if he hadn't, lots of times, but obviously not with another person looking on, sketching and humming and saying, "Doing okay, dear?" Worse than anything was the humiliating sensation of hardening, actual *hardening*, which might have been his exhibitionistic tendencies flaring up (unsuspected) or his oversexed nature kicking in (suspected but unconfirmed) but was more likely the automatic response of what he was holding onto finding itself in its favourite place: the amorous warmth of his closed fist. For months he'd been taking himself in hand nightly. It was the only way he could sleep.

He broke out in a sweat, the blood rushing to his head but not, apparently, all of it. Added to his physical discomfort—balls straining, groin buzzing, alternating hot and cold waves breaking over him—was the absurd fear that he'd have to go through with what he'd started or remain trapped that way forever, like the kid who'd pulled a face when the wind changed. Well, not exactly like that kid. More like a kid with a semi-hard dick in his sweaty hand, no wind involved. *Please*, he thought. *Please, please, please.* He'd be happy to die where he lay, one hand grasping the faulty rudder that was instrumental in running his small, wobbly craft aground. Dr. Jabbour could go right on sketching, sketching and humming, sketching and humming and glancing up and saying—

"Excellent! What a perfect coincidence!"

He wanted to tell her that the queasy hardening wasn't how coincidence generally worked, but she'd already taken out her calipers and snapped on her latex gloves. For one hovering moment, she hesitated. "You permit?"

Damp with humiliation, Charlie nodded.

"And—hold it," she said, laughing. "Hold meaning both to pause and to grasp. Isn't language wonderful?"

She sketched in silence for a minute then said all done, he could get dressed, she'd be back in a tick with Grandfather. Pausing at the door (*Hold it!* thought Charlie), she said she hoped that was okay, Grandfather being there, but she was obliged to report to the adult who had his best interests at heart. Luckily she could tell, even from their brief acquaintance, that Grandfather was that very person.

"Sure thing," Charlie said miserably.

Dr. Jabbour laid out the medical sketches on her desk. There were two, one labelled "Frontal View to scale" and the other "Anterior View showing position of Urethra." She'd used pencil on graph paper, painstakingly including a scale marked off in millimetres on the left-hand side of each di-agram. "Glad I got a chance to practise my sketching," she said. "Excellent idea, Mr. Minkoff."

"Happy to be of service, young lady," Oscar said, glaring at Nurse Imelda. "What are we looking at here, if you don't mind me asking?" He hooked his reading glasses over his ears and squinted at the graph paper.

"That's your grandson's genital area, Mr. Minkoff."

"Outstanding!" Oscar exclaimed. "Very nice genitals, Charlie. First class."

Dr. Jabbour smiled. "Quite right, Mr. Minkoff. That's what I've been saying since he was born."

"So what's the problem, may I ask?"

"Charles?" Dr. Jabbour prodded.

Charlie flushed. "They're too small, zeide."

"Small!" Oscar clapped a hand to his cheek as if he simply couldn't believe his ears. He whipped off his spectacles, polished them briskly on his sleeve, then replaced them on the bridge of his nose, peering closer. "What's too small? Who says too small?"

"Everyone, Zeide," Charlie said miserably.

Dr. Jabbour shook her head. "Size is relative, Charles. Small? Perhaps, taking averages into account. Too small? Certainly not."

"So, *not* too small," Oscar crowed. "Small but not too small. Sounds okay. Sounds handy. Good job, Charlie!"

Nurse Imelda clicked her tongue, making an exasper-ated *tcha*, but Dr. Jabbour said she agreed with Oscar. Oscar beamed and said evidently she was a smart cookie and also, if she didn't mind him saying, a very attractive young person. Elegant. High class. He brushed his palms together as if to rid himself of the last crumbs of dissent and wiggled his eyebrows at his grandson. *Ready to go, darlink?*

"Hold on there, Tiger," Nurse Imelda snapped. Everyone swivelled to look at her. She crossed her arms and stared them down. "Charlie needs help."

"Is Charlie sick?" Despite himself, Oscar's voice quavered.

"Not sick, but as you know he was born with a rare condition." Dr. Jabbour pulled out her trusty prescription pad and began scribbling combinations of Xs and Ys, explaining as she did so that XX was usually the chromosomal pattern for female babies; XY the one for males.

"Usually?" asked Oscar, smelling a rat.

Dr. Jabbour allowed that in rare cases an unequal chromosomal crossover occurred during cell division. Nobody knew why. Occasionally a female infant was born with undescended testes instead of ovaries; these weren't discovered until puberty when the parents brought their daughter for a consultation because she wasn't menstruating. Dr. Jabbour wrote XY in large letters and circled them.

She paused and asked Oscar if he had any questions.

Oscar shrugged.

Dr. Jabbour said she knew what he meant. It was difficult to understand how a beautiful young woman could be male, chromosomally speaking. But sex was more than just chromosomes. Sex was other things too: hormones and genitals, gonads and — and conviction. Conviction, she repeated, the inner voice that insisted you were one or the other. Maybe both, but that was a story for another day.

Oscar put up his hand. A question. "Who is this girl?" he asked. "Is Charlie this girl?"

"What? No!" Charlie said.

"Okay, okay. Honest question." In truth it wouldn't have made a difference. He loved his grandson whatever he turned out to be. It was too late for regrets. So why, if they didn't mind telling him, were they still sitting in this stuffy office?

"Wouldn't you rather be out with your fella?" he asked Nurse Imelda, who agreed that yes, she would, all things being equal. But, naturally, they weren't; for one thing her fella was a woman (she glared), for another they were on a break (glare). Just an experiment, nothing to get excited about, she added. Oscar said congratulations, young lady, he hoped that she and the girl-fella discovered a cure for love while they were busy experimenting.

"Whoa!" Dr. Jabbour held up her hand. "Let's keep our focus, ladies and gentlemen."

"Quite right," Oscar said smugly. "Focus is the key. Give us the whole works, Doc. All the modern conveniences."

So Dr. Jabbour explained that the same thing happened with boys: because of an unequal crossover between dad's chromosomes during cell division, a baby might be born with a female genotype and male phenotype. In large letters she wrote XX on her pad.

Oscar looked thoughtful. "Phenotype, genotype," he muttered, as if trying to memorize the words. "Quite a to-do, if you don't mind me saying. Makes you wonder who's in charge, eh, Charlie?"

Dr. Jabbour said perhaps she hadn't explained herself very well, but Oscar held up a hand. "Perfect explanation, Doc. Superb medical know-how. You should be proud. Just one question I have."

He paused for dramatic effect. When he spoke it was in the ringing tones of an orator. "Question I have is, why this mix-up with chromosomes? Answer is father. Father can't do his job, so baby gets the wrong letters. Right?"

"It's nobody's fault—" Dr. Jabbour began, but Oscar held up his hand again.

"That's okay, Doc. No need to apologize. Answer is father. That's what I want the boy to know. Nobody's fault but answer is father. Confidentially speaking, it doesn't surprise me. Charlie's father was mixed up about a lot of things. Doesn't surprise me he got his cell division wrong."

Nurse Imelda burst out laughing and Oscar, who liked to leave on a high note, smiled modestly and got up to go. But Dr. Jabbour was wise to him.

"One moment, Mr. Minkoff. I think Charles has something to say."

Charlie looked blank, so she tapped her finger on the diagrams. Good old "Frontal View to scale" and "Anterior View showing position of Urethra."

"Too small and wrong place," he mumbled.

Dr. Jabbour shook her head and sighed. What concerned her, she told Oscar, wasn't the size of the penis but the position of the urethra. As you could see from her diagram, it was on the underside of the shaft, low down.

Oscar said he knew where Charlie's pee-hole was. He'd changed his grandson's diapers, don't forget. He shrugged as if to say, what else is new?

"Long story short?" Nurse Imelda suggested.

"I want to make sure we're all on the same page, Mr. Minkoff," Dr. Jabbour said.

Oscar's voice was firm: "What does it matter, long story, short story? Same page, different page? Only one thing matters. Only Charlie matters."

"Agreed," Dr. Jabbour said. "I couldn't agree more." She gazed steadily at Charlie until finally the boy looked up. "I'm so sorry, my dear," she said. "This is hard work. You're a brave young man and you are going to have a magnificent life."

"Magnificent?" Oscar interrupted. "*Better* than magnificent. Magnificent ain't seen nothing like it, Doc. Magnificent is the best word currently available for the life my grandson is going to have. Magnificent is to apples like Charlie's life is to — to a much better kind of fruit even than apples. Kind of fruit you only get in Eden. *Terrific* fruit!"

But despite his bombast the old man was exhausted, drained. Tarrying for a moment, he mumbled a question to Dr. Jabbour; the answer seemed to weigh him down further. He leaned heavily on his grandson as they walked down the polished corridor, out the elevator, and through all the pipe-clanking underground passages leading to the exit, where the Handi-Transit van waited. Charlie could tell Oscar was downhearted because when Nurse Imelda pointed out the stencilled yellow footprints that would lead them out of Pediatric Endocrinology, he merely tipped his fedora. Clutching at Charlie's arm, he never once said *follow the yellow brick road* despite the persistence of the dumb yellow footprints that pattered alongside them as they left the hospital.

All the way back to the Seth Rowe, as the driver yelled into his Bluetooth, Oscar was subdued. He turned his head, gazing out the window at the black spool of the road winding them home. Charlie thought he caught the flash of a handkerchief.

He felt anxious, worried he'd let his grandfather down. Dr. Jabbour, still concerned about his stomach pain, had made an appointment for an ultrasound. Now he had to fret about the possibility of ovarian tissue growing in his abdomen, along with the things he already knew about: having to pee sitting down, his too-small penis, his too-large breasts. Dr. Jabbour had said not to worry about the breasts, embarrassing though they were. His body was adjusting to the hormones and he could have reconstructive surgery down the line. Then she said his penis was exactly the right size for what it was supposed to do: give pleasure to him and, one day, to others. What concerned her (slightly) was the position of his urethra and (greatly) the state of his emotions. Emotions were tricky, she admitted, but she was always there for him and so was Grandfather (warm smile). As for his hypospadias (pat on the arm), they could discuss the possibility of correc-tive surgery when he was ready. Not today, though. He had enough on his plate.

"Big plate, Charlie?" Oscar asked, spookily echoing his thoughts. Static from the radio crackled in the background, the dispatcher yelling at the driver, the bleak fall landscape whipping at the windows.

Oscar stirred. "So, Mr. XX, you want to know something?"

When Charlie nodded Oscar stretched out his hand. Charlie grasped it, feeling the loose handful of bone held together by sinew and skin. He looked down at his grand-father's hand, noticing the tremor, the swollen joints, the crushed knuckles, the Dalmatian splatter of liver spots. Oscar's index and middle fingers seemed to skew off in differ-ent directions.

"I wasn't born with this hand," Oscar said. With his other hand, equally disfigured by life's chaotic abundance, he pointed as he spoke: "Knuckles is from the war. Index finger got caught in a door. Middle finger I've forgotten what happened. Swelling is from arthritis. Spots and trembling is age. What am I saying, Charlie?"

Charlie shook his head.

"Doesn't matter how you start off. This is how you end up—very important point—how you end up *if you're lucky.*"

Oscar sighed. "I'm a lucky man. Lucky to survive the war, lucky to find my Chaya Rifke, lucky to learn a trade and provide for my family." He looked at the boy, wanting to say lucky to be here, darlink, lucky to look at your handsome face. Instead, with this same hand (trembling, swollen, painful), he reached over and, as lightly as he could, touched the boy's wet cheek.

"God laughs, Charlie," he whispered. "Might as well join in."

—

Handwritten letter
To: Mrs. E. Dershowitz
From: Mr. O. Minkoff

Dear Mrs. Dershowitz
Please forgive the handwriting, Mrs. D. For our generation, it is harder to type on a computer than to scrawl a letter with such arthritic hands that I wouldn't wish on my worst enemy. Not even Himmelfarb should suffer such pain, ha!

A letter? No, say rather a note, a tiny little not-important-at-all note. So what is this note about? What is so not important but still important enough to write about?

I will tell you in one word. Word is grandchildren, in my case only grandchild. But I know you have five. Five is a blessing beyond imagining. Five is riches descending from the hand of God. Five is why I am writing this note. Thank you, Mrs. Dershowitz.

In confidence,

Oscar Minkoff

To: Mr. O. Minkoff
From: Mrs. E. Dershowitz

See, it's not difficult to write a letter on computer. Also, on this computer you can make face-time with grandchildren if they are old enough, which all are except one. We must change with the times, is what I say. Your generation, my generation, we must *keep up*, Mr. Minkoff.

So what is it you would like to ask me? True, I have five grandchildren, *Baruch Hashem*. Five is a very good number of grandchildren to have, although one is also nice. Is that the question, Mr. Minkoff? It is not only your handwriting I am having difficulty with, as you can see. Also, please call me in future Esther, which is how I am

ending off,

Esther

P.S. Why don't you just *ask* me when you see me? Which is every day.

To: Esther Dershowitz
From: Oscar Wolf Minkoff

Dear Esther,
You are right (but not about computers). Right about grandchildren, right about keeping up. Right about saying

what you mean to say and not speaking in riddles.

For example, what has four legs in the morning, two legs in the afternoon, three legs in the evening? To such a riddle we all know the answer is man. But how to become one is an even better riddle. So this is my question to you, Esther: how to become one? Not just Charlie but all of us.

Also you are right about names. Please call me,

Oscar

P.S. Perhaps I will, dear Esther.

—

It was a day like any other when Charlie's world came crashing down around his prominent ears. *That's the way it goes,* Oscar would later say. *Out of a clear blue sky, lightning-city!* But although he'd tried to adapt himself to the variable weather conditions under which his grandfather seemed to live and thrive (lightning, thunder), Charlie was unprepared for the moment when Mickie Piper, the excellently proportioned, extraordinarily beautiful, and highly cool girl from the film set, sashayed into his Ancestry Studies class.

"Delighted you could join us, Mikayla," Ms. Kambaja said.

"Right on, Ms. K," the girl responded, giving the teacher a thumbs-up and catching Charlie's eye, whereupon she put both hands around her throat and pretended to choke, a dramatic re-enactment of their first meeting.

"Are you trying to tell us something, Ms. Piper?" Ms. Kambaja asked in a faux-sympathetic voice, the kind that implies that a kid called Timmy is stuck in a well and perhaps this girl could lead them to him? Mikayla looked as if she might do just that, might bark out the directions to wherever little Timmy was stranded. But she just sighed, shook her head, nothing to see here. False alarm, Ms. K, and sorry for your trouble.

"Anything you want to add, Mr. Minkoff?" Ms. Kambaja snapped, and Charlie, his heart in turmoil, shook his head dumbly and turned to face the front.

The rest of the class passed in a blur of disbelief, disbelief turning to incredulity, incredulity toggling towards uncertainty, uncertainty coming down eventually on the other side of credence and settling there. (*Mickie-Mikayla, Mikayla-Ms. Piper. So many girls, so many problems,* Weeza would later say.) One of the girls (but which one?) was waiting for him in the hallway when he stumbled out. It was the first thing he asked her, but she said she didn't care, he could call her anything he liked. She, however, would call him Three-Piece as a tribute to his flair for costume design. She gestured at what he was wearing, which was Oscar's exquisite jacket over a black T-shirt and jeans. He'd worn the same thing yesterday, and the day before (fresh T-shirts, obv); he was trying for an ensemble vibe, a stab at the sort of brand recognition that might establish him as a reliable presence on campus, the way Charlie Brown, for example, could be counted on to turn up in shorts and a polo shirt with a zigzag motif across the front no matter the occasion or the weather.

"Charlie Brown, huh. Is he your role model or something?" She narrowed her eyes, suddenly looking mean and Lucy-like.

Charlie Brown was not his hero, though, and he said so, making no bones about his contempt for that poor *schlimazel*, the world's most pitiful and poorly attired fall guy.

"Who then?"

"You see this jacket?" Charlie asked, taking a chance. When she actually held out her hand to feel the fabric of his lapel then whistled admiringly, he knew she'd be receptive to the answer, which was, of course, Oscar Wolf Minkoff. After all, she worked in the movie business and so might be expected to have a picturesque imagination and an appreciation for originality. So he told her about his beloved grandfather, not stinting on the praise.

As he talked, he examined her. Who and what was she, this girl who had turned up, willy-nilly, out of context, out of place, as if she'd just ridden in on the back of a twister? Something about the whole tornado-riding experience had changed her, subtly but unmistakably. Now the differences were greater than the similarities and so, however haphazardly, they carried the day.

Who she was was Mikayla Piper, a grade ahead of him, Ancestry Studies being an elective that any kid could pick up. What she was was smart, he'd later tell Weeza proudly, the best kind of smart, the kind that didn't translate to books. She'd set her heart on screenwriting, finagling her way onto the set of every movie that came through town, running errands, running lines, making herself indispensable. By the time anyone noticed she ought to be in school she was too valuable to spare. True, her attendance record was spotty, but her street cred was bankable.

Mikayla (like Mickie) was funny and smart, a rebel. And like Mickie, she wore a swishy ponytail high on her crown, although she'd cut herself bangs, which she was in the process of dyeing blue. She cultivated an edgy outsider status, a long-distance gaze that wasn't entirely convincing. She was too vigilant, always checking the perimeter for danger, her knuckles white. She was writing a screenplay that she might show him, it all depended, and was working on a homemade tattoo while saving for a real one. When Charlie told her that Jules had worked at River City Ink she was hooked, peppering him with questions.

So that was that, the opening credits of Charlie's life filmed as an after-school special. When she bothered to attend class or, more importantly, wasn't needed on set, Mikayla and Charlie hung out. After that first class they became friends, Mikayla waiting in the hall to poke fun at him, calling him Three-Piece and prodding him in the gut. Yet Charlie didn't mind the ridicule. It was nice to have a nickname, even a nickname that implied a waistcoat where none existed. And it was nice to have a friend too, of course. Sort of nice. Almost a friend. Since not long ago this would have been the fulfillment of his dearest wish, it was confusing to realize that being Mikayla's friend came a paltry second to declaring his love for Mickie. But he stifled this feeling. After all, there was more than one way to wear an imaginary waistcoat.

—

FRIDAY, NOVEMBER 8, 2019

Oscar waved Charlie over the moment he saw his grandson scanning the residents' lounge. He was sitting with Rabbi Spiegelman at a corner table. When Charlie hurried over he saw that his grandfather had already secured their coffee, an unheard-of event.

"Good afternoon, my outstanding friend," Rabbi Spiegelman greeted him, full of bonhomie.

"Sit, sit," Oscar instructed, barely glancing at the woollen overcoat the boy had worn especially to please him. "Himmelfarb's out with the gout," he explained. "Out with the gout," he repeated, pleased by the rhyme. "Gurgling with uric acid, as if you couldn't tell. What a golem, eh, Charlie? Could Hashem have made a worse man out of mud?"

The rabbi tried to look disapproving about this scurrilous view of his congregant but failed, as all noble endeavours inevitably failed when applied to Mr. Himmelfarb. All he could do was take issue with Oscar's inadvertent slighting of the God of Abraham and Moses, who most certainly could have made a worse man out of mud, if so inclined.

"Very true," Oscar said smugly. "I stand corrected, Rabbi."

Rabbi Spiegelman hit himself lightly on the forehead. It was astonishing that even when he tried to defend Himmelfarb he ended up maligning him and, worse, maligning the God who had created him. Observing the rabbi's discomfort, Oscar asked Charlie if he knew what a golem was, a cunning deflection designed to rescue the rabbi from his dislike of Himmelfarb, with which dislike Oscar fully sympathized.

Charlie said sure he knew what a golem was, and Oscar said why keep it to yourself, darlink?

Oscar always got a kick out of hearing the story of the legendary golem, the lumpy creature fashioned from mud and ashes, animated by the magical act of writing three Hebrew letters on its forehead. The letters spelled out *emet*, meaning truth. The golem could be stripped of power by removing the first letter, thus changing the inscription from *emet* to *met*, from truth to death. It was a silent creature, mute, a lunkhead. But useful, Oscar told Charlie. Useful for doing unpleasant chores about the house, useful for raking the ashes and taking out the garbage, useful for rescuing the Jews of Prague from a pogrom after their rabbi, a resourceful fellow, had sent his domestic golem on a rampage.

"Outstanding job," Oscar said when Charlie came to the end of his recitation. "Well, Rabbi, what do you think?"

"What's to think?" asked the rabbi. "A legend is a legend. Just a story."

Oscar reared back. "Just a story, Rabbi? Excuse me, what kind of foolishness is this? What we *got* is stories. That's *all* we got. No, wait—" he put out a trembling hand to forestall the rabbi. "I know what you're going to say. Torah, Talmud, word of God—not stories. Truth. Fine, good. Hundred and ten percent. But maybe Hashem doesn't want to be the only voice. Maybe He wants sometimes a...a conversation."

The rabbi stroked his beard as if to restrain himself from rash speech, but soon gave in to the didactic impulse and lectured them at some length on the purity of Torah which existed in and of itself, ipso facto and a priori and no need for kibitzing from the peanut gallery, thank you very much. Once again it was shaping up to be another debate about the superiority of truth over story, a sentiment Ms. Kambaja would have endorsed. But Charlie was growing impatient. Like his grandfather, he was partial to interpretation, to the sharp thoughts that cut the world into pieces. In his opinion, story beat truth like scissors beat paper—every time.

"Pickle-crack," he reminded Oscar, a private joke. Pickle-crack was their favourite word for what was extraordinary, better even than the tasty executive crack of a kosher dill when you first bit into it.

Oscar beamed. "Sure, Charlie. Why not? Torah is pickle.

Story is crack from the pickle. Can't have one without the other, right Rabbi?"

Rabbi Spiegelman contented himself with a Talmudic shrug and the terse observation that they'd strayed very far from their point. Golems and kosher dills were a nice detour if time was of no consequence but . . . he allowed his voice to trail off. Time was a touchy subject to a man in his nineties. Did he need to spell it out?

"Okay, enough with the chit-chat," Oscar said. "Listen, darlink, the rabbi wants to ask you a question." Caught wrong-footed, Spiegelman took a mouthful of coffee, swallowed the wrong way, choked and spluttered.

Oscar rocked back and forth in almost-guilty delight at the rabbi's discomfort. "Come now, no need to be delicate. We're all grown men here. Listen, darlink, the rabbi wants to know why you haven't had your bar mitzvah yet. Fair question, Rabbi. Well, Charlie?"

Charlie shrugged. Oddly, the thought hadn't occurred to him. He'd been so determined to secure a bar mitzvah for Oscar that he'd forgotten his own thirteenth birthday had just come and gone.

"Strictly on the down low, Spiegelman, I blame the mother," Oscar confided. "She's a fine girl. Oy, such a smile. It brings tears! But an artist, always an artist. Sometimes she holds opposing views."

The rabbi blinked, looking to the heavens as if searching for divine guidance. But his eyes reached only as far as the acoustic-tile ceiling of the residents' lounge. Yet even an expanse of perforated fibreglass may inspire those who seek grace with an open heart. "A pity," he murmured.

Oscar grinned at Charlie, obscurely gratified. "The rabbi

can't be expected to appreciate a woman like your mother. An artist. A rebel."

"I appreciate, I appreciate," Rabbi Spiegelman interrupted impatiently. He continued after a moment, his voice deeper, more profound. "We are all dreamers of the same broken dream. Which is to say, like it or not, flawed as it is, this world is our only home. The whole bill of goods."

"True, true," Oscar allowed. "What do you say, Charlie?"

Both men turned to the boy, who was blazing red. It wasn't that he didn't believe in God exactly, it was just that he didn't think God believed in him anymore. Oscar observed him sadly: the nerve-shimmer, the fidget, the slow leak of self-esteem as if some inner tube had been punctured. His heart smote him at the sight of his grandson's ungainliness and, as Charlie looked increasingly stricken, he relented. "Hoo-boy, it's like they say: youth is wasted on those who don't deserve it. Come on darlink, how about we make it a double bar mitzvah?"

His voice was cajoling, intimate. "You and me, Oscar and Charlie, together again for the first time. Don't wait until you're my age to become a man. Let me tell you, time passes, life goes on. What you need is a strong hand steering you. And what is this hand? Who does it belong to?"

When Charlie remained silent his grandfather replied. "The hand is God, Charlie. The hand is God."

GIRL

CES DEUX FOUS

Hand-delivered notes
To: Mrs. Oslavsky (3B)
From: Mr. Skerrit (2C)

Dear Lady,
It has come to my attention that you are the owner of a
certain bandy-legged permagrump of a grimalkin. I'm
assuming, from the odour in the stairwell, that we are deal-
ing with a feline of the genus "alley."

Apart from young Pyewacket's late-night swaggering
and irregular bladder control, he is prone to depositing
drifts of dander and fluff in the stairwell, the service eleva-
tor, and the laundry room. As a fellow resident of the GNC,
I must point out that you and your flea-bitten moggie are
in contravention of bylaw 33 of the tenancy agreement.

I trust you will take appropriate action. Yours, etc.

To: Mr. Skerrit (2C)
From: Mrs. Oslavsky (3B)

1) *Alexandra is most definitely female cat. Ha-ha Skerrit!*

2)   Don't try terrorize me with bylaw this and bylaw that. What is this? Gulag?

3)   Who are you? Questico landlord? (If so, I put curse on your head. Enormous curse, giant, king-size, big-time curse.)

4)   What kind of man sends letter about cat? Are you mad men?

5)   Charlie says you, Skerrit 2C, don't come out from apartment. Again I say Mad Men!

6)   Why you chuck shoes from window? Why you don't take out garbage? (What is the matter with you, Skerrit?)

To: Mrs. Oslavsky (3B)
From: Mr. Skerrit (2C)

Alexandra, by Gad! I might have known that's what you'd name that dreadful excuse for a sub-Garfield look-alike. You people are utterly predictable. Seventy-four years of Communism and the first chance you get, you resurrect some hemophiliac-carrying, Rasputin-loving Romanov.

However, you might want to rethink the name. From what I glimpse swinging between the legs of that tom-catting gigolo as he navigates the fire escape, Alexander might be more apropos. As a compromise, I propose we refer to yon cat's meow as Sasha, a nickname that salutes your people's sentimental attachment to slavish endearments when applied to either of the sexes.

Sasha it is, then.

To continue (taking up from point 2), I am not trying to persecute you, you paranoia-prone, oligarchy-loving muzhik. *You might want to preserve your ire, along with any spare curses you can summon, for our Questico over-lords (point 3). I am not the enemy, I assure you. Neither am I, as you delicately put it (points 4 and 5), a "mad men." Note, the correct nomenclature is "mad man," Mrs. Oslavsky.* Mad Men *is an American television drama about the exploits of alpha male Don Draper as he struggles to remain top dog in the high-pressure world of Madison Avenue advertising. It's quite good, I believe.*

If, however, you accept my grammatical intervention, then yes, I am indeed a "mad man." I can refer you to the appropriate DSM-5 classification should you be inter-ested, but I suspect you are merely nosy so allow me to recommend the relevant television program. Hoarders, *a so-called reality show on the A&E network, is a far less slick production than* Mad Men, *but it does give the viewer a glimpse into the lives of those benighted shlumps suffer-ing from what was once called "agoraphobia" but, in our ever-more-specialized world, has been given the grand designation of "hoarding disorder."*

There you have it, Mrs. Oslavsky: the answer to your elegantly framed final question (viz. 6). Fortunately, I am not as severely stricken as some. Indeed, I think of it as a lifestyle preference rather than a pathology. I can leave my apartment whenever I choose, I assure you. I simply do not, at present, choose.

At the risk of repeating myself, please be advised that your cat, the unlovely Sasha, remains in contravention of bylaw 33, and has more recently come into direct conflict with tenancy regulations 11–13. I hope you take appropri-ate measures (scrubbing the ground-floor landing with

*disinfectant ought to be the first order of business). Should
you fail to do so, I trust that the aforementioned Sasha
will remain untroubled by any "chucked" shoes that might
be flung his way.*

    I remain, yours, etc.

To: Mr. Skerrit (2C)
From: Mrs. Oslavsky (3B)

Ha, I knew it! Skerrit is crackers!

    *How I know is Why. For example: Why he is so busy
smelling and hearing and seeing what is plain not there?
Why he is giving cat wrong name completely? Why he
is threatening good neighbour and giving poor orphan
Charlie messages he must put beneath good neighbour's
door? And finally, why he is chucking smelly old shoes out
the window? Do you want to hit movie people? Do you want
to hit cameras? Do you want to hit pretty girl that Charlie
loves? (Don't worry, you will never hit speedy cat. Never!)*

    *Ha! Perhaps explains why neighbour's beautiful cat,
Alexandra Ivanovna Oslavsky, does her shit on the stairs.*

    *Remember, I only say perhaps. Try to prove it Skerrit
and you will be sorry. I am Mrs. Oslavsky from 3B.
P.S. Scared Skerrit? Fraidy cat, perhaps?*

To: Mrs. Oslavsky (3B)
From: Mr. Skerrit (2C)

*I know who you are, you crazy Slavic septuagenarian.
You're an old woman in ratty furs and cheap perfume.
Like your feline anima, you moult as you walk and your*

odious eau de toilette *makes my head ache even behind
the closed door of apartment 2C. I am watching you, Mrs.
Oslavsky. Next time you limp up the stairs in your ridiculous, bunion-producing heels, cast an eye at my door
and note the overlarge spy hole. I am watching you,* moy
kotensk.

By the way, I count two new errors of fact in your previous missive. Your cat, Sasha, is demonstrably not beautiful
and Charlie, our obliging mail carrier, is certainly not an
orphan. As to your triumphant bray regarding my mental
state, well there you have me dead to rights. I am, as you
say, utterly cracked.

Moreover, I am and remain, Mr. Skerrit (2C).
P.S. I am not in the least "scared" although I do admire your
sprightly postscript. Brava, Oslavsky!

To: Mr. Skerrit (2C)
From: Mrs. Oslavsky (3B)

Explain. Please!

To: Mrs. Oslavsky (3B)
From: Mr. Skerrit (2C)

Ah, the enigma of the Russian soul. As deep as the Volga,
as profound as the Steppes. I can only assume, other
matters being self-evident, that you are enquiring as to
young Charlie's parentage.

Simple, my dear Oslavsky. Jules Minkoff, our resident
visionary, failed tattoo artist, and part-time barkeeper,
is Charlie's mother, as I suspect you know. The fact that

Charlie addresses his mother by name rather than by some picturesque pre-Soviet patronymic doesn't erase their relationship. Neither, of course, does the fact that Ms. Minkoff resembles nobody's mother, least of all the mother of that ungainly youth.

I assume the boy has a father too, although when Ms. Minkoff and her pregnant belly moved into the GNC she was without companion, the reasons for which she failed to divulge. Perhaps she was silenced by circumstance, her condition, as I was taught to say. Pregnancy had boggled her mind and taken over her body. After all, she was positively bulging with life. With Charlie. Ah, but that was years ago. Years and years. And now you tell me that Charlie's in love and he tells me about his forthcoming bar mitzvah. O tempora, o mores! What a long time I've lived here as loci spiritus, the household god of our deranged commune.

I hope that satisfies your unseemly curiosity, Oslavsky. Yours etc.

To: Mr. Skerrit (2C)
From: Mrs. Oslavsky (3B)

Not so fast, Skerrit. Some questions I still have.
1) Do you know what is this bar mitzvah? Only know one kind bar, Charlie too young.
2) But never too young for be in love. (Not a question.)
3) Are you a fatty like Hoarders people?
4) If fat, what do you eat? If skinny, also what do you eat?
5) The boy has a father, you say? Where is he, my God?

—

SATURDAY, NOVEMBER 9, 2019

Weeza said sure thing when he invited her over. Then she said, "Cat's in the cradle?" and Charlie said looks like it. They were used to Jules and her vanishing act. Now you see her, now you never saw her before in your life.

Heloise Joyal, known as Weeza, was a sturdy woman with a hearty laugh, her trademark flaming red hair clipped short to show off beautifully adorned ears, their rims studded with silver. She was a long-distance trucker, drove a big rig, and had a ferocious sense of style despite the fact that she spent her working life in plaid shirts, jeans, and a selection of baseball caps. She and Jules had been friends since elementary school, when they met in Mr. Gallagher's detention room and realized they were kindred spirits. (*Kind Red*, the mural Jules painted on the side of the Lighthouse Mission, was dedicated to Weeza.) According to Weeza, their meet-cute had been cinematic in an indie art-film kind of way: two weird kids knocking heads in Mr. Gallagher's after-school detention class.

She once tried to tell Charlie what it was like to be a new kid: new to the neighbourhood, to the school, to the province (her parents having recently moved from Quebec), barely knowing a word of English, hot and itchy in her second-hand winter coat. Then Jules Minkoff turned up for detention in a tulle ballet skirt and a Ramones T-shirt, safety pin stuck through her right earlobe, half-eaten candy necklace shedding powder strung around her neck. And right away little Heloise Joyal realized that someone else was as weird and upside down and outside-the-damn-lines as she was.

"Darn lines," she corrected herself hastily. Weeza seldom swore, either in English or in the Québécois argot she slipped into when angry or excited.

"But *what* was it like?" Charlie nagged.

Weeza tried to put into words the feeling that had stayed with her all these years — that occasionally what somebody looked like coincided with an *idea* you had about yourself — even if this idea was fleeting, this fledgling self half-formed, improvisatory, still wobbly. She didn't want to confuse him, so in the end she said she just wanted Charlie to know that . . . well, lots of kids started out weird. *Ça vient de s'éteindre.* End of story.

That evening, Weeza came round at six, panting on account of having to haul a cooler and two takeout bags from Mr. Ken's Shanghai Palace up four flights of stairs. The elevator was out again, had been all week. "Can't Lenny do something?" she grumbled without conviction. They always had Mr. Ken's when Jules took off, when the message on the Wonder Wall read "Shouldn't take long!" or "Don't wait up for me!" or "Be back soon!" She'd be working on her invisibility machines, most likely sleeping on the mattress in her studio.

Weeza was indispensable to the Minkoff family, mother and son, and grandfather too. Without her they were separate planets spinning in their lonely orbits. Jules had her art and Charlie had Oscar, but they didn't have one another. With Weeza they became a family, although still an awkward one, bristling with poky, unconnected branches (Jules, Charlie, Oscar, Gellman, even the crazy neighbours, the ones she called *ces deux fous*). Somehow Weeza provided a critical mass, tipping the balance from not great to good enough.

Since Jules was so absent-minded that she was likely to

light a match and forget to blow it out, Weeza kept an eye on the boy. Actually, after having rescued them in a blizzard she was responsible for all of them, an idea she got from one of Mr. Ken's hokey fortune cookies— *You are responsible for the life you save*—but which suited her superhero inclinations perfectly. She did her share of post-rescue rescuing too, hustling Charlie to Emergency when he slipped on the stairs and broke his wrist, and hauling Gellman to the vet whenever the dumb dog swallowed what couldn't be digested. Mostly though, she was just around, in contrast to Jules, who seldom was.

Well, Charlie didn't like to point out, sometimes Weeza was around and sometimes she was a thousand miles away, honking her air horn and chasing down the highway miles. But it was Weeza who'd introduced him to thrift stores and weekend yard sales, where you could snag a pair of vintage Levi's or a military jacket for a couple of bucks. And it was Weeza who'd gotten Jules the bartending gig at the Sans Souci Hotel when her friend lost her temper, her mind, and subsequently all credibility at River City Ink. Ten years on and Jules still tended bar at the Sans Souci, her conviction being that she'd rather listen to sloppy drunks and half-assed pickup lines for the rest of her life than ever pick up a tattoo needle again. Weeza said that was good news for the fellow whose ass she'd disfigured with her spiteful doodling after he'd insulted her and passed out drunk on the table. Then again, you couldn't please all of the people all of the time.

And it was Weeza who told Charlie about his father, Jules having declared that she wasn't going to write a novel on the Wonder Wall. So it was Weeza who explained, three, maybe four years ago, that his papa had joined the Black Hats. When

Charlie asked if he was in a gang she laughed and said sort of, it was a religious gang, a Jewish sect. The men wore black hats and coats, the women had lots of children, and they all lived close together in big cities like New York. Straight off Charlie asked how you became a Black Hat, as if he were thinking of signing up. Weeza told him you were born that way. The Dervish family had always been religious, she explained, until his papa fell in love with Jules and suffered a crisis of faith, or whatever you called it. After which he did the whole thing all over again in reverse, abandoning Jules (who couldn't have cared less) and Charlie (who'd just been born) to return to his family and his faith and his God, all of whom were welcome to him. Eh, Charlie?

When Charlie was silent, Weeza hugged him and said he was the best thing his papa had ever done and not to forget it. One day when he was ready, she promised, she'd tell him the rest.

Four years later and Charlie still hadn't enquired after his crazy papa, for which she was grateful. Although resigned to her role as Charlie's story-keeper, she couldn't pretend sadness at the defection of his father, that deadbeat. Besides, she was temperamentally dubious about family and throughout her childhood had longed for her own crazy father to abandon his kids and take her aggravating mother with him. Of course, it was different with families you chose. Jules she had chosen, Charlie too. They were her family of the heart.

One day, she'd tell him about the doomed love affair of his deranged parents. But not today. Today, as always, she'd teach him about style, self-confidence, how to project who you hoped to be upon the flickering screen of not-quite-there-yet. She led by example, elegantly attired even when sharing a takeout meal with a boy and his greedy dog, looking very *le way qu'à hang* in her vintage bomber jacket over a crisp white shirt and stonewashed denims. Her hair was freshly cropped, so close to her skull it resembled red suede, and her silver earrings shone fiercely.

She sat herself down, huffing. Charlie was excited to show her the monogrammed cufflinks he'd found in Menlo's Pawn Shop, a steal at eight bucks, knocked down from ten. Weeza admired them, running her forefinger over the raised initials: J on one, M on the other. The cufflinks were a dull metallic gold colour, tarnishing to silver at the edges. They were chunky and bold, satisfyingly weighty, and clicked together in a friendly fashion when she jiggled them in her hand. "*Ma joyau,*" she said softly. M and J.

This had been her nickname as a child. It meant "my jewel," she told Charlie, although her mother's sarcastic tone when addressing her daughter had implied the opposite. Nothing to do with cufflinks, she reassured him. Charlie nodded. He hadn't been able to resist his mom's initials when he spotted the cufflinks in Menlo's dusty window. Jules didn't wear the kind of shirts you could cuff but it was lucky, right?

Weeza nodded. "Guess who I ran into on the stairs?"

"*Ces deux fous,*" Charlie said.

"Well *un fou*, anyway. The skinny one."

They unpacked takeout containers and spread them on the Formica kitchen table, shovelling Shanghai Palace ginger beef, chicken chow mein, and fried rice onto plates; gathering cutlery, water glasses, and napkins; all the time rustling through Styrofoam going, Damn, don't tell me they forgot to pack the celebration noodles again! But *whew*, false alarm: they hadn't forgotten. Everything at Mr. Ken's was primo, but celebration noodles was their signature dish. Until you tasted those warm noodles slick with garlic sauce, speckled with fragments of pickled beef and wisps of egg white, and crispy with pork crackling, you wouldn't understand what a catastrophe it would be to misplace a double order of noodles with extra garlic.

Charlie dumped wontons and fried rice into Gellman's bowl. The dog inhaled the lot in thirty seconds flat, then he stared at them as they ate, looking so mournful he might have been holding a sign: "HUNGRY AND HOMELESS. PLEASE GIVE." Charlie emptied the remaining wontons into his bowl along with another order of fried rice. Old Hungry and Homeless fell upon the bowl as if it was a food bomb about to go off unless he personally attended to its controlled detonation.

Weeza rolled her eyes. "You know dogs are supposed to eat dog food?"

Charlie shrugged. Gellman ate dog food all right. He ate dog food and human food and stuff that couldn't even be categorized as food (paint, shoes), though he was oddly temperamental about dog biscuits, devouring the bone-shaped treats but turning away in disgust from all others. Go figure. But for once Charlie couldn't muster the energy to complain about Gellman's absurd excesses.

Weeza sat forwards, alert. "What's eating you, *mon chum?*"

Charlie said nothing. Again with the shrug. "It's the Thunderbolt," he said finally.

Weeza knew all about the Thunderbolt. The Minkoff men, it seemed, were strangely susceptible to thunder. "Eh? I'm going to need more information."

Charlie was silent, damp with chagrin. He took a deep

breath and then, what the heck, another. "It's love. I'm in love with this girl and I don't know what to do."

Weeza lowered her fork. Without taking her eyes from his face she reached into the cooler, grabbed a six-pack, and thumped it down on the table. She cracked open a beer and tilted it down her throat. Charlie watched her neck muscles bulge as she swallowed.

"Here, catch!"

He caught the can and popped the tab, sipped. He didn't like the taste of beer but kept trying, giving it his best shot. After beer he planned to acquire a taste for cigarillos; after cigarillos, olives; after olives, irony. Becoming an adult was mostly a matter of willing yourself into requirement, Charlie believed. He took a slurp from the can, said *Aaah*, wiped the back of his hand across his mouth, then helped himself to one of the spongy pancakes Mr. Ken's wife always threw in with their order. Clumsily, he slid torn pancake around his plate, sopping up garlic sauce and bits of pork crackling. Whenever he thought about Mickie, the Let-Go girl, he felt both hungry and nauseous, a predicament that could only be *half* solved by stuffing himself.

"Who is she? The Thunderbolt?"

Charlie shrugged, at a loss. Weeza fished a checkout receipt from her pocket and turned it over. "Name?" she asked, her pen poised.

"She saved Gellman's life and . . . and she gave me a pen." He realized how lame that sounded so he filled Weeza in on what she'd been wearing, right down to her glittery red trainers. "Ruby red," he finished off.

"You're kidding?" Weeza was well acquainted with Charlie's obsession, although in her opinion the movie was vastly overrated. She didn't give a hoot about Dorothy Gale — a self-absorbed patootie if ever there was one — who, on waking from a bad dream, insisted on relating it in all its tedious detail without ever once enquiring about the wholesale destruction of the family farm.

"Tell me the deets. What's she look like?"

Charlie stuffed a folded-over pancake into his mouth. He chewed dreamily, his eyes glazing over, his mind going blank as the sensation of hunger overcome by satiation.

"Start with the bazoombas," Weeza said kindly.

Charlie took another swig of beer. It was beginning to taste a lot better.

"Let me get this straight. You met a girl. She was wearing red sneakers. She gave you a pen. That it?"

Gellman sat up, looking haughty despite the fact that he'd been pumping out nuclear-grade dog farts since wolfing down his second helping of fried rice. Weeza gave him a thousand-yard stare. "Oh yeah, she saved the life of that disgusting creature there. Gellman the Magnificent. Gellman the Fart-Artist. Nice one, dollface. You have my everlasting gratitude." Weeza wasn't fond of Gellman, and Gellman repaid her with his undying devotion. Hearing his name, he toppled over and rolled onto his back as if he'd been pole-axed. Even the family dog was a sucker for love, Charlie noted.

He crushed the empty beer can in his fist, psyching himself up to tell Weeza about the mind-bendingly trippy moment last month when Mickie Piper had sauntered into Ancestry Studies class, how he'd fallen in love with Mickie only to find she'd transformed into Mikayla. A reverse fairy tale: one click of the fingers and the beautiful, dog-saving girl in red sneakers metamorphosed into the tardy rebel sporting scuffed

THE FULL CATASTROPHE 129

Blundstones and a lousy attitude. *Ta-da!* Or like one of those tricky perception pictures. Once you saw the urn between the profiles you couldn't *unsee* it. Blink of an eye. No going back. You couldn't see them both at the same time, was the thing. You needed that tiny perceptual click, no matter how swift. That first day in Ancestry Studies, Charlie had actually heard it, the click. One minute Mikayla (ungainly, slovenly, mugging for laughs), next his stupid, manual-speed brain double-clicked on the other girl, on Mickie (poised, witty, perfect). They had nothing in common *but they were the same girl,* was the problem. They were the same girl *but he was in love with only one of them,* was another.

The problems multiplied. *Click, click, click.* The Thunderbolt had been decisive but not, apparently, comprehensive. He didn't love Mikayla but he still loved Mickie, as if the Thunderbolt had divided her in two. *Click, click, click.* One minute Mikayla, next minute Mickie. The effort of holding them both in his mind was an exhausting, nausea-inducing exercise in standing his ground while the world thundered around him. *Da-dum, da-dum, da-dum.* Two profiles, one urn. Herd of horses, herd of zebras. This, that. *Da-dum, da-dum, da-dum.*

As he talked, tears slopped down his cheeks. Sweaty with the combination of beer and despair, his nose manufacturing copious amounts of snot, he became infuriated by his inability to control the various liquids that leaked from him. Abruptly he gave up, laid his head on the kitchen table, and sobbed.

"Easy there," Weeza said. "*C'est pas si tant pire.* It's not so bad, *mon chum.*"

He swiped at his eyes and drew his sleeve across his nose,

cleared his throat, and tried to apologize. Instead he let out a burp. A tragic garlic-spiked burp.

Weeza smiled. "Ah, Charlie. The heart is a door. Who knows why it opens or shuts?"

He nodded, relieved. His heart was a door, swinging wide. Banging in the wind.

For a while they lingered there, Weeza and Charlie, Gellman sprawling, the smell of takeout food like a guest at the table. She pushed another beer towards him, drummed her fingers. *Whew.* Hearts and doors, hearts and doors. To comfort him, she tried to think of a story she could relate about a beautiful, kind woman. But the most beautiful woman she'd ever known was her mother, and Weeza found she still couldn't talk about her with kindness, the formality of distance being irrelevant in matters of the heart. Although her mother had been dead for years, she'd been mean for much longer.

Rubbing the suede nap of her head against the grain, Weeza stared into space, trying to make out the ghost that had haunted her for years. *Ah, mama, lâche-moi un wack!* Finally, she spoke: "Thirteen years old, eh. Already he's a man."

Charlie tried to follow. Wait—what? A man? Every morning he swallowed his pills, then examined his face in the cracked mirror above the washbasin, and every morning he flinched. His forehead and chin greasy, his crazy red hair flaming upwards, dry as kindling. A burning bush with nothing to say, no orders to give, no hope to bestow. And beneath the hair: a face. What was he supposed to do with such a face? He washed it in the hottest water he could draw, towelling it dry roughly. But you couldn't rub off ugly. Who would ever love that face? When people said only a mother, they didn't mean his.

Weeza popped another can, sluicing the beer. "Mickie and Mikayla, right?"

Charlie nodded.

"Two different girls?"

Nodded again. Caught himself, laughed sheepishly. They sure seemed like different girls.

"Why don't you go find Mickie?" Weeza suggested. "She's out there somewhere."

"No way! She doesn't want to—"

"She gave you a pen, didn't she?"

"You think I should write to her?"

"*Pfft.* Nobody writes letters. Except those two crazies you like so much." She canted her head down towards the lower two floors on which the crazies lived. "Think, Charlie! A pretty girl gives you something. A glance, a smile, a wink, a pen. Doesn't matter what. It's an *excuse.*"

He reached into his pocket for the gold cufflinks he'd found at Menlo's Pawn Shop: J and M, M and J. *Think quick!* Weeza plucked them out of the air with one hand.

She didn't want to take them. They were for his mother, no? But Charlie said they would suit her better. Besides, Jules didn't care for jewellery, hated gifts, didn't even own a dress shirt. (He'd been dreading the ordeal of presenting them, to be honest.) Yes, he wanted Weeza to have the cufflinks. She was a jewel, plain and simple. *Ma joyau*—however her mother had meant it.

—

When Weeza left, Charlie hauled the takeout boxes down to the garbage, stopping, as he always did, on the third floor to collect Mrs. Oslavsky's recycling. Mrs. Oslavsky had just taken a tray of *zefir* out of the oven and she needed somebody to taste them.

"Come in, Tzarlie, take off your coat and stay a while," she coaxed.

That's what she called him. *Tzarlie.*

Mrs. Oslavsky had moved into the GNC when her husband died and left her a poor, lonely widow. Yet she blamed him neither for the impoverishment nor for the solitude he'd imposed on her, because in dying he had become the source and substance of her fondest memories. Over and over she recalled his appetites and peculiarities, his insatiable, irrational, indiscriminating sweet tooth.

"What that man wouldn't do to get his hands on *zefir*," she confided to Charlie. "Oh boy, it was incredible." He'd loved chocolate halva, blini filled with sour cream and cherries, and even—God bless him—Guriev porridge sweetened with honey. He was partial to poppy-seed rolls and chocolate-covered prunes and charlotte russe, but his first love was the *zefir* that she'd made when they were newlyweds. As she spoke, she poured their tea into tall glasses, put out the dish of sugar cubes, and set down a plate of white and pink confections. The truth was, if you closed your eyes a white *zefir* tasted exactly like a pink *zefir,* both of which were shockingly good in Charlie's opinion. The prim rosettes resembled meringues but were neither brittle nor crumbly. Instead, the outer shell was crisp, like the crack of a heel on thin-skinned November ice, the insides gooey as marshmallows melting over a bonfire.

"Well, Tzarlie?"

He gave her the double thumbs-up. "First class, Mrs. O. Five-star rating!"

"You can recommend?"

"Highly recommended. A blockbuster for all ages!"

"Ha ha, Tzarlie. Very funny."

"Have one, Mrs. O?"

"No, Tzarlie, my God. I am still a young woman. I have to look after my figure."

Despite her self-ridicule, she acted like a girl, an illusion heightened by her voice, which was youthful, and her energy, which was vigorous. But in truth, she was very old, all bones and high fashion, her pallor thrown into relief by her hair, which was a deep glossy black, worn in the style of Cleopatra, she told him, running a ring-encrusted hand over her dramatic fringe. Her face had grown thinner, the cheekbones standing out like escarpments, and Charlie could see the webbing of her wig peeking out. Sometimes the wig slipped sideways and the old lady tugged at it while he pretended to gaze out the window or bit into another *zefir*, spraying crumbs. Yet somehow, in defiance of the antics of her hairpiece, Mrs. Oslavsky retained an air of dignity and faded glamour. She could have been a runway model for elderly people if there were such a thing.

There was no such thing, of course. The fact was she was a poor old woman, one of the last tenants of the GNC, and she kept her rundown apartment in scrupulous order. A demon for hygiene, she scoured the floors, attacked the grouting with a toothbrush, and polished up the fixtures, especially the brass doorknob that distorted Charlie's face into a Halloween pumpkin whenever he visited. She brought this same single-minded attention to preserving her ancient wardrobe, steaming and ironing, sewing alterations by hand to accommodate her steady weight loss, picking open her seams every few months to take in another centimetre or two.

"Peasy-easy, Tzarlie!"

Charlie worried that Mrs. Oslavsky was disappearing before his eyes. Soon all that would be left of his friend would be a doll-sized but impeccably tailored Chanel-style suit with perfectly stitched seams. She was so frail that anything might happen to her, none of it good. She could fall down the stairs or topple into the incinerator. She could be blown about on the wind or washed away in the rain. She could slip down a storm drain or tumble from the heights of her elegant heels, break her spine and die a protracted, lonely death. She wouldn't be found for days, and the cat would eat her face. Alexandra was exactly that sort of cat, Charlie was certain.

"What kind of scowl you are making, Tzarlie! Have another *zefir*."

"Gotta go, Mrs. O."

"Okay, okay. See you later, crocodile."

Mrs. Oslavsky had already packed half the meringues for Charlie to take home. She always ran the other half over to the Russian Orthodox Church on Jefferson, but today she shoved the package into his hands. "For the fatty," she said. He must have looked hurt, because she hastily explained, "Not you, Tzarlie. For him on the second floor. Mister Hoarder."

—

By the time he made it out to the garbage bins the wind had picked up and the smell of snow was in the air. *Any day now*, people were saying. For once there were no shoes on the ground, although a pair of sneakers hung by their laces from overhead electrical wires. Weeza had warned him that such sneakers meant drug deals were going down in the neighbourhood, but Charlie thought they looked innocent, even wholesome, turning idly in the wind as if they'd been tossed out of some teenager's messy bedroom in the sky.

Lenny looked up as Charlie approached, opening his mouth to display the ground-up remains of the takeout burger he'd been chewing. Nothing personal, just Lenny's way of saying howdy. His manners were lousy but his instinct for inspiring disgust was nuanced. From the overpowering smell of weed wafting from his direction, Charlie concluded he'd been there a while, burning through spliffs as he pawed over the recycling to check that nobody was sneaking Q-tips or plastic straws into the blue box. People were like that, always chancing. Lenny wouldn't trust them farther than he could throw them.

There were hardly any tenants left in the GNC, the old Glutt's Nuts and Cocktail Sauce Building. Most had moved out when Questico hiked the rent. Lenny was the meanest SOB in town, it was generally agreed, a puffy, beer-bloated version of his younger, even meaner self. Last winter he'd gone into overdrive, turning down thermostats, replacing hallway lights with twenty-watt bulbs, shrugging whenever the elevator broke down, and flatly refusing to come out on repair calls. No one complained, though; the consensus was that Questico was looking for any excuse to evict the handful of folks left living in the building chiefly because it was all they could afford. Cold and dark, liable to combust though it was, insect-ridden, rat-infested, and allegedly haunted, the GNC was still better than the alternative, whatever alternative was out there waiting for them: Through the door and down the street. Take a right at the first mean alley.

All that winter the tenants were certain their leases wouldn't be renewed, everyone except Jules freaking out. Mr. Skerrit said they'd have to drag him out kicking and screaming, by jingo. And one day Weeza found Mrs. Oslavsky sobbing in the stairwell because she'd twisted her ankle in the dark, weeping so copiously that her mascara left spidery imprints on Weeza's shirt. But in spring, to everyone's surprise, Questico renewed their leases, which probably meant that the planning permits hadn't come through (Weeza), that God was in a wish-granting mood (Mrs. Oslavsky), or that Lenny was a sadistic piece of shit who got his kicks by tormenting widows and shut-ins (Jules). Anyway, winter was bad, no question. Mrs. Oslavsky wore her moth-eaten fur constantly, like a second skin, and since among Questico's swaths of downtown properties was the warehouse space Jules rented, she'd had to cut the fingers off her gloves just to keep working. Charlie had been worried sick about Mrs. Oslavsky and Mr. Skerrit. By January he was knocking on their doors every morning — *Hey there, Mr. S! Anything I can get you, Mrs. O?* — to check that they were still alive. At night in bed, a sweater over his pyjamas, blankets piled up, and Gellman huddled in for warmth, he could see his breath unspooling in the cold room. Something white and tremulous seemed to be living inside him, a ghost boy.

"Get out of here, missy," Lenny yelled when he saw Charlie. "You're so damn ugly. How'd you get so damn ugly?"

That was another thing. Lenny persisted in addressing Charlie as if he were a girl, which was either the worst insult he could think of, or an honest mistake. If the latter (long odds but possible), it was a masterful stroke — he'd discovered a way of tormenting the boy that even he was unaware of. Charlie used to think it was weed that riled Lenny up, making him angry and mean. But one night he'd encountered the custodian sitting there, empty hands dangling between his knees. Instead of the sulphur-blue haze that habitually floated around his small, bald, matchstick of a head, Lenny had the mean reds, his eyes like pinwheels spinning trails of anger and spite into the dark. Right then and there Charlie decided that between the pinhead blues and the mean reds he'd take stupid any day.

"Hey! Watcha got there, missy? Don't dump that takeout shit in the recycle!"

"I know that," Charlie told him irritably.

There was nothing you could tell Charlie about garbage. It was like he'd *studied* garbage. Lenny was mad because ever since Charlie had taken over Mrs. Oslavsky's garbage run he'd lost a chance to terrorize her.

The wind was blowing stiffly, making a brisk cracking sound like the snap of clean sheets over a bed. *Any day now.*

"Haven't seen Mudder lately," Lenny said with that spooky sixth sense he had. He was so dumb he couldn't scratch his ass and chew gum at the same time, but let Jules slip out for a single night and a bulb lit up in his brain. A very dim, very dusty bulb.

"Can't help it," Charlie said. "She's around. Probably saw you first."

"Can't help it," Lenny mimicked in a shrill voice meant to imitate Charlie's. "Can't help being ugly either, but you could stay home."

Charlie left Lenny hooting at his lame joke — which, considering the source, was pretty ironic; irony in this case being just another way of pointing out that you were rubber and the other fellow was glue.

BOTTLE

LONG HAUL

An Exchange of Emails
To: Jules Minkoff
From: Heloise Joyal

Hey, cutie-pie. How long we been friends? Since third grade, right? So how come I have to hear about the big commission from Charlie?

Look, it gets lonely on the open road, only my laptop for company. I mean sure, the throb of raw, unbridled horsepower between my thighs makes me horny as hell. And yes, climaxing three times between Moose Jaw and Regina is terrific fun. (You know you can learn to come with your eyes open?) Hmmm, where was I going with this?

Write back, you lousy friend.

To: Heloise Joyal
From: Jules Minkoff

Listen kid, you've got to figure out whether you want to make your readers laugh or come. There's no such thing as Humorous Erotica, as your publisher keeps telling you. In my experience a dude with a boner's in no mood for a joke. That's pretty much a given, like God didn't make little green apples and it don't snow in Indianapolis in the summertime. Where the hell are you anyway? Last I heard you were heading down south to Jesus Wept, Missouri, or someplace.

Yeah, yeah. I got the commission. Whoop-de-do. *Dear Ms. Minkoff, we're delighted to inform you that your quinzhee design for our annual River Walk competition was successful. The jury was fucking awed by* Bottle Deposit, *your proposed warming-hut installation, which will be displayed on the Assiniboine River this winter. Congratulations on this extraordinary accomplishment. Go ahead and knock yourself out.*

I won't earn a plugged nickel, I have to get a grant to cover materials, and I'm not insured for accidents but hey, big, Big, BIG congrats! Ever think we'd end up like this, oh friend-of-my-youth? Me, a dumb bartender with a hermaphrodite son, and you, a lonely old so-and-so with a big rig for a lover? Sorry, sorry. Charlie's been down and, as you know, I'm nobody's straight-up shot of helium.

To: Jules Minkoff
From: Heloise Joyal

Don't try to soft-soap me, Jules. I'm not lonely and I'm not old. Being mute doesn't excuse terminal, bloody minded stupidity, my friend. And Charlie isn't a hermaphrodite. He has some intersex traits, is all.

I'm at a truck stop outside Spokane. Been driving all night in a sort of fugue state between sensory deprivation and sensory overload. Can actually *feel* thoughts streaming by like red tail lights in the dark. Not thoughts, sensations: whiff of diesel, shunt of wheels over concrete, burn of chew tobacco against gums. On and on, on and on. Crackle of radio fading in and out of local stations, wipers knocking drizzle across glass. After a while the highway becomes this blazing white birth canal pushing me forwards. By the time I pull into Darlene's Truck Stop (pneumatic hiss of brakes, goose-honk of air horn, drag of a million tons of inertia) I'm born again into the silence at the side of the road, into dawn seeping out over an industrial plant, into the homey funk of whatever Darlene's been frying up for breakfast. Hallelujah and draw up a chair!

Once I take down a plate of egg-and-sausage patties I'm climbing into my bunk and sleeping for the four-point-five hours to which I'm legally entitled and contractually obligated. I fucking love my life—the hemorrhoids, the artery-hardening cuisine, all of it. Nothing like schlepping other people's junk across the continent to free you from wanting anything of your own, to free you from *want*. It's art, Jules, the art of loading someone's crummy life—IKEA bookshelves, heirloom dishes, kids' drawings—all that precious and disposable *stuff*. End of the day? You get back in the rig and let the highway take you into its long grey arms.

And when you get to the other side—of the country or the continent or the world—the shipper's right there waiting, telling you you're late and he'll be watching you like a hawk. So what? Let him watch. You know what you're doing. You have a map in your head of every box, every dining room chair, every hideous garden ornament. You sink into your loading trance, press rewind. And at the end of the day you get to drive away, your load that much lighter, your bank account that much heavier, your trailer floor a mulch of boxes, burlap skins, and crumpled moving pads. So you pull into a lay-by, spend a couple hours cleaning. You hose down tarps and burlaps, secure dollies. You fold every moving pad into a perfect thirty-five-inch square and collapse your boxes. You collect the tools lying on the floor and repack them. What does it matter that your arms are buzzing and your pits are sopping wet? What does it matter that your blood is three-quarters energy drink to one-quarter nicotine? None of it matters because you have restored the world to its perfect shape.

So when it comes time to toot my last horn and hand over the keys, I'll be gut-shot. This is as good as it gets, Jules. Not every job demands a pee-in-the-bottle skill set. Okay, pep talk over. Down to business: what's the trouble with Charlie? Lord knows he has his cross to bear, along with adolescence, that cheery little crown of thorns. But he's always been a trooper. What gives?

To: Heloise Joyal
From: Jules Minkoff

What's the trouble with Charlie? Too many chromosomes and too few parents — could that be it? He's in a funk, no question. Goes about with a long face, stares into space. I hear him crying in his room late at night. And no, I don't go in there. It'd embarrass the hell out of both of us.

I keep remembering the night he was born, the nurse asking, Did you smoke a lot of cannabis during the pregnancy, dear? Well, faux-asking. She clearly thought she knew the answer. I was sitting up in bed feeling like a mile of broken road. They put him in my arms, squirming, trying to get a nipplehold. You're supposed to feel love, right? All that gurgling, nutrient-carrying, immune-boosting *love* letting down like milk. I'm sorry, dear, the nurse said. We don't know if your baby is a boy or a girl.

God. Imagine hearing that two hours after you've given birth. Blood, sweat, tears—so much *leakage*. My episiotomy oozing and milk seeping from ruched breasts. When they finally left us alone I put him in the bassinet, unfastened his diaper, began sketching. "Close-Up of Unknown Baby." "Still Life with Mixed Organs." "Portrait of the Artist's Biggest Mistake."

What's the trouble with Charlie? His father's a bastard and his mother's a bitch. (What d'you call someone so caught up in her art she doesn't realize she's pregnant until it's too late?) His best friend lives in a care home and his fairy godmother drives a truck. Hate to be the one to say it, but it doesn't help he's a weird-looking kid. That face. That hair. The custom-fitted jacket.

Going to end now because it's dawn. What is it with us? You on your never-ending highway, me forever coming off the graveyard shift. We're nocturnal creatures, I guess. Too much light and we fade away.

Good morning, Weez. Sweet fucking dreams.

P.S. You can pee in a bottle? Can't picture it but then again, don't want to.

To: Jules Minkoff
From: Heloise Joyal

You telling me you sat there sketching Charlie's genitals while he sobbed his little heart out? Dude, that's cold. And yeah, I'd call that person a bitch.

And to answer your question: Why, yes, I *can* pee in a bottle. All it takes is a strong pelvic floor, a funnel, and an empty pop bottle. Beats wrangling this monster into a truck stop and finding a public restroom free of loitering perverts and interstate serial killers. By the time I've wiped the birdshot-shit off the seat, coaxed my bladder to relax while I hover, thigh muscles clenched, above the bowl, I've lost half an hour pissing in a shithole off some highway near No Account, Neverville. And yeah, I know you'd rather not picture me hefting myself over a funnel shoved into a bottle. But you're an artist, dammit. Open your damn eyes.

Listen, take it from someone who's learned to pee while one-handing a rig at 120 klicks: you do the best you can with the worst you got. That's *all* you got. Don't be mad at me anymore. I love you, you gorgeous bitch. *Ça vient de s'éteindre.* P.S. The new book's called *Long Haul Layover*. Horny female trucker and her shenanigans on Route 66. My editor says she couldn't stop laughing. *Told* you women can do sex and humour at the same time. Besides, I wasn't writing it for your lot.

To: Heloise Joyal
From: Jules Minkoff

How can I stay mad at you? Steering your rig through Beating-Heart Country, counting the pro-life billboards and dictating lesbian porn while a bottle of pee rolls around at your feet. You're one of a kind, Weeza Joyal.

Up late with designs for the warming hut. Charlie's cooking up some scheme with Oscar the Grouch. All will be revealed in time. Gellman remains Gellman, which is to say a putrid sack of anal leakage and canine whimsy. Love you too, *ma joyau.*

—

SATURDAY, NOVEMBER 16, 2019

It was cold enough to bust out the old winter parka but Charlie was going a-courting, so he brushed down the woollen overcoat he'd snagged for a song at the Sally Ann. A song was what Oscar had called it, practically breaking into one. *Such fine stitching! Feel, darlink!* Naturally he instructed his grandson on the care and maintenance of a 100 percent wool overcoat, demonstrating how to pat it down with dryer sheets, remove dog hair with a rubber-gloved finger, and settle the nap with a nylon stocking wound around the hand. No Velcro, Oscar warned, no masking tape, absolutely no commercial lint rollers. Even a coat's got feelings, he half-joked.

His coat spruced, Charlie draped the red scarf that Mrs. Oslavsky had knitted him around his neck. He was going for a Toulouse-Lautrec effect, a bold pop of colour against the dark background of a night out at the corner cabaret. A kick of "who d'you think you are?" mixed with a splash of "why the hell not?" The old razzle-dazzle. On the whole he was jazzed with the effect, the scarf chiming against his hair with just the right note of careless disregard. *Huh, this old thing?*

Charlie had tried to flatten his vigorous, vertically inclined hair using lashings of gel. He cupped a hand over his mouth and sniffed, combed his eyebrows, examined his nostrils for boogers and his ears for wax. The pain in his stomach was back, a safety pin twanging open deep inside him. He was supposed to call Dr. Jabbour when that happened but had decided to ignore it as long as he could. Maybe longer. Luckily both nostrils and ears rewarded his scrutiny and he distracted himself by blowing into a Kleenex and chasing his pinky finger around the racetrack whorls of his ears. Then he slipped the pen she'd gifted him into his pocket.

The question was whether to take Gellman or leave his sorry ass at home. Charlie was inclined to the latter course because the last time they'd hit Water Street the big dope had conniptioned himself into a full-throttle panic over nothing more than a length of duct tape and a plastic bag. On the other hand, without Gellman's matchless hijinkery he might never have met Mickie Piper, his Thunderbolt, the amazing Let-Go girl. At least, not before he'd encountered her pale doppelgänger, the ungainly Mikayla.

"Ms. Piper," Ms. Kambaja called her, scooping her name out of the air as if it appeared in quotation marks: "Ms. Piper, perennial absentee."

The truth was, the more time he spent with Mikayla the more he liked her and the more he missed her. She was his friend, he saw her most days, yet sometimes he liked her so much and missed her so profoundly he thought his heart would break. But the fact remained that "Ms. Piper" of Ancestry Studies wasn't the same girl he'd fallen for on the movie set. Today he meant to find her, to prove that Mickie Piper was still out there somewhere, clicking her ruby slippers and trying to get home.

"Well Gellman, what's it going to be? Think you can behave yourself?"

Gellman launched himself at the door, hysterical with the anticipation of Charlie's absence, his utter annihilation as soon as he disappeared from the animal's anxious field of vision.

"Okay, but you gotta play it cool, dude," Charlie said.

Gellman yipped in frantic agreement. *Yes! Yes! Yes!* Certainly he would play it cool. *Yes, a thousand times yes!*

Charlie was dubious, but he clipped the leash to the dog's collar. Right on cue, Gellman choked dramatically, just as he always did. Sometimes he worked himself into such a lather over the leash that he scuttled his own ship, collapsing in a flop sweat of nervy despair. It looked like today might be one of those days, but at the last moment Gellman recovered from his death spasm and took himself firmly in hand, merely retching pathetically before standing up on trembling legs and casting a sheepish side glance at Charlie. *Good. I'm good.*

The elevator was out of order again, so they took the stairs at a run, Gellman's claws rattling on concrete. Outside, the wind whipped cigarette butts and newspapers around Charlie's ankles, yanking at the ends of his scarf. Gellman skittered and wheeled on his leash. He gawked at pedestrians and stopped to yawp at a city worker who was sweeping the sidewalk, at a homeless man hunkered in the shelter of an alley. It was colder than Charlie had anticipated, tall buildings creating steep ravines, the wind soughing through. For a moment he wished he were snugly packed in the goose down of his winter jacket. Then he glimpsed himself in a storefront window. Black coat, red scarf. Windy day in old Montmartre. Absinthe makes the heart grow fonder.

The first thing they saw when they turned onto Water Street was their old pal, Lanyard. Cigarette in one hand and a bullhorn in the other, he was putting first one and then the other to his mouth, almost hollering into the lit end of his cigarette. His words were garbled, the way grown-ups sounded in *Peanuts* cartoons, but his tone, as usual, was furious. *Take a fucking bath, Pig-Pen! Nice going, Lucy! Don't be such a punching bag, Charlie Brown!*

Huh? Charlie whirled around, but Lanyard wasn't speaking to him, wasn't in fact addressing the cast of *Peanuts* at all because the movie they were shooting had nothing to do with a bunch of quirky kids and the floppy-eared dog they hung out with. Charlie had glanced at the entertainment news earlier in the week and discovered that the movie was something of a big deal, featuring local talent and a genuine tip-of-the-tongue Hollywood actor. There it was in black and white: *Sleepwalkers*, a Kick-the-Can Production.

The same idling catering trucks and wardrobe trailers lined the street, the smell of diesel fumes heavy. A trestle table was set up with a coffee urn and takeout cups, a grease-stained box that had once held doughnuts, and a platter of picked-over sandwiches beneath cling film. Nearby, a warehouse was lit up with klieg lights and outdoor spots. It was an old building, derelict, ripe for a quick teardown-turnaround deal in which a shiny new condo would rise from the foundations seemingly overnight. The property had recently been sold to Questico, Weeza reported. She kept an eye on the area, especially for real estate news, none of which, in the last few years, had been good news.

"Another Waterfront Development brought to you by the Questico Corporation, a Shit-Can Production," she would announce.

Neither Oscar nor Jules received the news well. Oscar was testy at the thought of the old neighbourhood changing, Jules livid at the cynical profiteering that went by the name of gentrification. Outrage brought families together, Charlie sometimes thought. Oscar and Jules were so dissimilar they might have been members of different species, composed of different elements even. Oscar was earth, Jules was air, and Charlie was stranded in the middle with his wide-open prairie heart, his how d'you do tendencies, and his spend-a-penny, save-a-penny brand of Midwestern hopefulness. He was deep in these familiar thoughts while Gellman, deep in familiar odours — exhaust fumes, fast food wafting from the catering truck, cigarette smoke, hairspray, sweat — chased the scents down ecstatically.

"Hey! You there! HEY, I'm talking to *you*, Gellman!" Lanyard was bearing down on them, evidently thrilled to remember the name of the chubby dude who'd caused such havoc with his crazy, suicidal dog. Charlie noticed that his upper half was all Canada Goose jacket, state-of-the-art and much too serious a cudgel against the fall weather. In this city you paced yourself. Everyone knew that.

Overjoyed, Gellman galloped towards Lanyard, yipping his delight at finally gaining the recognition he deserved. *Here! Here! Here!* he barked; every snuffle and thrust, every moist slurp, every eager lunge at the fella's groin indicating that he was at the man's service.

"Quit barking!" Lanyard yelled. "Gellman, can't you get your brainless hound to shut the fuck up?"

Gellman immediately complied with this request by attempting to throw himself into Lanyard's arms as if he were the consumptive heroine of a period drama.

"*He's* Gellman, *I'm* Charlie," Charlie explained, as if accuracy was the solution to the chaos that resulted whenever Gellman and Lanyard went into their oil and water routine.

"Really? Is that SO? Tell me more, PAL!" With each unpleasantry Lanyard shoved his face closer to Charlie's.

Charlie could smell the man's coffee and cigarette–infused breath, the boiled-down essence of his aggression. He took a step backwards and Lanyard, as if on a pulley, took a step forwards. Backwards-forwards, backwards-forwards they danced a deranged waltz, Charlie retreating as his adversary advanced. Gellman was intrigued. He sat down abruptly, cocked his head, and thumped his bottle-brush tail. True to form, he sensed no danger despite the fact that the enraged man, having shoved Charlie up against a trailer, was now yelling profanities in his face.

"Let go, Floyd! Let him *go!*" a familiar voice called out.

Once again Charlie's presence on set had summoned the Let-Go girl. Once again a pair of glittery red trainers filled his vision. Once again the air thinned and his senses swarmed. Dizzy, he slid down the side of the trailer until he was sprawled on the ground, his head propped against the truck, whose idling engine throbbed through him.

"Mickie, it's that freak again!" Floyd yelled, trying to grab hold of Charlie. It was unclear whether Mickie had been going to cop to remembering Charlie because at that exact moment remembrance flooded the synapses of Gellman's tiny brain. He now threw himself joyfully into her arms, the girl who'd rescued him from his brush with mortality, his long-drawn-out death by plastic bag. *Oomph.* Mickie sat down hard, her arms full of Gellman.

"You see?" Floyd yelled. "Those two suck up all the gravity. The minute they walk onto my set everyone else falls down."

"Take a powder, Floyd," Mickie said. "I'll handle it." Even pinned down by Gellman, his wet tongue swiping a shiny circumference around her face, she sounded like she meant business. Tough. Ballsy. A street fighter with a clipboard, a pretty girl with a sharp left hook.

"Right you are, sweetie," Floyd said nastily. "I'll leave you to take out the trash. And *you*—" he wheeled to face Charlie, letting the cigarette smoke dragon from his nostrils before delivering his exit line: "I'll get you, my pretty, and your little dog too!"

"And—scene," Mickie said to Floyd's retreating back, pretending to take a bow.

Charlie snuck a glance. Except for her blue bangs and high-swinging ponytail she looked nothing like his school pal. For one thing she was wearing the glittery red trainers again. The idea that her footwear turned her into a different girl was so outrageous, so off the beam, so downright screwy as to seem the solution to a complicated riddle that couldn't be solved any other way. If it wasn't the trainers, what was it? What made them separate girls, occupying irreconcilable universes, never meeting, never merging, never even missing each other? It was as if thinking of one in the presence of the other involved a mental suspension, like holding a thought in a chemical solution, one part memory to three parts forgetfulness. The very impossibility of this conclusion made it believable. Everything in Charlie's life was impossible, yet everything was true.

"What are the chances of a house falling on him?" Mickie's voice broke into Charlie's reverie. She was still preoccupied with the demise of Floyd. "Until then you guys have to stay off the set. *Hey*!"

The exclamation was on account of Gellman, who, having expressed his undying gratitude in a variety of ways—licking Mickie, slathering over Mickie, dragging his sloppy tongue clockwise around Mickie's face — a gratitude that remained unsatisfied, now felt called upon to swallow the girl whole. Forepaws planted, jaw cranked to its utmost, Gellman was closing in on her right ear, a look of resolution on his goofy face.

"What? No, Gellman, *down*!" Charlie dragged the dog away, then slumped against the trailer. Gellman flopped into his lap, lifting his eyebrows and boggling his eyes in an unmistakable pantomime of canine chagrin. He appeared to accept responsibility for his part in the fracas but seemed unconvinced that Charlie felt a corresponding burden of guilt. Cocking his head, he encouraged the boy to own up to his desire. *You wanted to eat her too, didn't you?* But Charlie was distracted. The pain in his stomach was no longer a safety pin but a Swiss Army knife bristling with corkscrews and blades. Saliva flooded his mouth and fat drops of sweat broke out on his forehead.

"You okay?" Mickie asked, peering into his face.

"Swell."

"Hup bup. Don't lie to me, father of Gellman."

Damn. Lying was Charlie's Achilles heel. He'd always been a lousy liar. Best he could do was pull up the handbrake, wait for the pain to die down. He swallowed and swallowed, forcing down the sickness, congratulating himself on another victory against the vile vomit monster that lurked at the margins of his life, terrifying him in some indefinable yet utterly convincing way. But as the nausea receded, so too did his inhibitions. An abject feeling overwhelmed him, the impulse to confess his sins and be forgiven. He took a breath. "I'm sorry I crashed the set again. I'm sorry Gellman tried to eat you. I hope you don't get in trouble with, with —"

Fortunately Mickie had become distracted by a couple

of loitering techies who, under cover of doing nothing, were arguing about the difference between sleepwalkers and zombies. No difference, maintained the younger one, shaking his blond dreads. The other guy, older and wearing a beret, said yeah but you got to factor in motivation. Dreadlocks shrugged and said he thought the deal with zombies was they were unmotivated. Exactly, said Beret, that's the point.

Mickie rolled her eyes. "Lucky we got a couple of geniuses on the case."

"Is your movie about zombies?" Charlie asked.

"What? No! I mean, why does everyone— *Gah!*"

"Sorry." He was too.

"No, it's not your fault. It's just—okay, you want the pitch?"

It seemed he did. So: "All the children in this city wake up, um, asleep. And if you wake up a sleepwalker you kill them, right? So to save their kids the parents become soldiers of silence, basically, keeping the world quiet. If that means killing people, cool. Only they have to blow them away in dead silence, naturally, which ratchets up the tension. And while they're going full-out gonzo on anyone who breaks the Silence Barrier they have to figure out how to reroute trains and divert flight paths. Anything that makes a sound. Luckily you got winter, you got snow, you got the Muffle Factor. But then it's spring and right there's the crisis, Charlie, right there. Because what happens if there's a big-ass thunderstorm brewing? Which there totally is, by the way."

She peered at him. "You follow?"

Charlie nodded, yup, yup. He knew all about the dangers of thunder.

"So here's the question. What does it mean to wake up?"

She stared into space and Charlie stared over at her. Up

close she was even more beautiful than he remembered. There was an oily sheen to her forehead and late-night smudges beneath her eyes as if, unlike the children in the movie, she never slept at all.

"What you lookin' at, kid?" Mickie said, putting on a tough accent. She heaved herself to her feet and wiped her hands, gave him a friendly punch on the shoulder, and told him to keep the faith. Then she walked away, leaving him sitting there, head hanging, heartbroken. If this were a movie, she'd have turned back and kissed him on the cheek, and he'd have presented her with the pen. *Miss, you dropped something!* Cue the swelling piccolos. She'd kiss him on the lips then, she'd have to—it was in the script.

But it wasn't a movie. It was only a movie set. So instead she walked away, Mickie Piper and her ponytail both swinging. When she was too far away for it to matter, without looking back, she waved. A quick open-and-shut gesture, a waggle of the fingers. It killed him, that wave. It meant that she knew he was watching her, she was certain of it. So certain she didn't even have to turn around.

—

Wednesday, November 27, 2019

To: Parents of Ancestry Studies students
From: Maude Kambaja

Those of you who have been following our progress will know that we've embarked upon the autobiographical component of our project. Your children are preparing to "interview" themselves using questions in our learning rubric as prompts. Students will then work their self-administered interview into an autobiographical report or "story."

Your child may approach you with questions pertaining to their birth, early years, childhood, and so on. Do take the time to reply in full. Perhaps you might even initiate a dinner-time discussion about how stories imbue our lives with meaning, provided, of course, **they are true stories**. I appreciate how busy our lives are, but I assure you that the time you spend exploring these questions will be richly rewarded.

To: Ancestry Studies students
From: Ms. Kambaja
Subject: Interview Topics for Autobiographical Project

1) What is the story of your birth?
2) Describe your earliest memory.
3) What does your bedroom say about you? (Requires a description in the form of a written account or creatively drawn sketch. **No** Instagram photos please.)
4) What do your preferences and/or antipathies reveal? You might explore your favourite or least-favourite movies/songs/food. (Note: if you don't understand a word, **look it up** before coming to me for an explanation.)
5) What is the first historical event you remember? Do you feel "part of history"?

Due date: **December 16, 2019**
Remember our simile and metaphor exercises. Use vivid language to "paint a picture."

———

Autobiographical Project
by Charlie Minkoff

My earliest memory is of my mother leaning over my crib. Her face was blurred and unfocused like the moon coming out from behind clouds. "Poor baby," she said. "What am I going to do with you?" She tucked her finger into my fist, and I held on tight. Then she opened her moon-mother mouth and sang the rainbow song, *Where troubles melt like lemon drops.* My mother couldn't carry a tune in a bucket, I learned that day.

Slowly we got used to each other. She made me call her Jules and I made her tone down the singing and lay off the torch songs. Then she got into a fight with a river. They rescued her, but she hasn't been able to sing since.

My grandfather, Oscar Wolf Minkoff, says all questions are the reflection of a reflection, like looking in a vanity mirror. When you pull the flaps together all you see is mirrors vanishing into the distance. Every mirror is a door, he says, and behind every door is another question. For example, question: Why did Jules run onto the frozen river? Answer: She heard a kid crying, but—question—why was she out there in the first place? Answer: She was on her way to the store to buy Marlboro Lights and a tin of Altoids, but—question—why was she in such a hurry? Answer: The blizzard of the century was coming and we'd be snowed in for days. Weeza said, Trust your mother to be taken out by a cliché. When I asked what she meant she said running out to buy cigarettes was usually "just a ruse." (That's a quote. I've looked it up and it still doesn't make sense.)

Weeza Joyal, my mother's best friend, is a trucker. She turned around on the highway when Oscar got word to her that Jules was missing. If you ask me, the most important story of Weeza's life was when she drove back to Winnipeg with an undelivered truckload of low-fat fruit yogurt. An unstable product at the best of times, she points out. You should hear her go on about what it's like to be driving east on the Trans-Canada one minute then find yourself driving west five minutes later. Almost meeting yourself on the way! You'd think it was magic, instead of a case of hitting the brakes and turning into a handy truck stop outside Sault Sainte Marie.

Once she got herself turned around, Weeza floored the gas, and she rolled into the city, eight hours later, just before they closed the highway. Oscar and I were stuck on the fourth floor of the GNC. We'd been watching *The Wizard of Oz* on PBS and Munchkinland had just flooded into glorious Technicolor when the power went out, shrinking Oz to a buzzing dot in the middle of the screen. And, like that, the world was back to being a black and white movie. We spent the afternoon peering out of the window, watching snow static, seeing the world turn spooky and silent, waiting for Jules and her cigarettes to return. Oscar kept saying, Hoo-boy, we're not in Kansas anymore, looks like.

It was after midnight when Weeza found us. She scaled the stairs like a Québécois superhero, yelling, *Attache ta tuque! Attache ta tuque!* Hold on! Wait up! Stay put! As if we had a choice. I was asleep beneath the coats that Oscar had piled on me, and Oscar was too cold to move. Weeza hauled him down in a fireman's grip then scooted back for me. While she was at it, she got carried away and rescued Mrs. Shapiro and her dog, Gellman (2A), not to mention Mrs. Oslavsky (3B), who'd just moved into the building. She was so hopped up on adrenalin she even tried to rescue Alexandra and Mr. Skerrit (2C), but

Alexandra almost clawed her face off and Mr. Skerrit told her where to get off, thank you.

We spent the rest of the night in the high cab of Weeza's eighteen-wheeler, Weeza turning on the engine every hour to keep the rig warm. Nobody wanted to go back into the cold, dark building. Mrs. Shapiro, Mrs. Oslavsky, and Oscar huddled up front (you can divide three skinny old people between two seats just fine), while Gellman and I curled up in the snug under a tartan blanket that had been used to wipe up motor oil. Don't ask me where Weeza was. Securing the perimeter, she said later.

In the morning a police car fishtailed up the street and skidded on black ice, almost burying itself in a snowbank. Two officers pulled themselves out and slogged up to the rig. Oscar, Mrs. Shapiro, Mrs. Oslavsky, Gellman, and I peered through the window, watching the officers talking to Weeza. Oscar grabbed my hand and held on tight.

My mother hovered between life and death for a week. Weeza stuck around until Jules made up her mind then she was back on the road. Oscar went to live at the Seth Rowe, and so it was just Jules and me in our loft in the GNC. The only difference was she couldn't sing anymore. The river had taken her voice.

———

Handwritten note on returned homework for Ancestry Studies class

Mr. Minkoff:
I have read but not graded your "Autobiographical Project"

for reasons that must be clear to you. The instructions
were to compose a self-portrait using questions from the
rubric. Instead, you've handed in an improbable account
of other people's lives. If this were an imaginative exercise
you would have scored highly. In other words, ask yourself
<u>whose</u> story you are telling. If the answer is anyone other
than "Charlie Minkoff" then you have failed to comply with
<u>my explicit instructions</u>. To be clear, I'm not calling you
a liar, young man, but I would urge you to reassess your
supple relationship with the truth.

    Rather than assign a failing grade and risk crossing
swords with your vigilant and understandably partisan
mother, I will give you a chance to redeem yourself. See
me after class to discuss a make-up assignment.

    MK

P.S. I've been accused of <u>overu</u>sing the phrase "to be clear"
by students who enjoy mimicking their teacher. But clarity
is all, Mr. Minkoff; to be clear is to approach knowledge,
truthfulness, and self-regulation with open eyes and a spar-
kling conscience.

———

An Exchange of Emails
To: Heloise Joyal
From: Jules Minkoff

Want to hear a coincidence? Okay, pin back your ears: the
name of my quinzhee is *Bottle Deposit.* Crazy how we're both
obsessed with bottles! I've designed my hut as a bottle lying
on its side, entered by way of a bottle-neck tunnel, a neat

solution to crowd control. Imagine an empty wine bottle casually tossed aside. I've made these enormous curve-sided moulds out of silicone filled with water I pumped from the river in fall. Well, ice now, obviously. I rented an industrial meat locker the minute I got the green light from the Arts Council.

Hey, remember playing spin the bottle in Cindy Ricci's mom's basement? The anticipation, the bottle yawping from side to side, kids yelling *her*, no, *her*. Then two minutes in a cupboard with some boy and his anxious tongue. Yuk.

But there's something glorious about chance, right? Randomness. The fickle hand of fate, as Oscar would say. The point of *Bottle Deposit* is that the water's clear, so you can see bubbles and river foam and detritus, even fish bones (!) floating in the ice. I've learned how to suspend objects in water as it freezes, spookily floating there, almost…legible. See, it's a memory deposit, the memory of water, the river's layered, sedimentary history. I imagine visitors coming through the bottle neck, standing in that cold radiant light, peering into the past. I'm not afraid anymore, is what I'm trying to say. I'm not afraid of what happened on the river eight years and only three hundred metres downstream from the site they've allotted me.

There's still some give in the freezing process, Weez. Any time you want to come down to the meat locker and pee in the water just let me know.

P.S. I'm serious.

To: Jules Minkoff
From: Heloise Joyal

Wow. Talk about a message in a bottle! That's SOME PIG, as Charlie would say.

Glad you're not afraid of the past anymore. Apparently some spook lured you onto the ice and you nearly died, and your lungs are shot, and you still can't talk about it (hah!). I don't know what happened out there, but revisiting the river at the same spot you went through the ice is creepy yet liberating. In a word, art. Your kind of art, Jules. Besides, January ice is miles thicker than early-November river rind. They're two different rivers, as some Greek dude once said. Proud of you, girl. Always have been.

Um, you know we controlled the bottle spin, right? Why else did I always end up with the luscious Trista Bird, much good it did me. Two minutes of giggling in the cupboard with her glossy bubblegum lips pressed up against my ear. Torture. P.S. I know you're serious, you kook, but no thanks.

To: Heloise Joyal
From: Jules Minkoff

It wasn't a spook. I've told you, it was a lost kid calling for help. Sounded like Charlie, but it was a girl. She was calling my name. What would you have done?

To: Jules Minkoff
From: Heloise Joyal

We've been wrangling about that little bitch for years. Whoever she was, she caused a world of pain. And for what?

You think I don't hear voices on the highway? There's mama singing her angry songs and papa reciting the names of the horses he lost bets on; all the aunts arguing and yelling; my sisters, my brother, the ex-lovers. *I hate you. I love you. Go away! Come back!* One time mémé woke me just before I wandered over the median. *Aweille, la gras!* she hollered and pumped the air horn. *La gras.* Even to save my life she had to insult me!

We all hear voices, Jules. Just memory making another sad little clinking deposit.

To: Heloise Joyal
From: Jules Minkoff

Brilliant, Weez. Just fucking brilliant. SOME PIG! TERRIFIC! and RADIANT! all rolled into one.

You're right about the memory deposit thing. I'm kicking myself. We need a usable bottle deposit, maybe a pop-up recycling plant? Visitors bring empties in exchange for — what? Ten cents is the going rate for glass returns but what if they have something inside? A dead pet's collar, a sobriety bead. Anything — a postcard, a bus transfer, the butt from the last cigarette you're ever going to smoke. Whatever fits. *Fits.* Into a bottle or a memory. Then we've got that ship-in-a-bottle vibe going for us. And the payoff is I get to make *more* art with the recycled bottles. Genius.

BILLBOARD

INTERSEX FORUM BILLBOARD

Moderator: *Mel57*
Re: *Long Haul*
Replies: 9
Views: 312
Last Post: by *Homesick* >> Dec 3, 2019, 3:04 am

Re: *Long Haul*
by *BigRig64* >> Dec 1, 2019, 1:23 am

Howdy all, this is my first time posting. I'd appreciate any help you can give me. And apologies for getting things wrong or offending any of you. Like I said, first time.

Here's the thing. My godson is going through some troubles and I don't know how to help him. He was born with "ambiguous genitalia" is the term. I don't know much about this stuff. When he was born the surgeon wanted to operate because of emotional scars and so forth. Anyway, Dr. J said no way, let the kid choose when he's older.

You'd really like Charlie (not his real name). He's an amazing thirteen-year-old with a huge heart. Any advice gratefully received.

Re: *Long Haul*
by *Pinocchio* >> Dec 1, 2019, 8:09 am

The idea that doctors make us into "real" boys or girls if they make our bodies look "right" is giving them permission to torture us. We're seen as monsters. Society cuts us up, removes what's unacceptable and ridicules what's left. Surgeons are the real monsters, in my opinion.

Re: *Long Haul*
by *BigRig64* >> Dec 1, 2019, 9:10 am

Charlie isn't a monster. I never said he was. Sorry if I haven't made myself clear.

Re: *Long Haul*
by *Mel57* >> Dec 1, 2019, 8:09 pm

Greetings, *BigRig64*. Pleased to have you on board. Allow me to introduce myself. I'm non-binary, genderfluid, pansexual, and occasionally a-gender. A-gender without an agenda! Kidding. We all have an agenda. Mine is to educate well-meaning but clue-less cis folk about what it means to raise a child with intersex traits in a world where a binary understanding of sex is the norm.

If you want to know how to help Charlie then listen up. In our current woefully ignorant social climate, an infant's gender is based on what their genitals look like. It's as simple as ticking a box on a birth certificate: V for Vagina is F for Female; P for Penis is M for Male. But what happens when baby is born with an unusual presentation, say a "micro-penis" or an enlarged clitoris, a vaginal pouch or hypospadias?

The first recourse is so-called normalizing surgery, which *Pinocchio* correctly calls out. The medical "experts" wade in and basically select baby's gender. To be crass, they decide whether the penis is *viable* because, make no mistake, friend, the penis is king. The yardstick for viability is not more than 2.5 standard deviations smaller than average. If, heaven forbid, the penis is judged embarrassingly small, the next priority is reproduction. Where cervix, ovaries, and Fallopian tubes are present, a vagina can be created with little or no finesse. And little or no sensation too, is my understanding since vagino-plasty assumes that a vagina is merely a receptacle designed to accommodate a penis.

Once the docs figure out whether they want to prioritize phallic enhancement or reproductive capability they go in with scalpels drawn. It's a vile practice, evil beyond words. Charlie was lucky to have a guardian angel on their side. Of course, genitals alone aren't conclusive in assigning sex. There's also gonads (ovaries, testes), balance of hormones, and pattern of chromosomes. For instance, I was born with CAIS (complete androgen insensitivity syndrome) so although I have XY chro-mosomes a lot of people think I look female because my androgen receptors can't process testosterone. Neat, huh? Think of it this way: I'd totally get away with homicide, DNA-wise. The cops'd be searching for a dude and I'd be all, Officer, hold my handbag, would ya.

There's a condition called XX Male Syndrome, Klinefelter Syndrome, CAH, 5-alpha-reductase deficiency, and a whole whack of what the medical community calls DSD (disorders of sexual development) but we intersex folks just call life. Being born with intersex traits is more common than you'd suppose. It's difficult to get a bead on exact numbers, but the outside limit is 1.7 percent of the general population (at least if you trust certain biologists). Weirdly, that's the same statistic for redheads. You heard it here first.

We've come a long way from Aristotle's theory that the hermaphrodite is an incomplete twin with ambiguous genitals to signal that *almost* enough body was created for two babies. We've come even further from Plato's lost soulmates desperately searching for their other halves. If we search, it's only to come to an understanding of our perfect sufficiency. You can support Charlie by educating yourself about intersexuality in all its gorgeous, creatively unruly splendour. There's a world of info out there (I'm sending links). But it is categorically *not* okay to remain ignorant of what you dismissively call "all this stuff." Charlie's been exposed to thirteen years of heteronormal, cisgendered, binaried sexuality. They know all about *your* stuff. Return the favour.

Re: *Long Haul*
by *Busymom* >> Dec 2, 2019, 7:10 am

Dear Sir: The trouble with Charlie is he has bad parents or godparents or whatever you call yourselves. Unless you have ten-some years of medical school behind you (which I somehow doubt), who are you to ignore your surgeon's advice? Is Charlie supposed to select his gender as if he's choosing potluck at a church supper? The corrective surgery that your criminally negligent physician prevented him from having would have saved him from growing up hermaphrodital. This is a pink shirt/blue shirt world, mister. Deal.

Re: *Long Haul*
by *BigRig64* >> Dec 2, 2019, 8:32 am

Thanks for your two cents, *Busymom*. Quick correction in view of the fact that you address me as Sir/Mister. Don't let the name or the occupation fool you. I'm a female trucker of the lesbian persuasion. I wear flannel shirts in woodsy colours (neither pink nor blue) and although I don't possess a penis I pee both standing up and sitting down. I'll do you the favour of not assuming you're a smug, self-righteous busybody. Perhaps you mean well but since you ask — no, Charlie isn't supposed to choose his gender, since he's already done so. This is a plaid shirt/paisley shirt world, *Busymom*. No deal.

Re: *Long Haul*
by *Runaway* >> Dec 2, 2019, 6:15 pm

I don't usually post, but *Busymom* really triggered me. She reminds me of my mom, who told me I was a freak. She said I was like a kid with a forked tongue or an extra foot. But like the foot would be growing out of my butt or something. She tried to love me but it was too hard. I ran away when I was fourteen and I've been running ever since. I heard she died last year but it makes no difference. She's in my head. The only way to kill her is to kill myself.

Re: *Long Haul*
by *Busymom* >> Dec 2, 2019, 6:30 pm

You folks should be ashamed of yourselves. Be fruitful and

multiply, said the Lord. Genesis 1:28. He didn't say anything about addition, subtraction, or long division! One thing I know for sure: there's no hermaphrodites in nature. Canada geese mate for life, and so do swans. Anyone seen a lion shed his mane because the king of the jungle's suddenly decided he's really a queen? Settle down, people. Take a page out of nature's book.

Re: *Long Haul*
by *InterScience* >> Dec 2, 2019, 11:08 pm

Welcome to my house, *Busymom*. I don't usually engage, but you mentioned a couple of my friends. So here goes. Let's start with those much-quoted swans. A quarter of black swan pairings are male to male. They steal nests from females to obtain eggs, raising their cygnets to adulthood in, ahem, single-sex households. Ditto flamingos. Ditto American white ibises. Ditto mallards.

Next time you assert that sex is defined by biology, consider the female spotted hyena, whose penis secures her the status of official trans girl of the animal kingdom, the many varieties of cardinals and chicks with both male and female gonads, not to mention the tendency of clown fish to practise sequential hermaphroditism (born male become female).

I could go on (and on) but I assure you that no species has been found in which homosexual behaviour *doesn't* occur. Sorry your foray into biology has been so unfortunate. A word of advice: next time you read nature's book, don't skip the footnotes!

Re: *Long Haul*
by *Homesick* >> Dec 3, 2019, 3:04 am

Surgical intervention without consent is a hate crime. When I was a baby my internal testes were removed, my clitoris was surgically shortened, and my vaginal pouch was slit open and expanded by a butcher in a white coat. I live with the fallout from that disaster, including scar tissue, bladder infections, reduced clitoral sensation, and the fear that what's most important about me is what my genitals look like. That's what the guy who raped me when I was sixteen said.

Ten years ago I decided to transition. Apparently the wrong "half" had been assigned to me. But guess what? Surgeons are reluctant to reassign me. I was forced to have surgery I didn't want and now can't get the surgery I require. One of the worst things is when strangers ask what genitals I have. Or if I'm the kind of hermaphrodite that can fuck itself. Unquote.

Tell Charlie to hang in there, I guess. I've moved so many times, trying to give myself a fresh start. But there's no home if you don't feel at home in your skin. Tell him anyway. From me.

MAKE-UP

MONDAY, DECEMBER 9, 2019

When Ms. Kambaja asked Mikayla why she was late *again*,
the girl ignored her. She'd come crashing in from lunch,
swinging her backpack, stamping her Blundstones as if
she'd waded through six feet of snow, almost tipping over
the whiteboard on which Ms. Kambaja had written, in her
rounded teacher's cursive, *Everyone is the hero of his life story.*

Ms. Kambaja closed her eyes. When she opened them
Mikayla was still there, alas, banging her way down the aisle
to her seat at the back of the classroom, shoving desks and
yelling *Whoopsa daisy!* like some quaintly clumsy traveller
from an earlier century. Ms. Kambaja waited for her to reach
her seat, then she waited some more for her to rummage
through her backpack, slam her notebook open, and dive
back in search of a pen. When the girl finally settled, Ms.
Kambaja couldn't resist pointing out that once again she'd
missed the opportunity not to make a fool of herself. She took
her student's blank look as permission to rap on the board.
"*Everyone is the hero of his life story.* Discuss."

Mikayla looked up from the line she was gouging around
her wrist. She'd been working on her tattoo all winter, even
more enthusiastically once she'd settled upon her current

instrument of self-mutilation, a drafting compass with a wicked point.

"Or her," she offered.

"What? Oh." Slightly rattled, Ms. Kambaja inserted the obligatory "or her" into the sentence on the whiteboard. It now read: *Everyone is the hero of his >or her< life story.*

"'They' would be better. Then you've got non-binary, trans, and two-spirited covered."

"Thank you, Ms. Piper."

"No problem, Ms. K."

Mikayla made a doff-of-the-cap gesture, then, with hands concealed under cover of her binder, went back to scoring her wrist with the compass needle. Charlie admired her persistence, not to mention her nuanced feeling for symbolism. Ms. Kambaja had been discussing autobiography: it's not the story of your life, she explained; it's the story that gives your life meaning. Now here was Mikayla, working on the one story that gave her life meaning, the jagged wrist cuff she was etching into her skin. First she'd drawn an ornate barbed-wire bracelet on her left wrist and inked the lines with permanent marker, and now she was using a bent needle, pricking her skin until drops of blood beaded out. Naturally they confiscated her needle. Then they confiscated the needle she replaced it with. Mikayla thought it was hilarious.

"Watch them confiscate my geometry set next," she warned Charlie.

Predictably, no one did. That Mikayla Piper was failing Essential Math — failing spectacularly — was so far from requiring a compass set that none of her teachers had the heart to question her entitlement to one was precisely the point. She'd called their bluff and won, securing her the right to self-mutilate in public.

"Sure," Mikayla agreed when Charlie pointed out the irony of her victory. "But it's gross, right?"

Beneath the carefree rebel she pretended to be, Mikayla was seething, backlit by a bright, corrosive anger that found expression in the painstaking execution of her tattoo. Watching her dig into her flesh, deeper with every cut, Charlie understood that Mickie was gone for good — vanquished by the girl whose world had contracted to the tight circumference of her pain.

Performance art, Jules would have called it, but — honestly? Mikayla was right about the gross-out factor. Her flesh looked as if it was straining against the encircling wire. Yes, she was doing an excellent job on the *trompe l'oeil* front, though her wrist had begun oozing a cloudy liquid and her hand felt hot to the touch. Charlie hated the bleeding wrist cuff, but there were times when he fell into a dream as he watched her gouge at her flesh, angling the compass point and digging deep. She was a pain artist all right, and Charlie admired her transformative art. He had no such talent; sadness was just sadness, it did not take wing in him. These days he was sad all the time, despair ambushing him when he thought of Jules asleep with her boots on, or how Oscar's hand trembled, or when he remembered the dumb birthday card his dad had sent. The images blew about in his skull until they snagged on the barbed-wire strands of his imagination and then he could think of nothing else.

Mikayla stopped mauling her flesh and looked up: "Some people don't."

"*Every*body has a story," Ms. Kambaja repeated.

"Groovy. What's yours?"

"Nice to have you with us again, Ms. Piper."

"Thought so," Mikayla said, going back to the spatter pattern of her life.

But Ms. Kambaja couldn't let the subject drop. "We all have stories that give our lives meaning," she insisted. "Do you know what your name means, Mikayla? That might be a start."

"My name?" Everyone was listening, fascinated, even Ms. Kambaja, although she must have realized her mistake. "It's kind of a stinky-ass tea," Mikayla said. "Fermented yeast or something. *Eww*, right? What about your name, Ms. Kom*bucha*?"

The kids fell about laughing for five minutes, after which the bell rang for the end of fourth period. "Ancestry Studies was filmed before a live studio audience," Mikayla sang out, cementing her reputation as a comic genius.

Over the sound of students packing up and moving out, Ms. Kambaja managed to make herself heard. "Don't forget to hand in your make-up assignment on Monday," she called to Charlie.

—

WONDER WALL

Quick school-related question, Mom. Who was I named after?

Quick multiple-choice exercise, son.

A. Bucket

B. Bravo

C. Brown
D. *The solution is C*
Correct answer: D
You named me after a poorly dressed cartoon character?
You looked like the kind of kid who'd take it on the chin.
No matter how many times I land on my butt I'll always take another kick at the ball?
You believe in people. No one can knock it out of you.
Sounds like you gave it a try, though.
You know the story of the frog and the scorpion, right?
Which one am I again?
It ain't easy being green.

—

MARVELLOUS BEASTS

Before she fell into the river and lost her voice, Jules would read to him every night from *Marvellous Beasts*. The book was a gift from his father when he was born. Occasionally, people surprise you, his mother said. She didn't say another word on the subject, so Charlie never found out what was so surprising about the gift, let alone the man who'd gifted it. Over time the mystery of his father fused with the mystery of the book, which was an anthology of animal curiosities. *Why did Elephant grow a trunk? How did Zebra get his stripes?* The stories required much agile, out-of-the-box thinking. Oscar's favourite was about legs (four in the morning, two at noon, three in the evening) and Weeza's was about escaping a swarm of bees you had to imagine were trying to sting you to death. Once you knew the answer to Oscar's leg riddle it made sense (solution: man), Weeza's too (solution: quit *imagining*). Jules's riddle, however, seemed to have no solution. It concerned the logistical difficulties a farmer experienced in transporting a chicken, a fox, and a bag of grain across a river.

What does the farmer do? the book asked. *Remember: chickens eat grain and foxes eat chickens.*

Charlie and Jules attempted a dramatic re-enactment using a sketch by Jules of a branching river network. A nickel represented the bag of corn and paint tubes were the animals, the fox cadmium and the chicken purple madder. But whatever they did and wherever they moved their counters, they couldn't work out how to get the animals and the corn safely across the river.

Jules thought it was a hoot. "Don't trust easy answers," she told Charlie. He assured her that he wouldn't, but he was only five and apt to make reckless promises. His mother's fondness for difficult problems over easy solutions aside, Charlie didn't care if the chicken ate the grain and the fox ate the chicken and the farmer was left with nothing but one grotesquely bloated animal on his hands. What captured his attention was the story of the scorpion and the frog.

"You don't want me to tell that one again," Jules would tease. But he always did.

"'The Frog and the Scorpion,'" she read. "Stop me if you've heard this one."

What happens is a scorpion finds himself on the wrong side of a river, so he asks a frog if he can hitch a ride on his back. "No way," says the frog. "You're a scorpion."

"I promise I won't sting you," says the scorpion. "'Cause then we'd both drown."

Three times the frog refuses, but eventually he believes the scorpion's promise. "Hop on my back," he tells him, and off they go. Halfway across the river the scorpion stings him. As they sink beneath the water, the frog croaks out one final, pathetic plea: "Why did you sting me? Now we'll both die."

"I couldn't help it, dude. I'm a scorpion," is the answer. The end.

Naturally, questions arise. Such as: Can you change your nature if your life is at stake? If your friend's life is at stake? If your friend who's doing you a solid gets caught in the cross-hairs of who you are and what you want? Such as: What's the deal with all the animals wanting to get across the river? Such as: What kind of genius is this farmer, anyway? Such as: Why are rivers so darn dangerous?

And finally, *finally*: What the hell is wrong with that frog?

Dr. Jabbour: *Interesting that you blame the frog, Charles. Why is that?*

Over the years the story of the frog and the scorpion assumed mythic proportions. Charlie told it to everyone he knew, first in wonder — can you *believe* that crazy scorpion? — and, as he grew older, as a Rorschach test of friendship, the strange splatter-shape of scorpion-riding-frog conjuring up diverse reactions in the people he loved. Mrs. Oslavsky sided with the frog, Mr. Skerrit with the scorpion — no surprises there. Weeza claimed to be stymied by the whole murder-suicide deal while Dr. Jabbour, troubled, said anatomy was by no means destiny. Oscar understood, though. You couldn't teach a dog new tricks, he agreed. A dog was no cat. A dog was practically the *opposite* of a cat. What cat? The one in the box, remember?

Naturally, Mikayla had her own opinion. When Charlie told her the story, she said that maybe the scorpion should've hitched a ride with the farmer. He'd probably have stung the farmer too, Charlie pointed out. Nah, she said. The farmer had his own issues, sure, but for a legitimate frog-scorpion suicide pact to work you had to hit the exact right combination of spite and idiocy.

"Who's the idiot?" he asked.

"You are, Three-Piece," she said.

—

Everyone had a story, it seemed. A story that worked the wayward threads and unravelling fabric of the past into a sampler that read *There's No Place Like Home*. There was Weeza's beautiful, cruel mother, Jules's run-in with the river, Oscar's Thunderbolt. There was Abdulrahman's escape from a town in northern Syria, and Ms. Kambaja's father watching a man rid himself of a tapeworm in the jungle. Even Mikayla had a story. As a kid she was stung by a bee, went into shock, and died, she told Charlie, claiming to have risen above the city, where she hovered; watching rivers looping through fields, railway tracks and city blocks and parking lots; and far below, a paramedic breathing life into her small, temporarily abandoned body. He had a boil on the back of his neck, she reported, offering this unsavoury detail as proof of her out-of-body experience. The screenplay she was writing would begin with a slow pan out from that festering neck boil.

But try as he might, Charlie could never see himself as anything other than a bit player, a character actor without, strictly speaking, much of a character. What was *his* story, the story of Charlie Minkoff, a boy well on the way to being up to no good? Had his story happened yet? he wondered. Dr. Jabbour was always urging him to take notes, keep a journal, attend to the details of his changing physiology. *If you don't pay attention, others will,* she warned, adding sadly, *and even if you do*... But why would anyone want to write about him? And what could he write about himself? Like Mikayla, he'd floated free of the body others were labouring over and trying to breathe life into. Mostly he felt estranged from this body, as if it were a room in a long-term rental apartment. He'd lived there all his life but still couldn't ignore the cracks.

"Why don't you write about where you live?" Ms. Kambaja suggested. "What home means to you."

"Will do, Ms. K," Charlie said. He didn't think there was much of a story there.

On the other hand, perhaps he wasn't the best judge. For his money, Weeza's superwoman stunt, where she set out to deliver a truckload of yogurt to the depot in Mississauga and ended up rescuing three old people, a kid, and a dog, was a pretty good story. Weeza always reminded him to add in the cost of spoilage — vast summits of stir-from-the-bottom yogurt expiring past its sell-by date in the back of the rig.

Skin, she reminded him, by which she meant collateral damage, what you were prepared to lose in the process of saving the world. Weeza had lost her contract with Lucerne Dairy Industries and, until she decided to give up freight-hauling and become an independent contractor for Sweet Haul Van Lines, her livelihood. And Jules, being Jules, had gone that extra mile and almost lost her life. For Charlie's mother, skin was everything. Skin was the life she valued so lightly that she'd rushed across the brittle, newly skinned river in response to a voice nobody else could hear.

She hadn't lost her life, though; she'd lost her voice. The irony was cinematic.

—

SATURDAY, DECEMBER 28, 2019

Mikayla thought it was cool having a mom who couldn't speak.

"She speaks through her art," Charlie said.

"Is it spooky living in silence?"

"She's not *deaf*."

"So you don't talk to her, like *ever*?" Mikayla was trying to think of a way to get out of talking to her dad up in Stony Mountain. He wouldn't get out for another two years, minimum. She hated him and refused to visit, but he was allowed a phone call every Sunday night, and her crazy mom had flipped out and given him her number.

"I can talk. She just can't answer," he explained.

It was the winter break, the city frozen over and becalmed. Christmas had come and gone, a blank white day wedged between holiday specials and Boxing Day discounts. It was easy to be cynical amidst the retail-driven merriment, sales flyers, plinking shopping-mall carols, and cheap bunting but, as often happened, the weather took a turn. An Arctic wind funnelled down from the north, making it seem heroic to be out at all. Claiming that she missed Gellman, Mikayla had invited herself over and the three of them were hanging out in the loft, except that Gellman, ever-loyal to his perverse canine instincts, seemed to have forgotten who she was.

Of course, this might have been a function of Mikayla's latest incarnation, her demeanour caught between geisha and goth: face heavily made-up, lips thickly painted, eyelashes coated in mascara. Charlie thought she looked beautiful, but Gellman balked. Instead of throwing himself joyfully into her arms, knocking her over and slurping up her delicious face, he pitched her a shamefaced look and slunk off to hide behind the couch. Every few minutes he'd crane his head around to gaze at the girl, ears cocked. He was trying to place her, but, darn it, her name just kept escaping him.

"It's like I'm a completely different person," Mikayla said, which was so exactly what Charlie had been thinking that he blushed and tried to cover his embarrassment by whipping up a couple of peanut butter and chocolate syrup sandwiches with extra chocolate syrup. And extra peanut butter. Mikayla made a face but ate her sandwich and walked over to inspect the Wonder Wall. Today it featured a grocery list and the opening gambit of a Jules-and-Oscar chess match, along with a scribble informing the reader that the writer would be away. *See you when I see you*, an invisible hand had scrawled, making the throwaway words sound like a koan.

Mikayla was impressed by all the boho splendour, so Charlie showed her around the loft, pointing out features like the river-facing windows, the old-fashioned radiators, and the original pressed-tin ceiling. Such ceilings were hard to come by, he was saying, when Mikayla screeched to a halt. "Wait, is that your—?"

She was pointing to the photograph of Jules, the nude one, Charlie tucked up inside her, curled in her belly. Third-trimester Jules, not-yet Charlie. In the framed black and white photo, his mom was sitting at the loft window, half in shadow, half in light. She'd evidently moved her head when the shutter clicked; her face was concealed, her hair slightly blurred. Yet the rest of her was oddly still, her hands and her tight, hard belly a glowing sphere of light. The portrait had hung on the wall of the loft for as long as he could remember, and Charlie was so used to averting his eyes from the sight of his naked mother that he never noticed it. Almost never. Recently he'd asked Jules why she'd let someone see her without her clothes on. Shrugging, she ignored the question, but that night a corrective had appeared on the Wonder Wall:

Wrong question!

Okay. Why'd you let someone take a photo of you naked?

Try harder.

Nude? Starkers? Bare-assed?

Don't you want to know who? Who captured your mother in all her natural glory? Ripe with child? Replete with life?

Ugh. No, actually.

It was your father, Charlie.

———

MAKE-UP ASSIGNMENT

What Home Means to Me
by Charlie Minkoff

My mom and I have always lived in the GNC. I was practically born in the lobby, but Weeza got there just in time and whisked us away to St. B where I was *actually* born. GNC stands for Glutt's Nuts and Cocktail Sauce, and it used to be the distributing centre and national offices for, you guessed it, Glutt's Nuts and

Cocktail Sauce. You'd recognize the building from the dancing bottle of cocktail sauce painted on the side facing the railway yard. There's a loading dock out back and a freight elevator with quilted padding. The Glutt family was a big deal in this city on the basis of their toffee brittle and their secret recipe for Glutt's Seafood Cocktail sauce. They sold other sauces, sure, but ask anybody about Glutt's and they go all misty eyed about this magical cocktail sauce that just isn't the same anymore.

About thirty years ago, when the Glutt family moved east and Glutt's Nutco closed down their factories, some developer came over from the States, took one look at the GNC, and bought the whole deal for twenty cents on the dollar. He paid a local counsellor to rezone the area, bribed a guy at city hall to produce a bunch of phony planning permits, and ran an illegal gas line off the main circuit. Then he knocked down some walls, put up a whole lot more, and slapped magnolia gloss over everything.

The apartments are on the first three floors. The developer ran out of money by the time he got to the fourth and left it as it was. Which is perfect for us because Jules needs light, can't stand magnolia gloss, and thrills to the industrial vibe of exposed pipes, unfinished brick walls, and concrete floors. It's pretty cold in winter but where else are you going to find floor-to-ceiling windows, or a claw-footed bathtub, or those pneumatic tubes they stuffed mail in when the place was an office? We can't use the tubes because they turned off the suction, but you can still see the river and the tub is epic even if it didn't come with the building.

Actually, Jules found it on some demolition site. She got Weeza to load it into her pickup and haul it to the GNC even though it was cracked and one of the claws was loose. There was no place in the Gents so she installed it in the kitchen, running a set of hoses from the sink. She patched it up, tightened the foot and painted the claws with nail polish. It's a pain to fill and an even worse pain to drain, but she loves that bathtub. Mostly we use it for storage but sometimes, when I'm alone, I fill it with hot water then fire up the tea lights. You can lie in there forever, looking at the shadows moving across the original pressed-tin ceiling. You just don't get ceilings like that anymore.

———

Mikayla screeched when she saw the bathtub.

"It's just decorative," Charlie lied, embarrassed by Jules's eccentricity.

Mikayla whistled. So Charlie explained about the "Gents" on the third-floor landing, complete with urinals, toilet stall, shower, and a row of cracked porcelain sinks. Neither he nor Jules could use the urinals (an issue he had no intention of discussing with Mikayla) and the toilet had a tendency to clog. As for the shower, it was just a bunch of tiles centred on a drain beneath a broken showerhead, but Jules had installed a ceiling rail onto which they'd hung a waterproof curtain that she'd printed with a blow-up image from the movie *Psycho*, the one where the curtain pops off its hooks.

"Very meta," Mikayla said, admiring too how Jules had solved the showerhead situation by punching holes in an empty two-litre pop bottle and securing it to the rusty pipe. *Voilà!* Like everything else on the fourth floor, hygiene was a work in progress, Charlie explained. One thing that didn't need fixing, however, was the amazing acoustics, which were perfect for singing in the shower when you were alone.

The cracked sinks were a problem, though. Fortunately the wash basin second-from-the-end hardly leaked at all, although it still sported a pair of old-fashioned knobbed faucets, one emitting a stream of boiling water, the other running cold. Since the faucets were on opposite sides of the sink there was no way to mix the water to a bearable temperature. Charlie had to hold one hand in boiling water, the other in the icy stream, his body halved along an invisible dividing line. He couldn't bear it for long, not so much the heat or the cold but the sensation of division. The feeling that his body was alien to him and that this strangeness was something he had officiated.

Mikayla had stopped listening to his explanation and was examining the claw-footed bathtub with such intensity that Gellman, poking his head around the couch, was able to stare at her unobserved. She walked around the tub, her air of exaggerated concentration a side effect of the joint she'd inhaled so swiftly that Charlie had only managed to score a couple of hits. Suddenly she began throwing pots and pans out of the bathtub, unearthing a sweater and a foil of pill tabs, along with Squashy Green Ball, Gellman's long-lost toy. Charlie was embarrassed about the meds, but Mikayla had already left the tub and yanked open the fridge and was pretending to be overcome by the sight of a six-pack of Labatt's, the cans gleaming fiercely in the cold refrigerator light.

She grabbed a can, popped the tab, drained it, grabbed another, and then turned on the tub's faucet until the water roared. "Turns out," she said, giving him to understand she'd never bought his decorative-bathtub story. Gellman ran over joyfully when he noticed Squashy Green Ball. He had this *there you are!* look on his face as if he'd been searching everywhere for his lost chew toy although Charlie knew he'd forgotten it the second it had disappeared from sight. He worried about that dog sometimes.

"Fetch, Gellman! *Fetch!*" Charlie lobbed the ball across the room and Gellman sat up, following it with his head until it vanished behind the refrigerator. Then he gave an enormous, heartbroken sigh and slumped, head between his paws. Charlie started to tell Mikayla about Gellman's incredibly short attention span, which led to despair when his ball disappeared, even if it had just rolled away. It was as if the dog thought it had fallen off the edge of the world, rendering him permanently mournful if not borderline depressed. It was the same with people. Whenever Charlie left the apartment Gellman imagined him gone forever. You could hear him howling all the way down the stairs. Down the street, if you closed your eyes. Across the city and over the river and far away.

Mikayla said she didn't give a damn about his dog's PTSD. She was pulling her hoodie over her head as the bathtub filled and Charlie puzzled over the enigma of Gellman's mournfulness. Either the dog could remember Squashy Green Ball and miss it like crazy, or he could forget about it when it rolled away. *But he did both.* How was it possible to be devastated and amnesiac at the same time?

That's an interesting quandary, Charles. Is there anyone you don't remember but find yourself missing? Dr. Jabbour had asked when he told her about Gellman's problem.

"Maybe what he's so sad about is his shitty memory," Mikayla suggested.

"Hey!" Charlie said. And then, "HEY!"

The first Hey! was a brain-shimmer kind of thing, as in

"Hey, I never thought of *that* before!" The second HEY! was more of a shocked exclamation, as in "HEY, you're not going to strip, are you?"

—

MAKE-UP ASSIGNMENT (CONTINUED)

What Home Means to Me
by Charlie Minkoff

There's a ghost in the basement of the GNC but no one, not even Mrs. Oslavsky, is frightened of him. He's supposed to be a machinist from Poland who fell into the candy vat one night, drunk, and drowned in the toffee. "Nice way to go. Short and sweet," my grandfather says, but I think drowning in toffee is as bad as drowning in anything else.

"Those greenhorns couldn't swim," Mrs. Oslavsky wrote.

"Couldn't swim for toffee," Mr. Skerrit wrote back.

Mrs. Oslavsky and Mr. Skerrit are long-time tenants, so they've earned the right to make fun of the basement ghost. I feel sorry for him when I hear him clanking about amongst empty paint cans and old machinery parts. Jules thinks it's just Lenny making supper or fooling around with this whiskey still he's set up. But on Halloween, which is when the machinist was supposed to have died fifty years ago, you can actually smell toffee burning.

The thing about the basement ghost is how lonely he is. You don't often hear him knocking around, but you can't help thinking about him every day; this poor dude, lungs full of glop, hair sticky with toffee, and the stupid way he died, which would probably make a BuzzFeed list one day. Some nights when his loneliness is so terrible it clanks through the pipes and boils in the radiators and everyone, even Gellman, wakes up sweaty and sad, I wish he'd go away. Find another basement, find some other tenants to bum out. But even a ghost needs a home.

Anyway, I'm not sure how much longer any of us are going to be living here. Last week Questico sent out eviction notices: we have to be out by spring, no exceptions. Mr. Skerrit is taking it up with the housing commission, but Weeza says he doesn't have a leg to stand on. We've been living on borrowed time for years. Having to move out of the GNC has got me thinking about what home is. Is it the place you leave from or the place you arrive at? Is it where you were born or what you have to spend your life looking for? Is it what you've had inside you all along, or is it where you can't get to no matter what you do? Oscar says home is a promised land you can lead other people to but in the end God won't let you enter. God's not some soft-hearted dude with a loudspeaker saying click your heels together, Moses, or whatever.

This is meant to be a make-up assignment, and I just read it over like you're supposed to. It's not made up, though. It's all true. Even the ghost.

———

"Hey, you're not gonna lurk there watching me, are you?" Mikayla asked. Her voice was muffled in the T-shirt she was pulling over her head and her clothes were scattered around the loft as if she'd rolled each one into a ball then chucked it as hard as she could into a different corner. Blundstones, ripped jeans, socks, hoodie. He ducked as the T-shirt sailed over his head.

The water was roaring into the tub, where she was standing in her pale blue bra and thong. Then she was standing there in nothing at all, the thong floating in the water as the bra launched into the air, winging him as it landed. Charlie didn't want to stare; she was too fierce, too bright. She was an eclipse of the sun, and he was a couple of burned-out retinas. She was the Let-Go girl again, sprinkled with glitter, fizzing with life. As in the photograph of his mother, the sun was behind her. All he could see was light.

"What's the matter, Three-Piece? Haven't you ever seen a real woman before?" Despite the fighting words her voice came out wobbly.

He moved closer, away from the window. With an almost audible click the image of Mikayla changed, the pixels rearranging themselves into a picture that was diffuse and confusing, too grainy, slightly jumpy, the resolution poor. The first confusing thing was that she'd shaved her pubic hair to a narrow strip positioned like a bristly little moustache above her vagina. The second was that her foundation line ended abruptly, her face with its veneer of blusher and lipstick and powder seeming to float above her pale neck as if her head had separated from her body. The third and most confusing thing of all—this last dawning slowly as his eyes adjusted—was that her naked skin looked chafed, rubbed raw.

He moved closer.

Again he heard the click of his expectations resetting. Mikayla's skin, the parts he'd never seen, was minutely, painstakingly incised. Most were shallow nicks, light caresses of the razor blade, others went deeper, the surrounding flesh raw. And a few were scabbed with weeping crusts of blood as if they'd been picked apart over and over again. The cuts started at the tops of her shoulders and stopped mid-thigh. If you squinted, it looked as if she were wearing a sundress in a subtly flecked pattern.

Charlie shuffled from foot to foot, trying to get his bearings. His heart was pounding so hard he felt dented from the inside. He could feel the blood whooshing through his veins, his armpits prickling with shame. Somewhere far away, above the sound of water rushing into the tub, roaring like a river in flood, she was telling him to strip. It was only fair, she was saying.

"Don't make me ask you again, freak," she said. "Just don't."

The water was halfway up her shins. Someone should turn off the tap.

Charlie didn't know what to do, he really didn't. One of them was clothed, the other was naked. There were only two ways to right the balance.

"I'm warning you," she said.

Someone would have to climb out of the tub, dry herself off then get dressed, or someone would have to take off his jeans and T-shirt, his socks and (yes) boxers. He thought of running to get a towel but worried she'd misunderstand. One glance at her face (furious, flushed) convinced him that misunderstanding was a definite possibility. Instead, he did the only thing he could think of. He closed his eyes. There. Now he couldn't see a damn thing. Mikayla wasn't naked, Charlie wasn't a freak.

"Wrong," she said, as if reading his mind. "Wrong move, freak."

He opened his eyes when he heard that word again. The water was almost at her knees. Someone really should turn off that tap.

Mikayla was talking, telling him he needed to get over himself, he really needed to fucking get over himself. She just wanted to see what all the fuss was about. Some kids were saying he didn't have a penis, and some kids were saying he had a pussy, and some were saying he had both. Personally, she didn't care what he had between his legs, but it was a matter of trust, right?

Charlie swayed on his feet. The water was up to her knees. The bathtub was full, about to overflow. He could turn off the tap or watch the water cascade over the edge. He could take off his clothes or get Mikayla to put hers back on. He could keep his dignity or lose his friend. He could pull his T-shirt over his head and unzip his jeans and then slowly, reluctantly, shove down his boxers or he could just stand there staring at her.

"Take a picture, freak. It'll last longer," she said.

She shouldn't have called him a freak. That was the third time. It was getting to be a thing with her. It wasn't right. So he held up his phone and did just that. *Click.* Took a picture of her standing naked in the bathtub and sent it to her so she'd see what she looked like. Face flushed, eyes bugged. Makeup beginning to melt, mascara raccooning her eyes. Tiny moustache sneering above her vagina. The flecked sundress of her skin.

The minute her phone pinged she snatched it up. *Oh my god*, she kept saying. The water from the overflowing tub was puddling on the floor. He ran to the sink and snapped off the faucet. When he turned around she was crouched in the bathtub, sobbing. All he could see were her crazy blue bangs and the arm she'd flung up to cover her face. She'd done some work on the wrist cuff. It was more beautiful than ever. Almost perfect.

EMET

Monday, January 6, 2020

An Exchange of Emails
To: Heloise Joyal
From: Jules Minkoff

Okay, I brought up the subject like you told me. Turns out the kid categorically does *not* want to talk about his father. Satisfied?

To: Jules Minkoff
From: Heloise Joyal

What. Did. You. Do?

To: Heloise Joyal
From: Jules Minkoff

You know that photo? Me, gorgeously pregnant? I told him who the photographer was. Zero interest.

To: Jules Minkoff
From: Heloise Joyal

You mean he didn't ask about the man standing in front of his naked mother and saying smile? *Ben voyon donc!* I know you hate him but he's Charlie's father. Lord knows the boy deserves some of that—whatever they call it—closure.

To: Heloise Joyal
From: Jules Minkoff

He didn't say smile.

To: Heloise Joyal
From: Jules Minkoff

Don't go silent on me, Weez. I wasn't being a smart aleck. And for goodness' sake don't go off on another rant about the importance of accuracy when peeing in a bottle.

Here's the thing: I'm beginning to forget. I know I said I'd never forget a damn thing about the bastard, but when you started in about that photograph I remembered the feel of the sun on my body, the hard wooden slats of the chair beneath my ass, my belly glowing with light as if it were a mason jar full of fireflies. I'd just reached up to push away my hair. *Just leave it, Jules*, he said. Late summer, a wasp buzzing at the window-pane, drowsy sense of sap rising. The river flowing fat and slow, swollen with sun. Suddenly the child in my belly kicked me so hard I swear my diaphragm rippled. Light swarmed in the air, dust motes turning in every beam. *Hold it, Jules*, he said.

All afternoon he stood in the shadows, clicking away. Soon

after, he left us. He was my lover and Charlie's father and I'm beginning to forget him. You see the problem? I can't remember what Charlie doesn't (in any case) want to know.

As he'd have said, *Just leave it, Jules.*

———

Saved in Drafts
To: Charlie Minkoff
From: Heloise Joyal
Subject: Hang in there, Charlie

As you know, I would break down a door to save you. So I hope I have the courage to send you this. Trouble is I've been driving for twelve hours, writing you from a truck stop near Duluth when I should be catching a nap. I'm so dazed with highway fatigue that I've turned the corner on *exhausted* and I'm heading into the barrens of *never gonna sleep again.* I'm leaning against my rolled-up sleeping bag, laptop balanced on my knees. My eyes feel like they've been salted and my back is killing me.

But I have to get this out of my head and onto this page and off my conscience. Who else is going to tell you about your father? You know what Jules is like. She points to the Wonder Wall and shrugs. Translation: *You want me to write him a novel on that?* Who then? I ask. She makes a finger circle. The big O for Oscar. Oscar's old, I say, he's tired and heartbroken. She holds her thumb and index fingers apart, wriggling them to indicate her mastery of the world's smallest violin. Translation: *Cry me a river, pal.* Classic Jules. Bold strokes and crazy perspective. Just sign your name and walk away.

So it's up to me, *mon chum.* At least if I write it down it will exist somewhere. Somewhere in the outer galaxies of virtual space, floating above us in a drifting sound cloud: the love story of two people who made each other miserable and who, in the end, made you. You, Charlie Minkoff. Worth every tragic second.

There's something about driving on the freeway at night that brings on the existential heebie-jeebies. It's the emptiness, they say, the darkness, the lack of context. The experience of speed without effort, without friction, without even an awareness of the sensation of speed. Lights from oncoming vehicles approach, flare, recede. Again. Again. Again. The glare of street lights creates an uneasy rhythm—*whap, whap, whap*—the rhythm of light translated into sound. Red trails streaming through the darkness, the thin scream of metal fatigue. It's enough to bring on a fatal case of the freeway bends.

Not for me though, Charlie, never fear. (Sorry if I frightened you.) Sure, I get carried away sometimes. Not with speed or anxiety or the impulse to swerve into the oncoming lights of a false epiphany, but with the story that runs through my head on these long-haul drives. So where were we? Back to Nathan and Jules.

They'd known each other since they were kids, but it was only when Mort Dervish keeled over at his workbench, dead before he hit the pattern he'd been cutting out, that acquaintance deepened. Oscar had his hands full with Mrs. Dervish and her weeping daughters, so he sent Jules to find Nathan, who was living in some sort of socialist commune. The Dervishes were Orthodox Jews, but the son was a rebel, a photographer. How she found him is a story in itself, but the moment she laid eyes on Nathan, brand new fatherless son, what did she do but throw herself into his arms and soak the front of his shirt? She was overwhelmed by something she didn't understand, she told me later, but the time wasn't right. After all, the man had just lost his father; it shook him. He decided to return to the fold, become a good Jew, whatever.

Anyway, more time passes. Now that Dervish is dead, Oscar forgives him for not lending him money to buy an engagement ring, and the years go by. In a book, there'd be a row of asterisks to show time passing but you'll have to take my word. One day, who should walk into River City Ink on Jules's watch but this Hasid in a black coat and hat, long beard, the works. He's supposed to be getting married the following week, but he can't do it. He sits sobbing into his hands, his despair is terrible. What should he do? Naturally, Jules asks what business is it of hers, why should she care.

That's when he gives her this *look*. He has beautiful eyes: deep-set, dark, soulful. Only she can save him, he says. When he saw her again, he knew his life was in her hands. By now he's tearing at his shirt, wringing his hands, even thumping his head with his fist. It's such a terrible sight that Jules is moved, but still she wants to know why he turned from her. Why he left the commune and the socialists and the art collective. Why he became a religious Jew, a man so committed to holiness that even talking to a strange woman is frowned upon. Why is he here, she wants to know.

He shrugs and says she is his name.

His *what*?

He has the grace to look ashamed but out it comes. The whole rigmarole. Forty days before a child is born, as the psalmist says, before a soul descends to Earth, a heavenly angel calls out the name of this new soul's intended. And from the moment he met her, Nathan confesses, he knew whose name had been called out forty days before he was born.

Yet he couldn't accept it. Now, because of his foolishness, his cowardice, his stubborn-headed willfulness, he's going to marry the wrong woman. But he's seen the light. He'll do anything she tells him, anything.

Anything? asks Jules. Are you sure?

I'm tuckered out, Charlie. *Je mon voyage*. In the tradition of the best sequels, I'm going to end on a cliffhanger and say goodnight.

———

THURSDAY, JANUARY 9, 2020

She'd ghosted him. Charlie kept texting her even though she wasn't speaking to him. And to be clear, as Ms. K would say, he didn't expect a reply. Not after how he'd treated her.

Yet another thing that had become clear to him, *blinding* in its clarity, was that you couldn't subtract Mikayla from Mickie. It was apples and oranges except that apples and oranges had at least one thing in common (being fruit), more if you thought about it (being spherical, edible, seasonal, projectile, good for you, and so on).

But to get back to the human type of fruit, Mikayla was an entirely different species from Mickie: the one a fish, the other a bird; the one a clown, the other a trapeze artist; the one a girl, the other a woman. Perhaps subtraction wasn't the answer. In his head the two had merged, become one dense and extraordinary Mickie-Mikayla superbeing. But in his heart the opposite seemed to be happening: both Mickie and Mikayla were fading away.

Mickie went first, disappearing into the buzzing white noise of post-production. The film shoot was over and so was her fabulous, unsalaried, no-benefits internship. *So long, kid. See you next year.* Charlie would miss her, but he knew she wasn't real. She was a chimera, the afterimage of his flickering, cinematic desire. But the disappearance of Mikayla was more troubling.

For weeks Mikayla had existed in limbo, not *gone* so much as not there in some wholly philosophical interpretation of there-ness and its opposite. Ever since the film crew had struck the set and headed east with their giant canisters of film and miles of cables, their duct tape and clipboards and klieg lights, their streets full of idling trailers, ever since *Sleepwalkers* wrapped up, Mikayla had turned into one: a sleepwalker stumbling through her days, wandering dangerously close to high ledges, her eyelids fluttering. It was cold, getting colder — the season that production companies avoided. She had no one to be except herself. And then, not even.

"Does anyone know where our friend Ms. Piper is?" Ms. Kambaja eventually asked. No one replied, which could have been because they didn't know who Ms. Piper was. Or remember, or care. She was just the freak with blue bangs and a permanently seeping wrist cuff.

———

Saved in Drafts
To: Charlie Minkoff
From: Heloise Joyal
Subject: Hang in there, Charlie

In case you're interested, I'm near Tucson. Back in the snug, laptop on my knees. Tongue like chamois, oily stomach, eyes bubbling and day breaking. Where were we? Nathan has just thrown himself on Jules's mercy. Anything, he'll do anything to prove his love. Anything? she asks, is he sure? She's already flipping through her stencils.

She decided on the word "emet," the Hebrew word for truth, made up of the letters *aleph, mem,* and *tav;* the first letter from the beginning of the alphabet, the next from the middle, the last letter from the end. That was her truth: eternal, all-encompassing. When Nathan demurred, since it's forbidden for a Jew to defile his body, she turned on him. Was he with her or against her? If he was only for himself, what was he? And if not now, when? She was her father's daughter. To quote Oscar, the chip doesn't fall far from the tree.

In the end he gave in because he was crazy about her. Or perhaps he was just crazy, who knows? In short, he agreed to be her golem. He shut his eyes, waiting for her to tattoo the word onto his forehead. Fortunately, she took pity on him, told him to take off his shirt instead. Right there and then, in River City Ink, he stripped off his black coat and his white shirt, his fringed prayer garment, and his undershirt. He lay back on the table, naked from the waist up. Jules shaved his chest and proceeded to engrave the letters above his heart. Aleph, mem, tav.

She was angry. She wanted to teach this crazy Jew a lesson. How dare he turn from her? How dare he come back to her? She was glad when he winced in pain. She took her time, going slower than she needed to, pressing deeper. Tears welled in his eyes but he made no sound. He bit his lip until it bled. When she was finished she disinfected the area but refused to bandage it. Let his bride see what kind of man he was.

Yet something happened as she worked on his tattoo. It was as if, while engraving the word, she too was engraved.

Written upon. She cleaned the blood from his wound, but there remained blood on his lips. He opened his eyes and looked into hers. You'll have to imagine what happened next, Charlie. Some things remain private, we must avert our eyes (dot, dot, dot). There you have it. The Thunderbolt took them both down. In honour of truth and out of respect for death they decided to throw caution to the winds. To live for love.

But maybe it was a mistake to listen to the thunder. It didn't work, of course. And then it didn't work worse. Oil and water. Chalk and cheese. Love and laundry. She used to pose for him. He'd develop the negatives himself, hanging them over the tub to dry. Confidentially, those studies were terrible, the worst he'd ever done. He was never a great artist, but with Jules as his muse he lost all perspective. But that's love for you: it giveth, it taketh, it bendeth, it breaketh.

What was he like? Full of contradictions, like the rest of us. An earnest soul despite his lousy instincts. A terrible artist despite his ambition. He was a son and a brother, then he left his family. He was an Orthodox Jew, then he left his community and his God. He was a husband and a father-to-be, then he left his wife and unborn child. How can we know what makes such a fellow tick? But he didn't leave because of you, Charlie. Some people can turn 180 degrees, others have to go full circle. Nathan was one of those 360-degree spinners—a whirling Dervish! Rebellion was his youthful folly, not his destiny. He lives in Brooklyn now among the Black Hats. I believe he works in menswear like his father did. *Ça vient de s'éteindre.*

Reading back, I see I've made your parents seem like insipid, lovesick characters in a Hallmark movie. It wasn't like that. Nobody was charming or lovable. Lovers fell out of love, furniture got smashed, families stayed mad.

Charlie, I don't believe in Thunderbolts. There. Now you know.

On the other hand, what do I know? Your family's had its share of weather-related catastrophes, bless them. Jules fell in love with Nathan, but you know what she's like. Can't sing and won't dance. Zags when she ought to zig, crisses when she ought to cross, raises the stakes when all she has is a lousy off-suit. How could Nathan find room for such an extraordinary woman in his ordinary little heart? Like stuffing a ship in a bottle or, worse, shrinking a woman to fit inside a bottle. It couldn't be done, as he learned. So what does he do next but go right out and fall for God. This time for real, he said, an epiphany.

Your mother was pregnant when Nathan left but, true to form, hadn't even noticed. Well, she was preoccupied, having just started work on her *Invisibility Machines* series. Imagine Jules with a nine-month bump under her dungarees, wearing goggles and wielding a blowtorch. Click, right? But by then the photographer was ensconced in some humid yeshiva in Upstate New York and had vowed never again to photograph, paint, represent, or even so much as glance at the female form, every act of representation constituting a form of creation, creation being tantamount to mimicry, mimicry verging on blasphemy, and blasphemy being a big fucking deal to those folks.

You have to hand it to the Hasids. They certainly take art seriously.

Once again day has broken over another bankrupt Midwestern city. Good morning, Charlie. Glad we made it through the night.

———

FRIDAY, JANUARY 10, 2020

The rabbi had waved away Charlie's offer of payment. No need, he said. God forbid that a Jewish man, a Holocaust survivor no less, should be deprived of his rite of passage. And it was important that Charlie, a nice Jewish boy from a nice family, he could tell, should also be bar mitzvah. How else to make this world a home for Hashem?

"A home for Hashem," Oscar repeated admiringly. "Couldn't have put it better myself, Rabbi."

The double celebration — the b'nei mitzvah — was to take place three weeks hence, on the first of February, a Saturday. Rabbi Spiegelman had arranged to use the chapel at the Seth Rowe, as nothing could be more convenient. First Oscar would be called up to read from the Torah, then it would be Charlie's turn.

"Age before beauty," Oscar said.

"You'll be a hard act to follow, zeide."

"I'll warm up the crowd for you, darlink."

Good thing they'd started their religious instruction early, Oscar pointed out, recalling how he'd taught his grandson to read from the battered old Chumash. But when the rabbi showed Charlie the passage he would be reading from the Torah, the densely packed vowel-less lines of ancient Hebrew swarmed before Charlie's eyes. Each word, each letter, was a separate black fire, burning. Ashes blew about the page, collecting in bewildering little heaps. A spark from one of those fires could kill you, the boy thought, remembering the golem, the clay figure that could be changed from life to death, from truth to falsehood, by the rearrangement of a single letter.

"Ba — ru — u — u — uch," the rabbi chanted.

Charlie gave it a go, to the rabbi's distress, Mr. Himmelfarb's delight, and Oscar's encouragement.

"Try again, darlink. Don't give up!"

Rabbi Spiegelman was patient, but it was evident that the boy had a tin ear. A tin ear and a brass tongue and a frog in the throat, if he was being honest. However, when he tactfully hinted at Charlie's lack of musicality, Oscar was exultant.

"Like Moses!" he exclaimed, going on to explain that as a baby Moses had swallowed a hot coal handed to him by none other than the Angel Gabriel.

"What's to be proud of?" asked Mr. Himmelfarb. "Angel gives boy coal, boy should say thanks for nothing, not *ess gesunteheid.*"

"Like *you* would turn down a gift from an angel," Oscar gibed. "*That* I'd like to see."

"One thing gift, another thing breakfast. No need to put in your mouth whatever someone hands you. No need —" here Mr. Himmelfarb glared meaningfully at Charlie, "no need to be so damn *greedy.*"

The problem with Himmelfarb, Oscar thought, was that he considered himself a heavy, an enforcer. An angel wielding a sword at the entrance to the garden, no less. In fact, he was a nudnik, a mere thread of a man. Oy, a person like that! No matter where he found himself, whether in Eden or deepest suburbia, the other fellow's grass would always be greener. So lush it could be mistaken for Astroturf! Actually, Himmelfarb was the greedy one, not Charlie, an insight Oscar was more than willing to share.

As usual, Rabbi Spiegelman tried to restore order with exegesis. "Moses describes himself as a man of few words.

'Slow of speech and heavy of tongue,' as he says. Some commentators think he was a stutterer, but others point out that the Torah is silent on this issue. Therefore, since Moses is the only one to complain about his so-called speech defect, perhaps it didn't exist. Perhaps he was simply humble."

But Oscar was resolute. "Nope. Sorry, Rabbi. Not humble. Moses was a stutterer all right."

"Listen to the fella!" Mr. Himmelfarb shook with laughter. "So you know better than Moses, do you? Better than Rabbi? Better than God, even? Minkoff, give an inch," he said.

Oscar waited for the crackle of Mr. Himmelfarb's invective to die down before speaking. "Hashem wanted Moses to have trouble speaking. Serious trouble. Shy he could get over, humble he could work on. Same goes for slow, heavy, what have you. But stuttering? You think Pharaoh's going to wait while Moses breaks his teeth on a simple plague?" He paused before conceding. "Okay, maybe in the beginning. Maybe for the one-syllable plagues. Blood. Frogs. Lice. It's possible. But remember what comes after? Wild animals. Diseased livestock. Slaying of the first-born. For that you need a real voice. Deep. Loud. Magnificent."

Nobody spoke. The rabbi seemed to be processing Oscar's unusual division of the book of Exodus into monosyllabic and polysyllabic plagues. Finally, Mr. Himmelfarb whistled, "Holy Smoky, Minkoff, such *bubbe-meises* you talk. You should be ashamed. Tell me, Mister Real Voice. Why didn't the Lord just make Moses he should speak better?"

"Glad you asked, Himmelfarb," Oscar said, forestalling the rabbi, who looked as if he'd heard his cue. "Problem: someone needs to give Pharaoh a piece of advice. Solution: send for Moses. But—" Oscar held up an admonishing finger, "immediately arises another difficulty. Problem: Moses has slow tongue. Solution: why not cure tongue? Seems simple. Seems easy. Shortest distance between two points. So why not?"

When the company remained silent, Oscar gently prodded his grandson: "Come on, give it a try. Worse than Himmelfarb you can't be."

"Um, that's not how God works, zeide?"

Oscar whistled in admiration. "Exactly. Nail on the head. Not how God works."

Rabbi Spiegelman beamed. It had been a long journey full of twists and their corresponding turns, but they'd finally worked their way around to free will. However, before he could say a word or two about Moses, a fellow he had never warmed to but respected largely because of the man's pessimism in the face of so much to be hopeful for, Oscar again held up his hand.

"Charlie?"

"God wants us to, to..."

As the boy searched for words, Mr. Himmelfarb reared up in his chair: "Ha, slow tongue!" he yelled, pointing a crooked finger at Charlie. "Stutterer! Heavy mouth!"

Shaking his head at Himmelfarb, a man for whom the shortest distance between two points would always involve a detour into the scrubby terrain of sarcasm, Oscar continued. "Look, I'm not saying He couldn't if He wanted to. Easy as snapping your fingers. Like *that* He could have Moses reciting the Gettysburg Address. But no. Not how God works. Instead, He gets Moses's brother to help out. Moses opens his mouth, out comes Aaron's voice. Straight out of vaudeville. What do you say, Rabbi?"

Without waiting for confirmation, Oscar raced on: "Listen, what was in the Almighty's mind who can say? Maybe He wanted the brothers they should be closer. Not like they grew up together, not like they were buddies. Moses got the sweet end of the deal, living it up in Pharaoh's palace, but Aaron was the son of Hebrew slaves. Naturally he was a tough cookie. Separate, what have you got? The bulrush kid who's led a soft life and the street fighter with the golden tongue. Apart no good, but together? Who knows? Butch Cassidy and Sundance. Masked Ranger and Tonto. Oscar and Charlie."

It was clear where Oscar had been heading. The rabbi silently doffed his cap to him. But Mr. Himmelfarb, like a mouse caught between the jaws of a hungry cat, would always go down squealing. "Minkoff Shminkoff! Who do you think you are? A superhero, don't tell me. And the fatty is the sidekick."

"That's enough from you, Himmelfarb," Oscar said. "What about it, Rabbi?"

Rabbi Spiegelman, whose imagination had stalled on the image of Moses and Aaron charging from an ancient desert bunker, guns blazing, looked startled.

"The b'nei mitzvah," Oscar explained patiently. "Maybe there's no time to teach Charlie his Torah portion, but a blessing he can still make. That's kosher, right Rabbi?"

Grateful to be asked a question he could reliably answer, the rabbi agreed that a blessing was fine. Perfect, in fact. A blessing was sufficient to confer bar mitzvah status on Charlie Minkoff. Done. He gave his beard a fortifying tug. On the day of the b'nei mitzvah he would call the boy up to make the traditional blessing, after which Oscar would read his Torah portion.

"*Our* portion," Oscar said. "Charlie's and mine. It's only fair. Hey, pardner?"

—

To: Charlie Minkoff
From: Heloise Joyal

Hey Charlie, I'm hanging out on the west coast, the usual nightmare. You drive across the prairies and over the mountains and through the interior and there you are, staring out across Puget Sound, rain in your face and nowhere left to go. I mean if the east is where you've come from and the middle is where you are, then what the hell is the west? The future? The end of the line? Death?

Wish I was home with you and not just because my shipper is a mean SOB who's convinced Enzo and I want to steal his lousy collection of vinyl LPs and VHS cassettes. One thing you learn in this business is that the difference between what's priceless and what's worthless is a zero-sum game. Heads you lose, tails you lose.

Jules says you want to know about your father. The deal is I'll tell you whatever you want to know whenever you ask. I've been writing stuff down in case. Say the word, *mon chum*, and I'll press send.

—

"Does anyone know where our friend Ms. Piper is?" Ms. Kambaja asked again.

Once again nobody answered. The mystery of her absence

had become continuous with the mystery that her presence had always been.

"I'm worried about her," Charlie finally admitted. He'd stayed after class to talk to his teacher, but Ms. Kambaja seemed to have lost interest in Mikayla. Instead, she asked about his poor mother. Her words.

He told her Jules was excited about designing a quinzhee for the river walk.

"Of course she is," Ms. Kambaja said, pursing her lips. "How is the, um, the rehab going?"

Oof, he'd forgotten Jules's outburst and subsequent wild claims. "First class, Ms. K. She's getting all her rehab done *tout de suite.*"

"When will she be out?"

"Um, next week?"

"So soon?"

"Well, she didn't need a lot of rehab. Just, you know, a tune-up."

His teacher shook her head. "I don't want you to feel ashamed of your mother. Will you promise to forgive her, Charlie?"

Ms. Kambaja was so insistent that by the time he left her classroom he'd promised to absolve his poor mother, white-knuckling out her days in treatment. It was a shock to think of Jules at home right now, sucking Altoids and gazing out the window at the river that was frozen solid, frozen all the way down to its interlocking icy cells and plenty thick enough to take on the skittering weight of memory.

VOICE

SATURDAY, JANUARY II, 2020

Jules, Weeza, and Charlie were making their way along the frozen river to visit Jules's installation. Gellman had declined to join them because skittering about on ice wasn't his thing. Mutual, Oscar said.

Charlie wasn't lying when he said Jules was excited about the River Walk commission. The city held an annual design competition, with architects, landscapers, and environmental sculptors from all over the world sending in their plans for site-specific installations to be built on the frozen river. The quinzhee huts were places where you could warm up or tighten your skates or drink hot chocolate or just sit and watch other skaters swoop past. Weeza read from the brochure as they walked. "These warming huts are designed to be functional as well as aesthetically pleasing, original, durable, and imaginatively attuned to the environment."

It was cold and sunny, objects standing out crisply against glittering snow—bare branches, the rusty trellis on the railway bridge, a far-off church spire. The sky so blue it looked made up and the air full of frozen crystals, like mica chips whirling in hidden air currents. Charlie felt unexpectedly lighthearted, excited to be out with Jules, proud to be invited as her guest. *Bring something to put in a bottle,* she'd written on the Wonder Wall. After some deliberation, he'd slipped Mickie's pen into his pocket. Time to set it free, return it to the world, where it could live out the poignant but unremarkable life of once-beloved objects.

The River Walk was one of his favourite haunts. Designs in past years had been a riot, particularly last year's wind xylophone, which had been constructed of hollow metal cylinders set at unexpected angles. The wind played strange, otherworldly notes as you passed. *Random Music,* it was called. Not a tune you could hum, Charlie explained to the two women now. Just a series of random notes played over and over again.

"If they're random how can they repeat themselves?" Weeza asked.

Jules fumbled in her pocket and fished out a quarter, which she balanced on her thumb. She flipped it, plucked the coin out of the air, smacked it down on her palm: tails. Flipped it again: tails. Again: heads. The next sequence was: tails, heads, heads. Weeza and Charlie stamped their feet to keep warm as they stood there trying to work out what she was telling them. Jules flipped her coin again as Weeza pretended to interpret: "It's not random and it's not composed. It's a musical improvisation using wind, sound waves, and durational intervals. Every time you flip a coin you have a fifty-fifty chance of coming up heads even if it was heads the previous twenty times."

Jules held up a finger.

"*But,*" Weeza continued, "you only get two options. Heads or tails. So you have the *potential* for randomness limited by the *reality* of binary sequencing."

Jules lifted her right eyebrow. *Which is?*

"Which is what we call a coin toss, cutie-pie. Heads I win, tails you lose."

Jules poked her friend in the sternum — oh, *you!* — and Weeza burst out laughing, both of them getting a kick out of their goofy mind-reading act. They turned a bend in the river and there it was: Jules's quinzhee. From two hundred metres away it did indeed resemble a bottle come to rest on the ice, perhaps a discarded wine bottle at the exact point it had stopped spinning. The scale was extraordinary. Jules had taken into account the low-lying swoop of the river, the abrupt gradient of the banks tamped down with snow, and the fact that when you clambered down them and found yourself upon the broad, flat expanse of the river bed you lost perspective, your eye unable to rely on a hundred subtle markers of distance and scale that might otherwise have convinced you that the bottle was bigger than you because everything else — sky, river, wind — was larger and shinier and more important than the puny human figures standing before it. Site-specific point of view, Jules called it. She was famous for manipulating it.

But of course this strange imbalance of scale was an illusion that dissipated the closer they came to the warming hut until they were at its entrance, the sides rising in two high, curved arches. Suddenly, the human scale returned, aided by the fact that other humans were present, quite a lot of them, actually — clustered around the installation, peering through ice walls, reading the artist's statement, examining the pop-up bottle depository, and queuing to enter the bottle neck. Some of them looked like arty types with uber-stylish glasses and geometric haircuts, but others were just regular folk out for a jaunt with their bundled kids and panting, leash-tugging dogs.

Whoa! Weeza spun Jules around on the ice in a triumphant little twirl. Charlie put up his hand to high-five his mom, but she was distracted by a woman in blue leggings and glasses with cool cantilevered frames. The woman must have known Jules because she talked to her for a long time, apparently without expectation of reply. Charlie hovered nearby, listening to the woman's excited voice — "extraordinary excavation of memory," she was saying, "courageous reintegration of trauma" — but when a man came up and introduced himself as the critic for an art journal, Charlie wandered off.

There was a long line to enter the bottle neck. He thought he'd wait before joining it, anxious about his reaction. He wanted to say the most insightful thing he could, the one thing Jules would want to hear. It was a familiar anxiety, one that had plagued him ever since she'd invited him to her studio to show him *Memory Factory #7* and he'd said, "It's really nice, Mom." Immediately her face had fallen. Nice? He'd tried to make up for this lapse over the years — Nice? It's *nice*? — by reading about art exhibitions, researching stuff online, and developing a critical vocabulary. Weeza said you couldn't fake sincerity, you should always be honest — advice that confused him because he *was* being honest. He'd thought *Memory Factory #7* was perfect. The best, the most spectacular, the *nicest* combination of welded metal and moving cogs he'd ever seen.

A group of sightseers was clustered around a board on which the artist's statement was mounted. Charlie manoeuvred to the front and began to read.

An Art + Architecture Competition on Ice
WARMING HUTS v. 2020

Name: *Bottle Deposit*
Project Team: Jules Minkoff, Winnipeg
Material: Silicon, river water, hydraulic pump, tetrafluoroethane,
pollution, fish bones, iPhone 7, time, voice

A bottle is the container of its own perfect emptiness, just as
memory provides the form and outer structure of forgetfulness. But what contains the bottle? In this city the answer to
that question, perhaps to all questions, is winter. *Bottle Deposit*
is the response of the artist to winter, the container that we
live in and through which, like all captive creatures, we view
the world from behind distorting panes of glass.

Everyone was exclaiming, taking photos of the warming hut
and uploading them (as the brochure suggested) with the
hashtag *#bottledeposit*. Charlie fingered the pen and wished
he could be part of the excited, chattering throng. He felt
cold and lonely, a feeling he recognized from the time Jules
first went silent. Oscar had moved into the Seth Rowe and
Weeza was away updating her commercial licence, learning
to be a long-distance freight-hauler. In those days he imagined himself encased in ice, as if trapped in an Antarctic
floe or whirling through space, a lone astronaut adrift in
cosmic loneliness, a sturgeon hibernating at the bottom of
a river, or a lost mountaineer buried in a glacier. There were
so many ways to be frozen, he discovered, so many ways to
turn to ice.

A hand on his arm pulled him towards the entrance. "Come on, *mon chum*, we're being summoned."

He allowed Weeza to usher him dramatically into the bottle neck—*Déguédine! Mets tes snick!*—where Jules was beckoning. Folks in line made way; it was clear they were friends of the artist, VIPs with backstage passes. From a distance the warming hut looked uncannily like a bottle. From close up it looked convincingly like the *idea* of a bottle. But when you were inside, when you'd walked, stooping slightly, through the neck and into a high chamber constructed of perfectly curved, seamless walls of ice arching upwards, fusing invisibly overhead, all sense of proportion fled. You were bottle and container both, at once outer form and inner emptiness.

The ice was different from any he'd seen before. He'd been expecting kitchen cubes, the kind that turned opaque when wrenched from their trays. This ice was clear, so transparent he could make out fragile etchings of river scum in its depths—here a haze of silt, there a suspension of foam. The closer he looked the more he could see: a scrim of fish bones, a trail of bubbles, the current folding in on itself. Standing in the cold reflective light, gazing up at the cathedrals of ice, he suddenly heard a weird acoustical hum.

Everything went silent around him. Even Weeza stopped exclaiming. Charlie wondered if she was also trying to think of a word, the perfect word to offer Jules. The impression of silence wasn't the absence of sound; it was sound itself, an echoing, continuous hum that caught in your throat, freezing the words. Charlie worried he'd never be able to speak again, which would be a problem when it came to telling Jules how *terrific* her creation was, how *radiant* (*radiant* was good). Sunlight streamed through facets of ice, conjuring jewel tones — emerald, sapphire, amethyst — flashing rainbow scribbles, shimmering like oil puddles. It was a clear day, not a blizzard in sight, so he didn't expect to hear the voice his mother had once heard calling her. Not expecting it, he realized later, was the point. But it didn't make the air less cold or the ice less slippery or the ground less resistant when he tumbled down (fainted, Weeza claimed) and struck his head on it.

Weeza kept asking if he was all right and he kept saying he was fine. He'd tripped, he said, please don't call the paramedics (Weeza's phone was out, her finger poised).

Don't you dare! Jules mouthed, scribbling the words on her notepad, ripping out the page, balling it up and throwing it at her friend. *DON'T YOU DARE!* It was a coin toss whether she was on Charlie's side or whether she just didn't want emergency crews mucking up the entrance to her bottle.

"*C'es t'assez! C'es fucking t'assez!*" Weeza yelled, because the voice was still reverberating through the bottle, a spooky child's voice without words. *Aah-aah-aah* went the voice (Mama?) and then *Uuh-uuh-uuh* (Jules?) all of it set to a repetitive musical phrase Charlie was certain he recognized but couldn't quite name. But once he realized that Jules had created the disembodied voice as part of her installation and not to scare the heck out of him, he instantly felt better. He struggled to his feet, shrugging off Weeza's hand, and did a little two-step on the ice to demonstrate his fitness. *Ta-da!*

Attaboy! Jules high-fived him (finally) and did her own triumphant soft shoe shuffle.

Aah-aah-aah went the voice and then *Uuh-uuh-uuh.*

He definitely recognized the voice, sort of. It sounded at once familiar and strange, practically the definition of creepy. Weeza was pointing at the CCTV camera that had swivelled towards them. Some kind of voice box hidden behind it, she was explaining. Jules had randomly recorded that high-pitched, creepy-ass voice.

"Not random!" he interrupted.

Jules gave him the thumbs-up and blew him a kiss. He caught it in mid-air and pocketed it, proud of himself. She'd never blown him a kiss before.

No, of course it wasn't random, Weeza was still playing catch-up. *But whose voice was that? How had Jules...oh mon dieu!* Weeza's cheeks were flushed. She was yelling at Jules and Jules was beaming and demonstrating, in rapid pantomime, how she'd created the sound effects. Holding up her iPhone to show she'd made a recording, she pretended to pull out the voice, making snipping motions with her fingers.

"She recorded the voice and manipulated the sound," Charlie interpreted. "Good job, Mom, you finally found a use for that iPhone."

He was exaggerating his enthusiasm because the atmosphere was charged, electric sparks shorting between the two women. Weeza was glaring at Jules, her face redder than ever, and Jules was ignoring her. Instead she stared at Charlie, waiting for him to figure something out, which, after a long penny-drop moment, he did.

———

"Breaking the Silence: Jules Minkoff and the Human Voice Box Machine"
By J. Stanley Wintour
Published in *Flip Book: An Online Journal of Aesthetics*

Guerrilla artist Jules Minkoff's latest installation, *Bottle Deposit*, is located on the Assiniboine River Trail in Winnipeg as part of the city's annual International Art + Architecture Competition. The transient nature of these warming huts, or quinzhees, to give the Dene name, is heightened in the case of *Bottle Deposit*, which is constructed entirely of ice. As such it is exquisitely sensitive to seasonal variations (changing light, warming temperatures) as well as to the effects of extraneous features (visitors, pollution, weather) on site-specific artwork. When invited to be interviewed for this publication, Ms. Minkoff declined in writing, saying she would prefer the art to speak for itself. This preference, despite its retrograde air and hint of churlish refusal (Ms. Minkoff is the art world's most famous misanthrope), is significant in light of the artist's backstory.

Those familiar with Minkoff's *Memory Factory* series, in particular MF #5 – #11, will be aware of her Ur-story of creative self-knowledge through trauma. For those not yet familiar with these devastating installations, a quick summary. In the winter of 2011, the year of Winnipeg's so-called freak blizzard, Minkoff was lured onto the partially frozen Assiniboine River, later claiming to have heard a young girl calling her name (MF #7). In subsequent works she explores the etiology of this voice, speculating that it originated from an amniotic memory of her stillborn twin sister (MF #8) or, alternately, was the fugitive trace of the daughter she never had. (She has one son, an intersex child. See MF #11.) Although Minkoff maintains that the voice she heard was real, she has been inventive in interpreting the hallucinatory quality of voicing in her conceptual pieces, notably *Invisibility Machine* #13 and #18.

Because of injuries sustained while trying to rescue the *"Ghost Child"* (MF #9), Minkoff lost her ability to speak, a fact she parodies in numerous installations as the least interesting thing about her, on a par with Van Gogh's ear (IM #3) or Toulouse-Lautrec's dwarfism (IM #5). Despite these pseudo-heroic allusions, the issue of voicing remains central to her work, as may be observed in her manipulation of first-person narrative point of view in installations, beginning with her early and largely forgotten *Electric Light Box* series and continuing through various iterations in the machinery she painstakingly assembles to resemble the human voice box.

Until now Minkoff has refrained from allowing sound to alter the formal aesthetic integration of her highly articulate machines. She maintains that choice is paramount to her creative process, choosing, in effect, silence over speech, vocalization, and even ambient sound. Reportedly refusing to listen to music while working, Minkoff goes so far as to wear noise-cancelling headphones in her studio, and her exhibitions are noteworthy for the eerie silence that prevails. Visitors to the opening night of *Sound Stage* might remember that they were required to wear earplugs, don slippers, refrain from speech, and generally conduct themselves as undesirable guests at a particularly demanding Buddhist retreat.

In *Bottle Deposit* however, Minkoff breaks with tradition to resounding effect, shattering the silence that has haunted her art. This is a striking aesthetic choice given the site-specific nature of *Bottle Deposit,* which more than any work in her oeuvre imposes silence on the viewer: for once Minkoff doesn't have to compel silence through artificial means, since the isolation of the quinzhee, the muffling effects of snow, and the framework of winter as an actual and conceptual space create their own version of silence. Famously perverse, Minkoff has finally broken the artificial silence of her *Factory* series by manipulating sound in a "natural" setting.

The sound in question is a purposefully poor recording of a child's voice (whether male or female is impossible to say) singing what appears to be a snippet of the Harold Arlen classic "Over the Rainbow," which was recorded — according to the artist's statement — on an out-of-date iPhone 7. The effect is extraordinarily haunting, creepy in the way that disembodied children's voices tend to be. I can certainly attest to a visceral reaction; at the first deranged-sounding note of that well-known and utterly blameless melody, goose pimples stood out on my skin.

But why now? we might justifiably enquire. Why the contrived manipulation of auditory effects, why the schmaltzy soundtrack? And most pressingly, why this exploitation of the viewer's affect from an artist who has never engaged emotionally but simply presented her work and then, like her professed Joycean role model, stood back and pared her fingernails? As may be expected, when presented with these questions, Jules Minkoff responded with her classic brand of aesthetic disdain.

Otherwise known as silence.

You can visit *Bottle Deposit* online or in person until the end of February, when the River Trail closes.

—

HASHTAG #BOTTLEDEPOSIT

Fabulous day on the Assiniboine. One great city, one great river walk. #bottledeposit

Who told you to lick the ice sculpture, genius? LOL!!! #bottledeposit #winnipegfiredept #stupidhead

C'est trendy au boutte! #bottledeposit

Can't believe this crap is publicly funded! #bottledeposit

Youre publicly funded, asshole!!! #bottledeposit

You're #bottledeposit

Great own by Apostrophe Man! Im totally humiliated, Ass'hole!!! #bottledeposit

C'est pas si tant pire. Meh. #bottledeposit #bof

Who threw this bottle in the river? Amazing Art! #bottle-deposit #JulesMinkoff #onegreatcity #amazement

Love the pop-up depository! Check out this inspiring collection of cigarette butts and used syringes, peeps! #bottledeposit #publiclyfundedart #onegreatfuckup

—

WONDER WALL

So Weeza says I violated your privacy and took advantage of your trust and cannibalized your life for the purposes of art. Sound like something I'd do?

Don't go silent on me, Charlie. That's my thing.

I'm not. I just don't know what to say.

What did you think of Bottle Deposit?

Great, Mom. Really really really amazing, incredible, spectacular, and fantastic. Not nice at all. #bottledeposit

I'm sensing sarcasm here.

Like you always say, the problem with the medium is you can't read for tone.

I didn't walk in on you while you were showering, in case you're wondering. Just cracked open the Gents and held up my phone.

Yeah, no, totally. So no violation of privacy there.

Now I'm definitely getting a sarcastic vibe.

Sorry about the vibe.

Sorry about the violation.

That it?

Okay, okay. I'm sorry you felt quote violated. What can I say? I heard you singing and I thought <u>there</u> it is, <u>that's</u> the voice I heard. I mean all artists are monsters, right?

What can I do to make it up to you? Ask me for anything.

First off, quote violated doesn't even make sense. Second, do I really sound like that? High-pitched, girly? And third, why won't you tell me about my quote father?

Nobody likes the way they sound, Charlie. It's the shock of recognition transformed into some complicated defence mechanism shit. Same reason nobody likes how they look in photos (unless they're shameless like your pal Weeza). Who, speaking of which, is in charge of all father-related questions. Say the quote word and I'll yank her tail.

—

To: Heloise Joyal
From: Charlie Minkoff

Hey Weez, did you know I'm "intersex"? I'm putting in the quotes because that's what everyone else does. Not always with their fingers, though. Sometimes by their tone of voice or the way they look at you. "For want of a better word" is what this one therapist said. I told Dr. Jabbour I didn't want to see that shrink again and she said she understood. Nobody wants a name that acknowledges its inadequacy, she agreed. But when I asked why there wasn't a better name for me she said there was and it was "Charles." Funny, right?

It was weird hearing my voice in the bottle, I won't lie. But it was worse being described in that article as Jules's son, "an intersex child." Now everyone who reads it will know or *think* they know or (worst of all) *want* to know what I look like under my clothes. I wish I could go to the west coast with you. (I'd help you and Enzo, I don't care about the rain.) Sometimes I think of what it'd be like to go somewhere, anywhere. I bet there's some place west of west, you just have to find it. Or I could go east, where my dad lives. He probably wants to meet me, right? I mean *I* would if I had a son. Hey, maybe I could hitch a ride with you, Weez. I'd make sandwiches and a playlist with your favourite music. I'd be so quiet you wouldn't even know I was there, and I'd never ask for a bathroom break or a snack or if we're there yet. Promise.

I know you have stuff to tell me. I don't know if I'm ready and I don't know if it's the right time, is my answer. Truth is I've been flipping coins. Coming up with sequences and writing them down. Heads, heads, heads, tails, tails, heads, tails, is one. I'll spare you the rest. So yeah, whatever. Go ahead. Press send.

FACE

WONDER WALL

Ecce homo! Translation: Behold the Man!

Funny. Are you coming?

My father and my son becoming men? Wouldn't miss it for the world.

Oscar said you'd make fun.

I'm a fun gal, Charlie. Fun is mostly what I make.

Are you all kitted out for the big day? What accessories do you need to express your commitment to 18th century shtetl life? A large fur hat? A beard? An animal sacrifice?

Weeza's been hanging out on eBay. She found me a classic Sondergaard in charcoal wool. There's a hand-sewn loop for a boutonnière. Oscar's working out the kinks.

I'm supposed to ask you something…

I'm not a mind reader, sport.

Never mind.

I'm not a never-mind reader either.

The rabbi wants to know the name of the father.

You mean the name of your father?

It's a formality. Some crazy rule. (I mean I know his name but I thought you might not want me to. You know, give it to them.)

What do they do if you don't have one? A father.

You go with Abraham. Father of the Tribe of Israel.

Yo, Abraham.

Nah. Wouldn't want to be Abraham's son.

Ha! See what you mean. Hey, there's cash in the pig. Buy yourself a tie or something. For the big day.

Charlie?

Yeah, okay. Might as well use his name. That's all he was. Father in name only.

—

He was disappointed by his mother's reaction, despite the fact that he hadn't wanted to claim Abraham as his spiritual father, what with the man's oddly tolerant attitude towards infanticide. He'd only been trying to rile her, hoping she'd flip out and forbid him to associate with the crazy, tattooed, lovesick fellow in Weeza's story. His father. Huh.

A few nights ago, on impulse, he'd clambered out of bed, pulled the box of birthday cards from their hiding place, and shuffled through them. There they were: bunnies jumping out of birthday cakes, puppies holding balloons, a boy gazing at the stars. *Happy Birthday, Charlie!* Before he could think about it, he slid an invitation to his bar mitzvah into an envelope and addressed it to his father, Nathan Dervish. The address hadn't changed in all these years. Wherever Crown Heights, New York, was, that's where he lived. *Hope you can come*, Charlie had written. It was lame but true. Mostly true.

He was getting used to the idea of his father as a real

person, a lover, an artist, a rebel who'd loved his mother so passionately he'd betrayed his faith for her. The birthday cards with their neat addresses and goofy illustrations gave no clue to the sender's turmoil. *Do you miss your father, Charlie?* Ms. Kambaja had asked when he stayed after class to find out if she'd heard from Mikayla, who was still "away," no word from or about. He replied, as he always did, that you couldn't miss what you'd never had. It had a ring to it, certainly, and was more-or-less true. But Ms. K had given him one of her concerned looks—they'd been coming thick and fast of late—and allowed that it was none of her business, but she disagreed. For example, she said, she'd never been to the Congo, not even for a visit, yet she missed her homeland. She couldn't say how or why, she just did. Huh, said Charlie, his usual response to adults and their complicated demands.

It was possible he missed his father, he thought that night in bed. It wasn't the same as missing Mikayla, but it was a start. It wouldn't surprise him, because he was the Emperor of Missing these days. He missed everyone and everything—Weeza (when she was away) and Oscar (even when he was there) and buses and jokes and deadlines. He'd always been clumsy, a fumbler, forever blundering over one thing or another. The list of near-misses was endless: friendship, chromosomes, the ability to sing in tune, and (lately) to tune into his mother's ironic artistry. Once, just once in his life, he'd like to catch something the first time it was thrown.

—

OUR MAN, MOSES

FRIDAY, JANUARY 17, 2020

Charlie got the feeling that Rabbi Spiegelman was poorly disposed towards Moses. Nothing the rabbi would admit to, naturally, but it was plain he considered Moses a grudgy fellow, a kvetch, eternally complaining and demanding proof of the one theorem that could only be proven by the absence of proof.

"In the whole Bible no one is closer to God than Moses," he began. Oritsia had brought over a plate of cinnamon buns, still gently steaming, and Charlie had managed to eke out four cups of coffee, almost tilting the urn on its side. The rabbi gazed into the distance, imagining the stirring scene: "He, and he alone, climbs Mount Sinai to speak to Hashem. Face to face. But when he gets to the top, no dice. The Almighty gives him the Torah and turns His face away." Rabbi Spiegelman fell silent, imagining. Drumming his fingers, tugging his beard. After a moment, he continued: "I'm not saying Moses drew the short straw, I'm not saying *that*..." His voice trailed away unconvincingly.

"Look, he was a bulrush baby. That had to hurt," Oscar said, helping the guy out.

"Sure, sure." The rabbi took a tentative sip, made a face, took another. The coffee seemed to float a petroleum glaze like the surface of an oil spill.

Mr. Himmelfarb snorted loudly. "What's the matter with you, Minkoff? You want to make excuses for the ingrate, go ahead. But don't come with that bulrush bulldust!" Struck by his own *bon mots,* the old man grinned. "That's right. You heard me."

"Not bulldust," Oscar said haughtily. "Important to know where you come from. Very important to know who's family, right Charlie?"

"Right, zeide."

"Give me one good reason, darlink."

Charlie pretended to think, pulling at an imaginary beard and scratching his head like a rube before pronouncing: "Kidneys, zeide."

"Exactly. On the nose. Give the boy a hand." Oscar smiled, his heart in his eyes. It was smart to keep tabs on family, was his point, since a fellow never knew when he'd need the loan of a spare organ. The papers were full of stories of previously estranged siblings juggling kidneys between them. Matter of fact he might have a story to hand. Fumbling in his grotesquely distended wallet, he searched for the clipping he knew was hiding between expired coupons, offers of cut-rate gym memberships, and brittle paper fortunes from Mr. Ken's cookies. Eventually he gave up, handing Charlie a fortune instead.

"'It is better to lose the world than to lose face,'" Charlie read.

"Speaking of faces," Oscar continued, seeing his chance, "what does Moses say when Hashem appears to him in the burning bush? He says—and I'm paraphrasing here—'Who is this? Let me see thy face.' Naturally the Lord tells him to calm down and go free the children of Israel from Pharaoh. Chop, chop, you can imagine. So does Moses hustle and do the Lord's bidding? Nosirree, not this stand-up guy. He's got a new request. 'Tell me your name,' he nags. And the Lord, bless Him, says 'I Am Who I Am.'"

For the benefit of Mr. Himmelfarb, who was looking confused, Rabbi Spiegelman explained. "He's saying something pithy, quotable, but giving away nothing, which is pretty much standard for Hashem. *I Am Who I Am.*"

"'I Am Who I Am,'" Mr. Himmelfarb murmured. "Magnificent answer!"

Rabbi Spiegelman looked gratified. "So what does He mean?" he asked.

"Means mind your own business," Mr. Himmelfarb suggested. "He means Moses must stop asking questions and do what he's told. Fantastic advice, by the way. You hear that?" he turned to face Charlie, mouthing "Fatty Boom-Boom" behind the rabbi's back.

"Oy, Himmelfarb!" Oscar exclaimed, as if he was about to recite a Yiddish ode. Clapping one hand to his mouth, he covered his eyes with the other. He looked like a couple of monkeys called See No Evil and Speak No Evil. There was a third monkey, he'd probably have pointed out if anyone were interested. But the monkey called Hear No Evil was off on his own somewhere, listening to the music of the spheres. Or, more likely, *not* listening.

"'I Am Who I Am,'" Oscar repeated. "What does it mean? Means quit bothering me, Moses. Means don't you have something important you should be doing? Like leading the children of Israel out from the desert, hello? What do you say, Charlie?"

Charlie remained silent. He was getting a spooky vibe from that sneaky Old Testament God. In some ways God reminded him of Jules. When he was younger, he was convinced she'd talk as soon as she had something to say. He'd chat about his day, waiting for his preoccupied mother to put down her pencil and join the conversation. *Hmm, you think so?* she might ask. *Tell me more.* It'd be just like her to conceal herself in a burning bush or a whirlwind, to disguise herself as a pillar of fire or a splendid covenant-inclined rainbow.

"Darlink," Oscar was calling, breaking into his thoughts.

"Don't bother the darlink when he's thinking," Mr. Himmelfarb advised. "Doesn't happen often, ha!"

"Maybe God doesn't want to be—"

"Yes?" coaxed the rabbi.

"—to be known?" Charlie couldn't help the inflection that lifted the end of his sentence as if it was a bird about to fly off into the everlasting blue.

The rabbi looked thunderstruck, but it was Oscar who responded. "Bingo!" he roared. "Hole-in-one!"

Enraged, Mr. Himmelfarb mimicked the boy's high-pitched voice, his vocal uptick. "Doesn't want the people to know Him? Doesn't want say-so over life and death? Doesn't want kingdom come? Doesn't want the power and the glory?"

"Doesn't want a bandy-legged goat like you butting in?" Oscar suggested tartly.

"Gentlemen, *please*," Rabbi Spiegelman pleaded. "Let cooler heads prevail."

Mr. Himmelfarb was still grinding his teeth in anger when Oscar slammed his palm on the table, causing the remaining bun to jump nervously on its plate. "Okay, you want cool heads. Here's cool head," Oscar knocked the side of his head with his fist, sounding a hollow, mournful note, the distillation of two thousand years of exile. "Cool head says two sides to every story, right? On the one hand you got Moses, a fine fellow but a kvetch. Always second-guessing Hashem at the same time he's full of ire and whatnot at the children of Israel. On the other hand he does his best, which is all you can ask. You want examples? I won't go into detail about what they were up to at Sinai because I don't want you should plain pass out from shock, Himmelfarb. But one day Hashem loses His patience with His stiff-necked people. That's what the Bible calls them: stiff-necked. The Lord tells Moses to leave Him alone so His wrath can wax hot. Unquote. That's when our man Moses steps in and talks Him out of smiting every last stiff-neck — man, woman, and child. 'Why doth Thy wrath wax hot against Thy people?' he asks, calling Him out on aggravation. And what do you know? Straight away the Lord repents. Exodus 32:14. *Repents*. Strong word."

Oscar looked up from the Chumash, catching Charlie's eye. "That's Moses for you. A nag, a nooge, a nuisance. A stiff-neck like the rest of his people. But on the other hand a fine debater, not afraid to get into an argument with the Almighty, which, believe me, takes chutzpah. Next thing he's schlepping down from Mount Sinai and what does he see but the Israelites have got up a party. Drinking, dancing, fornicating — you should excuse the expression — even making a golden calf, which is the last straw. Immediately his wrath waxes so hot he's obliged to throw something. Unfortunately all he has in his hands are the tablets of the law. *Nu*, no need to go into detail. What's done is done. What's broken stays broke. It's a Humpty Dumpty situation."

Oscar put his head in his hands in a gesture of mourning. Nobody moved, nobody spoke. Angels danced on the heads of pins and a thousand years of silence passed in a heartbeat, followed by a thousand more. Charlie paused in his chewing of the remaining cinnamon bun, which had, in the melee, found its way onto his plate.

"Now, listen to this," Oscar said. "This you're not going to believe. Moses comes down from the mountain. Stiff-necked? You betcha. A little touchy? No question. Even something of a hothead? You're telling me! First thing he does is he burns that terrible no-good golden calf in the fire and grinds it into powder. But that's not enough for our man Moses. Far as he's concerned even the powder from the ashes of the golden calf must disappear. He wants every atom to vanish. So he throws the ashes in the water and makes the children of Israel drink up the water. Every last drop, I kid you not. That's the kind of man we're talking. Dedicated. An eye for detail. A maven of destruction."

Oscar shook his head. Something wasn't sitting right. He tried to explain: "Look, burn I can understand—who doesn't want to see the idol go down in flames? And grind? Sure, no problem. Even throw in the water? Fine with me. But drink up the water? Now you're going too far, Moses. Hoo-boy, now you're crossing the line."

The rabbi shifted uneasily. Like the others, he'd listened aghast as Oscar walked them through the annihilation of even the powder from the ashes of the golden calf. With some effort, he stirred himself to speak. "On one hand, Moses is overzealous, sure," he admitted. "Other hand, he's got a point. Don't put up a golden calf, he tells them. So what do they do?"

"Good thing he didn't tell them not to jump off a cliff," Mr. Himmelfarb observed sourly.

"Oy, such a stiff-neck," mourned Oscar. It was unclear whether he was referring to Moses, the Israelites, or even the Almighty, but it was a cinch he included Mr. Himmelfarb in the company of unbending ones.

Sensing his opening, Rabbi Spiegelman pounced. "The Torah teaches us that Hashem is all-powerful, all-knowing, all-seeing. But when they broke His commandments, they broke His heart."

"True, so true," Mr. Himmelfarb murmured, a brown-noser

to the end, prompting Oscar to roll his eyes and dig his grandson in the ribs.

But Charlie was silent, preoccupied. Something in the rabbi's words had unsettled him. He imagined the Almighty, profoundly unknowable yet longing to be known. *I Am Who I Am.* It was a feeling he recognized. While the men were arguing, he'd read ahead to the verse where, once again, Moses begs to see the Lord's face. No one can see My face and live, the Lord replies. But in the end, after more of that epic Moses-quality God-bothering, He relents, telling him to hide in the cleft of a rock, and promising to shield him with His hand so that Moses won't see His face.

What did it mean? Charlie puzzled. Had Charlie glimpsed a fragment of a sliver of a spark of the Almighty fire? It was only a glimmer, a gleam of understanding. But what if God was someone like him, he wondered, struggling to be human even though He lacked a body. Or at least a body that other people could see or understand or love.

It was a forbidden thought, transgressive and dangerous. Yet it fell, sweet as manna, from the sky.

——

TO BE CLEAR

An Exchange of Emails
To: Jules Minkoff
From: Maude Kambaja

Dear Ms. Minkoff,
I hope you are recovered and that your stay in rehab afforded

you serenity, courage, and wisdom, along with the knowledge of when precisely to use them. Having read over my previous emails I fear that I have not made myself entirely clear.

Our class has completed their biographical coursework and students are now writing their life stories. Despite a veneer of anomie, they enjoy this project mightily, little egoists that they are. In thirty years of teaching I've found adolescents to be eager first-person narrators, both in writing and in speech. In fact when I hear them chatting in the halls or at the bus stop, I wonder at their self-absorption. Whatever comes their way, of local or global importance, whether concerning unwelcome changes in the cafeteria menu or climactic changes in the biome, is interpreted via the looking glass of me-myself-and-I. However, this is emphatically not true of your son, who seems downright reluctant to share his story, writing instead about his grandfather, his neighbours, and even an alleged ghost.

I hope that in bringing this matter to your attention I have not distressed you,

Maude

To: Maude Kambaja
From: Jules Minkoff

I'm feeling much better after all my rehab, thank you for asking.

I don't know what's wrong with Charlie. He seems like a good kid. Everyone around here likes him just fine. I've heard that reverse psychology is effective. For example, you could give him a good grade for once. That would confuse him, but it'd get him off your back and I wouldn't have to punish him. Win-win, right?

To: Jules Minkoff
From: Maude Kambaja

Undoubtedly, Charlie is a "good kid." That should go without saying but since it evidently did not, let me reiterate that his character isn't in question. In the pursuit of clarity I've isolated the drumbeat of my concern to one persistent question: Why is he reluctant to write **his own** life story? What prevents him from seizing the galloping narrative horse by the reins? In short, why doesn't Charlie view **himself** as the subject of **his own** autobiography?

I ask only because I've grown fond of the boy. I sense his little motor of self-esteem ticking over, failing at first try to engage. Such is often the case with adolescents despite their "egotism"—but I don't need to tell you that Charlie is special.
Maude

To: Maude Kambaja
From: Jules Minkoff

If by special you mean weird then sure, Charlie's "special." Speaking of which, what happened to that friend of his? Mikayla Something. He says he hasn't seen her lately. Oh well, maybe she jumped into her little motor of self-esteem and drove away.

To be clear, that was a joke, Kambaja. Thanks for the heads-up, though. Will def put the screws to him re his lousy writing skills.

To: Jules Minkoff
From: Maude Kambaja

I know a joke when I hear one, Ms. Minkoff, but the comparison is apt. Self-esteem in adolescents is like an unreliable motor car with a sticky gear shift and a tendency to break down at the worst possible times. And you can't always predict which vehicle is liable to end up on blocks, wheels spinning. As any engineer will tell you, the newest models are often the most vulnerable.

Forgive the over-extended metaphor. As I may have mentioned, I've been an educator for many years and have stopped counting the young people who breeze through my classroom on their way to better things. At the beginning of each year, as I walk through the hallways, those evocative lines from Ezra Pound inevitably spring to mind. *Petals on a wet, black bough.* I remember the faces, but less dependably the names. Every now and then, at a parent-teacher conference, a preternaturally young mother or father will identify them-selves as a former student. *Don't you remember me, Ms. K?* And sometimes, of course, I do.

But the truth is, I've forgotten as many as I remember. And the ones I remember most vividly are those troubled students who've slipped from my anxious grasp. I've fumbled more times than I can say. Perhaps that's why I try to connect with parents when I can. I have a tendency to sound officious, interfering even, but my intentions are sound: to offer myself as a member of the village we are repeatedly told is necessary for the raising of even one child.

Oh dear. Please ignore the self-pitying tone. On days when

I learn that yet another young person has "fallen through the cracks" I tend to wax philosophical if only in defence. What an angry, raging river is adolescence! We parents, we teachers, stand on the banks, beckoning. We have taught them to tread water, to float, to swim. What more can we do? After all, most of them make it to the other side.

You asked about Ms. Piper. Administration has informed us that Mikayla is in intensive care at Health Sciences. Her arm became infected due to a "self-administered tattoo" that led her to contract septicemia. My outrage at our collective failure to help the girl has evidently overwhelmed my caution at sharing such private information, Ms. Minkoff, but some hypocrisies are difficult to bear. *What was her mother thinking?* our vice-principal exclaimed when she broke the news, indicating, in no uncertain terms, that the fault lay outside the walls of this institution. Ah, well. Perhaps it mostly did.

Maude

———

FRIDAY, JANUARY 24, 2020

Over the months, Oscar and Mrs. Dershowitz had grown close. When Charlie visited he often found them kibitzing in a corner, Mr. Himmelfarb glaring from afar. Today, however, Mrs. Dershowitz merely waggled her fingers at Charlie before hurrying to catch her three o'clock bridge game, and Mr. Himmelfarb was nowhere to be seen. Charlie was worried. Had Mr. H finally succumbed to his uric acid? But Oscar reassured him that the golem in question was still laid out on his sickbed, neither truthful nor dead.

"We'll have to manage without him," he said. "What you got there, darlink?"

"Just coffee, zeide," Charlie teased.

"No, in the *other* pocket."

Charlie took out the gift box he'd been concealing. He'd purchased the tie at Uomo with the money Jules had given him, choosing a subtle pattern in sage and soft greys. Pure silk, naturally. Oscar, his eyes moist, touched the rich fabric gently.

"For the big day, zeide."

"Beautiful tie, darlink. First-class. Best tie in the universe." Oscar took out his handkerchief and mopped his brow to indicate the emotional toll his grandson's generosity was exacting. He was pretending to be overcome, possibly to hide the fact that he really was in danger of losing it, of succumbing to the waves of emotion—jubilance, mournfulness, apprehension, nostalgia—that beset him daily. He was riding high, flush on the wave of his late-life blossoming: his dalliance with the widow Dershowitz and his invigorating study sessions with Rabbi Spiegelman, but most of all, with the excitement of the better-late-than-never bar mitzvah that was finally taking place, just in time to lay claim to his beloved grandson, knee-deep in manhood.

Late at night, after he'd gotten up to urinate for the third time, drowsy but unable to sleep, Oscar would ponder the strange confluence of accident and intention that had resulted, some eighty years after his stillborn coming-of-age, into an occasion for gathering his grandson into the ragged fold of history. At other times he remembered the starving child he'd once been who survived on brine-soaked crusts. The truth was that homunculus still lived inside him, deep in his heart, behind his ribs. After all, what could have liberated it from its bone cage? Love or death? A timely engagement ring for Chaya Rifke or a patent on the famous Dervish waistcoat? Perhaps the upcoming celebration, designed to usher the Minkoffs into manhood, would finally do the trick. If nothing else at least it would make the world a better home for Hashem, as the rabbi had said.

Nothing made Oscar as happy as the hours he spent debating theology with Charlie and Rabbi Spiegelman, Himmelfarb the comic relief that proved the solemnity of their enterprise. It was as if he was young again, full of plans and dreams, the human music rising and falling around him. Alone in his room, pacing, he practised his Torah portion. He was writing a sermon he planned to deliver to the congregation and sewing a suit vest for his grandson as a surprise gift. What could go wrong? he wondered, aware that the very fact of asking such a question might tempt fate.

His thoughts were interrupted by Oritsia, who came bustling up with a plate of warm cinnamon buns. "Ready for the big day, gentlemen?"

"*Born* ready," Oscar assured her.

"What about you, young man?"

"Charlie's getting there, don't worry."

Oritsia said she wasn't worried; she knew a couple of firecrackers when she saw them and what would they like for the party afterwards? Cinnamon buns, it went without saying, but what else? Any suggestions?

"Any *suggestions*?" Oscar repeated incredulously. "Suggestions I've got plenty, but the only thing essential is a cake. A big cake, mind you. Enormous cake."

"E-nor-mous cake," Oritsia pretended to write on an imaginary pad. "Got it."

"Not just any cake," Oscar clarified. "Kind of cake has vanilla inside, chocolate outside. On the front in big letters this cake must say"—he broke off to make a name-in-lights gesture—"'Wonder Boys!'"

"Wonder Boys," Oritsia pretended to write.

"Wonder Boys *exclamation*," Oscar corrected. "Don't forget exclamation."

Oritsia flipped her imaginary pad shut, shoved her imaginary pen behind her ear, told them to leave it to her, and walked away, chuckling.

"Wonder Boys, Charlie. It has a ring. What d'you think?"

But when the boy failed to reply, his grandfather grasped his hand. "Not feeling so wonderful, darlink?" he asked gently. Charlie shook his head.

Ever since their visit to the charming young doctor, his grandson had been downhearted, Oscar had noticed. Glum. It was to be expected, what with the wrong chromosomes, and sitting down to pee, and breasts where no breasts should be. None of it mattered to Oscar except for one thing. He'd stayed behind to check with Dr. Jabbour and she'd confirmed his worst fears. There was no chance of Charlie fathering a child, she told him, a sympathetic hand on his arm. None at all.

She was a nice woman, Oscar reflected, but she gave lousy odds.

Charlie felt his grandfather's hand tremble. The hand's slight palsy, its cruelly swollen joints, rendered him liquid-bellied with protectiveness. He squeezed Oscar's hand, feeling the bones beneath the skin. "Look who's here, zeide," he said, directing Oscar's attention to the door, through which a dynamo of activity approached. It was Rabbi Spiegelman, of course: full-bearded, barrel-chested, shedding drifts of paper as he strode up to them. "One week to go, gentlemen. Where's—"

"Himmelfarb couldn't make it," Oscar announced. "He's on the sick list. Can't even get out of bed to piss, you should excuse the expression."

"No matter," the rabbi said gratefully.

Charlie's recitation of the two-line blessing was perfect, the rabbi said. Then it was Oscar's turn. He adjusted his yarmulke, balanced his spectacles on his nose, and began to chant his Torah portion. He'd been practising, Charlie could tell. His intonation was precise, his delivery fluid. The boy imagined standing with his grandfather before the ark in the small chapel. They were as ready as they'd ever be: Oscar's formal suit back from the cleaners, Charlie's vintage Sondergaard altered and pressed, invitations sent out, dainties ordered, the wording on the cake finalized. Everyone Charlie had invited had promised to attend. Almost everyone. The jury was out on Mr. Skerrit, and Mikayla was a doubtful prospect since, according to Ms. K, she was still in hospital. But Jules, Weeza, and Mrs. Oslavsky would be there "with bells on," as the latter had promised.

Actually, Charlie was sick with worry about Mikayla, another emotion to add to the queasy roil of anticipation, terror, and fatigue. At night his anxiety translated into the sensations he dreaded—the room slopping heavily to one side, cold sweat breaking out, saliva flooding his mouth. *Swallow, swallow, swallow.* The thought of vomiting appalled him, his dignity breached, the loathsome secret of what was inside him suddenly revealed. But he managed to restrain himself, as he always did, the amazing No-Throw-Up Kid presiding. He was beset by a motiveless energy that hauled him out of bed and made him pace feverishly around the apartment before it deserted him abruptly. Then he'd fall dead asleep, a gravity-stricken lump, and wake up flat and dispirited in the morning.

"Still with me, young man?" Rabbi Spiegelman enquired. Before Charlie could reply there was a familiar disturbance, and who should come hobbling towards them, grimacing with pain but powered by outrage? Himmelfarb, none other, his voice pitched to the heavens. "Shame on you, Minkoff!" he roared.

Oscar licked his finger and held it up as though to calculate which way the winds of fate were gusting. Evidently Himmelfarb was less incapacitated than they'd been given to understand. Or else indignation had yanked him up by the scruff of the neck, hauled him from his sickbed, and sent him hurtling across the room.

"Here comes the great Echo," Oscar said as they watched the gout-stricken man hobbling forwards, panting and wincing and wheezing with audible pain.

"What echo? Who's the echo?" Mr. Himmelfarb howled.

"Oy, such an Echo," Oscar confirmed. "When Minkoff itches, Himmelfarb scratches. When Minkoff yawns, Himmelfarb sleeps!"

But Mr. Himmelfarb wasn't in a playful mood. Coming to a wobbly halt, he commenced his berating in earnest, although it wasn't yet apparent to whom he was addressing his fuselage of nuanced grievance. "You! You, a nothing! A piece of gum on the bottom of a shoe! You! Be ashamed!" With this last *mot juste* he lost his breath and was reduced to hanging onto the back of a chair, panting. After a minute he eased himself into it, gingerly propping his foot on a hassock.

"Himmelfarb, are you auditioning for *Swan Lake* perhaps?" Oscar enquired mildly. "What kind of fool gets out of bed specifically to holler at his friends?"

Mr. Himmelfarb pointed a trembling finger at Charlie. "Shame on you, Minkoff Junior!" he hollered again.

Rabbi Spiegelman shifted, as if trying to dislodge the thorn in his side. "Come now, Mr. Himmelfarb, remember our manners," he said.

"Remember!" roared Mr. Himmelfarb. "*What* remember? *How* remember? *Who's to say remember?*"

"Forget about remembering, Himmelfarb," Oscar advised, delighted. "Focus rather on breathing."

As always, Oscar's sarcasm had a bracing effect. Mr. Himmelfarb drew himself up to his full sitting height. Addressing the rabbi, he pitched his voice to the back of the room and beyond. To the furthest reaches of the Seth Rowe. To the four corners of the universe. In short, to whoever had ears to hear. "You want to make for this old man a bar mitzvah? Okay, so make. Does Himmelfarb utter a word? Does Himmelfarb say excuse me this is a bullshit idea? Not once, *not once*. But now for Minkoff Junior too you want a bar mitzvah? Ha ha, what a joke! A man he wants to be."

Himmelfarb brought his fist down on the table, making everyone jump. "*No*, I say. *Never*, I say. *Never in a million years*, I say again."

"My!" Oscar exclaimed in admiration tinged with irony. "First-class speech! On the stage you should be!" But Charlie, sensing trouble, pulled at his grandfather's arm. *Please, please, please.*

"By me are the old traditions best," explained Mr. Himmelfarb smugly.

"What seems to be the problem?" Rabbi Spiegelman asked.

"No problem," Oscar said, suddenly catching on.

"Problem is Genesis," Mr. Himmelfarb insisted. He grasped the edge of the table, pulling himself taller in his chair as he proclaimed, "'So God created mankind in His image; in the image of God He created them; male and female He created them.'"

In the uncomfortable silence that followed, Mr. Himmelfarb stooped to commentary. "Three times the Bible says exact same thing. First *create*, second *looks like*, third *male and female*."

Abruptly, he leaned so close the boy could smell the old man's aggrieved stomach acids. "Here's a question for you, Minkoff Junior. 'Create,' I understand. 'Looks like,' who's to say? But 'male and female,' *there's* the kicker. *There's* the whole ball of worms. Some people male, some people female. You got to choose, says God. Can't be both. Can't be man and woman in one body. Am I right?"

—

WHERE'S YOUR MESSIAH NOW, MOSES?

Later, they'd trace the genealogy of betrayals, both deliberate and inadvertent. Oscar had confided his sorrow to Mrs. Dershowitz, who, as a proud grandmother of five robust grandchildren, might be expected to sympathize with his heartbreak over his only descendant's inability to father a child. She, in an excess of misapplied sympathy had whispered Charlie's secret into Mr. Himmelfarb's hairy ear, and he, in turn, had taken the first opportunity to hobble from his sickbed, braying forth the news.

But the true beginning, Oscar couldn't help feeling, was Moses, pure and simple. Not the abandoned bulrush baby and not the privileged young buck growing up in Pharaoh's palace. Not the slow-tongued interpreter of his God's will and not the furious rabble-rouser descending from Sinai. No, he knew that the Moses of Himmelfarb's imagination was broad of chest and cleft of chin, a Hollywood matinee idol, a maverick. No doubt Himmelfarb had received this impression over the course of repeated viewings of his favourite movie, *The Ten Commandments*, a staple of the Seth Rowe movie club. Such was its interminable length that most residents decamped en masse after the first plague. Not Himmelfarb, though. Not that grudgy, touchy fellow, a natural contrarian, a collector of grievances, who'd stay up all night for the pleasure of watching Edward G. Robinson poke Charlton Heston in the vast savannah of his manly chest.

Where's your Messiah now, Moses? he'd mumble in misplaced wonder. *Where's your Messiah now?*

It was Edward G. Robinson's overseer who betrays Moses's Hebraic origins to Ramses, Oscar reminded himself. And Robinson who blames Moses as the Egyptians mass on the banks of the Red Sea. A betrayer, a blamer, that was Himmelfarb to a T; a tumour in the belly, a soul in need of repair, a terrible human-shaped cipher howling his eternal nothing-ing into the void.

After asking Charlie to step outside, Rabbi Spiegelman listened to Mr. Himmelfarb's accusations and Oscar's explanations, waiting until the end to enquire simply: boy or girl, which is it? It took Oscar back to the maternity ward all those years ago, and the cursed surgeon who thought all questions could be answered with one word—one syllable, even. Oscar did his best to explain the mysteries of chromosomes and the complexities of genetics, but in the end the Law was the Law, as the rabbi kept saying.

The Law was a line in the sand, the rabbi explained. The Law was a wedge against the slippery slope. As to the question of whether women were allowed to read from the Torah, the answer was swift and decisive.

The Law said no.

The Law said never.

It was an ancient edict. Ungenerous, some might claim. Unfair perhaps, the rabbi conceded. But it was not for mankind to question the ways of God.

"But Charlie is a boy," Oscar repeated for the fifth time.

"How can a boy be XX? Boy is XY. That's what boy means," the rabbi replied as he had the previous four times.

Cackling, Mr. Himmelfarb intervened. "How can a boy be XX? I'll tell you, Rabbi. Same way an animal has split hooves but doesn't chew cud. *Traif!* Unclean!" He spat on the ground three times. *Ptooey, ptooey, ptooey.*

Oscar leaned over and with elegant precision stamped on Himmelfarb's gouty toe. Bull's eye! Then he cocked his head and listened to the ensuing screams of agony as if he was a connoisseur of pain.

To his credit, Rabbi Spiegelman would have none of Mr. Himmelfarb's evil-mongering. Leviticus was not the way to proceed, he cautioned. Charlie was a precious soul, not an animal, of that there was no doubt. Perhaps it would be best for Mr. Himmelfarb to retire so that he and Oscar could get to the bottom of what seemed to be a very complex business. As he hobbled from the room, bent over in agony, sweating sourly, Mr. Himmelfarb got in one last zinger. "Draw a line in the sand, Rabbi," he advised over his shoulder. "Remember the slippery slopes."

Oscar was almost in tears. He blew his nose on his handkerchief, then sat twisting the white cloth in his hands. Rabbi Spiegelman shook his head sadly, eloquently. He held his hands out in front of him, wrists together to indicate that they were tied. But Oscar, head bowed, eyes wet, would not look up. If Charlie wasn't a boy, he could never become a man. And if he couldn't become a man, who was he?

After a while the rabbi patted his shoulder and left, but Oscar sat there, his heart drained of light as the winter afternoon darkened around him.

———

Correspondence
To: Mr. Skerrit (2C)
From: Mrs. Oslavsky (3B)

Dear Skerrit
One question. Did you get?
Reply please,
Irina (Mrs. Oslavsky)

To: Mrs. Oslavsky (3B)
From: Mr. Skerrit (2C)

To what are you referring, my dear Irina? In the last week I have received missives both welcome and decidedly not so. As to the first category I must acknowledge receipt of the poppy-seed rolled loaf you sent via our mutual friend, which, while not strictly a missive, was delicious. So soft and so sweet, as the poet almost said. Charlie left it on my doorstep, first knocking to alert me as per your instructions. When I'd extracted myself from my armchair and lumbered to the door, unlocked and opened said door, struggled to grasp the delivery in its receiving blanket of clean dishtowel, then worked my way creakingly upright again (the wonders of the sedentary life have been greatly exaggerated), when I finally held the fragrant bundle in my arms, bending to sniff deeply of that yeasty, newborn-bread smell, it occurred to me to ask myself—and now you, dear lady—why you bestow your largesse on this poor sinner.

No matter. That you do bestow is my good fortune. The poppy-seed loaf tasted as delightful as it smelled, I assure you. I now have enough morphine coursing through my system to be classified as an addict should the issue of urine analysis ever come up. And what's more, I'd count the world and my sobriety well lost. In fact I was sitting down to write a thank-you when Charlie pushed your peremptory note beneath my door. So yes, I "get," Irina, for which much gratitude.

In reply, Joseph (Mr. Skerrit)

To: Mr. Skerrit (2C)
From: Mrs. Oslavsky (3B)

Poppy-seed loaf not the issue, Skerrit. Poppy-seed loaf not what I am meaning when I ask did you get? Invitation, I am meaning. Also terrible Questico letter, my God.

To: Mrs. Oslavsky (3B)
From: Mr. Skerrit (2C)

If you refer, on one hand, to the invitation to Charlie's bar mitzvah celebration and, on the other, to the eviction notice from the Questico Realty Corporation, then I must shout a resounding Snap! Check and check, dear lady. However, I will not be responding in the affirmative to either of those beguiling enticements and would advise you to do likewise.

To: Mr. Skerrit (2C)
From: Mrs. Oslavsky (3B)

What is wrong with you, Skerrit, honest question? Has poppy seed lodged in your brain? Why not happy for little Charlie? Next month he becomes man? Together with dear grandfather, Oscar? And what to do about terrible Pack Up and Go Away letter from Questico Company? God in heaven, where will we go?

Here are some points not in order. One, Charlie is our friend. Two, also Oscar. Three, can Big Company throw old people out on street? Four, also beautiful cat, Alexandra Ivanovna Oslavsky? Five, where can old people go? Six, is legal? Seven, how can it be? Eight, Charlie is very nice boy. Lovely boy, actually. Will make good man someday. Nine, do not write to me about urine, thank you very much. Ten, poppy-seed loaf, pah, peasy-easy. Zefir, also. One day I will make for you charlotte russe with Bavarian cream. Eleven, but not if there is no oven because no kitchen because out on street, my God. Twelve, Skerrit, answer quick please.

To: Mrs. Oslavsky (3B)
From: Mr. Skerrit (2C)

I am tempted to write calm yourself, all will be well, but find I'm too fond of you to lie. Reassurances are convincing only if there is a glimmer of light at the end of the tunnel, an inch of water at the bottom of the well, a speck of hope, a flicker of maybe. Alas, in our case: no light, no water, no flicker, no speck. In other words, I'm afraid Questico, that heartless real estate conglomerate whose very name conjures the colonial enterprise, that whited sepulchre at the heart of our less-than-fair city, has every legal right to give notice at the end of the leasing period, which, as you know, fast approaches. Believe me, dear lady, I've scrutinized the tenancy agreement for a loophole, but to no avail.

No doubt our inconvenient, leaky, draughty, pipe-knocking, radiator-hissing, cynically neglected, inadequately heated and over-zealously patrolled home, our dear old GNC, is earmarked for demolition. I don't need to close my eyes to envision what will be erected in its place. Something resembling a Disney cruise line, I expect, with ludicrously staggered balconies and decorative portholes. There will be a state-of-the-art gymnasium in the basement so even our resident ghost will be routed unless he reconciles himself to the clatter of free weights and the desperate drone of muscle-building muzak. No, there will be no ghosts in the riverside condominiums, Irina. It will be as if we never existed.

My advice is to search out new digs for you and young Sasha, the sooner the better. As for myself, I have no intention of leaving. Indeed, I look forward to dying in my own squalor, if possible returning in spirit to witness the horror of the wrecking crew when they encounter the stink of my mouldering corpse.

Cheerily,

Joseph

P.S. Charlie tells me that due to some "technical error" he will not be honoured on Oscar's big day. Another reason to stay at home and plot my demise, eh Irina?

To: Mr. Skerrit (2C)
From: Mrs. Oslavsky (3B)

Get over yourself, Skerrit. Big Whoop, I say. Same what custodian Lenny say when I tell him this is broken, that is broken, can you fix? Ah, but I am not the Big Whoop around here. (What I am saying is you are the Big Whoop, Skerrit. You!)

So what out on street? So what have to find new place? So what new place not like cats? So what Alexandra Ivanovna Oslavsky not want move? So what bank sends red letter, so what knees hurt, so what can't sleep because worry, so what back hurts, so what more red letters, so what mouse in walls, so what maybe not mouse, so what stay awake all night? You not the only one have problems, Mister. Don't talk to me about ghosts.

What about Charlie, you ever think? No father, crazy mother. Even dog is stupidnik. Skerrit, in my country you get invitation, you go. Whether wedding, whether funeral. You go.

That is all,
Irina Oslavsky
P.S. Hope you like blinis. Is not a bribe.

To: Mrs. Oslavsky (3B)
From: Mr. Skerrit (2C)

Although I'm often moved by my own tender-heartedness
I am resolute in this instance. No, I will not be attending
Charlie Minkoff's spurious and apparently much-disputed
entry into manhood. Manhood is not, after all, such an
honourable estate.
Joseph
P.S. Thanks for the excellent blinis. They were most certainly
a bribe.

To: Mr. Skerrit (2C)
From: Mrs. Oslavsky (3B)

Eight in the morning, February first, I come. Wear suit
please. We go to Charlie's celebration. Also Oscar's cele-
bration. Eight sharply, Skerrit. I come to your door.
IO (Mrs.)

BO

CHARLIE

The morning was crisp and clear, air fizzing with ions, wind scouring away. But once again he'd woken up sad and dispirited. The last dragging week had seemed shapeless, baggy, and sprung at the knees. Every day felt worn out, like an old suit taking on the impression of its owner's body. He hadn't been sleeping well, trapped lying in bed listening to a nightly soundscape of breaking glass, sirens, happy yelling, angry laughter, car doors slamming, and drunken conversations about getting or not getting into various cars until the freight train rattled through the railway yard, its whistle ringing against cold, acoustic air. He'd fall asleep then, as if the whistle had released him, only to wake up shortly afterwards weighed down by complicated feelings, none of them pleasant.

For months he'd been anticipating Oscar's bar mitzvah, and then his own. As he envisioned it, the big day always began with a soak in the kitchen bathtub. He imagined lying back in the steam, all but submerged, half-dreaming, his face warmed by the sun, hair ablaze in flattering early-morning light, considering, with the seriousness that suited the day, what kind of man he'd grow up to be. Instead he had overslept.

Now he was a mess, his breath foul, eyes bubbling with fatigue. No time to soak in the tub. No time to take stock.

Put a bit of knuckle-crack in it, darlink, Oscar would have said. So he did, brushing his teeth, scrubbing himself down in the shower, rolling deodorant over his pits, and trying to tame his crazy Einstein hair with a couple of hard-bristled brushes, one in each hand.

If not now, when? Oscar again, chivvying him along. It was his favourite quote. *If not now, when?* Look it up, Charlie.

In the end, Rabbi Spiegelman had been kind but unbending. He'd consulted the Law; his conscience; his mentor, Rabbi Zalman; sundry clergymen of his acquaintance; even Seligman, the ancient shammes who'd been the synagogue factotum for as long as anyone could remember. Eventually he referred the thorny matter to his chief rabbi in New York, who reminded Rabbi Spiegelman of the Law that Moses had handed to Joshua, Joshua to the judges, the judges to the prophets, and the prophets to the rabbis. (*The rabbis to the shmendriks!* Oscar had retorted, furious.) And also reminded him that this ancient edict was, even in the present age of heresy and sporadic synagogue attendance, still the Law.

The consensus was unanimous, Rabbi Spiegelman had reported. While a young girl might observe her entry into Jewish womanhood, a ritual in which she'd be celebrated, blessed, and justly praised for such qualities as modesty and virtue, she could not be called up to read Torah, chant Haftorah, or offer an interpretation of the weekly Torah portion, the parsha. You had to be a man to do that, or at the very least a boy on his way to manhood.

He felt a piercing shame at the rabbi's words, a shame that intensified when Oscar pointed out, at first patiently, that his grandson was just such a boy. A boy about to become a man. Oscar had waited for the rabbi to capitulate, to say, I *know* he is, or perhaps even, *I* know he is. Instead Rabbi Spiegelman had stroked his beard and said that XX was a serious call. XX was all they had; it was scientific. "After all, we Jews value what is written," he said, attempting levity. But, realizing his mistake, he turned serious, explaining that to Orthodox Jews the separation of male and female was paramount. Strictly speaking, he added, a girl wasn't permitted to sit with male congregants but must take her place in the women's section.

"You're kidding me," Oscar exclaimed. "You want Charlie should sit with the women?"

The rabbi's face softened. No, he allowed, that would be unnecessary. Cruel, even. Charlie must sit beside his zeide, of course.

"Looks like a duck and quacks like a duck, eh? Seems you owe Charlie an apology."

"I'm sorry, young man," the rabbi said, but it was clear his apology was an expression of sympathy rather than the concession that Oscar desired. "These things are written. The Law is entrenched. What can I do?"

"Entrenched!" Oscar shouted. "What entrenched? How entrenched? On whose watch were those trenches dug?"

We both know the answer to that one, the rabbi's look said. But Oscar, galvanized, repeated his terms: "No Charlie, no Oscar!" Moses, that desert-reeking stiff-neck, had struck again. *No Charlie, no Oscar!* It was the hill his grandfather meant to die on, and it took all Charlie's ingenuity to coax him down. In the end he texted Weeza, who rushed over, and the two of them got to work on the old gentleman, arguing and cajoling and pleading, appealing to his best and worst instincts, the impulse to take the high road and the equally profound impulse to kick Himmelfarb to the curb. Nothing worked until, in desperation, he reminded his grandfather of the story of the frog and the scorpion.

Oscar's face lit up. Sure, he remembered.

"Go ahead, tell me," Weeza said, playing along. She'd heard this story along with the rest of the stories in the Minkoff family archive (cat in a box, how the farmer crossed the river, etc., etc.).

He related the story, giving it his best shot, even putting on a sinister scorpion voice. Weeza pretended to look puzzled.

"So they both drowned?"

He nodded solemnly, while Oscar guffawed, "Best friends to the end!" Demonstrating that he understood, his grandfather gave him the thumbs-up, then hooked his thumb over his shoulder, "Okay, climb on the old man's back, darlink. We're going across."

Weeza didn't want to put a spoke in the wheel, she said, but drowning was no kind of happy ending. Not for a frog and not for a boy. She had a point, so Oscar kindly explained: "Frog can't help being frog and scorpion can't help being scorpion. Frog can't help believing, scorpion can't help stinging. Is it their nature? Certainly, why not? Frog is a believer, scorpion is a stinger. Together you got yourself a little green tugboat with a suicide bomber on board."

Weeza let out a bark of laughter, signalling the end of hostilities. He wasn't sure why he'd brought up that old vaudeville routine, the frog-and-scorpion two-step. But he was glad he had because Oscar, mollified, went off to fetch the waist-coat he'd made for his grandson. His gift.

Now, he shook the heavy garment from its tissue-paper wrapping, held it up before him, and then slipped it on. It was a beautiful piece of clothing, a sleek three-button Dervish special with knife-pleat pockets. Oscar, who always preached the gospel of restraint, whose motto was that you never noticed what a well-dressed gentleman was wearing, had boldly broken with his tradition. He'd produced what was a suit vest in name but a fully-fledged waistcoat in execution, selecting a shimmery, figured brocade in morning grey and lining it in dark crimson silk. Of course you couldn't see the crimson silk; it was a secret blood lining, a pact between grandfather and grandson.

It had taken him two months to sew, Oritsia confided. Working six days a week, hunched over his old treadle machine, glasses smudged with concentration. He'd blocked out the pattern the day after they met with the rabbi. Oscar, who hadn't sewn a garment in years, still had the magic touch. The fit was perfect, there was a vent in the back with enough give to accommodate weight fluctuation — gain being the most foreseeable outcome. Standing before the bathroom mirror, he ran his hand gently over the mother-of-pearl buttons, tilting this way and that to admire the richly textured fabric that gleamed with a mineral light.

Jules walked into the Gents as he was struggling with his necktie, pursing her lips at his magnificent razzle-dazzle. *Nice vest!* she finger-traced on the steamy mirror. She was wearing a fifties-style navy frock with a tight bodice and swirling skirt, somehow managing to flatter and poke fun at herself at the same time. He'd seen the dress hanging in the window of Second Story, a clue as to where she'd sourced her crimson Mary Janes as well as the black fascinator she'd pinned to her head at a chic ascot angle. As usual, she looked both weird and beautiful, neither quality quite cancelling out the other.

Mazel tov! she wrote on the mirror and presented him with an envelope containing good folding money, a couple of twenties and a ten.

Thanks Mom! he wrote back. After a moment, he added, *You look pretty.*

OSCAR

Working swiftly, he pulled his new tie into a precise knot. How many times in his life had he performed this manoeuvre? Over and under, under and through, a swift yank. He winked at the handsome devil staring back at him, framed in the central panel of Chaya Rifke's mirrored dressing table. The soft greens and greys flattered his eyes, no question, but the cufflinks that Weeza had insisted on lending him were less than elegant. Yet he threaded them through his French cuffs, not one to refuse a gift from a horse. Weeza (not the horse) had said they were for luck. When he'd asked what the monogrammed letters meant, she'd shrugged. *What does anything mean?*

The Seth Rowe was a fully furnished residential facility, but folks were allowed to bring personal items from home to make their rooms feel less institutional — less like little boxes created entirely out of stain-resistant surfaces from which all traces of life might one day be wiped away. After some thought, he'd chosen his late wife's vanity table, the heavy, old-fashioned dresser topped with bevelled glass from which, on either side, hinged mirrors swung forwards. Every day of their life together, as Chaya Rifke settled herself before the dressing table, straight-backed and slim-ankled, he'd been granted the gift of watching her beloved reflection. As she brushed her hair or blotted her lips on a tissue, a hundred Chaya Rifkes bounced from one mirrored surface to the next before vanishing forever into the forever-vanishing distance. If he'd known she too would disappear one day, he'd have preserved every last crumpled Kleenex with its rosebud imprint.

He'd lost her in the mirror. Not immediately, but over time, which didn't surprise him. Time had never done him any favours. Time was an old man with a limp, full of aches and pains, eyes so wrecked that even hindsight was a blur. Time was the sound of footsteps following him down the corridor to the bathroom. Three, four times a night, his old man's bladder kaput. But mostly, time was the death's head grinning at him as he sat at his wife's dresser, peering into the glass. He was losing weight, bones hollowing out, flesh disintegrating. Only his memory was heavy and growing heavier by the day.

"*Nu*, get up, Oscar," he muttered, watching the lips of that ghastly ventriloquist move in time with his own. Who was the dummy now? He'd risen early, wanting to spend a moment communing with his beloved mother who'd turned him into a daughter and back into a son again, thrust the Chumash into his hands then pushed him out the door. *Run, flee!* She'd sacrificed her son not as Abraham had sacrificed

Isaac but as Jochebed had sacrificed Moses. Not as a father but as a mother. *Don't look back! Forget everything!* Like the mother in the court of King Solomon, she would rather give him up than let him be cut in half.

Ah, but had she sacrificed him or saved him? If sacrificed, to what God? If saved, to what purpose? On one hand, he thought he knew the answer, although it was always changing. On the other hand, it was possible that nothing had changed, nothing at all. In spite of his years he was still the boy who'd worn his sister's apron, who hadn't turned back to embrace his mother. The boy who'd lived in a forest, a cellar, a DP camp, who'd starved and dreamed, his teeth grown loose and his skin taut. And despite what he told Charlie, nobody had called him Wonder Boy. It was the name he had given himself.

Forget everything, his mother had urged. But how could you forget? It bothered him. *Forget everything, forget everything, forget everything.* Like an assassin, memory ambushed you when you weren't looking. He recalled a particular walk he'd taken with Charlie one fall, the boy's hand on his arm as they navigated slick sidewalks. One last stroll before winter's iron shutter clattered down. Peering up at the lowering sky, he saw a flock of geese, honking and lighting out for the cushy comforts of a retirement community down south, a snowbird's resort off the coast of Florida. Someplace warm. Suddenly he wanted to shake his grandson, for once to allow his fierceness to show.

"*And if not now, when?* Rabbi Hillel. Look it up, darlink."

"When?" he repeated, his insistency shaming him. *When?* Charlie had stared in freckled wonderment. "Now, zeide?"

"Very now."

What else could he say, what could he do? What piece of

advice stood the test of time? He was Oscar Wolf Minkoff, Charlie's grandfather, not one of those fair-weather geese. And when he left, he'd leave for good. In the end, he was glad he'd kept it old school. Patted the boy's jacket and settled his collar. Made a joke about geese and Florida. Hokey but apt. When Charlie laughed, he pinched his cheek lightly. *Sheyner punim.* That your luck should only be as good as your looks!

That day, like so many others, he bit back his words of warning and savoured the teeth marks in his tongue. Holding the boy's arm, he steered them into the narrowing afternoon. Lighting out for tomorrow.

CHARLIE

"*Garde ça!* Aren't you the little heartbreaker!" Weeza exclaimed when she saw him. She'd bought Jules a corny pink corsage to wear around her wrist, prom-date style, and for him she produced an elegant boutonnière, carefully threading the rose-and-fern spray into the custom-made loop on his lapel. She drove them to the Seth Rowe but wouldn't come in; she had a couple of other pickups to make. "Don't worry," she said in response to his anxious look. "I'll be back in time for Oscar's big solo."

The chapel was filling up with Seth Rowe regulars. Sitting in the front pew with Oscar, he heard the low rumble of conversation behind him, phlegmy coughs (a chest cold making the rounds), the *skritch-skritch-whir* of Mr. Weinberg's motorized wheelchair, as well as miscellaneous groans and grizzles, the sound of old age settling on wooden pews. From the corner of his eye he saw Jules taking her place in the women's section beside Oritsia. Jules looked awkward, a new look for her that, like the Mary Janes and the fascinator, was somehow flattering.

Oscar fumbled for his hand, popping his cuffs and flashing the cufflinks Weeza had lent him. Despite looking snazzy in his well-cut suit and new tie, yarmulke pushed to the back of his head and prayer shawl arranged neatly over his shoulders, Oscar seemed nervous. He polished his reading glasses and fumbled with a sheaf of papers, folding and refolding, glancing at them then stuffing them into his jacket pocket.

He sympathized with his grandfather's anxiety. After all, here he stood: Charlie Minkoff, sleek in his classic Sondergaard and gorgeous waistcoat; pants pressed, shirt starched; buttons, face, and shoes all shined. For once he looked as sharp and trim as a Swiss Army knife, yet he felt blunted and dull. He'd wanted to give Oscar the bar mitzvah he'd missed, to make up for all that he'd lost, but had only discovered new things for him to lose along the way. A loser, that's what he was! King of the Losers, in fact. His own father had sent a polite but disapproving reply to the invitation: Nathan Dervish was sorry to decline but religious considerations prevented him from travelling on the Sabbath. He wished Charlie a life filled with study and Torah.

All things considered, his father's refusal was probably a good thing. How much better, at this lowest point, to be overlooked rather than humiliated. At the thought of what he'd narrowly avoided he was overcome with nerves. Sweaty and slightly nauseous, he grabbed his grandfather's hand and hung on for dear life.

OSCAR

Gently he squeezed his grandson's hand. *Dear Life,* he thought, as if dictating a letter to God. He noted that Charlie's face shone with the pure light of virtue. As if he wasn't plenty handsome enough! And, as so often happened, he found himself addressing his late wife. *Well, Chaya Rifke, what do you think of your Wonder Boys now?* She'd have approved, he was certain. They had seldom disagreed when she was alive, even less so now.

Glancing around the synagogue, he noted the regulars in their seats behind him, hunched around canes or clutching at their pews. Barney Nagler snuffling into his vast handkerchief; Harvey Miller kibitzing with Simcha Zuckerman; poor Mrs. Rosenstein, confused as ever, settling with a billowy sigh into a pew in the men's section, heaving with effort before falling fast asleep. Down the aisle trotted Seligman, the ancient beadle, handing out prayer books and cough drops. Only Himmelfarb was absent. Where had the heir of Socrates gotten to now? he wondered.

As he craned, searching, he caught sight of a man he didn't recognize, a fellow slouched in the last row, enormously fat and sheened with exertion. He didn't look Jewish, but you never knew. He might be the last remaining member of some forgotten tribe, come in out of the cold to wait for the Messiah. He spotted Mrs. Dershowitz, comely in a lilac suit, waving from the women's section. She tried to catch his eye but he turned away, not wanting to be distracted by romance. The chapel door banged open and Weeza strode down the aisle, Mrs. Oslavsky in tow. The old lady was done up as usual in ratty furs and dangerously high heels, her cheeks hectic with rouge.

When Weeza saw him she blew a kiss, then jabbed a finger at Charlie, who still faced front, his head bowed.

CHARLIE

He couldn't believe that Mr. Skerrit, having made it out of his apartment, was now wedged sideways into a pew, from which it looked as if he'd have to be painfully extracted. Mr. Skerrit seldom left his apartment, and the fact that he'd done so today—however unwillingly, however cumbersomely—struck him with the momentousness of the occasion. Nothing short of finding Gellman in the seat beside his grandfather, his long nose stuck in a prayer book, would have surprised him more. But Gellman, prostrate with grief, had been left behind.

He didn't expect to see Mikayla either, and in this his expectations were not disappointed.

He'd visited her in hospital, but the nurse had waved him away, saying that Ms. Piper didn't want to see him. The next time he was refused again, and the next, but he must have worn her down because the time after *that* the nurse said, Charlie, right? She ushered him into a room where a girl lay beneath a thin hospital sheet. Her ashy skin made her look as if she was on the dead list, as Oscar would have said. He sat down beside her, heart pounding, only to hear a squawk of laughter from the next bed, where Mikayla lay—in bad shape, true, but not, as she pointed out, another girl entirely.

It was such a relief to see her, to finally be able to apologize in person for the photo he'd taken, that he ended up telling her what had happened, everything: Mr. Himmelfarb's calumny, the rabbi's decision, Oscar's despair. He even confessed to his own shame, although he downplayed this, being, naturally, ashamed.

"Don't turn up," Mikayla advised. "Boycott their ass, Three-Piece."

"Yeah, totally."

Wincing, she'd lifted an ironic freedom fist, her bandaged arm still swollen.

But not turning up had never been an option. Now here they stood, side by side, the handsome bar mitzvah boy and his weird grandson. From the bimah, where he was standing in front of the Ark, the rabbi found his place in the prayer book, cleared his throat, and began davening the morning service.

OSCAR

The day should have been joyful, but instead his thoughts kept returning to previous disappointments. At this very moment he was remembering the time he couldn't afford to buy a wedding ring for Chaya Rifke. He'd gone to Mort Dervish for a loan, but the SOB said that if he couldn't afford to buy a wedding ring he couldn't afford to get married. Simple as that. The Dervishes were tightwads, wallets ingrown like their souls, to a man. That included the boy's disappearing father.

Not Charlie, though. Never Charlie. Charlie was pure Minkoff, distilled from his grandfather's sweetest thoughts. Look at him standing there, he thought in wonderment. So good-looking, such a blessing! Maybe not tall, but getting there. His grandson was no longer the infant whose diaper he'd changed, marvelling, or the toddler climbing onto his lap to root in his pocket for a handful of Hershey's Kisses. He wasn't the kid practising Jules's signature over and over, or the boy peering through darkening windows, waiting for his mother to come home.

Ah, but look what had come of their endeavours! He tried to tell himself that progress was not all in one direction, an escalator leading from the Garden of Eden straight up to heaven. Sometimes the world faltered. Sometimes the people fell on their knees again, became like animals. Always there were times of destruction and disaster. War followed by plague, drought followed by flood, fire followed by famine. Such times were inevitable, waiting in the wings, yet they never failed to ambush humanity. After all, who could predict the future? The sages said that since everyone was born screaming, it was a blessing simply to die with one's mouth shut.

Think in shorter sentences, Chaya Rifke advised, breaking into his reverie.

He shook his head in wonder at his late wife's wisdom. She was right, she was always right. The past was a long sentence, the future an indecipherable one. The present was all there was because it didn't require a sentence, but could be summed up in a word or a pithy phrase. In a word, he, Oscar Wolf Minkoff, was heartbroken. So *nu*? So what? His heart had been broken before. Remembering that it was his duty to be stoic, to hide his sadness from the boy, he pulled his prayer shawl over his head and began to daven.

CHARLIE

It broke his heart to see his grandfather so sad. He did his best to clamp his smile in place with such conviction that by the time Oscar was called up to read from the Torah, he'd begun to believe in his own good spirits, his smile no longer a fluttering flag in the wind.

As he watched Oscar walk towards the lectern where the scroll was laid out, a pair of magic spectacles appeared to slide onto his own nose, so that the farther away his zeide walked the more fully he came into focus. With each step he saw things he'd never noticed before. Oscar had shrunk, eyes into sockets, flesh around bones. He seemed shorter, he walked with a limp. Without his trademark fedora his hair stood out around his yarmulke, thin and dandelion-fluffy. One hand trembled uncontrollably, the other fumbled at the sheaf of papers in his jacket pocket.

When Oscar got to the lectern he seemed confused, and the rabbi, smiling reassuringly, had to angle him into position in front of the Torah scroll. For one blood-thinning moment as he stood, head bowed before the congregation, it seemed his grandfather had lost it—the words, the tune, his composure. But the old man gave himself a shake, cleared his throat and, pressing a corner of his prayer shawl to the scroll, kissed the fringes and began the blessing. *Bor'chu es ado-noy ha-m'voroch...*

OSCAR

Boruch ado-noy ha-m'voroch l'olom vo'ed, the congregation responded.

He looked up, noting that Himmelfarb had scuttled into the synagogue when his back was turned. The old sack of piss and gout was bent over in his pew, he hoped in agony. One glance confirmed that Himmelfarb was frowning at the prayer book in his hands, pretending to read. The man was an Eeyore, pessimism his antidote to simple faith. Yet as much as he despised the villain, as much as he blamed him for the tragedy of what amounted to Charlie's excommunication, as much as he consigned him to the fiery pits of Gehenna, he was oddly relieved to see him. *Well, why not? Let him suffer before his enemy's triumph.* The one thing Himmelfarb couldn't stand was Oscar's storied ability to turn over the cards, coming up blackjack every time.

Don't try to reach him, Wolfie. He's got an unlisted number, Chaya Rifke cautioned. Smiling with love, his heart full, he began chanting the assigned passage from *Bo*, the fifteenth weekly Torah portion, taken from the Book of Exodus, which related the final plagues visited upon Egypt and the first Passover celebration.

CHARLIE

He longed to be true to the promise he'd made Oscar, to take part in spirit, to know that his grandfather spoke for both of them, to feel consecrated, lifted up and filled with the pure helium of spiritual joy. *Very now.* But despite the finger he moved along the lines of print, he soon lost his way in the dense black forests of Hebrew script and switched to the English translation on the left-hand page of his prayer book.

In this Torah portion he read, The Lord set the eighth and ninth plagues upon the Egyptians: locusts and darkness. Yet Pharaoh remained hard-hearted, refusing to free the Israelite slaves. Finally, God told Moses that the tenth plague would be the killing of all first-born Egyptian children. God commanded the Israelites to slaughter a lamb and paint their doorposts with its blood so that the Angel of Death would pass over their houses. All this the Lord did with *b'yad hazzakah*—a mighty hand. And so it came to pass that after the death of the Egyptian first-borns Pharaoh demanded that the Israelites leave the land, which they did, in haste.

Oscar chanted gracefully, his voice thin but not quavering, his delivery precise, melodic. He took his time as the rabbi had advised, since there was no train to catch, no Pharaoh to escape. Not once did the rabbi have to correct a mispronunciation as he had in their study sessions, not once did he tap the lectern with impatience. Every now and then Oscar shut his eyes and swayed on his feet, as if to commune with his deity. Then the room would grow quiet until even the rustle of candy wrappers ceased. Somehow his grandfather had silenced the coughers and the murmurers, the kibitzers and the kvetches, the fidgeters and the rustlers, the purveyors of hard candy and the sufferers of incurable throat tickles. It was a miracle.

When he finished reading from the Torah, when he'd kissed his prayer shawl, when the heavy scrolls had been painstakingly rolled up again, when the Torah was finally upright, arrayed in Sabbath splendour (golden crown, embroidered cover, brass plate), Oscar stepped away from the bimah with a modest smile that nevertheless acknowledged the success he had achieved and the accolades he was certain to receive.

He glanced at the women's section, where his mother, canted forwards in her pew, stared up at Oscar. Like the Hebrew script on the right-hand side of the page, her expression was difficult to read. Beside her, Weeza beamed with pride while Mrs. Oslavsky shook her head in disbelief. *Wonders!* she seemed to be exclaiming. *Who would have thought?* He was having trouble keeping it together and didn't want to catch anyone's eye, but he stole side glances at his mother until he saw Weeza pass her something white and fluttery that Jules twisted in her hand until it was nothing but a rag. It was as if she hadn't even noticed the tears trickling down her cheeks.

He felt a tap on his shoulder. Mr. Nagler leaned forwards, a folded handkerchief in his hand. "Here you go, young man," he said. "Wipe before you cause another flood."

OSCAR

"Let me set the scene: Seven plagues have come and gone. Water into blood! Frogs! Lice! Wild animals! Cattle disease! Boils! Thunder of hail and fire!"

With each plague he banged his fist on the lectern, rousing the congregation, who'd begun to slump and doze after they'd pelted him with handfuls of celebratory candy. *Thump, thump, thump, thump, thump, thump, thump.* By the time the hail and fire had passed, even Mrs. Rosenstein was awake, albeit grudgingly.

The Torah reading had gone without a hitch. Now, here stood Oscar Wolf Minkoff, newly bar mitzvahed, a Wonder Boy. But the real test was still to come—the sermon he was about to deliver, the privilege of which he'd wrested from

Rabbi Spiegelman by taking advantage of the man's well-deserved guilt in cutting his Charlie, the little prodigy, out of the picture. At first the rabbi had been reluctant to yield the floor. After all, the weekly sermon was the domain of the leader of the congregation, the rabbi. No, no, he couldn't possibly; Oscar, be realistic...

He shrugged, but the revolutionary impulse was upon him.

Ach, Wolfie! Chaya Rifke chided.

Once again he smiled, shrugged. *His beloved, his bashert.* Pretending to sympathize, nodding sagely, he lulled Rabbi Spiegelman into a false sense of security before delivering his ultimatum. "Pity if there isn't a bar mitzvah on Saturday. Terrible pity."

It was a bluff, a well-calculated one. The rabbi had spent too much time preparing his student, the event had been too widely publicized (write-ups in both the *Jewish News* and the daily paper about the ninety-year-old Holocaust survivor being bar mitzvahed) for him to lose his prize at the last moment.

But he, Oscar Wolf Minkoff, was aware that he had even more to lose: the debt to the past that might forgive his derelictions. His mother forever unembraced, his family turned to ash in the ovens of Europe, his conviction that in wearing his sister's clothes she had taken his place in the slow conflagration of history. The rabbi had a great deal to lose, but as a man bearing the weight of history he had everything to lose. Ergo, he must not lose. It was that simple.

In the end the rabbi conceded with good grace, even a joke. "Go ahead, Oscar, sermon's all yours," he said. "May it be the crack to your pickle."

So here he stood at the lectern, his papers fluttering, facing the congregation but addressing the two people he loved most in the world, one of whom was gazing at him with her narrow, glittery eyes, and the other staring at his feet.

CHARLIE

He was remembering the time the rabbi had asked them what "Bo" meant. Bo was the name of the Biblical portion they were studying, as when the Lord says to Moses "Come to Pharaoh," which He does frequently whenever He wants Moses to noodle the guy. Bo this, Bo that. So, what does Bo mean?

"Go!" Mr. Himmelfarb straight away yelled.

"Come," Oscar said.

"Same thing." Mr. Himmelfarb sounded indignant.

"Not same thing, Himmelfarb. *Opposite* thing. Opposite of come is go. Opposite of right is wrong. Opposite of Minkoff is Himmelfarb."

By this time, Mr. Himmelfarb having darkened unbecomingly, Rabbi Spiegelman intervened to say that although Bo did mean come, the locution "Go to Pharaoh," fell more naturally on the ear.

Oscar shook his head. "Bo means come. No question. Better question is *why*. Why say come when you mean go? Remember, this is God talking. This guy *invented* language. Well, Charlie?"

He tried to think of a reason, but all he could come up with was that come sounded more inviting than go. Kinder.

"Bingo! First-class answer," Oscar exclaimed. "Couldn't

have put it better myself. *Come* to dinner, *go* to the dogs. *Come* for a walk, *go* to hell. Right, darlink?"

When he nodded, Oscar continued: "Go is what you holler when someone is bothering you, say for instance, *Go away, Himmelfarb!* But come, that's another story. Come is an invitation. Come is a request. Come here, Charlie, I want to give you a kiss on the forehead."

He bent his head towards his grandfather, who reached up to brush away his hair, pressing his lips emphatically to his grandson's forehead. Still staring at his shoes, he couldn't help smiling. His grandfather made Moses seem like some shy kid the Lord had taken by the hand. *Come.*

OSCAR

Although delighted, he was surprised to see Charlie smile. He'd been describing the plague of locusts that invaded the land, followed by a darkness thicker than locusts. But a smile was a smile. He took courage from it, raising his voice as he continued to wrestle with theology, the old God magic.

"It's not looking good. Score is Pharaoh 9, Moses 0, when the Lord goes in for the final inning. Straight off He tells Moses that He's got one more plague up His sleeve, a surefire winner. Pharaoh will have no choice but to let the children of Israel go, once and for all. Goodbye and good luck.

"Turns out the Almighty's right, what d'you know. Comes the final plague and there's a cry throughout the land. I'm talking about the full catastrophe, ladies and gentlemen — the slaying of the first-born. In every house a child is dead.

"Every. Single. House." His voice trembled with emotion.

The image of Jules's stillborn twin assailed him. The infant whipped away before they could hold him. Or her. Nobody had said whether a him or a her. Eyes shut, swaying on his heels, he heard the congregation rustling in sympathy, immersed in their own losses, Mrs. Rosenstein sighing deeply, Seligman burying his head in his hands. Suddenly the sanctuary was filled with the children who'd gone before, as if the dog whistle of their parents' longing had summoned them. The infants who had been born with wings; the toddlers with swollen brains, treacherous blood; the teenage suicides. That a parent should say kaddish for a child — there was no greater tragedy, no bitterer pain.

After a moment, he leaned forwards. "I don't know about you fellows, but by me something doesn't add up. I don't mean to blaspheme or, God forbid, second-guess the Creator of the Universe, but if Hashem has a 100 percent guarantee, why not bring out the big guns to start? Why monkey around with frogs? Why punish the cattle?"

He whistled, took a beat. He'd been wrestling with Hashem's indecisiveness for weeks. Basically, every time Pharaoh says okay guys, get out of here, hit the road, what does the Lord do? He changes *His* mind, once again stiffening Pharaoh's heart.

He drummed his fingers, considering. "And I quote, 'But God stiffened Pharaoh's heart and he would not let the Israelites go.' Happens every time. Comes the blood; Moses says Let My People Go, Pharaoh sees the rivers run red and says okay, go. *But then* God stiffens his heart. Comes the frogs; Moses says Let My People Go, Pharaoh sees them dying and stinking up the land and says okay, go. *But then* God stiffens his heart. You name it — lice, vermin, boils — Moses wants to go, Pharaoh says go already, God stiffens. Wild animals, thunder, darkness—God stiffens. What to think? Why has He made Pharaoh's heart like a piece of liver that gets tougher every time it's boiled?"

He glanced around the sanctuary, pulling his prayer shawl close. The talk of liver had been a mistake, lulling some congregants into thoughts of the upcoming Kiddush lunch, sending others into a nostalgic daydream that had nothing to do with Pharaoh's indecisive heart. Enraged, he slammed his fist on the lectern. "I'm talking about *choice*, people. Free Willy. Letting the whale jump back in the sea."

CHARLIE

Gusts of laughter billowed about the room. *What whale? Which Willie?* He could sympathize. Study sessions had frequently centred on Mr. Himmelfarb's inability to wrap his head around what he persisted in calling Free Willy. What kind of Free Willy did Abraham have? he'd ask. God says kill the kid, *nu*, is he supposed to argue with the Lord? He'd expected Oscar to fulminate, to berate Himmelfarb, to relate his favourite story about free will (cat in a box) or offer another story, the one about not having as much free will as you thought (frog and scorpion). Instead his grandfather commiserated. Poor Himmelfarb, he said. It was terrible to suffer a crisis of faith at his age.

When Mr. Himmelfarb inevitably slammed out of the residents' lounge in a huff, Oscar would explain that the poor fellow had no children, no one to say kaddish for him when he died. This rendered him touchy, perverse, susceptible to anger.

Since the thought of dying—decaying, turning to worm fodder, failing to live on even in memory—was terrifying, the old man refused to imagine a world that would continue after he'd departed it. And much as he hated to admit it, Oscar said, Himmelfarb had a point. What was choice if not a stone in the shoe of Jewish history? But Rabbi Spiegelman, for once, refused to play devil's advocate. Hashem had given mankind free choice. No exceptions!

Oscar had scratched his whiskers against the grain thoughtfully, eliciting the sandpapery rasp that was his eternal murmur of dissent. *Perhaps yes, perhaps no. Who can say for sure? Not for me to decide.* Even though Oscar always returned to the whale trapped in his blubbery anguish, his grandson wasn't fooled. He was certain that his grandfather, even if asked by the Almighty Himself, would never put his head to the rock. And perhaps that's what Hashem had been hoping for, what He longed for with all His heart. That Abraham would disobey Him. That he'd refuse to sacrifice his son and so recognize God's fallibility. His oceanic and eternal loneliness.

RABBI SPIEGELMAN

Up on the bimah, where he was seated to the left of Oscar, he shifted abruptly.

Correctly diagnosing his impatience, the old man held up a restraining hand. "Don't worry, Rabbi. I got an answer to the question," Oscar said, to which he might have legitimately asked which of the *many* questions he was referring to, but did not, because he suspected that Oscar could filibuster all day and well into the evening until the traditional three stars appeared in the night sky to bring the Sabbath to a close.

"It's nice you should worry, Rabbi," Oscar conceded, interrupting his thoughts. He turned to the congregation. "Free Willy," he announced. "A couple words."

From the back of the sanctuary, from the general direction if not, indeed, the precise seat occupied by Mr. Himmelfarb, came a long-drawn-out sigh.

OSCAR

He'd been waiting for that sound. Himmelfarb's pneumatic exasperation goaded him on. Rustling through his papers, he found his place and glanced down at the heavily scored sheets; then, on an impulse, he swept the loose papers off the lectern. Time to ride bareback.

"Most of you know my story," he said, settling in. "It's no different from yours, Barney Nagler. Or yours, Esther Dershowitz. Anyone who lived through the terrible fire. Maybe your parents escaped and you were born here, first-generation Canadian, free country, a kosher chicken in every pot. But still you didn't escape. Which of us did? We all lived under Pharaoh, we all suffered. Then came the plagues. Cattle cars, showers, ovens. Auschwitz, Bergen-Belsen, Treblinka. Dead, murdered, martyred."

A ragged sigh travelled through the room, gathering and trailing off and swelling again, its irregular rise and fall like the fever spikes of grief. When the sound at last died down, he leaned forwards. "Not on the Nazis but on the Jews fell the plagues. Stones, torture, gas. Blood, darkness, wild animals. Slaying of the first-born and the mothers and the fathers. Slaying of the sister in the kitchen and the brother in the Beit Midrash. Slaying of the infants and the grandparents. Slaying of the six million."

He paused out of respect for the six million. Their invocation could be met only with silence. After a moment, he continued. "So tell me, where was Moses to give the people advice, to say go kill a lamb, go paint the doorposts with blood? Matter of fact, doorposts is where the Nazis looked for a sign that said once, long ago, the Angel of Death had passed over.

"What am I saying? Simple. In every generation comes a pharaoh. In every generation comes the plague. Sometimes it falls on the right people, sometimes on the wrong people. Sometimes painting the blood saves you, sometimes it kills you. Simple, right?"

RABBI SPIEGELMAN

"Wrong!" Oscar thundered, thumping his fist on the lectern.

As one, the congregation flinched.

"Wrong! Wrong! Wrong!" He continued to thump out his hollow wooden tattoo, his voice shifting out of the minor key, transforming from plaint to complaint, the universal currency of his churlish people. When the boy, who'd sat with his head bowed through Oscar's sermon, finally lifted his eyes, his grandfather was ready for him.

"Nothing is simple is the answer I'm looking for," Oscar said.

In the silence that followed, he forced himself to speak. "Um. Excellent, Mr. Minkoff. That was very—"

"Thank you, Rabbi," Oscar said modestly. "Wait until you hear the next part."

It was at this moment that his blood ran cold, which was not the dead metaphor he'd once thought it to be. On the contrary; it was as if he'd taken a whiff of Freon and his blood cells were icing over. He struggled to his feet, but the appreciative murmur from the congregation stopped him in his tracks. Shivering, he sat down again. It was unseemly to indulge in this colloquial back-and-forth on the bimah, the traditional place of prayer. So far Oscar had conducted himself reasonably well, hectoring and haranguing in the style of old-fashioned clergymen, but at least avoiding discussion, for which he was grateful.

It would be dreadful were Oscar to solicit opinions from the congregation as if he were taking some sort of spiritual poll, he reflected.

OSCAR

"Show of hands," he said. "Who here is a first-born son? And who"—he turned to the women's section—"is a first-born daughter? Speak up, no shame in coming first."

Blushing, Charlie raised his hand. All around the sanctuary men and women were sitting up, looking around, raising or not raising their hands. Oritsia had her hand up and so did Jules, the pink corsage sliding down her wrist. Mrs. Oslavsky, looking confused, was whispering to Weeza.

"What about you, Harvey?" he noodged a lanky gentleman in the second row.

"My mother, may she rest in peace, had a stillbirth before me," Harvey Miller said without rancour.

"Aha!" he exclaimed. "So Dr. Miller, here, would be saved. Good thing, on account of all the babies he's going to deliver. But some of you others—" he glanced around the room, shaking his head, "you should excuse me, don't be insulted, but for the rest of you I'm not seeing such a golden future."

From the back of the room a familiar voice thundered forth. "Get to the point, Minkoff. Some of us are living on borrowed time."

Pointedly ignoring the voice, he turned to regard the rabbi, who'd buried his head in his hands. "Don't worry," he told him kindly. "This you're going to love." He drew himself up like the seasoned pro that he was, raising his voice for the folks in the back.

"Killing of the first-born is a terrible thing, no question. Okay, *one* question. Question: Why did Hashem send down such a plague? Answer: How can we know what goes on in the mind of the Almighty? But question: Can we guess? Answer: Sure, why not? It's a free country. Want to know what I think? Educated guess, right?"

The congregation was all in. Cries of "Minkoff, spill the beans already!" and "What are you waiting for, Mister?" resounded.

Time for the old razzle-dazzle, Wolfie, Chaya Rifke prompted.

Standing tall, flashing his cuffs and snapping an imaginary hat brim, he obliged. "Ladies and gentlemen, family and friends, learned Rabbi, and most important, my fellow investiture, Charlie Minkoff; my guess is Hashem knew the only way to stop Pharaoh's heart from stiffening all over again was the final plague. Just imagine. Such wailing in the land, such sorrow. Mothers weeping, fathers tearing their clothes. All the first-borns dead, their little hands and feet cold."

RABBI SPIEGELMAN

He watched, fascinated, as the congregation rang to the tuning fork of Oscar's words. Eyes reddened, trembling hands groped for pocket handkerchiefs and tissues folded beneath watch straps, throats thickened and cleared themselves, harrumphing. In the women's section, an old lady covered her face and sobbed with abandon.

"All right, Oslavsky, take a hold," Oscar advised, patting the air in front of him. "So now you feel sorry for the Egyptians," he pointed out.

CHARLIE

It was true. He felt sorry for the Egyptians. *Mothers weeping, fathers tearing their clothes.* Listening to Oscar was like watching a movie. The world flared into Technicolor, the soundtrack swelled, and before you knew it you were seeing things from the point of view of some minor character you'd never thought about. Of course, you had a choice, his grandfather would be the first to point out. No one was obliged to listen to the narrator; or if they listened, to believe; or if they believed, to act.

He remembered the story of Abraham and Isaac, the son

who couldn't refuse his father and the father who couldn't refuse his God. Funny thing, Oscar said, but after the incident on the mountain they never spoke again. Abraham and Isaac, he thought he was talking about, but no, he was referring to Abraham and Hashem. Mind you, Oscar conceded, Charlie was right on the other count too. As far as the Bible was concerned, a pall of silence hung over the entire proceedings. He understood why Isaac had nothing to say to his father. Under the circumstances, he even understood Abraham's reticence. But God? Why was Hashem silent? Was He disappointed, angry, grief-stricken?

He thought about Oscar's words for a long time, pondering God's unfathomable silence, before realizing that it was the same old problem: there was just no way to interpret silence. He'd already learned this lesson from Jules, and now it was no use asking what Nathan Dervish would have done if Hashem had ordered him to put the knife to his son. Any choice he made or declined to make was eclipsed by earlier, less remarkable choices. To stay or go. To show his face or send a birthday card. To attend his son's bar mitzvah or plead a higher calling.

Sometimes he thought about other fathers, other sons. For example, who missed their old man more? Moses, whose father had sent him down the river to save his life, or Isaac, whose father took him up the mountain to exchange his life for an obscure currency? On the one hand you've got a father who loves his son enough to give him to the Egyptians; on the other hand you've got a father who loves his son enough to give him to Hashem. And then, at close hand, Oscar, who, according to the Bible, wouldn't even make a decent *pretend* father because he'd never send his son away or try to kill him.

What kind of father wouldn't risk their kid's life to keep him alive? he wondered sadly.

Everyone he knew had a conflicting opinion when it came to fathers. Mikayla never wanted to see hers again, but Oscar saw his dear father in his dreams. Jules had dipped a chopstick in garlic sauce and drawn a cartoon of Oscar on the side of her plate (hair sticking up like Einstein), but Weeza, for once disapproving, had wiped away the caricature. Mrs. Oslavsky said Charlie shouldn't feel bad — fathers were unnecessary, they left no trace — but Dr. Jabbour reminded him that his father's problem with cell division (smile) had left an indelible fingerprint on Charlie's life. Rabbi Spiegelman said ethics dictated that a young man was more than the sum of his parents, but Ms. Kambaja said any one of the apples on the family tree could change the course of history.

He didn't know if he missed his father. He longed to meet him, yet the thought of such a meeting terrified him. The man meant nothing to him, but his polite refusal to attend the bar mitzvah had filled him with shame. The birthday cards, once a source of speculation and pleasure, a secret covenant between father and son, now struck him as nothing but mere store-bought tokens. The love story Weeza had told him embarrassed him mightily, yet how many times had he reread her emails, his imagination stirred? Not a day went by that he didn't force his mind from the images her words had conjured: Jules and the Hasid at the tattoo parlour, ink seeping into skin.

The thought that he must somehow confront this man, demand to see his tattoo, had entered his mind and could not be expunged. *Emet, Emet, Emet.* Had he too become infected with the word, he wondered, was *he* the golem? He began to have elaborate fantasies about finding his way to New York (when?), persuading his father to meet him (how?), forcing him to show his son the forbidden tattoo (why?). None of it made any sense and so could not be reasoned away.

RABBI SPIEGELMAN

"Let me tell you a story," Oscar was saying.

"This story has everything. Pity, sorrow, tragedy, laughter. A little bit of monkey and a whole lotta shine. This story can be summed up in one sentence." Oscar held up a finger. "Fellas, would you like to hear? Ladies, what about you? Rabbi, you game?"

Against his better judgement, he nodded. Oscar, who seemed determined to proceed by consensus, immediately put the vote to the congregation. Naturally the room went bananas, his hitherto staid and sleepy congregants responding with a rousing chorus of "Tell already!" and "For what are you waiting?" and the ever popular but always apt "Spit it out, Minkoff!" Only Mr. Himmelfarb demurred. From the back, his voice harangued. "One sentence, Minkoff! *One* sentence? Excuse me, who are you to *summarize?*"

"Not my sentence," Oscar explained modestly.

"*Aha!* Then whose sentence are you pinching?" he roared.

"Sentence not *pinched*, Himmelfarb. Sentence was given."

Like the showman that he was, Oscar waited patiently for the noise to die down, for the sounds of coughing, throat-clearing, murmuring, kvetching, blowing of noses, unwrapping of hard candy, and the occasional soft-carpet thump of dropped prayer books to fade away.

Fascinated in spite of himself, he remained seated. To his surprise, he too wanted to hear the sentence.

OSCAR

Eventually convinced that he had everyone's attention, he leaned forwards and declaimed: "'Thus with a mighty hand God brought them out of Egypt,' is sentence. That's it in a nutshell, folks. *B'yad hazzakah*. Mighty hand. The rest is commentary. Bulrushes, plagues, Pharaoh's heart hardening and softening, killing of the first-born, not waiting for the bread to rise, parting of the sea, land of milk with honey—details!"

He thumped his fist on the lectern to emphasize this last word, making everybody jump. This time he addressed his grandson directly. "So why the details? Good question, boychik, glad you asked." From the corner of his eye, he saw the rabbi return his head to his hands. Good. He was finally getting through to the fellow. Taking a sip of water, he continued in a more modulated tone. "In the end comes down the mighty hand of the Lord. Next thing you know the Israelites are wandering in the desert. What's changed? Like an apple, the answer dropped on my head. *Like an apple*. Where does that come from, darlink?"

Charlie mumbled something indistinct so that he was obliged to amplify. "Mr. Isaac Newton, quite right. Good man, good story. Good story? What am I saying? Out*standing* story. Mag*nifi*cent story. Story that can't be beat. *Same with Exodus*. Sure, Hashem can get the children of Israel out from Egypt. No problem. With one click of the fingers He can do it. With a mighty hand, if you remember."

From the back of the sanctuary came an exasperated hiss, the worn elastic of Himmelfarb's patience snapping. "What do you remember, Minkoff? Were you there?"

"A*ha*!" he exclaimed, delighted. "Exactly. *Finally* you're asking the right question. Congratulations, Himmelfarb, hole-in-one! *I was there.*"

RABBI SPIEGELMAN

Observing that Mr. Himmelfarb had turned a deep mahogany, and fearing for his pulmonary health, he resolved to put an end to Oscar's sermon with the exercise of his own mighty hand. But before he could rise to his feet or even take a breath, Oscar held up *his* hand like a spiritual traffic warden. The murmuring assembly fell silent.

"We were *all* there. *All of us.* You, Irina Oslavsky, and you, Esther Dershowitz. You, Nagel and Seligman and Zuckerman, and even you, Marvin Himmelfarb. We were all there. Mind you, I'm not sure about the new guy at the back, but maybe." There was a pause for scattered laughter as the congregation craned to observe Mr. Skerrit's bemused expression. Oscar's voice was commanding: "And you, Charlie?"

When the boy finally looked up, his grandfather's voice was gentle. "You most of all, Scarecrow."

CHARLIE

Oscar always teared up at the scene, he couldn't help himself. Dorothy, kissing her old pal goodbye, whispering, *I'll miss you most of all, Scarecrow.* That was Oscar in a nutshell: he showed up and looked you in the eye. *You most of all, Scarecrow.* Over the years those eyes had grown bleary, a thin glaze growing over the corneas, imbuing their gaze with a milky sheen. But whenever Oscar looked at him, at Charlie, his eyes lit up. The sight of his grandson purely delighted him. He had lived his whole life centred in the old man's kindly protective gaze.

Love welled up in him like blood to a wound, and with it love's terrible twin. Now he understood how Gellman felt when they left him, when they shut the door on his howls and ran downstairs the better to escape the sound of abandonment, of utter loneliness without hope of rescue. As recently as this morning, he'd inched the front door shut, prodding Gellman's snout with his foot as the dog hurled himself against the sliver of vanishing light. Was this what loss felt like? Being trapped in a room while everyone you loved disappeared behind a door that closed over and over again? Why had nobody told him?

I'll miss you, zeide.

Take better aim next time, darlink.

In his distress he raised his eyes. Oscar was talking to him as if no one else was present. "Without stories there is no memory. Without memory, no identity. Without identity, nothing but a tattooed number on an arm. No rabbi and no shammes. No Spiegelman and no Seligman, it goes without saying. No Nagler, no Mrs. Dershowitz, no Himmelfarb, no Oslavsky. No Jules, no Weeza, no Oscar, and worst of all, no Charlie Minkoff."

With the sickening thud of an apple dropping on an unde-fended head, he understood what his grandfather was telling him. Loneliness wasn't just when everyone left the room, shutting you up or shutting you in, leaving you alone with your stinking doglike need. Loneliness was being the only one who remembered when the room was full of people who loved you, all of them laughing, their eyes shining.

RABBI SPIEGELMAN

"What two words do I have for you today?" Oscar was asking, he assumed rhetorically. The old reprobate raised his arm in the air and yelled "Mighty!" Then he punched the other arm high, this time coming down hard on "Just!"

There he stood, like Moses receiving the Commandments, arms aloft, his prayer shawl falling away to reveal the sleeves of his charcoal-grey suit jacket, each sleeve topped by the requisite one-and-a-quarter inches of blinding-white cuff, each cuff pinned with a chunky gold cufflink.

What now? he wondered.

OSCAR

He hoped insight would come to his grandson as swiftly as it had to Archimedes as he hauled himself from his bathtub, scalded. Sometimes a person relied on falling apples and sometimes a hot bath did the trick, but sooner or later it was up to the other fellow to take that leap into almost certain misunderstanding. To jam the plug into the socket and watch the whole world light up. To learn that everything is connected. What you could discover by monkeying around with a couple of letters! An M, a J. Pure Gematria.

Slowly he lowered his arms.

"Mighty and Just," he repeated. "How He brought us out from the land of dust and ashes. Mighty and Just. How He led us into the land of milk with honey. Two words."

Cupping one hand behind his ear, with the other he gestured to the congregation. "How did He do it?"

Mighty and Just! they roared. *Mighty and Just! Mighty and Just! Mighty and Just!*

RABBI SPIEGELMAN

It had become a concert, he thought, disgusted. He rose to his feet, determined to put an end to Oscar's everlasting sermon. His own children had been delivered in less time. These sour musings were interrupted by Oscar rapping on the lectern to silence the Israelites, as if he hadn't been the one to lead them in raucous song in the first place. Reluctantly, somewhat shamefaced, he sat down again.

"I only have one word left to say," Oscar was saying without a trace of irony.

"The word is story. Hashem instructs Moses to tell the children of Israel they are living in a story. A good story, a marvellous story. Such a pity for it to end, right? Simple solution! If you don't want story to end, keep telling. To your children and their children. To your children's *children's* children. But—big *but*—don't just tell, *live*. Tell the story like it happened to you. First-person, no disguises. Like it happened to *you*."

CHARLIE

His grandfather was tiring, he could see. His left hand trembled and the skin beneath his eyes seemed bruised. Worried, he glanced across to the women's section, where Mrs. Oslavsky was sobbing in enjoyment and Jules was fiddling with a thread on her sleeve. Only Weeza looked as anxious as he felt, Weeza the rescuer. As he watched, the starch went right out of Oscar. He swayed on his feet as if about to fall — the rabbi leapt up.

Weeza was already halfway down the aisle when he, moving without volition, shoved the rabbi aside to get to his grandfather. Sturdy and calm, she helped him ease Oscar from behind the lectern. His grandfather was sweaty, his cheeks flushed, his heartbeat visible in the vein at his temple. He slumped between them, fighting for breath. Together they managed to get him into a chair, loosening his tie and unbuttoning his shirt as Seligman ran up clutching a glass of water.

"Skip, skip," Oscar said, batting him away and doing likewise with Mrs. Rosenstein's smelling salts and various wrapped candies offered by members of the congregation. By now his breathing had eased although his colour was still bad. Harvey Miller, who'd once been an obstetrician, sat down beside him and took his pulse.

Oscar stirred. "What's the verdict, Doc? Am I in labour?" It took him a while to get the words out. Harvey Miller said probably not, since he'd just delivered the longest sermon in history. Then he said that the bar mitzvah boy should be checked out by someone whose patients were slightly older than his own.

Luckily Oritsia had already called the paramedics. They

listened to Oscar's heart and checked his blood pressure, asked him to raise his arms and follow a moving finger with his eyes, then said he'd almost certainly suffered a minor stroke. Working swiftly, laughing kindly at Oscar's attempts to waylay emergency with humour — *stroke of genius*, he kept muttering — they soon had him hooked up to an IV and loaded onto a gurney.

In the brief respite caused by Oscar's reluctance to leave until the candles on the magnificent Wonder Boys cake had been blown out, he fought his way to his grandfather's side and grasped his hand. Radiating love, Oscar looked into his eyes. He leaned into the words, still struggling to speak, but managed to impart a final piece of advice on this the day of his grandson's newly minted manhood: "Tell the story as if it happened to you, Charlie," he said. "First-person narrator, the whole works."

KNOCKS

The next time Charlie saw Mikayla (metal hospital bed, plastic water jug, tub of lime Jell-O)—which would also be the last time he'd ever see her—she was freaking out because the girl in the bed beside hers, the sick girl he'd once mistaken for her, had disappeared overnight. No one would say where she'd gone. "She's dead, right?" she kept asking, but the nurses wouldn't tell her anything. Patients had the right to confidentiality, they said, as if death were this big fat non-disclosure clause.

So to take his mind off that morning's other hospital visit with Oscar (ICU, breathing tube, machines beeping away), and to take her mind off the (possibly, probably, most likely) dead girl, Charlie asked how the movie had ended. Mikayla said she didn't know. They had shot two endings. In one the parents decide to wake their children; in the other they realize the only way to keep them alive is to let them sleep forever. In the first ending they get to hug their kids one last time (soft-focus montage, liquid piano soundtrack) but then, boom! they're dead. In the second ending they're not dead but they're not alive either—what Oscar would call a perfect cat-in-a-box scenario. The second ending was philosophical, she explained,

313

but the first had dramatic tension, which was probably the way they'd go if she knew anything about focus groups.

They agreed that the first ending (hope followed by despair) was a hundred times better than the second ending (no despair but no hope either).

"Hey Charlie," Mikayla said, "maybe that's what happened to Maybe-Dead Girl over there."

At first Charlie thought she meant that the girl had woken up and died (dramatic tension), or that she would remain alive so long as she never woke up again (philosophical), or even that she'd been moved to a bed in the Schrödinger Wing, where she was in no danger of dying ever (whoa!). But Mikayla shrugged and said she didn't know what the hell had happened to her and didn't care to speculate. Maybe-Dead Girl was only a plot device, a narrative problem that would be resolved in time. They just hadn't gotten to the end of the movie yet.

"Huh," said Charlie. It was a tough call but an accurate assessment: very callous, very Mikayla. She was being discharged that day and her mom was coming to pick her up in a U-Haul. They were setting out immediately due west to Edmonton to be closer to her mom's boyfriend, who worked up on the oil patch. Mikayla was resigned to the move since it would put an entire province between her and her deadbeat dad — not to mention any lasting vestige of the recent past and its shameful burden of self-harm, blood poisoning, burning bridges, failed tattoos, and subsequent skin grafts.

Indeed, the relief of not having to return to Assiniboine High was so intense, she told him, that it had released in her a flood of creativity. She'd completed the screenplay on which she'd been working for so long (boil on the back of the neck, slow pan out, the observant dead, remember, Charlie?) and had already begun a new one, a love story between the half-human survivor of an Armageddon-type full-on catastrophe, and some sort of yet-to-be-determined large-scale industrial mega-machine, an oil derrick or a pumpjack. Maybe a crane.

"Is your screenplay about cyborgs?" Charlie asked, at a loss.

"What? No! I mean why—okay, you want the pitch?"

It seemed he did. So: "It's the end of the fucking world. Dystopia-city. Only a small group of survivors, um, survive, and they have to get to the oil fields ASAP because they need parts. See, there's no actual humans anymore, everyone's had to become part-machine. I'm working this semi-brutal aesthetic—drained palette, no dialogue, killer soundtrack. Early death metal crossed with a post-punk sensibility, sixties folk for ironic counterpoint. 'Morning Has Broken,' say, when they wake up on the first day and 'Peace Train' as they're crawling across the tar sands, picking off weaklings and canni-balizing them for parts, etc. But, surprise! When they get to Fort McMurray they find this idyllic community of sentient heavy-hauler machinery—oil rigs and cranes, hydraulic power shovels, like that, living in total harmony and working together to extract the crude, which, turns out, is this truly excellent stuff, this elixir of life because it animates machinery and trans-forms CO_2 into oxygen or whatever. So what happens when the ragged band of just-barely-human, totally vicious, and ultimately self-destructive survivors confront a higher civili-zation of advanced machinery, is the question."

Charlie opened his mouth to reply, shut it again. "Um, chaos?" he finally ventured.

Mikayla burst out laughing. "Quite right, kiddo. Chaos ensues."

She was cagey about the ending, possibly because she

hadn't gotten to the end of her own story yet. It was a work in progress, she told him. She'd figure it out as she went along.

"Knock knock," said a nurse as she came in without knocking. She said it very loudly though, and kind of snidely. She didn't relish walking in on some sort of perverse semi-nude clinch, was the implication, so they'd better zip up, but since she was already halfway across the room by then it wasn't really any sort of warning.

Naturally, this didn't stop her from repeating herself. Louder for the folks in the back: "KNOCK KNOCK?"

"Interrupting cow who?" Mikayla yelled, disrupting the nurse's attempt at intimidation and demonstrating, once again, her genius for comic timing and freestyle anarchy. Then she flipped the nurse the finger, threw Charlie her tub of lime Jell-O that he'd been eyeing, blew him a kiss, and told him to keep the faith. So long, Charlie Minkoff. Goodbye and good luck.

—

Correspondence
To: Mr. Skerrit (2C)
From: Mrs. Oslavsky (3B)

What we are to do, Skerrit, my God?

To: Mrs. Oslavsky (3B)
From: Mr. Skerrit (2C)

Irina, milyy moy, how lovely to hear from you. As always, your dulcet tones ring through in the peremptory cadence of your rhetoric. Come right in, padrooga, *no need to knock.*

Ah, but what, after all is one to do? There is nothing to do. One must simply wait for the Heritage Committee to make their decision. Contacting that august institution was a brainstorm on my part, but, like all such storms, it requires a period of cooling off, of rolling up one's brolly and waiting for the clouds to disperse. In other words, of doing nothing.

In the meantime, I would advise the cultivation of a robust constitution and a steady nerve. Calisthenics before breakfast and a steep decrease in the number of cups of that bitter, over-caffeinated, samovar-tinkered beverage of which you are so fond.

Always yours,

Joseph

To: Mr. Skerrit (2C)
From: Mrs. Oslavsky (3B)

1) *Who is this one? If you then why not say me, I am one, I, Mr. Skerrit, 2C, who has in his life one good idea.*
2) *Okay, great idea.*
3) *What we are to do, Skerrit?*
4) *But not about Heritage Committee, foolish one.*
5) *About poor Oscar. That one.*

To: Mrs. Oslavsky (3B)
From: Mr. Skerrit (2C)

Ah, Irina, as always you bring me back to myself. Return me to my best instincts. What are we to do indeed?

One is inclined—excuse me—I am inclined to say all will be well. Trust in science, in faith, in guardian angels and knocking-on-wood and the competency of the medical profession to prolong life well beyond the point at which it is either comfortable or convenient to do so. But of course I shall do no such thing.

Instead I shall ask if you would consider meeting me one fine day on the bench that overlooks the river on Water Street. I find I am eager to get out and about and would enjoy a chance to practise my Rosetta Stone conversational Russian. What say you, dear lady?

Yours, as ever,

Joseph

To: Mr. Skerrit (2C)
From: Mrs. Oslavsky (3B)

Answer is perhaps yes but most no. No to terrible shrug of the shoulders for poor Oscar. No to mangling of dear tongue of Mother Russia, no to roll up umbrella and do nothing. No to disrespect for tea, no to practise Rosetta (what is?), no to call me by my first name (I did not say), no to all the big (very big, huge) words you like use.

Only one perhaps yes (small, tiny). Yes, I will meet you on the bench by Water Street. Two o'clock tomorrow. Fine or not fine, doesn't matter. Wear suit please. Two sharp, Skerrit. Or I will come knock on your door.

IO (Mrs.)

STAR

Name: "Star"

Project Team: Charlie Minkoff, young and old

Material: Email exchanges, medical notes and diagrams, interviews, biographies, Weeza's memory of her mother, Ms. K's story about her father, *Ethics of the Fathers*, the Wonder Wall, Genesis, Exodus, correspondence between Mrs. Oslavsky and Mr. Skerrit, letters from Oscar and Mrs. Dershowitz, study sessions with Rabbi Spiegelman, weather and weather-related catastrophes, *Marvellous Beasts* (an Anthology of Animal Curiosities), *Sleepwalkers* (a Kick-the-Can Production), *Long Haul Layover* (a road romp), "Crude Love" (a screenplay), "Over the Rainbow" (original ballad by Arlen and Harburg), the Intersex Forum Billboard, a thought experiment, the legend of the golem, theory of coin flips, *The Wizard of Oz*, *The Ten Commandments*, homework assignments, make-up assignments, River Walk Design Competition brochure, an artist's statement, real and recorded voices, Chaya Rifke's advice, stories, luck, divine laughter, a history of the GNC Building, journal article in *Flip Book*, "Hang in there, Charlie" (computer file), truth, death, more than one Thunderbolt, #bottledeposit, a sermon, photo of Jules and photo of Mikayla (both naked), winter, silence, a ballpoint pen, a steno pad, memory, and time.

Acknowledgements

The correspondence between Mrs. Oslavsky and Mr. Skerrit was contributed by Mr. Skerrit. Mrs. Dershowitz was kind enough to send the letters Oscar had written her. All other communications were obtained by the writer, at times in good faith, at other times merely in faith. Errors in fact, memory, and judgement, of which there are many, are his alone. The writer would like to thank Oritsia Hulchuk for the Wonder Boys cake and Oscar Wolf Minkoff for the tailored waistcoat. Both were magnificent.

Artist's Statement

If not now, when? Rabbi Hillel, that famously impatient sage, is supposed to have asked. As a boy, my grandfather made me feel the imperative in that phrase, the beating heart like an iron gong in the blood going *now, now, now.* Listen and you will hear the rabbi stamp his foot, he told me. There, where the comma is. Between *now* and *when.*

I first wrote what you are about to read when I was thirteen years old, in a white-hot frenzy of *if not now?* The world was about to change — suddenly and unexpectedly; there was nothing to compare it to. We were at the beginning of the first of the great pandemics. The ripples had begun, but who could predict the full catastrophe, the violent collision of past and future? This was the first time my generation felt ourselves to be part of history. We were like the Israelites, awoken on that terrible morning, dragged from our beds, and told to come.

Bo! Of course, we were given the opposite instruction: we were told to remain where we were, to stay home, to shelter in place. There would be no promised land, and no greater heroism than merely staying safe.

All this came later. Days later, but this was a time when a day lasted a week, a week a month, a month forever. March 2020 was the forever month. The months that followed would have their own heft, their own special density and inertia, but March was the first month, and we would take our orders from March.

At the time I was filling my notebook we did not know what life would become, how many would sicken and die, how the survivors would have to live with the weight of their knowledge, the knowledge that we were expendable, that those we loved were expendable, that governments valued profit over human life, and worst of all, that no overarching moral order prevailed in the universe. We did not yet know that the old stories were done, that we would have to make up new stories and find ever more creative ways to tell them. Predictably, this is not what was motivating me, thirteen-year-old Charlie Minkoff, who was barely aware of the state of the world when I set out on my journey.

Years later I came across the notebook shoved in a shoebox full of old birthday cards. We were enduring another quarantine year, every bit as horrifying as the first two had been. Having nothing to do, I reread the faded writing of that long-ago boy and found myself filled with purpose. I saw that what I'd written in the notebook (a cheap steno pad) was a sequence of events and their consequences, nothing more. Why not rewrite them, I thought, why not tell the story? And damned if I didn't hear it: a stifled expression of impatience followed by a faintly whispered question. *If not, if not, if not?*

I like to think that in the intervening years I've come to understand the difference between truth and story, between truth and interpretation, between truth and dare, although it's possible that what my beloved grandfather heard as a stamp of the foot was only a drum of the fingers, an indrawn breath, a sigh. What follows is the revised version of that earlier testimony, rewritten by an older version of Charlie Minkoff, who, in order to navigate the treacherous river that flows between *now* and *when,* had to hop aboard his younger self in the optimistic hope that somehow they'd both make it to the other side.

MARCH 2020

When I woke, the truck was pulled up in a lay-by and Weeza was holding a downward dog on the mat she'd unrolled on the side of the highway. Yoga is how she keeps herself fit on the road, the road being the only place she could still do it. She had to stop going to yoga classes at the Y because women were always falling in love with her. It's a family curse, she says. I would flipping love to be cursed like that, but you can't choose your family curse is one thing I know by now.

Gellman woke up as I watched Weeza swing into a back-arching cobra then tilt her ass in the air and plant. He yawned in my face and farted, filling the snug with the exhaust fumes of his putrid canine butt and even more putrid canine breath. "Aren't you a disgusting little stink-sack?" I whispered, careful to sound admiring so he wouldn't freak out. For good measure I scratched the sweet spot behind his ears. He rolled his eyes in ecstasy, a sucker for a friendly voice, and let out yips of pleasure and excitement. He was unaware that we were stowaways. We'd spent the journey beneath an ancient tartan blanket whose familiar odour of motor oil reminded me of another night Gellman and I had huddled together, wind shrieking and snow falling, my world about to change.

I hadn't wanted to schlep the dumb animal along on my great adventure, but what could I do? I didn't know how long I'd be gone, and Jules would never remember to feed him or put out fresh water. By the time I came back, *if* I came back, he'd be dead, dried up and shrunken so small she could have stuffed him in a bottle. On the other hand, if we both left home she might not notice we were gone. She was absorbed in her stupid quinzhee hut (the idea of it, since the reality had long since reconstituted itself into the puddle at the end of winter), the articles and write-ups, the bottle deposits still pouring in. Turns out people had really creative ideas about what could be put in a bottle. She was currently in negotiations with the Bank of Canada about "the status of currency when used in an artwork" and with the office of Cleaning and Sanitation Procedures about just what exactly constituted human waste.

These were her favourite kinds of negotiations, ones she couldn't win, which was one of the reasons she wasn't in a noticing mood. The disappearance of her son and his dog was just one more example of a phenomenon I like to call Where the Hell Did Squashy Green Ball Go? I mean, the woman didn't even know that school had been cancelled. She probably thought I was still going to class every day and that Gellman had taken to walking himself because that was the sort of enterprising fellow he was.

Nah. Truth is she didn't remember we were there. We'd rolled out of sight beneath the sofa and fallen off the edge of the world.

On the other *other* hand, it had only been ten hours. So maybe.

I couldn't help worrying about her, though. People were freaking out and stores were running out of essentials. I'd stocked the fridge before we left and bought a container of black olives from the Greek Market, careful to leave it on the kitchen counter so as not to alert Jules to the absence of her insensitive-to-olives son.

Weeza was still bent in half with her ass in the air, which was getting her a lot of attention from passing traffic. The sight of a woman doing yoga on the shoulder of the road brought out the opinionated side of motorists. Opinion seemed to be divided as to whether she was a *bitch* or a *total fucking bitch*, but she bagged an air horn salute from a passing trucker and none of the flying empty beer cans or takeaway containers scored a direct hit. I was grateful for the open window because we needed the air circulation, but I was scared she'd hear Gellman whimpering the way he does when he needs to pee. I needed to pee too; it was all I could think about. This wasn't what I'd anticipated when Oscar told me to find my story. So far my story was ten hours of sticky sleep in a moving truck, waking up beside a reeking dog, and praying we wouldn't wet ourselves.

I'll be honest, it didn't look good. Gellman kept trying to raise his leg to pee in a corner of the snug. I grabbed his hind legs, hoping it would bamboozle the poor fellow. "Hold on, big guy," I whispered. He gave me a hurt look, the skin above his sad, doggy eyes wrinkling into a dozen wavy ridges, ears flipping in confusion, one up, one down.

"I know, I know," I said. "Soon as she comes out of her downward dog she'll go get supper." At the word dog, Gellman looked confused. Was I calling him a bad one or telling him to stay down? Was I talking about some other dog we both knew or was I confirming what he already knew, what he'd always known: that he was trapped in this four-legged, itchy, foul-smelling, lousy Halloween costume of an existence, that life would consequently be all trick and no treat? I felt bad for him. I knew how it felt.

By this time the feeling of needing to pee was an arrow starting in my mind and ending in my bladder. It was all I could think about. I hung on to Gellman's hind legs with one hand and with the other grabbed at myself. He swivelled his great shaggy head, gazing at me over his haunches. *So what's the plan, Charlie?*

I shrugged. The plan was what it had always been: a triumph of split-second timing, meticulous organization, and a whole lot of luck. Mainly luck, though. We would stow away in the snug, hiding out until Toronto, where we'd break cover, light out for the border, catch a Greyhound to New York, and make our way via subway to Crown Heights, Brooklyn, and the father known as Nathan Dervish.

That's it? Gellman looked appalled. *That's all you got, bro?*

"What, you wouldn't have come if you'd known?" I asked.

What about food, water, cash? What about peeing when you need to pee? What about avoiding contagion and sheltering in place? What about border security, what about passports, animal quarantines, body-cavity searches? What about Weeza?

"Don't worry," I told him. "We'll figure it out as we go."

* * * * *

Don't you love asterisks? They're stars, indicating that time has passed and day is night and stuff has happened that might be too boring to relate. Don't worry, though, the narrator will catch you up if you have faith and finish the damn book. There was this one book, Oscar told me, where the narrator committed a murder during the asterisks that *he himself put there.* "Such chutzpah," he said, shaking his head in admiration. "Comes out after the stars, acting like nothing happened. Whistling, even!"

Oscar pointed out that asterisks were a post-biblical invention that he particularly appreciated, having had occasion to wish that time would pass more swiftly when he hit the battles and the begats, the abominations and the thousand-and-one rules about what constitutes an unblemished peace-offering and what is in no way acceptable to the Lord.

"Stars mean et cetera," he told me.

I was a kid and inclined to be distracted, and the book we were reading made an occasion of those stars, printing them in red ink in the middle of a story about a river and how to get across if you were a scorpion who turned out to be a murderer.

"Et cetera, et cetera, et cetera, et cetera, et cetera," Oscar said, tapping his finger on each star in turn. "Means cut to the chase. Means don't get hung up on details."

Don't worry, I haven't killed anyone. It's evening now: moon up, stars out. The neon sign reading Pulley's 24-Hour Truck Stop and Weigh Station is buzzing in the distance. All the etceteras are in place, in other words.

What happened before the stars came out was that after a long time hanging upside down, Weeza inched herself upright in a final salute to the sun. Then she rolled up her mat, flung it through the cab window, and swaggered off towards Pulley's 24-Hour Diner. Gellman and I jumped out of the rig, darted across the highway, and dived into the ravine on the other side, both of us dribbling squirts of pee before we made it to the cover of the ditch. Gellman only had to lift his leg, but I had to crouch in the dirty snow with the beer cans and cigarette butts. At times like this I thought about the operation that Dr. Jabbour said was possible but not advisable. *What does it matter in what position you urinate, Charles? Sit or stand, as long as there's a good flow and a felicitous outcome. Everything else is details.*

After about five minutes of steady drumming (good flow) I was finished, my bladder reduced to a deflated balloon (felicitous outcome), the snow where I'd been squatting transformed into a soggy yellow streak of Charlie Was Here (details). Suddenly all business, Gellman bustled over to investigate, letting out yips either of surprise or disgust, a mystery that wasn't solved by his decision to lap at the soggy puddle I'd made. After a moment, he threw back his big, shaggy head and howled.

"What did you expect?" I asked, irritated by his expressive regret. But, as always when the world failed to conform to his hopefulness, Gellman was inconsolable. The fur on his neck rippled in surges and he buried his head between his paws and shook so violently I thought the highway above us was shaking in response. But it was only the eighteen-wheel rumble of a passing semi-trailer, reminding me where we were. Unfortunately, this was nowhere near where we should have been because when I peered out of the ditch I saw Weeza emerging from Pulley's, shaking her hands dry as she hurried towards the rig.

* * * * *

Oscar always said luck is the difference between what you need and how you deal with the world's misunderstanding of that requirement. I never knew what he meant until I found myself crouching in the waterlogged, piss-soaked ditch, holding on to Gellman with one hand and my pants with the other, watching Weeza climb into the truck and turn on the engine before edging into the stream of vehicles heading east. It took about two minutes to watch the last trace of her tail lights disappear, blinking like the red consoles on the Starship *Enterprise*, good for nothing except a slow fade-out.

"There goes our ride," I told Gellman, in case he'd missed the point.

He sighed and buried his head, aware that he was in the doghouse again.

"That's right," I told him. "Think about what you've done."

With his snout wedged between his forepaws, he lifted his eyes, the effort of raising his eyebrows making him look unexpectedly sardonic. *Really?* he seemed to be saying. *This is my fault? I'm the one who wants to find my father? I'm the one who wants to be the hero of my life? I'm the first-person narrator who wants to write the end of the story? Huh. Could have fooled me, Charlie.*

* * * * *

The real stars were in the real sky by the time we figured out what to do. By *we* I mean *me*; Gellman's no good in the trenches. If it were up to him we'd have thrown ourselves on the mercy of the first person we encountered. *Help us before we die of starvation and loneliness! Save our stupid-ass souls!* That kind of thing.

Nope, I told him, no way. First thing they'd do is send for

the cops. That'd be the end of the story. Nice try, Charlie, good luck with the quest narrative. Next time you stow away make sure to keep your wallet in your pocket when you jump into the ditch to take a piss. That was the kicker, you see. My wallet with the money Jules had given me was inside the truck that had been driving away at a hundred kilometres per hour for the last eleven minutes and forty-two seconds. That's the kind of math that makes no sense until it's happening to you. Luckily I still had my phone in my pocket, along with a miniature box of treats for Gellman and a dollar fifty-five in change. But a dollar fifty-five buys you nothing if you have nowhere to spend it, and I couldn't get a signal for the phone. All it could do was indicate how much time had elapsed since we watched the rig chugging off into the future without us. Mathematically speaking, we were in deep shit. I offered Gellman a bone-shaped dog biscuit, the only kind he'll eat, but he panicked, snatched the box, and devoured them all. Then he ate the box.

"Think positive, Charlie. Think about what you *have*," is what Oscar would say. But the answer wasn't encouraging. At 8:06 in the evening, standing in a ditch on the side of the road out of Thunder Bay—the *wrong* side of the road—all Charlie Minkoff, our hero, had were the clothes he was wear-ing: jeans, T-shirt, sneakers, along with the beautiful waistcoat he'd buttoned himself into at the last minute. For luck. Plus a leash at the end of which the most disgusting dog in the world was trying to cough up the cardboard box he'd just devoured, hanging his head in shame and lapping up snow and occasionally gagging dramatically.

On the other side of the luck scale, I now realized, was my wallet and winter parka, with Weeza's spare key in the pocket, along with a plastic bag filled with supplies: three cans of Pedigree Ground Dinner, a can opener, Squashy Green Ball, a packet of peanut butter and chocolate syrup sandwiches, and a notebook and pen. These last were to record my heroic adventures in search of my father, mostly to show Oscar but also because Ms. Kambaja said I still owed her a family crest, and I had some vague idea that the notes I intended to take could substitute for the missing family crest that I could neither imagine (at present) or draw (ever).

For a moment I stood there, lost in wonder at my fore-thought, until I remembered that all these items were concealed beneath the blanket in Weeza's snug, which snug was by now many algebraic miles from where we were stand-ing in the ditch on the (wrong) side of the highway, cold, hungry, and whooshing with panic. I told Gellman to chill while I climbed the ravine and popped my head up. Pulley's Truck Stop was where we'd left it, a squat concrete building framed by sodium-arc street lights, dimly shining now that afternoon had clicked over into evening as we were noodling in the ditch, emptying our bladders and piddling away our futures. The only thing I could think to do was cross the road, a calculation even a chicken could make but one that sent Gellman into such a spiral of terror (eighteen-wheelers floom-ing past, airstreams blowing grit, panicky whiffs of diesel) that I had to pick him up and carry him across the double-lane highway while he whimpered into my chest, drooling.

A string of saliva swayed like a suspension bridge between us before detaching from his slathering jaw and soaking into my waistcoat. A stain in the shape of an asterisk formed, one more footnote to a story I hadn't yet written. Suddenly angry, I had to drop Gellman and stuff my hands into my pockets so I wouldn't hit him. It was a terrible feeling. I'd never wanted to hit anyone before, and the poor dog hadn't even chosen to come along. Not wanting to be left alone isn't the same as volunteering to be dragged along on someone else's heroic quest, especially when its purpose is a mystery and the transportation is iffy.

We'd hidden in the dark, smelly garbage run behind Weeza's apartment for hours before she arrived with the rig fully loaded for a household move to Toronto, a corporate gig she'd been talking about for weeks and wasn't going to put off for some lousy virus, no matter how famous.

Knowing her, I reckoned she thought she'd do one last run before whatever happened next (highway closures, martial law, full-out zombie wars). There would always be one last run in Weeza's estimation. She counted herself an essential service, the custodian of other people's moral worth, their dearest summing-up of themselves: their *stuff*. Besides, she loved her work. The money was good, and she got to pack and load everything, then do the whole thing in reverse order (unpack, unload) at the other end. She worked with local crews, of course, but she was the one who jigsawed thousands of household items into tiers two feet deep that hung in dozens of neat rows in the moving van. Like creating an art installation, she'd tease Jules. Taking the most three-dimensional thing there is—a house!—and packing it flat.

I'd been studying Google Maps and comments on Tripadvisor for weeks, but the best plan I could come up with was to "stay open to possibility" as some dude on Reddit recommended. He wasn't talking about the cheapest way to get to New York if you were a cash-strapped kid and his neurotic dog, but it was the only advice that gave me a fighting chance. We were still a week away from border closures, so the thought of not getting to where I was headed or being turned back never entered my mind. Basically, I figured that as soon as we hit the Don Valley Parkway into Toronto we'd bail and strike out for the nearest Greyhound station, where we'd hustle cheap tickets to New York City. I hadn't worked out the kinks yet (I had to convince folks I was over eighteen, that for some reason I didn't require a passport, and that Gellman was a service animal), but that's where possibility came in, along with my staying open to it.

Waiting for Weeza in the garbage run with Gellman, I worried briefly that she'd driven to the depot, ready for a quick getaway in the morning. I comforted myself with the thought that, unlike those truckers who spend more nights in their cabs than in their crummy apartments, Weeza hates sleeping in the rig. She's not into the whole urban cowboy ethos, the cheap rentals and heavy metal and CB-radio lingo, the road-wrangler myth of not owning a thing and not giving a damn. She says myth just weighs you down. Like most of what she packs it's not worth the price of the box.

When she came eventually, Gellman was so exhausted he didn't even lift his head to bark but just sighed heavily. From the shelter of the garbage run we watched her wrangle the moving truck into a parking space that looked too small to accommodate it. Weeza jumped out and ran up the stairs of her apartment building, not even glancing back. Two in the morning, so cold I could feel my bones clenched in their sockets, my teeth ringing with the tension of their chattering. It was snowing lightly, small kernels of dry-as-popcorn snow settling on Gellman's rough coat and in my hair.

"Ready, big fella?" I asked him.

* * * * *

"Ready, big fella?" I asked when I'd finally calmed down.

I forced myself to unball my hands and unclench my shoulders. The waistcoat was probably ruined; not only was there a gigantic drool stain across the front, but my exertions with Gellman had made sweaty half moons rise in my armpits. I could smell myself now, the flop-sweat of fear hormones rising from the damp cloth. Perhaps I could stop off at a dry cleaners when I hit the Big Apple, get myself spruced up before I set off to find my father. New York was the real-life equivalent of the Emerald City, I figured, a magical place of requirement. You could get whatever you needed provided you had a good heart, a clear head, the courage to use them, and a faithful dog. So far all I had was the dog but, once again, I was open to possibility.

An eighteen-wheeler sped past, sucking the air out of our lungs so efficiently that we could neither inhale nor exhale, our collective fur and hair and thoughts flying up over our heads. Grit blew into our eyes and Gellman's ears streamed out behind him as if he were on the trail of the Red Baron. When the dust settled, I could see again, mainly the folly of my ways because I was as far from that magical dry cleaners as I'd ever been. The smell of fried food wafted from Pulley's, making water flood into my mouth and my stomach gurgle. From the road, I noticed the fluorescent buzz of a soft-drink dispenser beside the service station. I pulled Gellman into the shadows, and we made our way across slushy asphalt to the vending area, where he cowered before the humming machine as if it were an ancient road god. I stuffed my dollar fifty-five into the coin slot and gazed into the display window, unable to choose. In the end I lost my head and pressed H, E, L, P on the keypad over and over. After an interval of clanks and hollow bumps deep within the machine, a can detached, hung poised, tumbled down.

Plink. The tinkle of the nickel in the coin-return slot was the saddest sound I'd ever heard. It made me want to hurl myself into a snowbank, pull Gellman over my head, and die. Gellman, seeming to anticipate this impulse, skittered away on fear-stiffened legs. By the time I grabbed him and convinced him not to succumb to his despair, I'd forgotten my own.

I also spied a storeroom off the rest area, its door ajar. Peering in, I saw silhouette outlines of moving supplies piled up against the wall, an assortment of folded pads and burlaps, dollies and cartons, straps, tarps, and winches.

It wasn't stealing, I told Oscar in my head. It was acknowledging what the Lord had provided.

* * * * *

We'd been walking along the shoulder of the highway for hours.

I was shaking with cold. My muscles ached from clenching against the wind that blew through the trees towards us. That's all there was on either side: trees, lumpy fields, rocky outcrops all covered with trees, trees, more trees, windbreaks of shivering trees. Evergreens laced with snow, pine needles glinting in the moonlight, ice crystals hanging in the air. Silent wings unfolding overhead followed by the death cry of some small creature being blooded in the dark. Thick sprinklings of stars in the sky, so many and so bright that they looked like the stars you see on the planetarium dome when they turn down the lights, bring out the laser pointer, and try to make you believe that a bunch of random stars are shapes just waiting for you to recognize them: Orion's belt and the Southern Cross, an archer, a goat, some fish. You can make a shape out of anything if you have enough stars, a magical pointer, and a bunch of kids with sore necks.

There were no street lights on this stretch of road, but the moon was almost full. In another night or two it would be complete, a weird reflective disc in the sky. I was learning that anything looks strange if you stare at it long enough: the moon, trees, even words. (I'm having trouble with the word "weird" right now. It just *looks* wrong.)

Writing is hard, I'm finding. You start with an idea and three more grow off the same stalk. I was trying to express how cold it was, the cold like an object rather than a feeling. As if a gigantic optometrist's lens had clicked across the landscape making everything look hyper-real and over-focused, making every detail stand out: ice crystals in snow, the shadow of ice crystals in snow, the crisp outline of the word "shadow" in blue ink on a white page. I was going to say my breath billowed loose as if my soul was trying to tug free, that when I inhaled, cold air entered every tiny air sac in my lungs, when what I wanted to say was that two hours in I'd warmed up considerably. So much so that I could feel a light sweat on my upper lip, a trickle of moisture between my shoulder blades.

It was partly the heavy-duty mover's overalls I'd taken from the storage room, worn over my clothes with the ankle and wrist cuffs rolled. And it was partly the effort of moving through the frozen landscape, my heart racing every time a truck roared past. They were always coming up behind me, headlights blazing. I felt like a goldfish in a glass bowl, lit up and pulsing with light. I was certain one of these trucks would screech to a halt beside me, and the feeling of abandonment when they passed by was worse than the terror of discovery. But mostly it was the exertion of pushing Gellman on the mover's dolly, inching over divots and up gradients, hauling hard on the way down, my forearms burning with effort, shoulders straining in their sockets.

It was the only way to proceed. Gellman had lost heart, slumping into the dirty grey sludge bordering the rest stop, burying his muzzle between his paws, and playing dead with more conviction than he'd ever brought to the role before, method actor that he was and all-round drama queen. I waited for him to stir so I could catch his eye when he shot me a goofy look as if to say, convinced yet? But Gellman stayed pat, nose buried in paws and eyes shut tight. I couldn't just leave him there, could I? So I darted into the storeroom, grabbed a storage container, a burlap sack, a dolly, and put them together—burlap into box, box onto dolly—then tried to cajole the dog to climb aboard. In the end I had to lift him up and dump him, floppy and whimpering, into the box. Immediately, he burrowed under the burlap, trying to disappear from the world. I couldn't blame him. Like the Cowardly Lion, he had been born without conviction, and I could already tell we weren't in the kind of movie with a ruby-slipper ending.

What kind of movie are you in, Charlie? Oscar would have asked. I had to smile. He was always trying to get me to think like a hero, like a narrator.

First-person, zeide, I whispered. *Wonder Boy all the way.*

* * * * *

Da-dum, da-dum, da-dum. The zebras were back, galloping alongside the horses, keeping pace with my heart. If I were into the whole family crest thing I'd draw a zebra in the first quadrant, rampant on a magenta shield. In the second, this same zebra would be sidling up to a horse that was grazing and minding its own business. The next few quadrants would feature a conversation, zebra challenging horse to a race.

"Don't be a jerk," says horse. "You're faster than me."

"No way!" says zebra, not bothering to go into detail, keeping up the pressure.

"Fine," says horse eventually, pretty worn down by now.

You know the story. Quadrants eight to ten show zebra kicking horse to death, stomping on his broken body, succumbing to exhaustion and dying. Just before he dies (quadrant eleven), horse, with his last breath, croaks, "you promised you wouldn't kick me to death and stomp on my broken body!" And his galloping pal replies (quadrant twelve), "yeah, mate, but I'm a zebra."

Ms. K would flip out and say a quadrant, by definition, can't have twelve sections, Mr. Minkoff; and Mikayla would say sounds more like a comic book than a family crest, Three-Piece; and Oscar would say magnificent comic book, darlink; and Dr. Jabbour would say zebras and horses both have the potential to lead happy and useful lives, Charles. And Jules? Jules would say nothing because silence was an artistic choice, a free pass. Then she'd go right ahead and use my comic book in one of her installations.

I was still walking down the shoulder of the highway, pushing the dog in the box and listening to all the voices in my head except, of course, for Jules's. Don't worry, I wasn't going mad. I knew they weren't real. The only real voice was Jules's not-voice. For years I'd thought she was listening, giving me her full attention because she wasn't always thinking of the next thing to say. She was like God, a witness, a listener. Then I had a crisis of faith and realized she hadn't been listening at all. Like God, she had more important things to do. You couldn't blame either of them; they were both creative types. So it was a shock to learn she'd been eavesdropping all along, one ear pressed against the bathroom door.

Gellman hadn't moved for hours; I didn't even know if he was alive. So long as I kept going he couldn't be dead, I comforted myself. I was so tired I was hearing things (hoof-beats, imaginary voices), so tired I wanted to curl up on the side of the road and sleep. I knew about the dangers of dozing off in the snow, though, so I kept plodding, moving one foot in front of the other like a sleepwalker, like one of the kids in Mickie's movie, the ones whose parents were trying to save their lives by not waking them up. Every now and then I'd look at my phone to check the time — 3:02, 3:07, 3:10, 3:25, 3:26 — but I stopped because my eyes were burning. It was as if I'd been staring into the sun, and time was burning my retinas to ash.

There was no sun, though. Only a moon, a moon so far away and high above us it was like a coin flipping in the sky. *Heads you win, tails I lose.*

* * * * *

My phone was down to 13 percent when the eighteen-wheeler stopped.

It was 5:03 in the morning, grey light, fog drifting between trees, thin skin of ice hardening on the ditches. Freight trucks and rigs had been passing us throughout the night. At first I'd dive into the ravine, dragging the dolly with me, but the ditches were slushy and deep, and the effort of wrangling the contraption with its dead weight of wet dog, soggy cardboard box, and flapping burlap rapidly grew impossible.

I soon stopped fleeing for cover when the trucks passed. Instead I'd crouch down behind the dolly, arms wrapped around the box as I tried to prevent us being sucked into the slipstream of whatever monster vehicle had roared past, the wake of its momentum buffeting us like the loose debris on the side of the road. It was terrifying: hair whipping around, breath vacuumed from lungs, headlights rising out of the darkness with such intensity that even when they passed, the roar of articulated metal dopplering away, I could see nothing but flashing lights. No one stopped or indicated either with blast of horn or courtesy wave that they noticed us. Although I didn't want to attract attention, although I shuddered with fear whenever the concrete beneath my feet began to sing with the anticipation of approaching wheels, I felt sad every time a truck barrelled past. Were we invisible? Had we, sometime in that interminable night, simply disappeared from the world?

So when an eighteen-wheeler, with a shattering screech of air brakes and a grinding mesh of gears, shuddered to the shoulder ahead of us, I was shocked. Surely the driver hadn't seen me labouring over the dolly that had become increasingly difficult to manoeuvre, its wheels jammed with gritty slush, the weight of dog compounding with every hour. Clearly he had, though. He tooted his horn, and when I (huffy, sweaty, hopeful) drew level with his rig— "Van Fleet Vending Services" emblazoned on its side—he cracked the window, letting fly such a stream of abuse that I was grateful Gellman was either dead or asleep, in neither case being in a condition to respond.

The trucker cursed for what felt like an hour but was probably only a few minutes, blowing in his own headwind. His point being that I was a no-account fellow who didn't know diddly from squat, although the words he used were considerably harsher. By the time he paused for breath, the air was so full of son-of-a-* * * * *-this and mother-* * * *-ing-that that if I were to transcribe what he'd said, write it down on this page, there'd be so many stars it would look like a thousand asterisks lighting up the dawn sky.

For some reason I told him my name.

"What the Starring-Star you got in that Mother-Starring stolen dolly of yours, *Charlie*?"

He sounded so sarcastic that I protested. "It's my real name," I said.

"No kidding," he yelled. "By name and by nature, you God-Starring, Mother-Starring, great big Star-Starring, Son-of-a-Starring Star piece of *Star*!"

Gellman woke up and shoved his head out of the burlap, took note of his surroundings (roaring man, monster truck sweating diesel, cold grey dawn), threw back his head, and howled. The trucker looked startled, probably because Gellman is such an ugly Mother-Starring, Son-of-a-Starring *Star*, but also because he'd obviously been expecting a haul of stolen vending-machine supplies—a jumbo box of Twinkies, a crate of cherry-flavoured Dr. Peppers—and whatever you could say about Gellman, he wasn't anybody's idea of what you'd swipe if you had the choice.

With a vicious jab of his horn, the trucker angled into

the highway, his airstream blowing clouds of dirt. But when the red flare of his wavering tail lights blinked once before disappearing, such a sense of desolation claimed me that I wanted to fling myself down on the side of the road and die of heartbreak. I'd never felt so lost, so abandoned. Nobody in the whole world knew where I was except for the trucker, and he didn't know who I was, or, I was reliably certain, care. The whole who-where axis was off; those who knew *who* I was didn't know *where* I'd got to, and the one witness to my lostness didn't give a Star-fucking damn who I was.

Oscar was the only one I'd told about my plan. He was in a coma, hooked up to a bank of machinery with a breathing tube in his mouth, but I had held his hand and imagined, with all the hopefulness I could summon, the reciprocal pressure of his fingers against my palm. Then I whispered in his ear that I was going to New York to find my father. Yup, I've got his address, I reassured him, patting my pocket. I thought I saw his eyelids flutter, thought I felt his hand grasp mine although he remained silent.

It didn't matter. I knew what he wanted to say.

"First-person, zeide. The whole works," I promised.

Keep in touch, darlink.

I told him I'd write down my adventures and read them to him when I returned. The only sounds in the room were the gurgle and whoosh of machinery amplifying the inner workings of his body, the drip of IV fluids, and a heart monitor's intermittent beeping. His breathing tube slipped, sucking air. A nurse poked her head around the door and gestured at me to leave. That had been a day ago.

So much had happened since I'd kissed his forehead. *Bye, zeide, I'll miss you.*

Aim better next time, darlink.

I was also going to write my adventures for Ms. Kambaja. She'd refused to assign me a grade for the Ancestry Studies course until I turned in my family crest. "Four symbols, Charlie," she said when I told her what a lousy artist I was. "Four symbols to represent your family. How difficult is that?"

I had lots of symbols, none I wanted to share. For Jules: a quinzhee made of bottles, a neon cocktail glass swizzled with olives, a mouth without a tongue. For Weeza: the rig, an order of celebration noodles, a flare of red hair. For Oscar: a burning village, a battered Chumash, a pocket of Hershey's Kisses. Even Gellman had Squashy Green Ball and a bone-shaped dog biscuit. But the trouble was that nobody's symbols related to anyone else's. We were a family of separate stories, and until I found a way of telling *this* story — which I suspected was about our collective inability to inhabit the same story — until I joined the dots with my magical pointer, there'd be no family crest. I'd developed a sneaky respect for Ms. Kambaja, tireless in her pursuit of what she called my "God-given potential." I didn't believe in God anymore, let alone my potential, but you had to respect a teacher who wouldn't close the book on a kid, assign a gentleman's C and call it a day.

My phone was dead. I checked it reflexively, but all I saw was my face reflected in its shiny surface. Another useless mirror. With or without the means to precisely track it, however, time had passed since the trucker flipped us the bird and hightailed it into the future. For one thing, the sun had hoisted itself above the horizon and was managing to hang in there, wobbly and weak but *up* at least, a defining characteristic of being a sun. "Morning Has Broken" was playing on a loop in my head as, on either side of the highway, snow-covered fields shivered awake, small creatures rustling in the undergrowth. Far above, a hawk riding the high thermals twisted in the wind.

I was stumbling along, pushing the dolly with its boxful of dog. Every now and then Gellman poked his head up and looked tense, like a canary being hauled through the mines. Evidently, he'd breathed in so much emotional carbon monoxide he was on the point of death. He gazed at me, letting me know that he was hungry and thirsty, that this had never been *his* idea, that I was a lousy caregiver, a poor excuse for a hero, an all-round loser. Traffic was rising to a slow boil: freight-haulers and rigs passed us, along with logging trucks and pickups and the occasional car driven by an early riser on the way to whichever town came next. Nobody stopped or turned their head as they roared past, knocking brumes of grit-laden dust in my face. Overnight, drivers had grown surly and skittish. Locked in their private bubbles, they stared grimly ahead. I was invisible. Daylight had turned me into a ghost, a ghastly cyborg—half boy, half cumbersome dog-box on wheels.

I was so tired I had started hallucinating, convinced I was really a ghost and that if I stepped off the shoulder into the path of an oncoming truck the vehicle would pass right through me without damage. I grew so obsessed with this idea that I promised myself I'd put it to the test the moment I was close enough to read a certain billboard that loomed in the distance, its image obscured by the low-hanging sun. In a landscape devoid of language I could understand (no signs on buildings or restaurants, no buildings, no restaurants, no traffic lights or street signs or graffiti) I was convinced the billboard held a message. Like the voice of Oz behind the curtain or God speaking to Moses in the wilderness, it offered signs and wonders, advice, direction, and sagacity. At the very least a helpful weather report: *Stay alert for columns of cloud and fire! Watch out for flying monkeys!* Something to guide my journey.

But the closer I dragged myself forwards, the farther the billboard receded into the thin grey seam between white fields and white sky. I began to think I'd die before I reached it, a comforting realization until I remembered that I was a ghost and therefore tragically incapable of dying. I had become the golem, a being more dead than alive, a creature others marvelled at because of its ability to exist when the conditions of existence were so bleak. The concrete highway began vibrating again. I felt the intersection of wind currents and shrinking distances pulling at me, indicating a vehicle's approach. Sure enough, a dot on the horizon became a field of dots, gradually transforming into a pixelated mirage and then a shimmering silhouette. A truck was barrelling towards us.

Counting to ten, I took a deep breath and stepped into the road.

* * * * *

"*Mais pourquoi diable me fait ça?*"

I opened my eyes then closed them hastily. I was lying on the highway, the world tumbling around me in fragments: giant metal grill looming, steam pouring out, sun swinging like a yo-yo, light glancing off the surface of the billboard. Someone was shaking my arm. Someone was shrieking.

"*Quelle bêtise as-tu fait la?* Charlie? I don't believe it, *ben voyon donc…*"

I opened my eyes, thinking I'd heard my name. The sun exploded into a thousand pieces, all of them shiny, all of them sharp. *Star, stars.*

Jerking my head from side to side I tried to shake the stars out of my eyes. The motion made me feel sick, sicker than I'd ever felt. I swallowed, forcing down the terrible sickness inch by inch. What was inside me was oceanic and surging, but also dirty like water at the end of the rinse cycle. Swallow and swallow and swallow. I tried to press a hand against my mouth, but it was stranded at the end of a boneless arm. After a long time fumbling in empty sleeves for an arm that might work I gave up, lay back. Waited for the world to stop twitching. A crow rattled down off the hydro line and stood at my feet, cawing. Was I dead? Was I roadkill? Was some filthy scavenger about to peck out my entrails?

And where was Gellman? Who was looking after the dog?

"*Check moi l'es donc!* Just look at the guy! Charlie, *je mon fucking voyage!*"

I'd definitely heard my name. Strangely, someone on this deserted stretch of highway not only recognized me but was determined to call me back from the dead, tugging at my arm and hauling me into a sitting position, a foolish response to a spinal injury, as this idiot trucker should have known.

"*Ferme ta gueule!* Shut up, you don't have a spinal injury," the trucker said.

"Am I thinking out loud?" I asked.

"Wouldn't exactly call it thinking. You're just saying random stuff."

"Hey!" I yelled, insulted. Then, realizing who it was hanging over me, her expression a delicate balance of fury and concern, I jerked myself upright. "*Hey!*"

"See. No spinal injury. Look—" Weeza shook me hard, presumably to demonstrate that my spinal cord was intact, but roughing me up convincingly in the process. At the sound of the beloved voice, Gellman popped out of his box and lunged at his old pal, goofy with love.

"*Fourer le chien!* Dude, take it easy, chill!"

Despite her angry words, Weeza suddenly saw the humour in our situation. She leaned back on her haunches and laughed until she hiccupped. "Charlie, you should see your face," she said. "Such horror. Did you think I ran you over?"

I did, actually.

"No way. You fainted, mister. Nothing to do with me."

Apparently I'd fainted again. Always with the fainting.

"Were you looking for me?" was all I could think to say.

Weeza sighed and said it was a long story, too long a story to relate while hanging out on the highway with freighters blasting by, their drivers sounding their horns and hollering helpful suggestions as to how we might want to move our fat fucking asses out of the way.

"Now you care?" I remembered her downward dog in the face of oncoming traffic as Gellman and I did the dance of the exploding bladders. It was so long ago. Decades, centuries, an ice age of continental drift and dying species separated the boy with hope in his heart and the freak I'd become—filthy and starving, exhausted, wrapped in a greasy jumpsuit, sneakers hemorrhaging slushy water. My muscles ached and my teeth were chattering so hard they sounded like castanets dancing a tiny dental flamenco.

But Weeza only laughed and told me to stand up, *mon chum*, she had to get me out of my wet clothes and into a warm place so I could thaw out. She helped me to my feet and pulled open my snaps, making me toe off my sneakers and climb out of the jumpsuit. Then she held up my old friend the tartan blanket like a screen, telling me to strip and passing me clean overalls from her stash. But when I tried to fasten the snaps I discovered that my fingertips had thickened in the night and I could no longer perform the simplest task. Ugly tears slid from my eyes. I'd made a mess of everything. I would never find my father or the story I was supposed to live or the centre of my life, the place from which that mysterious force—narrative—gushed like an underground stream. I'd never be the Wonder Boy that Oscar had tried to conjure, the creature he'd coaxed into existence with nothing but a clumsy kiss on the forehead in place of the letters that sometimes spelled truth and sometimes spelled death.

Not wanting to miss out, Gellman flung his head back and howled into the wind. *I'm sad too,* he howled. *What about me? What about ME? WHAT ABOUT ME?!*

Weeza did up my snaps, gave me a one-armed hug, told me to *lâche pas la patate* and stay positive, rummaged in her duffle and extracted woollen socks and a sweatshirt, handed them over, cuffed Gellman, cuffed Gellman harder, got him to clamber into the rig and snuggle down beneath the blanket, climbed in after him and wrestled the long-lost packet of peanut butter and chocolate syrup sandwiches away, told him if he was a good dog she'd feed him soon, jumped out and ran back to where I still dawdled, urged me to get a grip, *mon chum,* tugged the sweatshirt over my head, bundled my waistcoat over the sweatshirt, dragged me to the rig and boosted me into the cab, fitted the seatbelt over my shoulder and buckled it in place, pulled the socks onto my feet, hopped down again and collected the dolly and the soggy moving box, the jumpsuit, and my discarded clothes, stashed them in the back, jumped into the driver's seat, blasted the heat, and without waiting for a gap in the traffic, swung confidently into the left-hand lane.

It sounds like a lot when you write it down, but it took no time at all because Weeza was honed and ready. She was doing what she did best. She was saving the day.

A moment later she threw back her head and laughed. We'd just drawn level with the billboard. Pointing, she indicated the image of a vast baby-like fetus blown up in its shiny bubblegum-pink womb. Another pro-life billboard; there were tons out here. The caption read: *Before I formed you in the womb I knew you. Signed, God.*

"Glad he signed it," she said as she manoeuvred into the fast lane, still laughing as if something in her had finally broken.

* * * * *

I devoured my sandwiches while Weeza caught me up. I wasn't feeling too good. Some fragile mechanism in my brain box was jammed and the pain in my head had gone stereo. It felt like a ball bearing had come loose and was rolling around my skull. Weeza passed me her sunglasses, said I probably had concussion from hitting my head on the concrete highway.

"Such a sore head," I moaned.

"*J'ai mal des fesses,*" she replied coarsely, indicating that she had an equally sore ass and that I might want to *ferme ta damn gueule* for a while.

I didn't blame her; she'd had a long night. After loading up the contents of a large two-storey, she'd crashed briefly, got back in the rig, and driven straight into the sun for ten hours before stopping off for a few shoulder-releasing downward dogs and a hot dog to go.

"That's when you lost us," I told her.

"Good to know," she said, glaring at me.

She was pissed off, I could tell, so I kept the commentary to a minimum and just listened. The way she told it, after visiting Pulley's she drove to Wawa, making good time. Just outside town she pulled into a lay-by to catch some shut-eye. She reckoned she'd make it to Sault Ste. Marie before dawn, easy, hit Wiley's Full Service, where she'd grab a shower, take down a plate of eggs and a gallon of coffee, and settle in for the final haul, cruising into the city by noon latest. She'd eased into the lay-by, climbed into the snug, and was already half-asleep when she discovered my wallet under the blanket, along with my bag of supplies and my parka.

"I could have used the parka," I said.

"I could have used the sleep," she snapped.

She didn't know the details but could join the dots, she said, and tried not to panic. Instead, she turned and headed back to Thunder Bay, the last place she'd stopped, where she assumed we'd jumped ship for our own not-necessarily-sane reasons.

"We needed to pee," I said.

She rolled her eyes so dramatically we almost skidded into the median. So there she was, heading back from Wawa, no idea how she'd track us down. The cloud cover was thick, making it difficult to see, but the emotional register was thicker and she was having difficulty thinking straight. Panic and anger kept her going through the night. She had to find us before someone realized we were missing and called the cops. The addition of the cops never improved any situation, was Weeza's firm conviction. She fell silent, drummed her fingers on the wheel, then cut me a sidelong glance. I knew she felt bad because here it was, the next day, and no one had discovered we were missing yet.

"Jules is really busy with the quinzhee," I told her. "And Oscar's still in hospital."

"Oh, Charlie," she said, her eyes suddenly much too bright.

Around five in the morning she hit Thunder Bay and was looking for an off-ramp when this trucker came through on the radio raving about a fellow who'd stolen a bunch of moving supplies and was proceeding east on the highway, presumably towards a centralized haven of moving-supply bandits. The trucker was a mean son of a gun, she confirmed. He called himself the Lone Ranger and subscribed to the myth of the open road and the ten-gallon, rig-wrangling cowboys who cruised it. Usual bullshit. She'd almost tuned him out when she was struck by his description of a dude pushing a mover's dolly along the hard shoulder, five klicks east of Pulley's.

"It was you, Charlie," she said. "I knew it was you."

I didn't ask how she knew. I didn't ask, but it wounded me that the cruel description I was certain had been provided by the mean son of a gun so perfectly coincided with her conviction.

* * * * *

The metal ball had gone rogue, whizzing around my skull like a pinball. *Boing-boing!* Wherever it landed, the inside of my head lit up with the promise of another free game. *Jackpot! Jackpot!* Weeza's voice wasn't helping any. She was yelling, *ben voyon donc*-ing and *je mon voyage*-ing, asking a stream of questions (*but how were you going to* and *why did you think* and *dammit, what about school, Jules, Oscar?*). It felt as if her voice was activating the flippers, slamming the ball from one side of my head to the other.

"Jesus, kid, you look like shit," she said.

I didn't want to tell her how lousy I felt; my words would be just one more inducement for slamming on the brakes. We were still travelling east. I figured so long as we were pointed in the right direction I had a chance to make it to New York and find my father. But I kept expecting her to swing around and haul me home in disgrace, a lumpy good-for-nothing might-have-been.

"Why do you want to meet him after all this time?" she asked.

"Um, closure?" She howled with laughter, continuing to guffaw no matter what I said — curiosity? family feeling? spare kidney? — until she ran out of patience and threatened to turn around and deliver my sorry ass back home so swiftly we'd collide with ourselves on the way.

"Well?" She slammed on her indicators as an off-ramp loomed. So I told her what Oscar had said. *Tell the story as if it happened to you, Charlie.* Shaking her head, she said the old man had a lot to answer for, she wished... but she lost the thread of her wishfulness, falling silent or at least not talking for the next five minutes, during which she hit the steering wheel four times, the dashboard twice, her forehead once. We were still driving east, the sun hitting me square in the eye, my head feeling at once dented and bulgy. But I didn't care about the rolling-pinball pain, or the sharp-edged light pouring through the windscreen, or the nausea blowing up inside me like a full-body balloon so that even my fingers and toes felt like puking. East was why. It was the direction we were headed, all Weeza's browbeating and banging on steering wheel and dashboard not being sufficient argument to convince her to turn around.

I leaned my head against the back of the seat and watched the highway off-ramps flip past. East, East, East.

* * * * *

Weeza was lobbing questions again. *How did you get into the rig? Whoa, you stole my spare keys? Jesus, Charlie, do you even have a conscience?* She reminded me of Oscar's Sphinx, not in the same league, obviously, but with the same zero-tolerance policy for error. One wrong answer and she'd yank the wheel around, she threatened, whenever I took a moment to think. But, unlike my grandfather, Weeza didn't much care for Greek mythology. Her focus was strictly contemporary. *What's Jules going to say? Come on, Charlie, why'd you say that? Of course she does.* (I knew she didn't, though, I'd known since I looked up at the towering ice with its freight of river memories and detritus. I'd stood in wonder, wondering even as I heard that shrill voice singing the off-key version of a song that had once been a covenant between us.)

On and on she went, firing off questions, about my father (*have you contacted the dude?*), about my plans (*when were you going to?*), about my prospects (*you know what's going on in the world?*). I tried to answer her (sort of, pretty soon, yeah some) but my heart wasn't in it. I knew enough to know that they were the wrong questions, although I didn't yet know what the right ones might be. All my life I'd been a stranger to myself and to others, as if I'd fallen asleep and been teleported to another land. And even though everyone I met there was someone I already knew, they were all in disguise. So how would I recognize them? And how would they recognize me? I was wearing the right shoes but my chromosomes were all wrong. I was wearing the wrong shoes but maybe if I clicked them? I'd started out a boy but now I was never going to be a man.

Dr. Jabbour had made it clear that the operation to correct my hypospadias was risky, unnecessary, even foolish. But I was the one who'd have to think about sitting down to pee for the rest of my life; who might discover I had ovarian cells growing in my abdomen; whose penis was in her damning words "functionally adequate." All morning, travelling into the sun, I obsessed about that billboard, brooding over the baby who'd been known, signed off on by the big guy who didn't make mistakes. I couldn't speak for that baby caught forever in its half-blown bubble, but if I wasn't a mistake, what was I? The question rolled around in my brain, yet another pinball, lighting up the pain centres but illuminating nothing.

Not knowing the answer didn't surprise me. I was so used to getting stuff wrong and making bad decisions and generally screwing up that even when I worked backwards from the answer, which was, as always, Man, I couldn't figure out the question. But I was pretty sure it had nothing to do with the Sphinx and its weird obsession with counting legs.

* * * * *

East. We were still travelling east.

I must have dozed and woken five or six times, my head so sore I felt the pain in my sleep, as if a dense black star had lodged in my brain and was pulling light through my eyeholes. The brain-star was infinitely heavy, the light razor-edged. Amid the fog of exhaustion and nausea I heard Weeza talking. She was relating a tale of highway cowgirls and lady truckers, chuckling and exclaiming. But when I tried to reply she waved me off. "Don't need help, Charlie. I know where I'm going with this story."

Great, I mumbled. Good to know that someone else was in charge of a story for once. I had no idea what she was talking about, what story she was telling or who she was telling it to, but the murmur of her words was comforting, the rise and fall of her voice lulled me as we drove past burned-out spruce forests and clear-cut pine barrens, through a landscape of shale and brush, melting white fields, billboards and windbreaks, the silver gleam of railway girders flashing in the distance. We passed logging towns and steel mills and ashy, grey industrial fields, occasionally pulling up to a rest stop, where Weeza climbed from the rig, cracking her jaw and rolling her shoulders. Once I woke up alone to find she'd wrangled Gellman outside. She was pulling him along by the scruff of the neck, his front legs stiff, large paws planted in the dirt.

The farther east we travelled the fewer people we saw. The dwindling numbers imbued our journey with a spooky sense of intentionality, as if something—the past or the future—was nosing alongside us. Perhaps because neither of us was able to explain these changes, the silence grew oppressive, eventually overwhelming us, and Weeza halted her story in mid-sentence.

I was so tired I was barely conscious, waking only when we stopped moving or Weeza shook me to ask if I needed a restroom break or a snack, if I wanted to stretch my legs or wash my face. I needed nothing and wanted less. Sleep was the only imperative, the warm place I burrowed into through the swooping hope and despair of the days and weeks and months that had preceded Oscar's bar mitzvah, arriving at the moment when we'd taken a deep breath and, together, on the count of three, blown out the candles on the magnificent Wonder Boys celebration cake.

* * * * *

We spent the night at the North Star, a dingy motel out-side Blind River (curtains a thin film against halogen sky, all-night buzz of neon Vacancy sign, curly black hair stuck in the soap). The room had the makeshift look of a stage set thrown together moments before an actor sticks a key into the keyhole of a rickety plywood door. Inside were a couple of beds, a battered side table, an empty bar fridge that wasn't even plugged in, and a lopsided bureau with an old-fashioned, curved-screen TV balanced on top. The bath-room door was shut but, like everything else in the room—skimpy bedspreads, too-short curtains—didn't quite fit its frame, the gap between door and floor giving it the look of a toilet cubicle in the kind of diner where parents are always bending down to check on their kids.

Weeza looked like she could use some time to herself, so I grabbed Gellman and pulled him into the frosty, neon-buzzing night with its stink of parking-lot gas and takeout and the pneu-matic shunt of freight-haulers on the highway that had become the soundtrack to our lives. But when we returned from our walk along a frozen, rutted path that petered out at a line of porta-cabins, we found her frowning at her computer screen.

"Jules says hi," she said.

"She didn't know I was gone, right?"

"Sure she did. She was worried sick. You know how she gets when you're out of sight for, what? Twenty-four, thirty hours?" Weeza glanced at her watch and shrugged.

I was glad she didn't try to explain that my mother loved me. To be honest, I wasn't all that lovable, so my mother's patented brand of guerrilla love was probably the best I'd do. Weeza was still frowning at her computer. "Um, Charlie? I know you don't want to talk, but it's not going away."

I told her I was going to take a shower and locked myself in the bathroom. I needed to shower. I stank like someone who'd been pumping out pure adrenalin for thirteen-and-a-half years. But when I confronted the rust-stained, mould-blooming room that reeked of drains and bleach, I slumped. I turned on the faucet and shower full blast, then hunched on the toilet seat and wept. She rattled the door but I ignored her, even when she yelled that I was now personally responsible for emptying about an acre's worth of ocean down the drain of a lousy motel off the Trans-Canada Highway. At least turn off the shower, she kept yelling. But my body had filled to the brim with wet cement.

I heard Gellman whining and Weeza begging him to hush up. You'll get us evicted, she said in a faux reasonable voice. But the prospect of eviction seemed to thrill Gellman, and he pitched his signature whine a couple of frequencies further up the scale until she cracked and hurled something against the wall. She didn't hit him but what she'd thrown was made of glass, and the sound when it hit the outer threshold of her tolerance held the unmistakable ring of conviction. I wanted to tell her to find Squashy Green Ball, but I couldn't put the words in the right order. They changed shape, moving about in my head like wooden blocks painted with random words:

Green Ball, Bean Gall, Bash and Fall. There was swearing from the other side of the door, the sound of furniture scraping and Gellman whimpering. I worried she'd go into rescuer mode, break down the door, throw me over her shoulder, and haul me out in a fireman's hold. Yet still I couldn't move. *Ashy Brawl, Sassy Ball, Gashy Squall.* The wooden words bumped against each other.

Time passed, I don't know how much, then more. Eventually I heard a scraping sound at my feet. Weeza had pushed a folded paper beneath the door. It was torn from the motel notepad, the North Star logo on top. Inside she'd scrawled a sentence in her untidy writing.

We need to go home. Jules says it's

The paper was damp and puckered, the last word obscured. I sat on the toilet seat, squinting at the note for a long time before summoning the energy to push it back. "Can't read your writing," I mumbled.

"Time," she yelled. "It's *time.*"

She pushed the note under the door again together with a ballpoint pen, same ugly North Star logo emblazoned on its side. The gap was large enough to accommodate a pen, large enough to accommodate a computer, probably. I stared at the paper for what felt like a year before I picked it up. Seeing took time, and so did moving. You wouldn't think such things took time, is what I learned that day. You'd be wrong.

Beneath the sentence she'd written another.

He's not going to get better, Charlie.

It took forever to pick up the pen, grasp it, press it to the paper. I was suddenly transported back to that long-ago afternoon, shadows moving across the loft towards that clueless kid who was trying to imitate his mother's signature. Once again, I was lost. What could I write on the note that Weeza had pushed under the door of a crummy motel on the side of a highway in the middle of an unknown province in a country and a century and a world that had become strange to me?

Jules Minkoff, I wrote. *Jules Minkoff Jules Minkoff Jules Minkoff Jules Minkoff*

* * * * *

Oscar had never warned me that you could find yourself in the wrong story, that when you set out on a quest to find your father you might discover that you didn't give a damn about the guy who'd abandoned you because the guy who'd always cared for you was on life-support with a DNR order pinned to his chart and a living will that said "enough already."

Don't ask me why I'd bailed on him. I was counting on the fact that Jules wouldn't pull the plug if I wasn't there or that Oscar wouldn't die, despite the massive stroke he'd suffered the day after the bar mitzvah. That he'd live forever because I was out in the world having my adventures, discovering my story, finding my father. Not letting anyone else steal my voice. It broke my heart to say goodbye, to lean over the hospital bed with its smell of antiseptic and starched linen and kiss his thin cheek. *I'll miss you, zeide,* I whispered, waiting for him to respond in a silence broken only by the beep of machinery.

Somewhere amongst the stroller-laden streets of Crown Heights, the brownstones and walk-ups, the row houses and crowded sidewalks where black-frocked men hurried, eyes averted, my father lived. I pored over Google images, finding photos of the Hasidic neighbourhood and its denizens, imposing fatherhood on one curly-bearded stranger, then another. There was no way to tell, *no way to tell on the surface*. But under one of those black coats beat a telltale heart. Somewhere my father walked the streets with his forbidden tattoo, the scarlet letters of his renegade love.

"Or you could just write to him," Mikayla said. "This isn't a fairy tale, Three-Piece. The guy's got a LinkedIn account."

So I wrote to Nathan Dervish, Dervish Tailoring and Men's Apparel, and in time received a reply that was noncommittal in everything except its writer's assurance that all would unfold as the Creator intended. Obeying the Orthodox imperative not to write the Lord's name except in its abbreviated form, he said that if, G-d willing, I was ever in the neighbourhood, I should feel free to contact him. He included a postscript to the effect that the tattoo I'd written about so imaginatively no longer existed. He'd had it removed, at great expense, so he could return to the fold and become the observant Jew that he'd always been. He would appreciate my never mentioning the aberration again.

"He doesn't even have the tattoo anymore," I now told Weeza. But Weeza didn't care about my father and his disappearing tattoo. She advised me to forget about him for the moment. Maybe one day we'd meet, thrash out the ending to our particular story over a plate of matzo ball soup in a kosher restaurant off Kingston Avenue.

"Hope you enjoy the soup," she said, making it clear that lunch was the only thing that could reasonably be expected from such an encounter.

Whoa. I turned to look at this new straight-shooting, no-bullshit-talking version of Weeza. She lit up, the headlights of an oncoming vehicle making her seem brilliant with truth-telling. The headlights bloomed, slid over the roof of the cab, then dwindled and disappeared. We were on the road again because when I'd emerged from the bathroom at the North Star (Weeza rushing in and wrenching the taps shut) neither of us felt like sleeping. Might as well hit the road, she said, try to make it back home in time.

Weeza had decided to turn around, as she'd done only once before, and drive back to Winnipeg to deliver Gellman and me like the unclaimed baggage we were. But she wouldn't make the same mistake twice, and so while I had been having my moment in the bathroom, she'd been radioing for assistance in the form of a colleague who could take over her freight and deliver it safely to the shipper. Fortunately, what with the new restrictions and the imminent threat of border closures, truckers were going rogue, driving helter-skelter down the highway, picking up short-haul gigs where they could. She soon found a fellow, an independent contractor, who cut her a deal—although it was not one that she profited from. And there in the parking lot of the North Star Motel, working without finesse or regard for cleanup, the three of us transferred the contents of our rig to his.

"*Allons-y!*" Weeza said as she watched his tail lights lengthen the distance between us. She did not sound happy. It was clear that Gellman and I had become burdensome, an awkward load. And we would be driving home empty, deadheading across the Canadian Shield.

It was an exercise in economic mismanagement she made certain I understood.

* * * * *

We fought all the way to Sault Ste. Marie, where Weeza exited the highway. Cranky and red-eyed, she drove through the town, the lights from oncoming vehicles lighting her up, making her shine in orange and black stripes before they slid across the roof and disappeared into the night. I was terrified by this new tiger-striped, heat-seeking truth missile, this straight-up gospel version of Weeza, but the headlights kept coming, blooming and dwindling, lighting her up so that she flashed on and off, on and off. I closed my eyes, which only made it worse, as if the light and the darkness had entered me and were playing themselves out on the screen inside my mind. Yet I kept them shut, purely to waylay some unspeakably violent collision of opposites — truth and dare or truth and death — that I didn't want to see looming out of the night towards me, headlights blazing.

Mostly we wrangled about the current state of the world, about Jules, and about my beloved grandfather. Weeza refused to weigh in on the question of plagues and punishment, God and His mighty hand, saying that the metaphysics of cause and effect ought not to be imputed to what was, after all, a simple virus, the smallest of microbes. As for Jules, she was Jules, take her or leave her. She wouldn't play well in a focus group for a movie in which you saved your son by sacrificing him in some existentially ironic way, but, credit due, she'd never forced her agenda on me. Then Weeza cleared her throat and said she wasn't going to insult my intelligence by telling me that Oscar would be fine so long as no one opened the box, so to speak. Taking off the way I did had made it easier to pretend he was asleep and would wake up refreshed, raring to go, a new and improved Oscar, but that simply wasn't true. Understand, Charlie? she asked finally.

The truth was I did not understand. The truth was I understood nothing. That the essence of the person I loved so much was already gone was one thing I had not understood. Another was that the body lying in the hospital bed, hooked up to costly machinery that pumped blood into its heart and breathed air into its lungs, was all that was left of my grandfather. I'd run away because I couldn't bear the inevitable collision of these misunderstandings — his barely-there body catching up with his already-gone soul. But understanding came eventually, as it always does: a shot of adrenalin to the heart, grief pulsing through me.

By now Weeza had found the late-night convenience store she'd been searching for. She told me to sit tight and went off to make her purchases. Through the window I watched her stride deserted aisles, shovelling tins and boxes into her basket, piling them in front of the cashier, who wore a bandana over his mouth and nose and seemed to be instructing her to stand back. It was an odd scene, made odder by the exaggerated gestures and the silence, as if we'd wandered into the opening sequence of a movie about the end of the world. The small store was so brightly lit and the night so dark that, for a moment, what I knew to be a view through two windows — windscreen and storefront — became a cube of fluorescent light floating free into the night, its human inhabitants trapped forever.

I was still gazing at this lit-up diorama when she returned with a couple of bags containing cans of off-brand dog food; generic dog biscuits; a cooked chicken under a moulded plastic dome; two prepared salads from the deli counter, both coated in Jell-O (one red with marshmallows, one lime-green); three Gatorades, and a two-litre bottle of Coke. She'd thrown in bleach wipes and a packet of Hershey's Kisses. Gellman flipped when he smelled the chicken and wouldn't look at the dog food or biscuits (they weren't even bone-shaped), so Weeza shared with him the whole greasy mess of goose-pimpled skin and sinew-strung bones. For the first time in my life, I wasn't hungry.

"You have to eat," she said. "I got you salad. Red or green?"

There was a picnic table chained to a stake at the edge of the car park. As I walked towards it, my eyes filled with flickering neon rods and fluorescent cones, and the brain-star lodged inside my skull began imploding in slow motion. I staggered and almost fell. Weeza made me sit on the cold, damp bench while she fed me tender spoonfuls of one of the jellied salads, I couldn't say which. Moments later, without warning, it all came up again.

It was the red salad. Deep ruby red and studded with tiny marshmallows.

* * * * *

I knelt in the parking lot, throwing up in volcanic waves of acid-red lava. I'd hardly eaten all day so it was a mystery what was coming up, but eight years of swallowing stuff down was my guess. Weeza crouched beside me, her hand on my back. "That's right, get it all out," she murmured.

After a while, though, she got impatient and told me to wrap it up.

But I couldn't have stopped to save my life. Every time I thought I was done another wave of sickness hit, the under-tow dragging me, convulsions rippling out like earthquake tremors until my whole body was engaged, everything in me trying to squeeze out of my stomach and escape through my throat. It was as if I was vomiting myself up, getting rid of the boy who'd made a mess of his life, who went limp when he should have fought, who ran when he should have stayed. Gellman was going crazy, barking his head off. Naturally, he assumed I was dying. If this was death, it was at once painful and humiliating. My hair was wringing wet, my eyes bubbling in their sockets, my throat stripped raw.

"Finished?" Weeza asked hopefully. I shook my head and bent over again. Thick loops of saliva hung from my lips. Nothing came up but I couldn't stop convulsing, dry heaving and straining and retching.

"Come on, *mon chum. Mais en pas* fucking *trop*. This is just symbolism now," she muttered.

She wanted to start out for Winnipeg, drive as long as she could, pass out in a lay-by when she no longer could, then press on. The thought of Oscar hovering in the limbo from which only we could release him spurred her on. Jules had said she'd wait for us before telling the doctors to "um, go ahead," Weeza fudged. But still I knelt there, the ground boggy, steaming in the cold air like the entrails of a slaughtered animal. Gellman snuffled up and shoved his cold nose in my hand. We stayed like that until the world stopped jerking. I couldn't bear to look down to see what new damage I'd inflicted on my waistcoat, so I closed my eyes as Weeza swabbed me down with a roll of paper towels and about a gallon of water.

"Ready?" she asked finally. But the thought of getting into a moving vehicle made me heave again. From the back of the rig she pulled out the adjustable deck and said I should lie down and compose myself.

"You just need some fresh air and a sugar hit," she said, handing me the bag of Hershey's Kisses. I was to eat the chocolate slowly but not too slowly because we really needed to get going. We were late already.

When I opened my eyes, I saw stars. All I saw were stars.

I was lying on my back on the deck of a truck pulled onto a deserted stretch of road. The darkness was so thick it had weight to it and the sky was sizzling with stars, some bright and distinct, others a veil of swarming light. Behind the veil, I knew, was another veil spangled with light, and behind that another. The stars shook and shook, making a gentle sound like maracas.

I felt washed clean by pain and sickness, my body fragile as a soap bubble. I was a stranger to myself, a small, soft-boned creature birthed on the side of the road, eyes seeing light for the first time as if at the creation of the world. I wondered if God would speak, and then I knew He was, my heart filled with such wonder I was dissolving, my skin and bones and marrow dissolving into a sky filled with a billion points of light. I didn't yet know that stars are composed of the same carbon-based element that connects us all, stardust coursing through the veins of leaves and elephants, through the wings of hummingbirds and bats and flying fish, and through every human soul, but this feeling was flooding my veins, making my bones glitter and my blood shine. And as I looked into the vast, unaccountable sky I imagined the Minkoff family crest, each perfect symbol of our relatedness outlined by a magical laser beam, a planetarium pointer connecting the dot-to-dot stars, rendering them legible.

It only lasted a moment. Even as I gazed in wonder, I felt the joy ebb, the sky shrink, the stars recede. In a moment they were just stars, chilly and beautiful, light years away. I sat up and put a Hershey's Kiss on my tongue, letting it dissolve slowly as I remembered being small enough to sit on Oscar's lap and burrow in his pockets. The crazy star-joy shifted and made way for grief.

Weeza came round the side of the truck looking harried, a streak of dirt on her cheek, red hair standing up in funny little tufts. She'd been tidying up the rig while I had my moment. The trailer was a disaster of exploding boxes, rubber bands, and runaway dollies, the floor a mulch of wrappers and takeout containers, ashtray jammed with butts. We don't have time to clean up, she kept saying, but I knew what Oscar would say.

"'Who makes time *saves* time.' *Ethics of the Fathers*," I said. "Look it up."

She gave in eventually, showing me how to fold moving pads into squares and sort rubber bands by size. Working only by the truck's light, I collapsed boxes and stacked them, figuring out how to secure the dollies while Weeza wiped down tarps and burlap skins. We collected screwdrivers and wrenches, hammers and drill bits and every last nail, packing them in the tool box. We funnelled receipts and takeout containers and plastic bottles into a garbage bag, emptied the ashtray, swept the trailer front to back. Then Weeza said it really was time.

I climbed into the passenger seat and buckled myself in. She started the engine, blasted the horn, banged her fist on the roof. *Ready, mon chum?* Gellman was snuffling beneath the blanket, letting out yips in his sleep. I reached for the supply bag, empty now except for a pad and pen.

The pad had a stiff back, easy to write on, and the pen was the one Mickie had given me. It was the sort of cheap ballpoint that writes for a short time then peters out. I didn't know how long I had before the ink dried up, so I thought I'd better begin.

*

ACKNOWLEDGEMENTS

My deep gratitude to Rachel Letofsky for her calm good sense and enthusiasm, to Janie Yoon for balancing sage warnings with encouragement, and to Mark Libin for being the gentlest of readers. Heartfelt thanks to the wonderful folks at House of Anansi who took this book from my shaking hands and ushered it into the world, in particular my extraordinary editor, Joshua Greenspon, and Debby de Groot, whose exuberance is a joy. Gratitude to Hans Lindahl for medical knowledge and to Aviva Cook and Agata Kesik for their buoyancy and humour during times of partial to extreme catastrophe.

This book is for my *bashert* and our three children, rollicking companions along the yellow brick road. Oh yes, and the little dog too.

ACKNOWLEDGEMENTS

MÉIRA COOK is the award-winning author of the novels *Once More With Feeling*, which won the Carol Shields Winnipeg Book Award; *The House on Sugarbush Road*, which won the McNally Robinson Book of the Year Award; and *Nightwatching*, which won the Margaret Laurence Award for Fiction. She has also published five poetry collections, most recently *Monologue Dogs*, which was shortlisted for the 2016 Lansdowne Prize for Poetry and the 2016 McNally Robinson Book of the Year Award. She has won the CBC Poetry Prize and the inaugural Walrus Poetry Prize. Méira has served as writer-in-residence at the University of Manitoba's Centre for Creative Writing and Oral Culture, as well as the Winnipeg Public Library. Born and raised in Johannesburg, South Africa, she now lives in Winnipeg.